OUTCASTS

A STARCROSSED NOVEL

JOSEPHINE ANGELINI

SUNGRAZER
PUBLISHING
LOS ANGELES

For my family, given, found, and chosen.
You know who you are.

THE FOUR HOUSES

House of Atreus
Upper East Side and Central Park

Elara Atreus - Head of House

Polyduces (Deuce) Atreus

Daphne Atreus - Heir to House

House of Thebes
Washington Square, The Village and Alphabet City

Paris Delos - Head of House

Jordana Lycian

Tantalus Delos - Heir to House

Castor Delos

Pallas Delos

Ajax Delos

Antigone Lycian

Pandora Delos

House of Athens

Downtown, the Waterfront and Tribeca

Bellerophon Attica - Head of House

Ladon Attica

Daedelus Attica - Heir to House

Nilus Attica

Lelix Attica

House of Rome

Upper East and Harlem

Melia Tiber - Head of House

Leda Tiber - Heir to House

Adonis Tiber

1

DAPHNE
HOUSE OF ATREUS

I'm not used to being happy.

I wasn't raised to believe happiness was an attainable goal for me. My uncle Deuce disabused me of any hope of it at a very young age. Not to be cruel, but to give me a leg up on what was almost certainly in the cards for me.

I remember him telling me that for our kind, fairy tales were often true. Not the sanitized, pink-and-glitter version of fairy tales that they make cartoon movies of in Hollywood, but the original ones that are more like those Scared Straight presentations from ex-convicts. The princess usually suffers a hellish childhood where her whole family dies and she's either locked in a tower or forced into indentured servitude. In most cases, she not only doesn't get the prince in the end, but they also both either die or get turned into animals. Being turned into a swan sounds romantic until you consider the fact that you'll probably get eaten by a fox.

I admit it. Being happy was never something I considered, and because I'm not primed for it, I'm waiting for the other shoe to drop. Maybe I'm paranoid, but I can't help but feel like there have been too many accidents, too many near misses for me to swallow them as coincidence, and when I hear Ajax gasp and curse under his breath I think, *this is when I lose him.*

I run across the deck of the *Argo IX*, our home since faking our deaths two months ago, to where Ajax has been painting all morning.

"It's nothing," he says, wrapping a rag around the gash in his wrist.

"I'll get the kit," I say, and rush below deck to our medical supplies. When I come back topside Ajax's blood has already seeped through the rag and started to run across his hand.

I open the kit and he peels the rag back away from the wound. It's deep. I meet his eyes. "Do you need a Healer?" I ask. Not that I can take him to one. We're supposed to be dead.

"I'll be fine. Just give me some clean gauze and I'll put pressure on it until it closes."

I do as he asks and stand back, my fists clenched around the lightning in my fingers. "What happened?" I ask.

"There was a gust of wind and the mast swung. I put my arm up so it wouldn't knock me across the head, and cut myself."

While he presses down on his wound, I check the mast of our ship. "Cut yourself on what?" I ask, baffled. There's nothing sharp anywhere near the sails.

He shrugs. "I think it was the edge of my easel."

Ajax's easel has been tipped askew and there is some blood on the top corner, though how he managed to cut himself on it so badly is beyond me. I look out over the calm waters of the Aegean Sea. The steady, light breeze hits my face from one direction. There are no gusts of wind now. The mast is a bit loose, but it's not swingingly violently. I yank on the ropes, pulling them tighter anyway.

"It was just an accident," he insists, watching me.

I double check my knots before I turn to face him. "How many accidents have happened to you since we ran away together?"

He smiles through a sigh and comes to me. He doesn't try to tell me I'm jumping at shadows anymore, but he's still not ready to be convinced, as I am, that the universe is trying to kill him. Holding onto his wrist, he loops his arms over my head and pulls me against him. He kisses my temple until I go from stiff to pliant in his arms.

"You can't fight the wind, Daphne," he says.

I wrap my arms around him, wishing I could unzip my chest and stuff him inside me. "That's what scares me."

TANTALUS

HOUSE OF THEBES

Words are tools. I've always understood that.

The whole course of my life has been shaped by words, and I have used them to shape others. They are the hammer and chisel of the human psyche. I size people with my words, making their egos bigger or smaller to fit into the roles I need them to play. I know that makes me a manipulative person, but I've been given a part to play, too, and I never had a choice about it. Scions don't get choices. We get roles.

Words have shaped me from the moment I was born, and though I take no pride in the prophecy that was made at my birth, I know it's unavoidable. I *know* that the war between the four Scion Houses is inevitable. I *know* there will only be one House left at the end of it and I am going to make sure it's my House that survives. The House of Thebes. My family.

I guess that's the difference between me and my brothers. I don't think they've ever truly accepted what it means to be fated like I have. Quite honestly, a part of me doesn't want them to. I love my brothers, and I protect them from fate as much as I can. I let them forget that the ending has already been written so they can pretend that the end doesn't matter as much as the steps they take to get there. They still believe they have a choice about what steps they take, clinging to the notion that there's such a thing as right and wrong, but there isn't for Scions. How can there be if we don't have a choice about anything we do?

The best we can hope for is plausible deniability, like Oedipus killing his father and marrying his mother—at least he didn't know what he was doing while he did it. I can give my brothers that kind of conscience-sparing ignorance and later, after all the horrible shit we're fated to do is done, they can blame me for it. They can believe they were good men because Tantalus made them do it.

It's been three months since Ajax's supposed death. Our family is officially coming out of mourning, and I've been asked to say a few words. The Fates are always handing me more chances to shape those around me, and my family desperately needs shaping. They've all fallen to pieces since losing Ajax, and now it's my duty to put them back together, the way I need.

I can't say I planned it that way when I suggested to Jax that he and Daphne fake their deaths. At the time I was trying to understand what the Oracle, my cousin Antigone, had told me. She'd had a vision that I would kill Ajax. She saw me cutting off his head. But there's nothing in this world that would make me kill Ajax, and visions are notoriously misleading. They are not like prophecies. Prophecies are the Fates speaking directly through the Oracle as they possess her. Those are incontrovertible. Visions are more like dreams the Oracle has, and they do come true, but their meaning is often hidden. Like watching a movie on mute, the Oracle might see two people arguing passionately, but for all she knows they could be arguing about how much they love each other.

Helping Daphne and Ajax fake their death was the only explanation for Antigone's vision, and it has proven to be extremely useful in other ways as well. It has been just what my father and I have needed to convince the last few holdouts in our House to strike first, strike hard, and win the war that is fated to come in my lifetime. Castor, especially, has come around. Believing he's lost one person he loved has made him afraid he could lose everyone, and fear has made him dangerous. He's like a loaded gun now. All I need to do is point him at our enemies.

My father, Paris Delos, Son of Apollo, Head of the House of Thebes, motions with a flick of his fingers that it's time for me to speak. I stand in front of the Hundred Cousins (an exaggeration. There are only forty-two of us) and my family goes silent.

Half the time when I make one of these "rally the troops" speeches I don't even know what I'm saying as it's happening. Maybe I have a bit of my cousin Antigone's talent and the Fates speak through me. Or maybe I just need to believe that because it's my form of plausible deniability. I'm still a good man because the Fates made me do it.

After delivering my rousing words about love and family and the need to protect our own now more than ever, I find Castor.

"Dad wants you to parlay with the House of Rome, tonight," I tell him.

"With you?" he asks.

"Leda knows I'm a Falsefinder. If I talk to her, it will be an interrogation," I remind him, trying to put his misgivings to rest.

I don't need to ask the Head of the House of Rome about Ajax's death. I know what happened to him. "She likes you. She'll tell you more without me there."

"*If* there's anything to tell," he replies. "I don't think the Romans had anything to do with Jax."

He still can't say *Ajax's death*. After three months he still can't accept it. I put my hand on his shoulder and pull him closer to me until our foreheads are nearly touching.

"My guess is that what happened to Jax is way more complicated than just the girl," I say. "Rome knows something, I'm sure of it," I lie. "Be charming."

"That's Pallas's job," he replies, uncomfortable with this new role.

"Then just be yourself," I say, knowing that my brother's raw emotions will be much more effective on Leda than any planned seduction. She can read hearts, and his is broken. He has no idea how attractive sadness is on him, but some women love that. I'm betting Leda does.

Getting Rome on our side will accomplish two goals. Isolating Athens—the only House that could give us trouble in a fight—and keeping my family in the dark about what really happened to Ajax. We need to take the other Houses down one at a time or we won't win, not if Athens and Rome team up to fight back. Castor with his big, broken heart is the key to winning Leda's sympathy, and therefore Rome.

"Should I take Pallas?" he asks.

"No. Best to go alone. Less threatening."

He acknowledges and leaves. My father joins me.

"Leda isn't stupid. She'll read him like a book," he warns me. He doesn't think my plan to deceive the Romans while we divide and conquer will work, and he has a point. The House of Rome are descended from Aphrodite, and they can read, and even control emotions to varying degrees. While they are not the strongest physically, they are expert politicians, and they rarely get outmaneuvered by the other Houses. But I understand Rome better than my father ever did. I'm a Falsefinder. In a way, I can read hearts too, in that I always know when someone is lying to me, and because of this I know what it takes to deceive me. It takes the truth.

"I'm hoping she does," I reply. "Castor doesn't have ulterior motives. The only thing he's thinking about right now is getting justice for Ajax."

While I may feel a twinge of guilt for using my brother this way, my father's misgivings are for a different reason. He dislikes the idea of working with any of the other Houses, no matter how temporarily, but he doesn't fight me further because he'll do anything for a chance to kill Bellerophon, Head of the House of Athens. Even allow one of his sons to get friendly with Rome.

"The girl," my father says. He's still stuck on Daphne, or rather her face—the same face her mother, Elara, bore some twenty years ago. He saw Elara come to get Daphne the night Ajax killed Polydeuces, and he won't let that connection go.

"She's dead," I lie for the thousandth time. "The House of Atreus is extinct."

"You killed the girl, but Elara could still be alive," he insists, but he can't meet my eyes when he says it. Even he knows he's just looking for a reason to say her name, and a reason to believe she's still out there.

"Possibly," I reply, though I know it isn't. I saw Elara die on a beach to save her daughter's life. I helped bury her. But I can't tell him that, and if I say that one of the other Houses may have killed her, he'd want proof. He's obsessed. He'd go to the other Houses and demand to know who took her life.

"He should ask about Elara," he repeats, unable to let it go.

I walk away from him like I'm fed up with this subject, because that's what I should be feeling, rather than sympathy. Because the truth is that I feel the same way about Daphne.

🜲 3 🜲

ADONIS
HOUSE OF ROME

It's generally believed that the members of my family are heartless, but the truth is that when it comes to the heart, it's all or nothing with us.

There are members in the House of Rome like my cousin Corvus who are devoid of empathy, but I'm the opposite—the "all" as opposed to the "nothing". Thank the gods, too, because Corvus is truly a monster. I've been *called* a monster often enough, usually by ex-lovers who would rather be current lovers, but nothing could be farther from the truth. I feel too much, pretty much all the time.

It's exhausting to be constantly dragged into other people's emotions, and it's usually not worth it anyway. Most of what people think of as heartbreak is nothing more than a bruised ego, and given a few years, and possibly a good therapist, most people would agree. My blasé approach to matters of the heart is often taken as an insult, which has earned me something of a reputation for being heartless, but it's all in self-defense. I'd go crazy if I allowed myself to get sucked into the bottomless pit that is everyone else's melodrama, and *crazy* is something my family is prone to. The House of Athens may have the rare physical monster in it every now and again, but in the House of Rome, monstrosity is on the inside and much more common. Ever heard of Nero? Caligula? Yeah. That's the kind of monster I mean.

Real loss, however, is never melodrama, and Castor Delos has lost someone he loved dearly. It's quite beautiful to see his heart twisting in his chest, though it breaks mine a little. It's breaking my sister Leda's heart, too, even if she is a bit less sensitive than I am—though, let's face it. Everyone is a bit less sensitive than I am. I brace myself against the peaks of anger and the valleys of sadness oscillating out of Castor as he speaks with my sister. I try to look bored. That usually makes people aim the pain away from me, but Castor isn't paying attention to my artful look of disdain as I lounge in a leather chair across the cocktail table. He doesn't care what anyone thinks about him right now. It's admirable, like everything else about him, which is so annoying. You're supposed to hate your enemies, or at least dislike them, but this guy makes it nearly impossible.

"Bellerophon claimed he killed Polydeuces Atreus nearly twenty years ago—his father even threw him a Triumph," Castor is saying. "So how is it that Polydeuces and his niece Elara invaded my home a few months ago?"

Invading the family home of the Head of any of the Houses is an open act of war. Leda and I share a nervous glance. "Help me connect the dots here," I say, feigning misunderstanding. "Atreus invaded your home, not Athens. And now you say that Atreus is extinct. So...what's the problem? Why do you want our support against Athens?"

Castor takes a calming breath. It's not the Furies—I've got the bloodlust they rile in Scions when we are in mixed company firmly in hand. As the children of Aphrodite, some members of my House can manipulate emotions so well that we can practically erase the Furies, but this talent, even among us, is rare. I happen to have loads of this talent, though. So does my sister Leda. But I'm better at it than she is. And as attuned as I am to the emotions at this table, I can tell that Castor's anger is sorrow, masquerading as something more tolerable.

"Bellerophon lied. We all know that now, but what else has he lied about? Did he help hide Atreus all these years?" Castor looks down at the forgotten highball of whiskey sweating in his hand. "Athens is behind this somehow. We're sure of it." He looks up at Leda. "You could be next."

Dang. This guy. I don't even have to look inside him to see his emotions. He is genuinely concerned about Leda, and she's getting sucked into his soulful blue eyes like frigging Charybdis. I wave down a cocktail server.

"This wine is corked," I snap, holding up my glass.

Poor girl's face blanches with fear. My sister and I not only own this classy supper club, with its oak paneling and its exclusive member's only list, but we own half the night spots and hot trendy restaurants in New York City. The girl's scared out of her mind, thinking she's going to get fired and never work again. But I'm just using her to distract from Castor so my sister can think clearly, which admittedly is dickish of me.

I soften my tone and calm the girl with a brush of my fingers on the inside of her wrist. "How 'bout you bring me a bottle of Veuve instead?"

"That's c-champagne, right?" she stammers, blushing furiously.

I repress the urge to roll my eyes. Apparently, we're now hiring bumpkins. "That's right," I say nodding and smiling at her. "Off you go." I may have overdone it a bit. She hustles to the bar, her heart all aflutter, while Castor tries to bring the conversation back on topic.

"We all have secrets, Castor," Leda says, eyes narrowed. She's back to her mistrustful self. Thank the gods.

Castor narrows his eyes, mirroring her. "Not like this. Hiding Atreus from us—"

"We don't know if that's what Athens did," I interject, trying to derail him one last time.

"Then we should find out," he counters, unruffled. He looks at Leda. "Thebes has enough support already to start a war."

She nods, and I abandon my attempts to deflect because Castor is right, and Rome won't survive another war. Divided from within, with our cousins Corvus and Phaon openly opposing Leda and me every chance they get, we're barely hanging on as it is. Never happy with being cousin to the Heir and not the Heir himself, Corvus has been staging a coup of our House since he was old enough to think, which has made mine and my sister's life an absolute horror show. All Corvus wants is to be Head of the House of Rome, and for the past ten years or so he has had Phaon to help him realize his murderous ambitions. Phaon couldn't give a rat's ass about being the Head of the House. All he wants is to hurt people, and Corvus' rather astounding deviousness allows Phaon to do so, while protecting him from annoying little details, like getting caught. As long as he does the majority of his maiming and killing to further Corvus' ambition, Corvus keeps covering for who Phaon really is, a psychopath.

The only thing stopping them from flat-out shoving a stiletto

13

into mine or my sister's back is the fact that it would make them Outcasts, and then Corvus couldn't be Head of the House. Basically, Rome is a vipers' nest that has weakened itself from within so terribly that my House's only chance is to try to diffuse this situation between Athens and Thebes before it gets started. We wouldn't last a week if an inter-House war broke out right now.

"I'll help you," Leda promises, and then she tacks on a list of stipulations like she always does. My sister never gives a favor without asking for double in return, bless her. "But just you and me. We do this quietly, and if we can't find a connection to Athens, Thebes will back off."

Castor nods. "Thank you," he replies. My sister and the golden boy stare at each other for too long.

Our House has always had to be more vigilant about the Truce with the gods. Not only are we more prone to love affairs because of our descent from Aphrodite, but the ability of some of our numbers to silence the Furies has made relations with the other Houses not only possible, but downright inevitable. Romans have been known to dally with members of the other Houses from time to time, but the rule that Rome has lived by for centuries is, no falling in love, and absolutely no offsprings with the other Houses—on pain of death for both you and the child.

Children who are born of two Houses are called Rogues. If they are created, we do not allow Rogues to live for long.

Harsh though that may seem, there can be no joining of the Houses, and every Roman with the ability to silence the Furies swears this on pain of death for both them and the child. I would rather die than kill my sister, but I'd have to do it. There's more at stake here than my love for my family, or the oaths we took, or any of that shit. There are only three Houses left now that Atreus seems to be extinct, and if it ever occurs that there is only one House remaining, the gods will be released from their prison on Olympus, and then we can kiss our collective asses goodbye. Earth would be knocked right back into the frigging Bronze Age, where those savage gods prefer it, and I for one refuse to live in any time or place where I'd have to shit in a bucket.

"Is Noel still working for your family?" I say, breaking their eye-contact.

I don't care if my sister has some occasional fun with Castor, but she's starting to care for him, and that I can't allow. She is Head of our House. She must put Rome first, not Castor with his shiny honor and his gorgeous pain.

Bringing up Noel was a cheap shot. We both know that Castor is in love with her, and that Noel doesn't want to have anything to do with him for some reason. From the looks of his heart when I said her name, he would give anything to be with her. That's the whole reason my sister started her flirtation with Castor in the first place. She just can't resist a guy who's in love with someone else, because it means she never has to worry about things getting serious. Though she has been changing lately. I think she's gotten tired of the game, like I have, and she's been wanting to get emotionally involved with someone. Which is exactly why I have to keep her and Castor apart. My sister may want to strangle me right now, but all's fair in love and war. This is both.

"She isn't," he replies, his mouth tight. He can't resist asking about her, though. "Is she still working for you?"

"She and Aileen," I reply. "Patrons love them. Both so easy to look at. Plus, they're excellent bartenders. They pretty much run the place. I never see you and Pallas visit anymore."

That rubs him the wrong way. And it pisses Leda off too, because we both know there's no way he'll be able to stop himself from going to Noel's bar and check up on her. Playing the white knight to Noel's fair maiden—saucy barkeep is more like it, but that's not the way Castor sees her. My sister is shooting daggers at me with her eyes, but I'm not going to make things easy between her and Castor.

"I should go," Castor says, standing.

Yes. He should.

"I'll be in touch," Leda tells him, then we both watch his broad shoulders angling through the crowd on his way out the door.

My sister and I regard each other, each of us waiting to see who is going to talk first.

"I have two words for you," I say. "Shit. Storm."

Her pillowy lips slide into a wide smile. "Sure is," she says. What the hell was *that* I just saw flitting through her heart?

"Wait. Have you already slept with him?" I ask.

She ignores my question, taking evasive maneuvers, which is never a good sign. "Do you still have that friend in Athens?" she asks instead.

"He's not technically *in* Athens," I reply. Ladon is an Outcast, but Leda doesn't need to know that, or anything else about him. I love my sister, but she would tear through Ladon like a kid through a candy wrapper.

"He's given you information before, and this is something we need to solve fast."

"I'll talk to him," I say. "No promises though."

"Why won't you tell me who he is?"

I stand just as the cocktail server comes with the champagne bucket. "You can bring that back," I tell the girl, handing her a hundred in tip. She's devastated, thinking she's displeased me, but the money helps.

I avoid my sister's appraising look and leave. She'll set a tail on me. I'll slip it and come back with the information she needs, and we'll pretend the subterfuge never happened. Just another day in the House of Rome.

❧ 4 ❧

DAPHNE

It happens again a few days later.

Only this time it wasn't a gust of wind that pushed the mast that made him lift his arm, so that he would cut the tender underside of his wrist on the only sharp edge at the corner of his easel. The next time the universe tries to kill Ajax is even more convoluted than that, and it happens the only time I ever drop my guard nowadays. When Ajax is making love to me.

We've weighed anchor off the coast of a tiny spit of sand that could hardly be called an island. Ajax had wanted to come ashore to finish a painting without the constant rocking of the sea, and he does get some work done before his eyes find me standing in a tide pool, observing the creatures. He comes to me and, already pulling up the skirt of my sundress, brings me into the shade under the trees.

In the midst of it all, a rotten branch above us falls, smashing on the rock beneath, causing the rotten branch to explode in a spray of sharp splinters the size of daggers. The only thing that spares Ajax is that I have just happened to roll him beneath me, and the improbably formed shrapnel peppers my impenetrable skin in lethal places instead of his.

Bleeding from a few minor cuts where my arms and my back haven't shielded him, Ajax rolls me back under him and checks my body, his face frozen in shock.

"Are you hurt?" he asks, his voice shaking as he runs his hands over me.

"No," I reply, touching the powerful charm from the goddess Aphrodite around my neck that makes me impervious to weapons. There isn't a scratch on me. Propping myself up on my elbows, I look at the detritus around us. "I don't get it. The Cestus only protects me from *weapons*. Not natural causes."

He pushes back on his heels, goes to run a hand through his hair, sees that there is a pencil-sized splinter sticking out of the back of his hand and pulls it out instead. "How could the branch be a weapon without someone wielding it?" he asks, trying to be logical in an illogical situation.

"Intent." I say. I've been watching this happen for weeks now, and it's like the world has been turned into a giant mousetrap.

"How can a branch have an intent?" he counters.

It's not the branch that kills someone, any more than it is the sword or the arrow or the bullet. "The fact that the Cestus stopped those splinters proves that there is an intelligence behind this somehow."

Ajax is angry. Who wouldn't be to learn that the universe is trying to kill them? I wait until he finally drops his eyes and nods, accepting the impossible.

"Okay," he relents. "We'll go back to New York and talk to my brother."

. . .

Weeks of sailing and multiple near misses later, we dock the *Argo* at a marina in the Bronx. Now we're on the 6 train, headed downtown. Traveling nearly the entire length of Manhattan to get from the Bronx to the Village has me edgy. We have to go through Roman territory on the Upper East Side, then Atreus territory in Central Park—my own—and then down to Theban territory in Greenwich Village.

My Uncle Deuce explained to me why the Houses were all crammed onto this tiny spit of land when I moved here with my dad a year ago now. The Furies bring the Scions together. It's unavoidable. Over the centuries, the countries and cities have changed, but wherever the center of Western Civilization is, there we are. At one time it was Paris, another time Venice. You name a time period, and a city at the apex of Western Culture—and the Scions we were. We have always divided up these cities into territories so we wouldn't accidentally run into each other, and start lopping off each other's heads in public. This century, it's been New York City.

As we travel through these enemy territories, I can use the Cestus to change my appearance, but Ajax can't. Even in a Yankees baseball cap, which is the standard uniform of nearly every New York male under the age of fifty, he stands out. Tall, broad shouldered, and tanned even though it's autumn, men appraise him and back down, recognizing someone they don't want to mess with, while women appraise him and sway closer, recognizing someone they do. Everywhere Ajax goes he snares eyes.

"Maybe you should go back," I whisper in his ear.

His expression saddens. "I miss him," he replies, not asking to come, but giving me the reason he wants to, knowing it will work better on me than any argument.

I angle myself in front of him as we hang from the strap overhead, trying to block those prying eyes. It isn't safe. He knows it, I know it, but he can't come this close to his family without seeing at least one of them, and I can't bring myself to tell him not to.

Ajax feels the Furies first. We're coming into a station on the Upper East Side, and I hear him pull in a breath. His hand presses on the small of my back, sealing me against him. I feel the rage sweep through me and see the flicker of a gore-stained girl with ashes clumped in her tatty black hair out of the corner of my eye. But the Fury suddenly disappears, and the rage drains out of both Ajax and I at the same time, like magic.

The doors to the subway car open. Ajax and I look at each other, but neither of us can explain the Fury's disappearance. A tall, gorgeous man steps onto the train. I've seen him before. I grab Ajax's wrist.

"Hades," I whisper.

Ajax shakes his head, confused. "Can't be."

He's right, of course. It's impossible. The god Hades never leaves his domain, and I see no helmet, no clouds of black shadows curling around him like smoke.

The gorgeous man who looks like Hades but can't be him looks right at us, his eyes widening with shock, and then away with a small smile tilting up one side of his full lips.

He's got to be a Roman. And he's powerful enough to control the Furies so completely it's like they're not even there.

"Adonis Tiber," Ajax whispers, never taking his eyes off him.

This is bad. Very, very bad. It's also borderline ridiculous. There are eighteen million people living in this city. The chances that we would run into one of the few dozen individuals that we needed to avoid in the first *hour* we'd come here are vanishingly small. If I had any lingering doubt that the universe had painted a giant target on Ajax's back, it's gone now.

"We can't let him live," Ajax says, his lowered voice shaking a little. He doesn't want to do this anymore than I do, but his eyes are hard.

I nod, swallowing down the lump forming in my throat. I'm thinking as fast as I can. Do we follow Adonis? He could bring us to more Romans, dragging us in deeper. I'm not scared to fight. Ajax is a better fighter than anyone I've ever seen, and I can level an army with my lightning; I just can't believe I've been this stupid. How many will we have to kill tonight because in my blind panic to keep Ajax safe I didn't stop to consider that the mousetrap wasn't on the boat, or at sea, or on some distant island? The mousetrap is everywhere, and it will follow us wherever we go.

We glance at Adonis, who seems unconcerned that two enemy Scions are hawking him. The doors open at the next station and he stands back to let other passengers on. The intercom gives its *bing-bong* signal that the doors are about to close, and then Adonis quickly exits.

Ajax pulls me with him, and we barely make it out through the closing doors in time.

We weave through the rivulets of people, following someone who couldn't hide if he tried. His clothes are expensive and flashy. He's tall and his shiny, chestnut hair is like a glowing crown. People part in front of him, their faces turning to his beauty, like flowers striving toward the sun. But despite his surprise dash through the closing doors moments ago, it appears Adonis is no longer trying to get away from us. He's even smiling to himself, like he's having fun.

"He's leading us somewhere," I murmur to Ajax, suddenly not sure we should be following.

Ajax nods, aware that this is probably a trap, but does not give up the pursuit. At this point, we don't really have a choice.

Adonis doesn't go through the turnstile to get aboveground. Instead, he strides all the way to the end of the platform, where he stands as if waiting to catch another train heading downtown. He doesn't get on the next train, either. Instead, he waits until it pulls up. Waits until everyone who wants to get on is on. Waits for the doors to close. And then, just as the train starts to pull out, he disappears in a flash.

"He jumped!" I bark, grabbing Ajax's hand and pulling him down with me behind the receding train and onto the dark tracks.

We run, but we don't have to. Adonis hasn't gone far, just far enough so that someone gazing down the tracks looking for the next train wouldn't be able to see us. He's waiting for us with his hands up. Though it's a gesture of supplication, he doesn't look afraid. He's just letting us see there's nothing in his hands. I feel a flood of calm, happy feelings inside and, hearing my Uncle-Deuce's voice in my head (*always strike first—damn Romans will have you half in love with them before you can scratch your ass*) I know that even if there isn't a sword in Adonis's hand, there is most certainly a weapon.

"This is so strange," Adonis says, like we're running into him at the deli or something. "I just had a drink with your brother, Castor, about fifteen minutes ago. It's Ajax, isn't it?"

Ajax freezes next to me. Hearing his brother's name is like a blow to the chest to him. He's wondering now if he should be worried about Castor.

"It *is* Ajax. And you're supposed to be dead," Adonis answers for him, like he understands he's going to have to do a lot of grunt work to make this conversation happen.

"What did you do to my brother?" Ajax demands.

"I just told you. I had a drink with him," Adonis repeats. "Ironically, he was asking our help avenging you, as a matter of fact."

"Who?" Ajax asks.

"My sister Leda and I. You remember her, from the inter-House meeting? The one we had about some strange Scion girl who was so strong she beat the kingdom-come out of four Athenian knuckle-draggers all by her little self?" Adonis looks right at me. "I'm guessing you must be her, Daphne, daughter of Elara. The Atreidae Tantalus was supposed to have killed."

I look at Ajax, thinking I'll find the same shock and fear I'm feeling, but instead I see resolve. Ajax is going to kill this Roman, and he's going to do it to protect me.

"Wait," Adonis says, looking into Ajax's heart. Reading the murderous intent, he becomes serious for the first time. "I know you don't want to kill me. In fact, I can tell that even hearing me say it is making you nauseous. So instead of the standard fight to the death, why don't we do something completely outrageous and talk. I mean, we didn't just bump into each other. Scions don't have accidents. We have irony, which sucks so much harder."

I pull on Ajax's arm. "The mousetrap," I say. Out of the corner of my eye, I see Adonis react to the word. "It brought us here to him to kill him."

Ajax looks at me, unsure. Still gearing for a fight.

"What if we *don't* do what it wants?"

Ajax looks at Adonis, finally coming to his senses, seeing the logic in what I'm proposing. "Okay," Ajax says finally. "Let's get off the tracks before the next train comes."

"Excellent idea," Adonis says, relieved. "There's a lovely spot right up here." He goes to one of those recessed service doors and pushes it open. "Watch out for rats," he says with a rakish smile as he goes through it.

Ajax and I look at each other, questioning our decision. We know there's more than just rats in those service tunnels. There are monsters of all kinds, including a dismembered and partially rotted Hundred Hander, and the Witch Titan, Hecate.

We go down a few levels, each one making Ajax more tense than the last, until he finally says, "That's far enough."

Adonis stops and turns to us with a winning smile. "Just a little farther. I promise it's worth it."

I feel another push of calm inside, and I shake my head to clear it. Stepping away from Ajax I call my lightning to hand. "Stop it," I order Adonis. "Stop manipulating us."

He glances down at my glowing hands, a combination of fear and awe on his face. "My apologies. I'm only using my talent to keep the Furies at bay. It's hard to draw the line sometimes."

He hurries forward, bringing us to another recessed alcove. Inside, there is a reinforced steel door with a wheel lock across the middle, like a submarine. It's hoary with frost, though not cold enough to warrant that. Adonis grips the wheel and I see a flash of gold on his wrist buried amid all the other chunky, mostly silver rocker boy jewelry. This thick shackle-like cuff is special. It encircles his wrist with no visible clasp to remove it. It has a leaf and vine etching on it, and it appears to be very old. Whatever it is, it's not just a simple bracelet, any more than the charm I wear around my neck is just a necklace. His cuff has the luster of power.

He opens the thick door, and we pass through a veil of bone-chilling cold, and into a sumptuous living room plunked down in the middle of a cavern hewn from the granite. The walls look like they've been clawed out of the rock by some titanic beast, and an underground river flows past a silky-looking Persian rug, leather club chairs, and solid oak coffee table. There's also a well-stocked chrome bar cart off to the side, and after firmly shutting the door behind us, Adonis goes to it, already helping himself.

"Drinks? Snacks?" he offers, holding up a crystal bottle of brown liquor and a fancy silver dish full of nuts.

There is no way in this world a dish full of uncovered nuts would last unattended in the rat-infested lower levels of New York.

"Where are we?" I ask.

Adonis smiles at me, tipping his head as if I'd just scored a point. "Not in Kansas, Dorothy," he admits. "Not anywhere, in fact. It's sort of an *in-between* place on the edge of the Underworld." He sits with his drink in one of the deep, leather chairs. "Please," he says, gesturing for us to be seated. "The Furies can't come here, which makes it much easier on me. Even I have limits, and first encounters between enemy Scions can be... touchy. Probably why we usually kill each other on sight. But if given a little time together, we can learn to tolerate each other quite easily, actually."

Ajax and I both know what he's talking about. That's what happened to us. After our first meeting Ajax and I found ways to get around the Furies to some extent. We kept our eyes closed. We talked about silly things. We managed the Furies to some extent before we fully freed ourselves, but we've just never heard it spelled out so succinctly. I guess it's silly to think Ajax and I were the only ones.

We take seats on either side of Adonis, flanking him.

Adonis addresses Ajax. "Your family thinks you're dead. Castor was not faking his grief. Can you tell me why you did it?"

Ajax looks at me, still unsure if Adonis can be trusted.

"We didn't have a choice." I take a chance.

"Ah," Adonis says, leaning back with a knowing smile. "Star-crossed lovers. You're bound to get a lot of people killed, you know."

"That's not our intention," Ajax says.

"Your brothers are about to go on a rampage across the city. They're looking for evidence that Athens is behind your death."

"They won't find it. Castor and Pallas will stand down if there's no proof. They don't want a war," Ajax replied. He suddenly leans toward Adonis, a supplicant. "I'm expendable, but Daphne isn't. She's the last of the House of Atreus. And my father... he has this *thing* about her House."

"What *thing*?" Adonis asks.

"If Paris Delos knows I'm alive, he won't stop until I'm dead," I say. "My mother killed his brother, but he's also obsessed with her... it's complicated."

"It always is with us." Adonis lets out a long breath. "But four Houses is a damn sight better than three." He looks between us. "If you two have a child, Thebes and Atreus will be united anyway. The Truce with the gods will still be endangered."

"*If* we have a child?" I reply. "We're eighteen."

"Anyway, why are you here? Why aren't you on top of a mountain in the Andes, or hiding in the Amazon jungle? You two need to stay dead, so what are you doing in New York?"

Ajax and I share a look, both of us deciding if we should tell this guy anything.

Really, what do we have to lose?

"We've got a problem," I say.

"I would argue you have a few."

"It seems the universe it trying to kill us."

I don't say it's just Ajax the universe is trying to kill because I have two choices here. Gain Adonis' confidence so that he'd be willing to keep our secret, or kill him. Adonis might not side with us unless he thinks I'm in danger, and that by helping us he's helping to keep the Truce, and stave off a war between the Houses. My Uncle Deuce always told me that in a war between the Houses, Rome has always tried bargaining first and violence last, and that Rome more than any other House tries to avoid the ultimate war with the gods. They would certainly lose an inter-House war, and quite simply, they like things the way they are. Decadent, my Uncle Deuce had called them. The only way for Rome to avoid a war is to keep the Houses separate and, in my case, alive. Adonis might help us just to preserve the House of Atreus, and the Truce, and therefore his cushy life.

Adonis narrows his eyes, studying us. "The mousetrap you mentioned, is that what you mean?"

I nod. "It's like a chain reaction of things that ends in something innocuous nearly killing us. It keeps happening."

"A Rube Goldberg machine. Except it's not a machine, it's the world doing this to you?" I nod again, and he makes a rueful face. "That's a problem. But what help were you thinking of getting here in New York? Your family is gone," he says to me, "and *your* family thinks you're dead," he says to Ajax.

We both know we can't tell him about Tantalus. "That's our business. And the fewer people we involve in this the better," I say.

He's obviously curious, but he shrugs it off. "Your mousetrap problem is fate working against you, and that is above my pay grade. We need to speak with the Oracle."

"Antigone is my cousin. She can't find out that we're alive." Ajax says.

"She's the *Oracle*," Adonis replies in flat tone. "Don't you think she knows already?"

A glance at Ajax tells me that he never considered this, and neither did I.

"She must be keeping our secret for some reason," I say, though I have no idea what that reason could be.

"Maybe because she has a lot in common with the two of you," Adonis replies. But does not explain.

I look over at Ajax. "If he's right and she knows we're alive, then we *have* to go see her," he tells me.

"Well, no time like the present," Adonis says, standing.

Ajax looks alarmed. "You know how to get to her?"

The Oracle is the most protected Scion in all the Houses because she is the most valuable. If our lives were a game of chess, and it often feels like it is, the Oracle would be the queen. The House of Thebes guards her incessantly. The fact that Adonis, an enemy Scion, could just stand up and go to her is deeply troubling.

"Friend of a friend," Adonis replies in a breezy fashion. "Shall we?"

5

ADONIS

All right. I admit it. I'm a sucker for love.

And Ajax and Daphne are totally in love. And by "in love" I mean once in a lifetime, souls-entangled, keeper of each other's conscience's kind of love. I don't even allow myself to think this word often, knowing what I know about the gods, but their love is *sacred*, and if I don't at least try to help them, then what's the point of any of this malarkey? I'm not being romantic either—no one's ever accused me of that—I'm just talking about basic meaning of life stuff for me. I've come to terms with the fact that I'll ever have the kind of love they do, but knowing it exists, and doing what I can to make sure it isn't trampled underfoot gives me some solace.

Okay. Maybe I am being romantic.

The edges of the Underworld have all kinds of trap doors and secret tunnels that span space in creative ways. Sometimes you are farther from your goal than actual geography would dictate, and sometimes you are steps from something that should be miles away. It has something to do with your mindset when you enter the Underworld, and it's taken me years to learn how to control the Bough of Aeneas. It's the actual bough of a tree that Sibyl cut and gave to Aeneas, the founder of the House of Rome, to enable him to traverse the Underworld while still alive. How a tree branch can do that is beyond me. But it's Greek. It doesn't have to make sense.

The Bough is in the guise of a gold cuff around my wrist because it can also change its shape. Again, it's Greek. Doesn't make sense, doesn't have to. The cuff was put there when I was a baby, and it has grown and changed with me my whole life. It will only fall off when I'm dead. Which hopefully won't be soon. Although, if I keep hanging out with people like this I probably don't deserve to live. Darwin's Law applies to all beings, including Scions, and it isn't kind to idiots.

"Think happy thoughts," I tell the Starcrossed couple as I bring them through the winding caverns to Ladon's cove—and, coincidently, toward another Starcrossed couple.

Yes, I realize that this makes me doubly screwed. "Starcrossed" literally means unlucky, and right now I'm surrounded by so much bad luck I wouldn't be surprised if the tip of Manhattan caved in over my stupid head.

Despite pondering just how big of a hole I'm digging for myself, we make it to Ladon's cove, which is deep underground at the very end of Manhattan Island, in just a few minutes. The Underworld apparently wants me to get these two cursed couples together, and I wonder (as I often do when I muck around down here) if Hades has anything to do with it. Not the place, the god. Never met him, but I've read he's rather a nice guy. God. Whatever.

I somehow get the feeling Hades is hurrying us along because he wants to help Ajax and Daphne. Or maybe Hades is just kind to idiots, as Darwin is not. Which would explain why so many idiots like me aren't in Hades when natural selection should have killed us.

Whatever the cause, we get to Ladon's cove unmolested by any of the scads of monsters that slip between our world and the worlds of weird that border Hades. Much like my little subterranean haunt, Ladon's cove is dug right out of the bedrock, and is bordered by water, although it is not *in* the Underworld, as my place is. Ladon's cove exists in the real world and you don't need a glowing bracelet to get to it.

It's much larger than my hidey-hole, with more living space; it tapers down to a subterranean beach that leads out into the place where the East River, the Hudson, and the Atlantic mix in a briny swill deep down beneath the surface. Only members of the House of Athens have the strength and skill to swim at those depths and in such dark and turbulent water. I take the tunnels from the subways to get to him, but either way Ladon is hard to reach.

Ladon Attica, Firstborn of Bellerophon, Head of the House of Athens, was born half dragon and must live hidden. At his birth he was shunned by his father. Poseidon had all kinds of fishy, scaly, multi-appendaged, and sometimes downright creepy offspring, and the House of Athens has something of a monster problem in its gene pool. The House was founded by Cecrops, who coincidently, was half dragon himself. But the modern world is much less accepting of monsters in general, and there's now a law within the House that dictates that any monstrous offspring are to be left exposed on a mountainside until they die. They have the same rule for Earthshakers, which is another problematic talent that plagues the House of Athens, although one of those hasn't been born in generations. Lotta babies left to die in that

House. Luckily, Ladon didn't. Die, that is. For which I am grateful, because he is my friend.

Ladon also happens to be in love with Antigone, the Oracle of Delphi, and cousin to Ajax. But this Starcrossed couple will never consummate their love because Ladon, though human and quite handsome from the waist up, is a very pointy and sharp dragon where his tender manly bits would normally be. Their love is completely platonic, which is a good thing, or the Houses would be one step closer to being united, and then down come the gods to smite us in a pre-Biblical, totally Greek, and therefore shockingly violent and barbaric fashion.

As I lead Ajax and Daphne across metal gangplanks and through abandoned subway lines complete with hundred-year-old trains still sitting on the tracks, I am aware that the potential combination of these two pairs of Starcrossed lovers means that *three* of the Houses would be united, and that's the main reason I'm forcing this meeting. Apart from the fact that I am an idiot.

We Scions need to get on the same page. All this clandestine running around means that we're dangerously close to freeing the gods—and that is something I will never allow to happen, romantic idiot that I am or not. If the *Iliad* taught me anything, besides my family history, it's that no love affair is worth starting a war over. The Scions did that once before and it didn't end well. Just ask the Trojans—not the warriors who attained everlasting glory, but all those peasants, farmers, and cute little village people who died brutal deaths—if they think Paris' and Helen's great love was worth it. And now imagine that happening to, say, London, or Tokyo, or New York. Not such a great love story anymore, is it?

I call out to my friend, alerting him to the presence of strangers in his home, although I know from experience that he can smell us coming. I'm not worried about Ajax and Daphne ever being able to find their way back here uninvited. I took them though too many passages through the Underworld for them to ever be able to accomplish it without me. Or without dying first.

We see a flash of scales unwinding in the recessed shadows at the edge of Ladon's cove, and the hiss of his hide as it slides over itself. Ajax and Daphne startle at the sheer size of him and go on guard, though if Ladon were really attacking them they would have already been too late. In a wink, Ladon has bounded before us. He is extremely fast, even among Scions, and I hurry to speak.

"It's okay! Everyone calm down," I say, standing between them as I wrestle inwardly to contain the Furies.

Since saving Antigone's life Ladon can be around anyone in the House of Thebes without exciting the Furies, but Daphne is House of Atreus, and I wasn't kidding about how the first meeting between two members of enemy Houses is often the last. First contact is always the most dangerous moment between the Houses; if we can get through that it gets loads easier. The Furies wail insistently, but after taking a calming breath of my own—I am not completely impervious to them, either—I manage to get everyone to back down.

I make quick introductions before Daphne can throw that bolt in her hand. She controls *lightning*. Damn. I've heard stories, but I've never actually seen a bolt-thrower. It makes me wonder what else she's got in her arsenal, though lightning would be more than enough.

"Why did you bring them here?" Ladon asks, looking at me as if I'd betrayed him. This guy with his big, innocent eyes. He just kills me sometimes.

"They need to see Antigone," I reply, which elicits the response I'd intended.

Ladon looks abashed, and Ajax is quick to recognize what's going on.

"Oh no," Ajax says, palming his head and pacing in a tight circle. "Athens and Thebes?" he asks me.

"She's just a friend!" Ladon insists.

"How?" asks Ajax.

"I saved her life. Cleared my blood debt with Thebes."

While it's true his feelings for her started as strictly platonic, I've noticed a shift in him recently. She's aged slightly in the past few months that they've been in contact, but she's still young, and this has put him at odds with himself. Antigone on the other hand is madly love with him and couldn't care less about the decade or so difference between them.

"You see the problem now? Athens and Thebes," I say. "Thebes and Atreus," I say gesturing at Ajax and Daphne. Ajax gets where my math is going, and so does Daphne.

"This can't be," she says, shaking her head.

"No, it can't," I agree. "Antigone's the only one who can help you with your little mousetrap problem, but I'm also hoping she can see a better way forward because this Starcrossed lover thing isn't going to work."

"Thebes already knows the way forward," Ajax says, though he doesn't seem happy about it. "The Oracle before Antigone made a prophecy at my brother Tantalus' birth."

That is new information.

Of course, Thebes has never shared prophecies with the rest of us. That's why they are the most prosperous of all the Houses, and why they have an army in the Hundred Cousins while the House of Rome is clinging to existence by its fingernails, and Atreus is pretty much gone.

Athens is doing okay. Except for the fact that they have more brawn than brains. This is something I've always found particularly funny—strange funny, not funny-funny—what most people misidentify as ironic. Athena is the goddess of wisdom. She and Poseidon fought for generations over which of them was the true patron of Athens, but because she's a virgin goddess, she has no offspring. By default, the House of Athens are all the descendants of Poseidon, and it seems like almost out of spite that Athena made them all a bunch of cretins. Excluding Ladon, Daedalus, and a handful of others, Athens is full of dumbasses.

Right now, they are the second largest House after the House of Thebes. I'm not too worried about Athens being the last House standing, though. Dumbasses may get lucky for a while, but that luck always runs out because, well, Darwin.

"I'm guessing she didn't prophesy a hundred years of Halcyon Days?" I say, trying to keep it light so I don't lose my grip on the Furies.

"She did not," Ajax replies. "The blood of the four Scions Houses will become one in Tantalus' lifetime. The final war with the gods is coming."

Not even I can act blasé about that. "I'm guessing that Thebes has been secretly preparing to make sure that their bloodline is the one that's left?" I ask.

"My father and my brother Tantalus have. Castor and Pallas view the prophecy differently. They're against killing off the other Houses," Ajax says.

I raise an eyebrow. "What, they think the Houses will be joined in love and not war?"

Ajax narrows his eyes at my sarcasm. "They know the Furies won't allow that. They think—and so do I, by the way—that there's another path that we haven't considered. The Fates tell you the ending, but the actual story is always a surprise. Our fate may be set, but how we arrive at that fate depends on what kind of people we want to be. We don't have to be killers."

Huh. He is surprisingly deep. Daphne gets it. She's watching him with eyes that I'm pretty sure aren't her own. Yet, when she looks at him with so much love, I can almost see her true face behind whatever magic she's using to conceal her identity.

There was another girl who did that. Helen. Now *there's* some bad luck. What Scion would be cynical enough to name their daughter Helen? I'd think Helen and Daphne were the same person, except the feeling I get from them is nothing alike. And Helen loved Lucas. They can't be the same girl, but there is something about them... It's making me crazy. I have to see Daphne's face. But I'll tackle that later.

"Your father is still Head of your House. Castor and Pallas are good little soldiers, and they'll do what he tells them to," I say, steering my brain back to the conversation. "If he orders them to kill other Scions, they will."

Ajax cocks his head, considering. "Not blindly. And they have a lot of support in the Hundred Cousins. My father won't do anything that will divide his House."

Good to know. Castor is about to be spending a lot of time with my sister as they investigate Ajax's death. Leda could influence him. Keep him arguing for peace, or at least peace with Rome. A prophecy is a prophecy—it's going to happen—but nobody knows *when* any prophecy will be fulfilled. At this point, that's our only hope. Delay, delay, delay. Scions have been putting off the return of the gods since the fall of Troy thirty-three hundred years ago, and hopefully we can pull it off for a bit longer.

"Okay," I say, making up my mind.

Ladon and Antigone are not going to be having any kids. The

Houses won't be joined by them, so that's one problem solved. And Daphne and Ajax? Well, she has to have a kid, or Atreus will be extinct anyway, but she doesn't have to have a kid with Ajax. I can make sure their *union bears no fruit*, as they used to say in the old days. House of Rome has about a thousand potions for fertility and contraception. I just need to get some crap together, slip it into his drink, and Ajax will not be fathering any children. In the meantime, I need them to stay here with Ladon where I can keep an eye on them.

I feel bad for them. Ajax has "great dad" written all over him, even if he is too young for the job right now. I don't relish the thought of making him sterile, but someone's got to save the world.

"It's all going to work out," I tell them.

Daphne laughs bitterly. "How do you figure?"

"We're going to appeal to Castor's better angels. He'll keep Paris from going to war with the other Houses," I say. I turn to Ladon. "You need to tell your brother that Leda and Castor are going to be poking around his territory. Tell Daedalus he's got to let them. Make Athens stand down, be helpful even."

Ladon's jaw slackens as he stares at me, probably thinking I've lost my mind. "My brother will never do that."

"Tell him it's out of respect for the dead," I reply.

I quickly lay out Thebes' suspicion that Athens was involved in Ajax's death, and why Ajax and Daphne must stay dead to protect Daphne, the Last Atreidae, from Paris Delos. But we've still got to clear Athens from any suspicion in Ajax's phony death or Castor will go to war to avenge his brother. It's complicated, but Ladon's a smart guy and he catches on fast.

"If Athens allows Thebes to investigate out of respect for their dead brother, Castor will remember it. He's an honorable guy.

He'll speak up for Athens if his father tries to make a move against them," I say. "And as for Rome, well... my sister will take care of that with him."

"Yeah, I've seen how Leda would like to take care of my brother. I don't think that's going to keep the Houses separate, though."

"My sister's smarter than that," I say with confidence I don't necessarily feel. I'll make sure she's smarter than that, or we're doomed.

My stomach growls. All this Machiavellian scheming is making me hungry. "Anyone want take out?"

6

DAPHNE

"I'll go with you," I tell Adonis when he suggests food. "I have to anyway, right?" I add when I see him pause.

Ladon can be near Ajax, or anyone from the House of Thebes, without inciting the Furies because he cleared his debt with the House of Thebes by saving Antigone, but I'm House of Atreus. I can't be around Ladon without Adonis there to control the Furies between us.

"Right," Adonis replies, remembering. I can tell this has thrown a wrench in the works for him, and now he's reconsidering his next steps.

I don't trust Adonis. I think he's on our side for the moment because he's trying to avoid war, but I have no illusions about whether he'll stay on our side if his loyalty gets tested. He's up to something. Scratch that—he's up to *several* things. I can practically hear the gears in his head spinning from three paces away.

"Stay here and wait for Antigone?" I suggest to Ajax. He

nods, already anticipating this. After all, the less he shows his face in public, the better.

"She might not come today," Ladon says, trying not to sound mournful and failing.

"Antigone? *Really*?" Ajax asks, which sends Ladon into a flurry of slithering tail and prancing claws. His dragon half is quite emotive, which is unfortunate because it is also covered in razor sharp scales and dagger-like spikes.

"She is my *friend*," Ladon says.

I feel Adonis say close to my ear, "He'll agonize about this for another half an hour at least."

I give Ajax a look. He nods me away, his attention occupied with not getting impaled on any part of Ladon, and I follow Adonis out of the cave.

I notice his golden cuff glowing softly on occasion, glints that are coupled with flashes of bone-aching cold. I've felt this kind of cold before. I question Adonis about the cuff, but he's elusive, saying it is a family heirloom. We Scions don't like to reveal our abilities to each other. You never know when one of them will come as a surprise and give you an advantage in a fight.

"The cuff allows you to go through the Underworld," I guess. He glances back at me, surprised.

"Been here before?" he asks.

"Not exactly here. I've been to the Dry Lands, though."

His eyes widen in genuine sympathy. The only way to get to the Dry Lands is to die. "How'd you get out?"

"I was sent back."

Adonis stops and stares at me. "Did you meet *him*?"

There is only one "him" he could mean. Hades. I nod and debate whether I should tell him about their resemblance to one another. What would knowing that do to someone, I wonder, and does it have a deeper meaning that I can't quite grasp yet? It can't be random. There is a reason the Head of the House of Atreus looks exactly like Helen of Troy. There must be a reason Adonis looks like Hades.

Adonis is staring at my heart, watching my flailing emotions, but he can't read my mind. He lets out a held breath as he turns back to the path. "Did he give you that disguise? That face you're wearing over your real one?"

"No," I reply, surprised he can see past the Cestus, though I probably shouldn't be.

The Cestus was a gift to Helen of Troy from her sister Aphrodite, and Adonis is descended from Aphrodite. No one else from the House of Rome—or any other House—has ever been able to see past it, though. He must be extremely powerful.

"Family heirloom," I say, grinning.

He chuckles. "Touché."

We come out in a subway station on the Upper East Side after a relatively short amount of time, hop up from the tracks at Scion speed so no one sees us, and in moments we've joined the flow of foot traffic aboveground. We're headed toward a corner pizza place.

"New York City pizza," I groan with pleasure.

"Missed it?" he asks.

"You have no idea."

"This place is my favorite. Doesn't look like anything special, but the *sauce*..." he trails off, like there are no words to describe it.

Adonis saunters into his pizza place and orders a few large pies from an older lady who's as wide as she is tall. She beams at Adonis, surreptitiously patting at the gray-shot black hair she's got caught up in a net, and rushes to fill his order. Hands stuffed in his pockets as he waits, Adonis keeps glancing over at me.

"You gotta let me see it," he says.

I shake my head, knowing he's talking about my real face.

"Come on!" he cajoles. "Is your identity some big secret or something?"

I debate whether I should just tell him the truth. "It's cursed," I say. "Most Scions react to it... poorly."

Most Scions react to it by falling madly, obsessively in love with me. That's the last thing I need.

"Like Medusa?" he asks.

"I wish."

It's niggling at him, burrowing into his mind. I've seen it before. He won't let it go, and soon he'll resent me for keeping it from him. I'm torn as to what I should do. I've learned the hard way that withholding my face can be worse than just letting that person see. We get the pizza and a couple of bottles of soda and pay up. He leaves an exorbitant tip, and I can tell by the way the staff reacts to it that he always does. As we push back out into the crowd, I allow the shift so he can see a glimpse of my real face. I hear him gasp.

"You're *her*," he says. "Helen of Troy."

"A copy," I reply, assuming my disguise again.

"No—wait," Adonis says, wanting to see it for longer, but I shake my head.

"It's better for everyone if I keep it hidden." I wave a hand at all the people we're passing. "For them, for you. Trust me, it's not safe."

Adonis looks down at his feet. "Immediate obsession. That's terrifying," he mumbles. After a few blocks he asks, "Has Paris Delos seen your real face?" I nod, and he frowns in thought. "But you said he was obsessed with your mother."

"We all get the Face. Mother to daughter. I told you. Atreus is cursed. There's nothing we can do about it, and it's never done anything but start wars."

He walks next to me, lost in troubling thoughts until he seems to decide something. "Don't worry. I won't tell anyone."

"Not even your sister?"

"Gods, no!" he exclaims, his expression casually horrified as he shifts the pizza boxes stacked in his arms. "If Leda had a hamster, she'd find a way to weaponize it. Telling her about your face would be like giving her launch codes."

I laugh despite myself. I don't want to like Adonis.

"You don't have to worry about me, either," he says when he notices me putting more space between us. It's habit. I can't help it.

I look over at him so I can read his face.

"I'm really good at controlling my emotions, especially the more insidious ones like obsession and covetousness," he tells me. "I never would have survived in my House if I wasn't."

I believe him. I know a thing or two about having to survive a messed-up family.

We take the expedited route back down to Ladon. I start to feel uncomfortable before we get there. Edgy. Irritated. It's the Furies. I hear him curse under his breath.

"Of all the days..." he says to himself.

"What is it?" I ask.

"Daedalus," he mutters. While Ladon can be with Ajax, or anyone from the House of Thebes, and not incite the Furies, the same doesn't hold for his brother. Ajax and Daedalus will attack each other on sight.

It's in my head, I know it is, but I imagine I can almost hear the gears of the mousetrap advancing into the next phase in the chain-reaction. A quick glance at Adonis, and then we drop every-thing and run.

When we reach the end of the tunnel that leads into the back of Ladon's cave, Adonis shoots out an arm and clotheslines me, stopping me from charging headlong into the cavern. His other hand he holds up imperiously as he scrunches his eyes shut, concentrating as he wrestles against the Furies. We can hear raised voices. Ladon's, and someone else's—I don't know whose—is saying, *how close is that subway line?* I don't hear Ajax. And then it's like I can't feel my body anymore.

"Just calm down!" Adonis hisses at me.

I realize he's tackled me from behind and put me in a bear hug. I struggle against him as he wrestles me to the ground, pinning me beneath him.

"Please, trust me!" he says close to my ear. "Ajax is hidden. He's *safe*. But I can't keep him that way unless you stop fighting me!"

Trust him? Trust my enemy? I look up at Adonis as he battles to keep my wrists immobilized on either side of my face. He looks frantic. I could get out of his hold. I'm stronger than he is. I could electrocute him. Kill him.

And then what? I'd have to go in there, kill Ladon and kill whoever else is in there with him. That's what the Furies want. That's what the mousetrap wants, for me to open up my light-ning and rain down death until there is only one House left standing.

The voices in Ladon's cave are no longer shouting. I do the unthinkable. I nod. "Okay," I whisper between panting breaths. "I'll trust you."

7

DAEDALUS
HOUSE OF ATHENS

My brother is yelling at me through the red haze of rage in my head.

"Daedalus, stop!" Ladon calls. "One of the other Houses must be on the subway that comes near here! It happens sometimes."

And—poof—the Furies are gone.

Ladon still has ahold of my shoulders, and his tail is tightly coiled around his lower body to protect me from the sharp scales that run in a line down the side of his serpentine half. I relax a little. Not a lot.

"How close is that subway line!? Which one is it!?" I ask. Shout, really.

I can still feel my heart heaving around in my chest. If one of the other Houses ever found Ladon... The Delos brothers would probably skin him and put his head on a wall in their showroom. Pack of pretty boys, so polished and well spoken. They think they're the heroes of old reborn, and they would hunt my brother like he was some prize. Like he was the Thespian Lion, or the Minotaur.

"I don't know," he answers.

I send the water still soaking my skin and clothes away into in the air to dry myself. "They shouldn't be in our territory."

"They're probably passing through it. On a train. How else are they supposed to get off the island?" he asks.

He's always forgiven others so quickly. I can't remember him ever getting angry. Not really. After watching him my whole life, I've decided that the Furies influence him less. A few times now I've seen things that make me think they barely influence him at all.

When I was sixteen, my father ordered me to hunt down some Athenian Outcasts that he wanted to put to death. I found them and nearly killed them, but my brother was watching my back when all this went down and he intervened. I was overtaken by the Furies and I would have slaughtered them all, which would have made me an Outcast myself, but Ladon was fine. He kept me in check and we managed to get the Outcasts back to my father alive.

I still can't believe my father did that to me. He would have let me become an Outcast just so he could have his revenge. In the end my father had the Outcasts killed the old way—which is to force them to take their own lives so no more Outcasts are made.

I don't know if it's because Ladon is part dragon and that gives him powers we don't possess, or if it's because he's already suffered so much that the Furies have granted him some grace in this one aspect, but he can remain calm even when anyone else would be screaming with rage.

Ladon shuffles up to the living area instead of bounding with his usual gait which makes him look like he's swimming on land.

He's keeping his tail coiled tightly to his lower body. He's being careful. Staying contained.

"You can relax," I say. "I'm in control. I'm not going to cut myself on you."

He gives an indeterminate grunt like he doesn't believe me. "Are you hungry? Thirsty?" he asks.

"No," I reply.

Ladon stares at me with his eyes narrowed. I'd call his look mistrustful, but that's not quite it. Or if it is, it's not me he doesn't trust. "I was hoping to speak to you, and here you are," he says. "Isn't that strange?"

I guffaw. "I guess we're telepathic now."

He laughs and shakes his head in that bashful way of his. Makes him look younger, and I guess he kind of is. Harsh as his life has been it's also been sheltered, at least from other people. He hasn't had to learn how to fit into the world the way the average twenty-something would have. He hasn't had to pretend to be cool, or act like he's always right, or hide the fact that half the things he feels scare the shit out of him. Like I do.

Sometimes I think my brother's maybe sixteen in terms of maturity. And then other times he says something so wise it's like he's a hundred. He may be young inside, but he's never been dumb, and he's the only person in my family who makes it worth it for me to be House of Athens.

Though I still wish I was just a normal person. Every single day I wish I was normal. And he's probably the only one who wishes that more than I do. Maybe that's why we've always been so close.

"Not telepathic," he says, like I was serious. He thinks some more. "Led by fate. Linked in our destinies," he finally decides.

No idea what he means by that, but I kinda like it. "Sure. We're linked," I allow. "What did you want to talk to me about?"

"It's been three full moons since the youngest son of Paris Delos was killed. Thebes will be coming out of mourning now."

"Yeah, I've been thinking about that too," I say, sighing. Freaking out about it is more like it, but I can't tell Ladon that. "They'll be out for blood."

Ladon tips his head to the side. "Maybe not. They killed the girl who did it."

"They'll still find a way to blame Athens," I say, shrugging. "Though the way Nilus responded to her makes me think she was Roman."

Four Athenian soldiers had a run-in with the Atreidae who killed Ajax, and who was then later killed by Tantalus. Even though she beat the stuffing out of all of them *and* half killed Nilus, he hasn't stopped talking about the girl with the most beautiful face he'd ever seen.

"Is he still obsessed with her?" my brother asks.

"He still talks about her," I say. "I don't get it."

Ladon smiles at me. "You would if it was Leda."

"Gods, let it *go*," I groan, standing up so I can move away from him. Just hearing her name makes my skin hot, and my brother can sense even a minuscule change in temperature through air or water if he's close enough. He really is amazing. The perfect hunter, though it makes it hard to hide emotions from him. "She and I aren't going to happen for about a thousand reasons."

"True. But denying it isn't going to make you get over her any quicker," he replies, then he laughs at himself, like he should be taking his own advice.

I look at him, surprised. He's definitely thinking about a girl. "Who is she?"

"Does it matter?" he replies. He gestures to his still-coiled tail.

How he manages to not be bitter about that, I'll never know. I don't say anything. There's nothing he can do about the way he was made. Not a lot of half-human, half-dragon women running around, and unless Ladon were to find one, he will never find a mate. The top half of him could never couple with a beast, and the bottom half, well. He'd kill a human girl. Though, Athenian men rarely do much better when it comes to mates. The male Scions in the other Houses have always managed to bring mortal wives home and keep them for a while, sometimes into old age, but Athenians don't have it that easy. Almost all our mortal women die in childbirth—if not before. It's tough for a mortal woman to carry any Scion baby, but Athenian babies are especially brutal. Even in the womb we're a bunch of savages.

"But we were speaking about the Delos brothers," he continues. "They will want proof Athens wasn't involved."

"The rest of us don't owe them anything," I snap.

Ladon's eyes soften, like he's disappointed in me. "They are in mourning still, even if they've stopped fasting by day and wearing ashes on their foreheads. If *I* were to be killed—"

"You're going to live for about three hundred years," I say. He starts to say something else, but I get where he's going with this. "You think we should help them find out who that girl was in an act of good faith. Easy. She was House of Atreus. The Delos family claimed the Aegis of Zeus off Polydeuces' body and displayed it for all of us to see. Case closed."

"Yes, except our father was supposed to have killed off the last of the House of Atreus twenty years ago."

"He lied," I scoff. "He does it all the time."

"So why should Thebes believe that Atreus is extinct now? Because Athens, the liars, say so?"

I kind of knew this was coming. I nod and sigh. "I've actually thought about that, too. They might think we were helping Atreus hide, and that we still could be if there are any more of them out there."

Ladon nods. "I'm surprised they haven't called a meeting already."

I pace around my brother's neat living area. He likes shiny stuff. It's a dragon thing, I think. Little curios glint inside carefully dug out niches in the granite walls. His furniture, which he can't sit on, is polished to gleaming. I don't know why he has all this furniture. I rarely ever sit on it, either. I think he just likes to have civilized things around him even though all he can do is look at them.

"So what do we do?" I ask.

"Let them search for Atreus in our territory. Help them, out of respect for the dead."

It really is the only way to avoid a war, though I hate Thebes more for it. If that's even possible. "Why do those golden boys always get what they want? If one of our brothers—Nilus or Lelix —got killed, do you think Thebes would let us prance through their territory, implying that they were involved?"

It's an unfair comparison. The Delos brothers love each other while Ladon and I have no affection for Nilus or Lelix who are, in complete honesty, a couple of dipshits whose stupidity is eclipsed only by their cruelty. But how much the sons of Attica love or don't love each other isn't the inequality that matters here, and Ladon knows it.

"Their father does not lie," he says. "Ours does."

And that's the heart of it. My father is a dishonorable man

and as his Heir I'm always left cleaning up his messes. This is a big one.

Bellerophon Attica's reputation as the greatest fighter of his generation is based on his assertion that he's the Scion who killed Polydeuces Atreus decades ago. Acknowledging he lied about that even though it is clear that Polydeuces only died a few months ago would shame him. Up to now he's been denying that it was Atreus that attacked the House of Thebes, despite all evidence to the contrary because how could it be if he killed off the last of that House? Allowing Thebes to search for Atreus would be tantamount to admitting he lied. Which, of course, he did. I scrub my hands over my face so I don't scream.

"I would have to convince father to open his territory to the enemy for some other reason than they have the right to search because he's a liar. That should be easy."

Ladon meets my sarcasm with a weak smile. "Or. Don't tell him."

🐚 8 🐚

ADONIS

Seeing Ajax peel himself out from between Ladon's coils after Daedalus leaves, looking half suffocated and wholly shell-shocked, almost makes the threat of getting electrocuted to death by Daphne worth it. At least someone knows my pain. Ladon hid me in there once, and it felt like I got swallowed.

Daphne rushes to Ajax as he falls in a sweaty heap beside Ladon's unwinding tail. I can see the way her body echoes his. Distress in him creating real, physical pain in her.

"Are you okay?" she asks him, trying to help him to his feet before he's ready.

"Give him a minute," I advise.

I've been where Ajax is right now, and I gotta say it is no fun. Not that Ladon hurts you when he hides you in his coils; he doesn't at all, but being completely wrapped up by something that very much resembles the King-Kong of anacondas is something human beings have an atavistic aversion to. Coupled with the terror of not being able to move a literal muscle while you're in there and the knowledge that Ladon is so shockingly powerful he could break every bone in your body if he so much as coughed... well, it's a unique experience.

"That was awful," Ajax says, deadpan. He looks pale.

"He's got a particular musk, doesn't he?" I muse. "Very oud-y. Gets into the back of your throat."

Ladon's back talons scraped against the granite floor in agitation. "I'm sorry if I frightened you. I didn't have much of a choice."

Ajax shakes his head and allows Daphne to help him to his feet. "Thank you," he says graciously.

I go back into the tunnel to salvage what I can of the pizza, which got dumped on the ground in my struggle with Daphne. Luckily, the boxes held together.

When I return Ajax is asking Ladon, "Does your brother visit often?"

"Couple of times a week," Ladon replies, shrugging. "But I wasn't expecting him today."

"Another example of your mousetrap at work?" I guess as I lay out the pizzas on Ladon's coffee table.

"If it were, we would have ended up fighting Daedalus. Bloodshed has always been involved with the mousetrap prior to this," Daphne says, shaking her head. Then she frowns. "I think it was *almost* the mousetrap, though. Like it got thwarted somehow."

"Perhaps it has something to do with how Antigone doesn't feel the Fates around you." I say to Ladon as I bite into a slice. Dammit. It's cold. Still good, though.

"What do you mean?" Daphne asks.

"Antigone told me that she always hears the Moirai whispering to her, except when she's with me. She never hears them or feels them when we're together. She said it's like they can't see through me," Ladon says. "I presume that's why she likes my company so much."

Ajax turns to me. "You think it's the Fates that are after us?" he asks. "Not some other small god or random curse we hadn't thought about yet?"

"Oh, it's definitely fate. Starcrossed couples are doomed to end in convoluted ways. Didn't you guys read *Romeo and Juliet*?"

"They were Scions?" Ajax asks.

"Of course they were. Romeo was from House of Rome and Juliet was Theban. Anyway. All that business with the sleeping draft, and the lost message and the poison? Very mousetrappy," I reply. "They were trying to fake their deaths and run away together just like you guys did."

Daphne and Ajax share a falling look with one another, and I get why they feel like this is hopeless. We've been taught that there's no way to avoid fate. I mean, Oedipus is one of Ajax's direct ancestors. I'm sure they've considered that everything they're doing to extend their lives is futile and that this trip to New York will probably end with them meeting their fate on the road they took to escape it. But before Daphne and Ajax can throw in the towel and hurl themselves off the nearest tall building, which would deprive the world of the last member of the House of Atreus, I put down my cold slice and let them in on what I've been brewing in the back of my head.

"Lucky for you guys, there might be way around it." I point at Ladon. "That fine half-man, half-dragon right there is the only Scion I've ever heard of who the Fates can't control. And when you're around him, they can't control you either."

Everyone stares at each other for a moment. This is a Doug Flutie-sized Hail Mary I'm throwing here, but I don't let them see me sweat it. There are no lengths I won't go to in avoidance of a future that ends with the world being overrun by gods who came into being before there was a concept of morality. The only real rule the Greek gods have is *don't feed anyone your own children,* but apart from that, it's open season as far as they're concerned.

"I guess it's worth a try," Daphne says.

"How do you feel about having roommates?" Ajax asks Ladon. It's a joke, but Ladon isn't great at reading social cues.

"My brother, and sometimes even the other members of my House, they just come here uninvited..." he says.

"We know," I tell him, holding up a hand. "These two can't stay here for the rest of their lives. That's not a solution. But if it's okay with you, they should stay here most of the time while we try to figure this out. I'll make sure to be with Daphne to control the Furies in case you have any visitors."

That seems to make sense to everyone. Which is good because I'm still trying to convince myself that it makes sense to me. There is a voice in the back of my head that says I'm bringing together not one, or two, but all three of my enemy Houses, and if Rome is to stand a chance at survival in the coming war my best bet would be to set them against each other. Of course, this voice sounds like my sister's, and therefore, I know the advice it's giving me is terrible.

"This pizza is not going to eat itself," I remind them, and they finally join me. Except for Ladon, of course, whose diet runs strictly in the uncooked and usually still bleeding meat department.

Ajax and I are pleasantly discussing what it's like to live on a boat and spend your days painting and sailing around island paradises, when Daphne's nerves get the better of her and she finally decides that waiting for Antigone to show up isn't going to be the best use of her time.

Her leg has been bouncing for about ten minutes before she stands up and declares, "I'm going to find Antigone."

"There's a guard with her nearly all the time since Ajax's death," Ladon warns. "If you're seen by someone from the House of Thebes, won't they recognize you?"

Daphne alters her face and hair slightly and Ladon gasps. I almost gasp, too, because it really is shocking.

Then she turns to me. "How do I get out of here?"

9

DAPHNE

Ladon tells me of an underground route that will lead me directly into Theban territory and I take it, noticing that it's well-worn. Clean, even. I smile to myself, debating inwardly about who uses this path more—Ladon or Antigone?

The tunnel brings me to the tracks of a subway station. I time the trains going by and jump up onto the platform. I come above-ground on the other side of Washington Square Park from the Delos brownstone.

It's strange to be here again. Bittersweet. I miss who we were when Ajax lived on the other side of that third story window, and I would rush here after school to be with him.

I can hear Castor in there. I don't catch who he's talking to before the two of them move to the back of the house and use the elevator that brings them down to the lower levels, but I *feel* that it's Tantalus.

I could ring the bell. Figure out some excuse to be there. I know Tantalus would recognize me immediately and he would play along. The original plan, the whole reason we came back to the city, was to ask Tantalus for help, but now I'm reconsidering. With Adonis, Ladon, and soon Antigone involved I'm not sure we should bring anyone else into this. But more important than that, and this is why I stop myself—Tantalus would be too happy to see me.

Even if I showed up on his doorstep disguised, he'd still know it was me. He'd make some excuse to Castor and take me to his study. He'd give me one of his enveloping hugs and hold me to him just a little too long. He'd tilt his mouth toward my neck, press his hand against the small of my back and ease my hips closer to his. Not a lot. Not so I feel caged or like he's taking advantage, but just enough to let me sense the edge of that yawning space inside of him that's been empty since I refused to fill it. And then he'll pull away, ask about Ajax, and hate himself a little bit more for wanting me. I can't just walk up to him without warning. It's not fair.

It's gotten dark out. I head west into the Village toward the Lycians' brownstone, where Antigone lives, convinced now that this is a better plan. We came back to New York to get the only help either of us could think of, but now Adonis has offered us another possibility. I haven't spoken of it with Ajax—how can I, considering it means talking about how Tantalus wants me for himself?—but if we can get help that doesn't include his brother it might be better for all of us. Also, I want to keep Tantalus in the dark about Ladon. And Adonis in the dark about Tantalus. What a mess. There are too many people involved already, and I can practically feel the mousetrap clicking and whirring around me.

I watch Antigone's house for about an hour, walking by

multiple times as unobtrusively as possible before I pick my spot in the shadows and settle in. I hear snatches of conversation from inside. A woman is speaking to a man, but I can only hear pieces of their exchange. It takes me a while to discern that it's Ceyx, the Healer, speaking to Jordana, Antigone's mother. I don't really understand what's going on apart from the fact that apparently Antigone is tired and wants to sleep all the time, but Ceyx can't find anything wrong with her.

"Depression often masquerades as fatigue," Ceyx says at one point.

"But she's been happy lately," Jordana replies, like she can't figure it out.

They talk for a while longer and then Ceyx leaves. I mark his tall, thin frame as he goes, careful to keep well out of his line of sight. And then, about half an hour later, I see Antigone sneaking out. She looks taller, more grown-up than I remember her. She goes into the middle of the street, looks at a manhole cover, and then taps on it five times.

I'm thinking this is the moment when I should call out to her, and then it hits me, what if Adonis was wrong and she never foresaw that we were still alive? What do I say to her? *Don't run, I didn't kill your cousin? Oh, and I'm not a ghost?* Neither of those options seem really appealing and they'll probably just make her start screaming.

Before I can figure out the least panic-inducing way to accost her, she starts running toward Washington Square. I follow. She slows to a walk around 5th Ave when she gets to that more well-lit area around the park. She avoids the Delos brownstone by going a block out of her way and circling the north side of the park to get to the subway station. The same subway station that has a tunnel to Ladon's cave. Ah. I think I've discovered Antigone's reason for wanting to go to bed so early.

The park is closed, forcing me to go around it and split the distance between Antigone and the Delos brownstone, bringing me a little too close to both for my liking. I've decided it's a bad idea to approach Antigone on the street. I've met her before and she and I got along well back then, but she might still believe I'm dead even if she is the Oracle, and I don't want to scare her and cause a scene out in the open. I'll wait until we're in the tunnels.

I'm so focused on how to go about initiating a conversation without freaking her out that I don't notice I'm being followed, too.

"Daphne."

Tantalus' voice is rough and full of longing. We stop a few paces away from each other. His back is to the subway station. He doesn't see Antigone steal down the steps, and I wonder if he even noticed that she snuck out. But I know the answer to that question as soon as I think it. All he sees is me.

"I'm sorry I surprised you like this. I was going to send word first," I say, but Tantalus is already shaking his head.

"Don't worry about that," he replies. "Did something happen? Are you okay?"

"No—yes. I mean, a little bit of both." He smiles at me while I sigh and try to order my thoughts. It's impossible to lie to a Falsefinder, but that doesn't mean there can't be a right truth to tell him. "We're not in any immediate danger," I clarify.

"Good," he says and falls silent again, just looking at me from five feet away. He did not try to hug me like I thought he would. That's worse somehow. Like he doesn't even trust himself to give me a hug anymore.

"How did you know it was me?" I ask. I was expecting this,

but I'm still curious to find out if I've got a specific tell that would give me away to anyone else.

He responds with a tired laugh, shaking his head. "Your walk. The way you hold your head. I don't know. It's just a feeling." He watches me a little longer. "What's the matter, Daphne? Do you need help?"

"I'm not sure anyone can help us," I say, still trying to decide what to tell him and what to keep hidden. I have no choice but to involve him now, and somehow leave Ladon, Antigone, and Adonis out of it. "I need some advice," I finally decide.

"Come inside," he says.

We walk the short distance back to the Delos brownstone. We don't talk on the way, but we keep shooting each other expectant glances like we're leaving an opening for the other to talk. It's not awkward, per se, but it isn't comfortable. He's guarded and I'm apologetic. Neither of which makes any sense unless you first admit it's because there's more going on between us than there should be. Which we can't do or this whole thing falls apart.

He doesn't take me downstairs to the lower level where I know there are a few offices, a master suite, vaults for their unbelievable art collection, and even a fight cage and gymnasium. He brings me upstairs to his room instead.

I've never seen inside his room before. I pause, glancing over my shoulder and down the hallway to Ajax's door. They haven't changed it at all. It's still covered in graffiti, an explosion of riotous passion and grit in the otherwise immaculate and expensively decorated house. I look back to see Tantalus watching me.

"Everyone's downstairs for a House meeting," he explains. "I can't take a stranger down there."

"This is fine," I say and follow him into his bedroom. "Do you still live here?"

I know he's married now. He did that to protect Scions from exposure, but really, he did it to protect me. I wonder how much of this she knows.

"Mildred and I have our own place in Soho," he replies, looking down. There is no warmth in the way he says her name. "I still stay here a lot, though."

I don't press him for details, though I have questions about his wife. About how much she knows, how involved she's become with the House of Thebes; but I don't ask any of these things because I know he isn't happy with her, and it's all my fault. He pushes the door open and goes in.

His room is like a gallery. Spare and well lit, clean lines, bare wood floors, and white walls unimpeded by anything but a few carefully chosen works of art. I know enough about art now to recognize a black and white Frank Stella on one wall, and a Rothko in fierce pinks and reds on another. I stare at this hypnotic color field, which is positioned opposite Tantalus' bed. Covered in a white duvet, two pillows, and nothing else, his bed looks hard and flat like a platform not meant to be shared with anyone. I feel him watching me and meet his gaze.

"My wife hates it," he says with a wry tilt to his lips.

I frown and glance around at how open his bedroom is. How straightforward. How it answers the need in him for truth. "It's painfully honest."

I hear him let out a breath and I look back at him. I know I've said too much or said the right thing, which for us is the wrong thing, because his guard is down now, and that empty space in him with my name on it opens a little wider.

"Sit," he says, indicating a corner where there are two Mies chairs in white leather and chrome facing each other. There is no table near them. This is a place to talk, and only talk, not hide behind a drink.

Leaning forward, elbows braced on my knees, I tell him about the mousetrap, and he asks detailed questions about each incident. I leave nothing out. Not even that part about Ajax and I making love on the beach. How I was on top, and how my body curved over his to protect him. I see him swallow, his eyes turning inward as he pictures it, but he doesn't interrupt. It's better for me to be brutal. Painfully honest.

"I don't know if I should even try to fight this, or if I'm just digging us in deeper," I say, my voice catching as I start to wrap it up. The insistent clamor of managed panic has been droning in my head for weeks now. Talking about it has been steadily turning the volume up until I can't take it anymore. Shit. I think might cry. "And I'm so sorry—I'm just realizing that if it *is* fate we're up against, I'm probably dragging you down with me."

Then he's kneeling in front of me and pulling me into his arms. My head falls on his shoulder and he cradles the back of my neck in his big, warm hand.

"Don't worry about me," he whispers. "I'll fix it. I'll fix everything."

It's an insane promise. Impossible for him to keep, but I believe him anyway. At least, I believe that I'm not alone in this anymore which is almost as good. The more I try not to cry the hotter and harder the tears push to get out. Finally, I give in and pour a river down Tantalus' neck. It helps, and as soon as I let the tears go they peak, then start to ebb. I sniff and laugh at my foolishness as I pull away from him.

"Sorry," I say, wiping my eyes with the backs of my hands. "I'm not afraid for myself. But... "

He nods in sympathy. "Being afraid for Ajax is unbearable. I know the feeling."

Tantalus and I have tacitly agreed, without ever having so much as mentioned it in passing, that Ajax was meant for better, more beautiful things than we were. It's not that Ajax can't look after himself; it's that he shouldn't have to, and loving him means shielding him so he can make art. If Tantalus and I can't do that, then what the hell are we good for?

"We think it's fate working against us," I say.

"No," he replies immediately, pushing even the suggestion away as if he won't even consider it. "If it was fate that wanted Ajax dead, he would be already. Fate is driving you back to New York, that's all."

"But—it's like the world keeps collapsing in on him," I begin, like he didn't understand, couldn't grasp what I did because he hadn't witnessed it firsthand. "I've never seen such a collection of improbable things happening one right after the other—"

He stands and starts pacing around the small area. "This is about you, not him. Think about it. Ajax being in danger is the only thing that could have brought you back to New York, and here you are. Exactly where fate wants you." He stops pacing and looks down on me, his gaze holding mine with so much conviction I can't even look away, let alone disagree with him. "Fate isn't something that is *going* to happen, it's also what *has* happened and what *is* happening. This right here—you being here in my room with me—is fate. Now we just have to figure out why the Moirai brought you back to New York so we can understand what you're supposed to do next."

I can't see a way to argue with him. Maybe I shouldn't. Maybe all of this has been fated and I'm meant to be here. Maybe what was wrong was my running away from the conflict that has been brewing in this city, and the Fates used Ajax to bring me back to it.

I turn my hands up, at a loss. "I don't understand anything right now," I admit.

"Where's Ajax?" he asks.

"Safe," I reply.

Tantalus narrows his eyes at me, trying to peer into my head and discern why I'm being cagy about Ajax's whereabouts.

"I'm keeping him away from you on purpose," I say. I gesture to our surroundings. "You're never alone. One of your brothers or cousins is always in the next room and in my experience, they always come barging through bedroom doors at the worst moments. I can change my face, Ajax can't."

All these statements are true. None of them fit together in a way that explains why I'm keeping Ajax's location a secret, but hearing no lie, Tantalus accepts them. And this is his blind spot, I realize. He relies so heavily on his ability to hear lies that he believes misleading truths unquestioningly. But only if I'm careful. Only if I craft my lies from the absolute truth.

"No one can see him, or you'll be exposed," he agrees. Then he looks up at me. His expression is so vulnerable and so much like Ajax it startles me. "You think I should stay away from him, too?"

"For now," I say. "He misses all of you so much. It would be hard for him."

"And dangerous," he agrees. He nods to himself, accepting my terms. "We should get you out of here," he says, then he smiles and looks back at me as he leads me out. "Before someone barges in."

He walks me all the way to the subway station. It's dark. He's unnecessarily escorting me as if I were a mortal girl, but it's still sweet.

"What's the plan?" I ask before I go below ground. "Do we even have one?"

"Not yet," he replies, laughing a little. "I need some time to think about it."

We set a time and place to meet again before we part ways. He does not try to hug me or touch me in any way. He just nods and steps back. But as I go down the steps, I can feel his eyes on me. He watches me until I disappear.

10

TANTALUS

Daphne goes and half of me goes with her. The better half, I suppose, because once she leaves a thousand bitter thoughts creep in.

I held it together at the start, but I can only pretend for so long I'm not gutted by seeing her. And then when I'm done pretending to myself, I have to touch her. I have to hold her. I have to get a promise from her that we'll see each other again. Then, when I get these things, I'm back to hating myself and making promises like an addict. My mind saying things like, *this is the last time* and *all I want is to look and not touch*. It's bullshit. I can hear every lie, even when I'm the one telling it.

I watch Daphne go down the subway steps and I have to hurry back to the House meeting. Rome has contacted us. Athens will allow Castor—and only Castor—into their territory to have a look around for any more Atreidae. I run back and make it as the meeting is breaking up and everyone is either leaving the brownstone or going to the upper levels.

"Where were you?" Pallas asks as I enter.

"What happened?" I ask in return.

He frowns at my obfuscation, but does not pursue it. "Dad wants Castor to find something, even if he doesn't, if you know what I mean," he replies, boiling down the meeting to what is most important to him and Castor.

"Caz," I call out as he passes us. "When are you going?"

He shrugs. "Whenever Leda gets here," he replies, heading up to the conservatory, probably. He likes to play the guitar when he's in a mood, and right now he's in one. I'm pretty sure our father pressed extra hard to get Castor to fabricate something, anything to justify going after Bellerophon. I leave him to it, knowing he won't listen to anything I say right now. Castor won't pretend to see something he didn't, no matter how much our father or I wish he would.

I go down to the lower level to speak to our father alone and find him talking with Mildred. I give them both a look, surprised to find them here.

"When you didn't show, I asked Mildred to join," my father tells me.

I look to her. "I didn't know you'd be stopping by tonight."

"I drove up just as you were stepping out. I noticed you were preoccupied so I came down to attend the meeting in your stead," Mildred says, barely lingering over the words *stepping out* to hint at another meaning without crossing the line between us.

The line is that I don't love her and I never promised her fidelity, just discretion. She obviously saw me with Daphne—disguised of course, so she has no idea who the young woman beside me was—but the result is damaging enough. She's brought it to my father's attention in a way that I cannot fault her for. And I didn't even notice that Mildred was there. Her chauffeur could have all but hit me and I probably wouldn't have noticed. Daphne blinds me to all else, which is dangerous for both of us.

"That was thoughtful of you," I say. I angle myself back out the door, indicating it's time for us to go. "You can tell me what I missed."

My father has been watching our exchange with narrowed eyes from behind his desk. There will be consequences to my actions. He does not approve of sex either before marriage or outside of it for the men of the family, and with good reason. Fathering children with mortal women who are not our wives endangers our House. Mildred knows this. What she doesn't know is that I will have to lie to my father and say that I have been involved with a mortal girl, when I haven't been. I'll have to say that I've just ended it and that's why I was walking a pretty girl to the subway. He'll set a tail on me if I can't convince him that I didn't end it completely.

The last thing I need is for my father to have someone following me right now. Ajax needs my help. And I need to see Daphne again.

Mildred stands with a satisfied smile, content with her revenge, but with no idea of the true damage she's done to me. "Always happy to help," she says, waving back at my father as she follows me out.

DAEDALUS

I'm not used to things going exactly the way I planned them.

In fact, no matter how many ways I've imagined a given situation could pan out, I've never gotten it completely right before, so it throws me a little when Leda calls a meeting at the amphitheater in Central Park, and asks me for the very thing Ladon and I thought she would.

She's staring at me blankly. Waiting for me to answer. "You want me to let Castor Delos into my territory, so he can look for signs that Athens was involved in his brother's death." I repeat.

"I'll come along, of course. Dampen the Furies."

"What does he think is going to happen?" I scoff. "My territory is all of Lower Manhattan. Does he think he's just going to bump into someone from the House of Atreus out on the street?"

She purses her lips. "We don't have to actually bump into anyone, you know that," she says, not taking any of my crap. "If we get so much as a block away from an enemy Scion, the Furies will let us know."

"And you can tell the difference between feeling the Furies toward my House as opposed to someone from the House of Atreus?"

"I can," she replies. "If you hadn't noticed, they whisper different names."

I *hadn't* noticed that, but I guess it makes sense. The Furies are there to punish us for our ancestors killing the ancestors of the other Houses back when all the Houses were related, and it was tantamount to kin-killing. It would make sense that I would be held responsible for different deaths than Castor or Leda, or whoever is left in Atreus.

"If Athens was hiding Atreus, why wouldn't we just ask them to go to Jersey for the weekend?" I ask, trying to poke a hole in this.

"Come on, Dae. It wouldn't just be for one weekend."

"You want me to give Thebes unlimited access?" I'm getting angry now, and it has nothing to do with the Furies. It's the nickname that bugs me. I refuse to let her get comfortable.

"That's not going to happen. And don't give me any of that respect for the dead shit," I add quickly when I see her take a breath to say something. "That's too big of an ask for too small of a reason, and you know it. We've *all* lost people. The Delos family isn't special." I know the plan was for me to let them search, but now that she's here, begging for Castor, I can't stop myself from fighting it. "Don't you see how stupid this is?" I ask. "Why doesn't Castor search *your* territory?"

She bites her lip. For a moment she looks worried. She rarely lets her emotions show, so I know this is a big deal. I press the point.

"I'm not going to allow a search in my territory if you won't allow one in yours," I say.

"Fine. Tomorrow."

"Uh-uh. Right now. Unless you've got something to hide."

I can see a muscle in her jaw jump. She's a grinder. Bet she chews ice, too, but only when she wants... *Easy, perv boy.* I'm going to need one of those frigging collars that'll give me a shock every time I think something dirty about her.

"Tonight it is," she says.

"Well, that just about killed you," I say, smirking. "Why do you want this so bad? Is it for him?" I hate myself for asking, but I can't help it.

"Are you serious!?" she answers, a little too defensively, so yeah, it is for him. "I don't know if you've noticed this or not, but we're on the brink of war. Paris and Tantalus Delos are looking for any reason to wipe out both our Houses."

"They can try."

I'm still fighting this plan when I shouldn't be. But it digs at me that I have to do this for *him*. One of the precious little Delos princes. She sighs and looks at me with those big green eyes of hers. She's disappointed in me.

"We'll all go together. My territory, your territory," I say, quickly just to get it over with. "It'll be one big dumb field trip around Manhattan, like we're a bunch of geriatric tourists. And when that's all done with, the Hundred Cousins will find another thing that pisses them off and start their frigging war anyway."

Leda surprises me by laughing. "Maybe," she says. "But that will be *later*."

"So that's the game plan, huh?" I reply.

"Yup. Always later."

"Trying to procrastinate your way out of a war won't make it go away."

"It's worked for three thousand years," she replies, shrugging.

"So far."

She's smiling at me, weighing what kind of an effect she's having on me. I turn away from her to hide what I'm feeling. My dad told me that she has to be able to look right at my chest or my face to read my heart clearly, but it's also easier for me to pull myself together when I don't have to look at her. For probably the thousandth time, I tell myself that she does this to everyone. What I'm feeling isn't real, or special, and neither is she. She's just House of Rome.

"So, what are you waiting for?"

"Right now?" she replies.

She's stalling. She's definitely got something to hide. "Yes, now. And we'll do Rome's territory first. Wouldn't make any sense to give you a chance to send Atreus to Jersey, now would it?"

When we exit the park, there's a limo waiting for her. It's brand new, with tinted windows and leather seats. It even has a mortal driver who looks like he's happier sitting behind the wheel than he would be in a hot tub. I slide in next to Leda while she tells "Carl" to take us downtown, and wouldn't you know it, but "Carl" is pleased as punch to do anything Leda tells him to.

I wonder what it would be like to go through life knowing that anyone you spoke to would do just about anything to see you smile. She arranges her long legs, demurely crossing her ankles and tucking them beneath the seat, angling her knees toward me. I sit as far to the other side as I can and try not to fidget with the buttons on the arm rest, feeling like a bull next to a thoroughbred. Everything about this woman screams money and taste. The car and driver, the outfit, the hair and manicure, even the way her skin looks all dewy with some kind of yummy smelling cream.

She's naturally gorgeous, of course. A stunner even if you were to take away all the designer labels and the expensive haircut and make-up. Beauty is something that most Scions have in abundance, including me. But there's a difference between the way she's beautiful and the way I am. She's tended, like a garden. Well bred. The kind of person who knows what all the forks are for at a fancy dinner. I'm a plastic spork kind of guy because I never had anyone to teach me any better, and it bothers me.

In its long existence my family has amassed and lost more fortunes than some continents have. Athenians have always excelled at warfare and because of that we have taken hordes of treasure over the centuries. And then squandered it. Every now and again the House of Athens will be led by someone who can actually make a good business deal and not blow it in a fit of temper or stupidity, but my father is not one of those leaders.

When I started taking over some of the duties of the shipping industry my family runs out of the Port of New York, I was shocked at how poorly run our company was. How many mistakes there were in the books. How many opportunities and resources were being wasted. I'm trying to get everything back in order, but it's an uphill battle against my father who thinks he knows what's best in every situation, even when he doesn't know what the hell he's talking about.

Money comes in, then I'll discover an old debt that needs paying. I'll fix that with an influx of more money, only to stumble over another problem and another bad deal my father made. His answer to every problem is to kill his debtors because that's what his father did, but you can't do that. Not anymore. Mortals don't disappear without causing more trouble than their death solves, and I can't tell you how much cash I've dropped to keep some average mortal alive after having the gall to insist my father pay his debts. So we've never been poor, exactly, but there's more to class than money and my family has always found itself running short on both. But not Leda's family. And not Castor's.

We pull up in front of the Delos brownstone on Washington Square Park. I can hear music being played somewhere inside the house. Not on a stereo. Someone is playing the guitar, but like, Spanish style I think? It sounds hard to do. Bet they all sit around listening to Mozart and shit like that, eating caviar with their pinkies sticking out.

Leda takes a black object about the size and thickness of a sunglasses case from her purse and starts pressing buttons. A cellphone. That brand new kind. "Nokia" it says beneath the green-glowing window that's right above the buttons. They're smaller than other models. Those look like you're holding a toaster to your ear. I've got to retire my pager and get one like hers. Leda says a few things into her sleek cellphone, hangs up and then makes another call.

"You don't mind, do you?" she asks me while it rings. I shrug and she says to whoever picks up, "It's me. I'm with Daedalus, and Castor will be joining us. We'll be coming to Roman territory. Nothing I can do about it now." She waits a moment, listening, and then says, "I think that would be best," before hanging up and putting her cellphone away.

A few moments later Castor comes down his front steps and gets in the limo dragging with him a cloud of scented air. He's not wearing cologne, but he was near cologne recently. Or maybe his house and his clothes just smell nice like that. Music, beauty, art. The sons of Apollo probably take baths in rose petals while someone recites poetry to them.

Before Leda can silence the Furies completely, I hear a faint whispering in my head. Names. The names of the people in my family that his family have killed. I try to pay attention to them this time, but I can't quite make them out. The Romans must be better at it than me. As Castor takes a seat across from us he nods at me. I nod back, both of us with tight jaws and narrowed eyes.

"Thank you for agreeing to this," he says to me. Such good manners.

"You're welcome," I growl back. His jacket stays smooth across his shoulders even when he's sitting while mine bunches up around my neck. The sleeves are too short. I tug them down to try and cover my wrists and he watches me do it.

Leda gives Carl directions, then she smiles at Castor. "I'm afraid it's going to be a long night," she tells him. "I've promised Daedalus that we would also go to my territory. Only seems fair," she adds when he looks surprised.

Castor looks between us suspiciously. "That wasn't what I asked for."

I can see him thinking, testing scenarios in his mind to see if it makes sense for Athens and Rome to team up against him and take him out. It's smart of him to be wary, but when you turn it around it's also self-centered. Like all of this is just for him and I'm supposed to waste my time for his peace of mind without asking for anything in return.

"This isn't just about what *you* want, Thebes," I say, sneering. "If there are more members of the House of Atreus knocking around out there, I want to know too, and my House isn't completely convinced that Rome wasn't involved."

Castor nods and leans back in his seat, looking at me like he's smelling something bad. Annoyed, he glances down at his watch. It looks heavy and expensive but not gaudy. It isn't a Rolex, but I couldn't tell you what kind of watch it is because I don't know any other expensive watches.

"Let's get this over with," he grumbles.

Leda laughs to herself, looking between the two of us. I know she's reading our hearts, but I have no idea how much she sees.

When I get back to Ladon's cave, Antigone is there, and she, Ajax, Ladon, and Adonis have been talking for a while.

I let them know about my run-in with Tantalus—I can't wiggle out of it, seeing as how I was supposed to be getting Antigone and I don't have any other explanation for my long absence. It seems like every time I try to avoid involving anyone else in this mess, more people get dragged down with me. It's like I'm caught in quicksand, or one of those tar pits that swallowed all those saber-toothed tigers. Anyone who tries to haul me out ends up getting trapped with me.

After everyone panics for a moment, asking rapid-fire questions about how Tantalus helped me and Ajax fake our deaths, I assure them that I managed to keep Ladon and Adonis out of it, though there is considerable doubt about whether I'll be able to continue to do that.

"I'll have to make it work," I say, shrugging. "It's not like I could avoid it. I was shadowing Antigone, and he just walked up behind me, like he knew I'd be there or something."

"Mousetrap," Adonis muses, looking fretfully between Ladon and Antigone. He truly cares about them, I realize. It's... touching.

Antigone looks much better since the last time I saw her. Back then, when Ajax and I had just met, she seemed so frail I didn't think she was going to live much longer. One look at how she stares at Ladon, and I can guess why she's so much stronger. She's got something to live for. Though she is much more self-possessed and confident, and somehow older than the few months that have passed would allow, this situation has derailed her. She hasn't had enough time to let it sink in that Ajax is alive. Every now and again she reaches out and touches his hand or his knee with the tips of her fingers to make sure he's real.

"You really didn't know he was alive?" I ask. "What about your prophecies?"

"I don't *see* anything when I make a prophecy. The Fates possess me and speak through me. I don't even remember what I've said. You know that," she replies in a tight voice.

I do. I was there one night when she made a prophecy about the Houses being joined by blood, and by blood alone. I was the only one who heard the prophecy, and the only person I've told is Ajax. I didn't even tell Antigone what the Fates said through her. Ajax and I chose to interpret "blood" as "bloodline", and that our child would join our Houses, but we know what Tantalus would think. He would take that prophecy as his cue to start killing the other Houses in the streets.

"But there are things about the future you can see that others don't," I say, pressing for clarity. The House of Thebes has always withheld the prophecies from the other Houses, and they have never explained to the rest of us how their Oracle goes about seeing the future. I've witnessed it once, but there is obviously more to it.

"Sometimes I have visions of the future, and those I remember. But visions are different from prophecies. They're hard to interpret," she continues.

"Why?" I ask.

"They're... dreamlike. Everything's jumbled together, and I *have* seen Ajax," she glances at him again fearfully, "but I see lots of things. I didn't know it meant he was alive."

As she speaks, she won't meet my eyes for long, barely glancing up at me and then away. She still doesn't trust me, but she's trying. I would imagine that it's hard to have any faith in me after believing for months that I murdered her favorite cousin.

"What did you see about me?" Ajax asks.

"The death you faked, I think," she replies. "Daphne is there, Tantalus is there, but my vision looks nothing like the way your death was described to me. I told you. My visions are often scrambled, and they can be misleading. For instance, I've seen *you*, but not you, many times, and I didn't understand why until recently," she tells me.

I know exactly what she means as soon as she says it, and I nod. "You've seen my face because it's The Face. The one that launched a thousand ships. It's passed from mother to daughter in my family. You've probably seen a future descendant of mine."

"Yes, that's what I've come to understand. But I've also *met* someone else who wears it. Your future daughter, I think," Antigone says. "Her name was Helen."

"Woah! That was your daughter!?" Adonis says.

"That's impossible." I exclaim.

"Apparently not," Antigone insists. "Because she was here."

She looks back at me, but I'm frozen in shock. "And I know she was your daughter."

"I met her too. Few months back. Wait, are you talking about time travel?" Adonis asks incredulously. "Never in the history of anything has a Scion, or even one of the Olympians, been capable of time travel. That's not one of our talents."

"It's the talent of the Titan Cronus," Ladon says.

There's dead silence for a long time. Cronos, like Hecate, exists somewhere, we all know that. They're immortal so we know they've all got to be out there somewhere, but to think of him being directly involved with us in some way is terrifying. Even for people who grew up with gods for sires, the Titans are too elemental, too prehistoric, too damn titanic for us to wrap our heads around. All I can think about is that Goya painting, *Saturn Devouring his Son,* and my stomach slips with fear.

Adonis must be thinking the same thing as me. "That's it. I'm out of here," he says, standing up.

"Dude, what is *wrong* with you?" Ajax asks, holding out a hand to stop him.

"I am not killing my grandfather!" Adonis yells.

"What the hell's that supposed to mean?" Ajax wants to know.

"It means I'm not screwing around with Titans and time travel, okay?" Adonis clarifies.

"No one's asking you to," I say. "We're just talking here. Trying to make sense of it all."

Ladon tips his head to the side thoughtfully. "When you consider it, how much different are seeing the future and time travel anyway?" he asks. "Saying what will happen in the future is like bringing the future into the past, isn't it?"

Adonis stands there for a moment, staring at his friend. "I

have no idea what you're talking about," he says, nonplussed, before flopping back down into his chair. But I suspect he does. Adonis is much smarter than he lets on. Tactically, it gives him an advantage to play the gorgeous dumb guy. But I'm not buying it.

"All prophecy is the future interfering with the past, but there's something we're missing, still. Something about that girl Helen," Antigone says, suddenly standing and pacing. "With Ladon here blocking the Fates it's almost like we can work around them. Work toward a future we want, if we figure out what it is they're trying to do first."

"Maybe avoid the war altogether?" Adonis asks hopefully.

"Maybe," Antigone allows.

We discuss it until all our heads hurt. We know there's something there, something about fate and knowing the future, but the concept is elusive. How do we use an Oracle, who is the mouthpiece of fate, to avoid the future we don't want? Basically, avoiding fate is what Scions have been trying to do since Oedipus, and look how great that turned out for him.

Eventually, Adonis announces that he can't stay any longer, which means I can't stay any longer either, not without him there to silence the Furies. Ajax can stay because Ladon has paid his blood debt to Thebes, and he won't incite the Furies in Ajax, but Ladon has not paid his debt to Atreus, nor I to Athens, so Ladon and I can't be together without Adonis. It's confusing, and even though we've all had a lot of practice with this, it still takes us a beat to sort it out sometimes.

"Should we both go?" Ajax asks me quietly. He glances over at Adonis, who is making hurried plans with Ladon for tomorrow.

"No," I reply immediately. As soon as Ajax leaves Ladon's presence, the mousetrap will try to catch him. "No, you need to stay here."

"But where will you go for the night?" he argues. "Not all the way back to the *Argo*?"

He's right. It's too late and too far for me to go back to where we docked our boat. Plus, I'd have to go uptown to Queens, through Roman territory. I don't really have a lot of options. It's not like I have a ton of friends. In fact, I only have one.

"Harlow's," I say, already smiling at the thought of seeing her. Even though I haven't contacted her since Ajax and I left town, I know she'd love it if I showed up on her doorstep. "I can go there."

He nods and then pulls me into a hug. "Be careful," he says, then he kisses me.

"Let's go, lovers!" Adonis calls out to us.

"I'll be back first thing tomorrow," I tell Ajax before pulling away and joining Adonis and Antigone on our way back up to the surface.

When we're on the streets again, Adonis looks at a little black gadget he has in his jacket pocket and curses. He dials the thing— it's a cellphone, I figure out. I can't believe how *little* it is—and listens for a while. Then he mumbles a string of foul curses under his breath and returns his phone to his pocket.

"Something wrong?" I ask.

"I've gotta be somewhere," he replies.

"So go," I tell him.

He looks at me, frowning, and shakes his head. "It can wait," he says.

We see that Antigone gets home safely and undetected by her own family before Adonis turns to me and asks what my plans are for the night. I give him a vague answer about going to see a friend and he persists in asking me where she lives.

"Around Central Park," I reply.

"You can't go up there alone," he says. I frown at him. Central Park-adjacent is my House's territory.

He draws to a halt, puts his hands on his hips and sighs like he really doesn't want to tell me what he's about to tell me. "Rome has been encroaching on patches of Atreidae territory since you supposedly died. So has Athens. We both say we have the right to be there for a whole bunch of bullshit reasons. We're supposed to be settling one of those disputes tonight."

"You mean, like, who gets which blocks of *my* territory?" I say. I don't really have the right to be angry about it. It's not like the other Houses are going to leave the most valuable blocks of New York City unaccounted for, but it still bugs me. Plus, I was looking forward to seeing Harlow.

Adonis gives me an understanding smile. "Yeah."

"I guess it was bound to happen," I admit. I look around and shrug. "Well, I could stay here. I'm safe in Thebes."

Adonis shakes his head and stiff-arms his fists into the pockets of his jeans. Even though I'm fully taken, you'd have to be dead not to notice how attractive he is.

"You can stay at my place." I hesitate and he barrels on: "And I'm not coming on to you."

"I didn't think you were," I retort, but my voice is unnaturally high, so obviously I was thinking that.

He gives me a wry smile. "I'd have to be an idiot to try something with you," he says.

"I know plenty of smart guys who've gotten caught up in this." I gesture to my face, and let it change back to my real one.

I face him full on and smile up at him, looking right into his eyes. I suppose it's a test, which may be unfair of me, but I don't care. I need to be sure he won't lose his mind like others have. I need people I can trust, and I need to know now if

Adonis is going to turn on me, because I'm starting to trust this guy.

He regards me under the beads of lamplight while cars go past us down Christopher Street. He's not losing his mind and I get the sense that he knows I'm testing him.

"I get it. I really do, Daphne," he says.

And I bet he does. Nearly all Scions are attractive, but this guy has something else to him. Something that others don't just want, but that they *covet*, which is another thing entirely. I know what it is to be wanted. Ajax wants me, and it's wonderful. But being coveted like an object is different because behind covetousness is not admiration, but jealousy. And behind all jealousy is hatred. I can tell Adonis knows all about it. He's lived it, just like I have.

"Come with me." He grins and nudges me with an elbow.

I grin back. I really don't have any place else to go right now. "Okay," I relent, sighing.

He steps to the curb and hails a cab. "It'll be fun," he promises.

I sincerely doubt that, but I get in the back of the cab with him anyway. We go to the Upper East Side and Adonis pays the cab driver as I step out onto 92nd St. The neighborhood is quiet at this hour. I change my face to someone else's when the cab pulls away.

"I'm glad you're going to be here for this," he tells me as he goes to the call box and punches in a number. "It should be a good fight."

I stop and grab his arm. "Wait—what fight?"

"Relax," he says. "It's not a fight to the death or anything."

He pushes through the buzzing door and into the building, forcing me to trail along after him. "And how are you going to

keep Athens and Rome from killing each other if they fight?"
I ask.

"This is a sacred space."

It certainly doesn't look like a sacred space. I give him a doubtful look.

"You'll see," he assures me. "Just act like you don't know anything."

"I *don't* know anything," I say.

"Atta girl. You're my mortal date and you have no clue about Scions—don't worry there will be plenty of other mortals here who don't know. We met at the club. You came to New York to be a model."

I glare at him.

"Singer?" he tries again.

"Photographer," I decide. "I travel a lot."

"Nice." He nods appreciatively. "No one will ask. Everyone will think you're a mortal and ignore you, but aren't cover stories fun?" He leads me on, enjoying himself.

We've entered what appears to be a normal apartment building on the Upper East Side, and Adonis leads me downstairs to a subbasement. There's a long, wide hallway ending in double doors that say *Valetudinaria* on them. To my left is another set of double doors that say *Thermae*. He pushes through them without pausing into what appears to be the reception room of a voluptuous spa. Scented air wafts around enveloping chairs and small end tables meant to hold up refreshing drinks that I imagine would have cucumbers or bubbles in them.

"The *ludus* and amphitheater are in the back. We have to go through the locker rooms to get to them." He leads me toward the back wall where a giant cursive M is emblazoned on the tiled wall. "The genders are more of a suggestion then a rule," he adds as he passes the M and brings me around a corner and into the men's locker room.

Warm, wet air lays down on me. I can hear the sound of a small crowd that gets nearer as we pass through the many rooms of showers, saunas, and hot tubs. We reach the rotunda of the gymnasium, which I assume is the *ludus,* or school for gladiators to the Romans. It's a huge, round room with a domed ceiling—almost like the Pantheon, except there is no oculus open to the sky. We're many levels underground. There we find several dozens of Scions bunched into smaller groups, making side bets, and sliding mistrustful glares toward other huddles of Scions.

I notice Scions—wearing some article of clothing in Roman purple—standing around the perimeter like sentinels, not talking to anyone. They have a faraway look in their eyes. I nudge Adonis questioningly and he explains that they're keeping the Furies at bay. I wonder how long they can last. Some of them have beads of sweat standing out on their foreheads.

"What a powder keg," I say under my breath.

Adonis agrees, taking far too much pleasure it that, then raises a hand in greeting to another Roman, about Adonis' age, who is approaching us quickly with a tight look on his face.

"Phaon," Adonis says in an indifferent tone. The two Romans clasp each other not by the hand, but by the forearm—an ancient way of making sure your "friend" isn't concealing a dagger. These two obviously do not get along.

"You're late, cousin," Phaon replies. He releases Adonis and turns his pretty face to me. "Who's this?"

"She's cool," Adonis assures him.

"Not what I asked," Phaon returns, giving me the once-over with reptilian detachment. "Is she of age?"

"I'm eighteen," I snap. "And I can speak for myself."

"Pity on both counts," Phaon says, which makes me recoil in surprise and disgust. "Leda isn't very happy," he continues, addressing Adonis. "You were supposed to be here an hour ago. Some of our cousins are practically dead on their feet."

"Well, I'm here now," Adonis says. He approaches one of the sentinels. "You can stop," he tells the red-headed girl gently.

The sentinel practically falls over with relief. She waves at the others, and they visibly crumble as if collapsing under a heavy burden. Some of them take a knee, shaking. Others clutch at their heads like they're having a migraine.

I have some understanding of the Roman ability to manipulate emotions because I possess the Cestus, and with it I can marginally influence hearts for a short time. So I know that what Adonis is doing is as close to a miracle as Scion abilities can get. While he may not be able to do anything as flashy as summon lightning like I can, or fly like Ajax, it occurs to me that by single-handedly suppressing the Furies when there are dozens of members of two enemy Houses in such close confines, Adonis might be the most powerful Scion I have ever encountered.

Phaon would probably agree with me. His envy for his cousin's display of ability is palpable.

Adonis doesn't even need to stand in concentration like his cousins were doing. He leads me under an arch that's inscribed in Latin. My Latin is a little shaky, but I think it says something like, *to be made from the spoils,* though I can't be sure. The arch looks very old and worn.

"The original. From the Colosseum. That's why this place allows me to control the Furies for so many. It's been consecrated," Adonis tells me.

"Translation: a lot of blood has been spilled on these stones," I rebut.

"Same thing," he says. He jumps up and grazes the bottom of the marble keystone with three fingers as he passes under it. Phaon does the same. It doesn't seem to be expected of me, so I refrain. It's probably just a Roman thing, and I'm supposed to be mortal.

Through the arch is the amphitheater—a sandy, oval fight pit that's surrounded by tiered rows of benches. On one side I see Scions wearing purple somewhere on their persons, and on the other side are Scions sporting something in blue. Romans versus Athenians. I watch curiously.

The Athenians are cut from the same cloth physically, with very little deviation from their standard phenotype. They are all tall, broad, and most of them have dark hair, pale skin, and blue eyes. The Romans, however, are a riot of different ethnicities, from deepest ebony to alabaster pale and every size, shape, shade of skin, hair, and eye color that people can come in. The one thing they all have in common is that they're all indescribably alluring.

Scions take after their Scion parent, not their human parent; in other words, each of us tends to look a lot like some other Scion from history. I once asked my uncle Deuce why the House of Rome was so varied. He said that everyone was someone else's idea of perfect beauty, and as the descendants of Aphrodite, Romans had to be a little bit everything. I always liked that.

As I peruse the stands, I notice that there is a distinct lack of red among the spectators.

"Where's Thebes?" I mumble to Adonis, my eyes on Phaon. He's not with us, but he hasn't left us yet, either. He's just lingering on the edge, waiting for Adonis and me to start a private conversation that he can overhear.

For the first time, Adonis looks worried. His eyes are scanning everywhere. "I feel them," he says in a distant way. "And I shouldn't. This bout tonight doesn't concern them."

I move us away from Phaon. "How can it not concern them?" I ask when we're out of earshot. "Wouldn't they want a chance to compete, too?"

"Of course they would. *If* they knew about it. Which Athens and Rome agree would be a bad idea."

I frown at Adonis, but he waves my objections away. "Look, Thebes is powerful enough as it is. With centralized territory added in, they would crush us."

"But that's not fair," I say.

He gives me a candid look. "As long as the Houses are equally matched, no one would be dumb enough to start the war. Do you want things to be fair, or do you want peace?"

He goes back to scanning the stands and finds who he's looking for. He grabs my arm and starts to climb the steps up into the Roman section toward a beautiful woman with auburn hair.

"Ready to meet my sister?" he asks me.

"Ah, no," I say, grabbing his arm to stop him. "Won't she feel the Furies and know who I am?"

"Course not," he says with a cocky half-smile. "I'm stronger than she is, than all of my House put together, actually. I've got you covered." He waits a beat. "You should be *really* impressed by me right now." This last bit makes me laugh. He laughs with me with charming sheepishness, and continues. "Honestly, though? I'm hiding it, but this is hard, and I couldn't do this if we weren't in the coliseum. This place allows for Scions to fight honorably with each other without being overcome by the Furies, as long as we stick to the rules. This is how our kind has resolved territory disputes for thousands of years without destroying each other, and I wouldn't have brought you here if I thought you'd be in danger. You can relax."

"I'm not going to relax," I say. But I do a little. I realize Adonis cares about me. He's not obsessed or getting possessive or anything "Face" induced, but I can tell that I matter to him, and I know that he wouldn't allow me to get hurt.

"My sister's pretty awesome. You'll see," he says, holding my hand as he walks me up the stairs.

Leda Tiber is Head of the House of Rome, but I would find her an impressive looking woman even if I didn't know her title. She's tall and curvy, dressed all in black except for a purple scarf tied around the toned muscles of her left upper arm. When we join her, she hands her brother a matching purple scarf—while staring daggers at him. Adonis takes off his jacket and ties the small scrap of silk around his upper arm like his sister.

"Should I ask where the hell you've been?" she asks Adonis with arch sweetness while glaring at me.

Adonis faces his sister and takes her by the shoulders, clearly deciding between giving her a hug and shaking her until her teeth rattle. "Why is Thebes here?"

Leda rolls her eyes and groans. "You have no idea what I've been through tonight. Castor—"

"The Theban is *Castor Delos!*?" Adonis shouts back into his sister's face, releasing her shoulders.

I stiffen and freeze, then remind myself to breathe. I'm feeling several emotions simultaneously: shock, worry for Castor, and anxiety to see him for Ajax's sake. But I have to act neutral, or Leda will become suspicious.

She launches into a lengthy explanation about how she had Corvus (who I assume is Roman) challenge the House of Athens tonight, thinking it was the perfect time because Daedalus would be with her, unreachable and unknowing of the challenge, and therefore he wouldn't fight for his family. But then, totally out of the blue, Daedalus insisted on a search of Roman territory, in case Rome was hiding Atreus for Thebes. Leda then tried to get Corvus to call the fight off, but it was too late. Bellerophon had already accepted. As soon as Castor arrived at the *ludus*, he figured out what was going on.

"He freaked out. And rightfully so," Leda concludes. She runs a hand through her thick hair, knowing how badly she messed up. "And who the hell is she?" she demands, trying to deflect.

There are quite a few mortals here. Some of them are the spouses of Scions, and so they know what's going on, but the others, most of them dates, have no idea what this is about, and they stick out like sore thumbs. Luckily, I look like one of these clueless mortal girls to Leda, and from her perspective, I'm hearing far more of the inner workings of Scions than I should.

"I vouch for her," Adonis replies, taking a seat and pulling me down beside him. "What does Castor want to do about it?"

It seems Adonis vouching for me is enough for Leda, and she answers him as if I'm not here. "He wants to fight. I couldn't say no."

Adonis wraps his fingers around my wrist, and I feel my skyrocketing tension and worry for Castor ebbing out of me. I know he's using his influence on me to calm me down, but I welcome this. If Adonis could sense my panic, it's possible Leda could as well. I don't know how powerful she is.

"A three way?" Adonis asks as I feel myself relaxing into his touch.

"He said he'd fight the winner," she replies, shaking her head, and Adonis barks a laugh at Castor's presumption. Even I can't help but smirk at it. Invisibly, of course. "He caught us trying to cut Thebes out of it. How could I deny him anything at that point?" Leda adds.

"So how many blocks are we fighting over?"

"Lincoln Center all the way to the park."

That's probably the most valuable few blocks in the entire city. And my personal favorite. I have to let it go, though. My life isn't in New York, but it does piss me off a little.

Adonis looks skyward for help he doesn't expect to get. "Who's fighting?"

"Corvus against Daedalus. The winner against Castor."

"*Daedalus* is going to fight for Athens?" he asks.

The Houses can pick their own champions. It's a tradition that dates back pre Trojan War. I think it's odd that an Heir would be in the ring. Usually, picking a champion is to avoid putting Heirs in danger, but I guess this is Bellerophon's call.

Leda nods, looking despondent. Adonis glares across the fight sands at Bellerophon, who is pawing at some poor mortal woman who has no idea what she's gotten herself into.

"I guess we can kiss culture goodbye," Adonis says.

"Corvus would have stood a chance against Doris, who would have been Athens' champion. But Corvus can't beat Daedalus," Leda agrees. "That's why I wanted the challenge to be tonight while Daedalus was supposed to be busy and stuck in Athenian territory with me, escorting Castor around." She chuffs, shaking her head. "And it couldn't have worked out worse."

Adonis gives his sister a quick side hug. "It really couldn't have," he says, teasing but also absolving her, and she smiles up at him gratefully from under his arm.

I watch them with a familiar twinge of envy. Seeing Ajax and his family together always left me wondering what it would be like to have a sibling I loved that much. Now, having some sense of what Ajax has given up for me, glimpsing this moment just makes me feel guilty.

"It's about to start," Adonis says in a hazy way, like he's reading emotions from someone far away.

For a moment, I see the strain this situation is putting on him. Adonis drops his forehead and touches his temples with his fingertips. His eyes close, as if he's concentrating deeply. The crowd quiets and takes their seats, as Phaon enters the ring to announce the fight. With his free hand, Adonis reaches out and takes his sister by the wrist. Like his, her eyes slide out of focus into the middle distance as they share the burden of the Furies.

13

ADONIS

Hungry. Angry. Aching.

Everyone has feelings, and most of those feelings are unpleasant. Tonight is weird, though. I know there's something off as soon as Phaon enters the ring and announces first the stakes, and then the fighters.

Yearning. Spiraling. A bright trill of fear.

There are nearly too many hearts here for me to control them all. To be honest, I'm struggling.

Disgust. Lust. Suffocating frustration.

I reach out for my sister, and she lets me push a little bit of the chaos off onto her. She is strong and she helps me. I arrow her toward Phaon... *smug, amused, bitter...*

And she knows now there's something off about his emotions, too. But he feels her prodding at the edges of his desires... *no, no, no...that's too much Leda... too clumsy...* the ones that tangle with our intentions and almost become our thoughts, and he blocks us both. Dammit. If I didn't have the Furies to contend with, I could force my way in, which is abominable, but Phaon is practically asking for me to break into his mind. He should know better than to block me right now. What is he hiding? He shouldn't be hiding anything right now.

Screaming rage. Centuries of loss. The torment of injustice.

The Furies start pounding on me as Daedalus and Corvus enter the ring and I almost lose my control. They are in a tizzy tonight. Two sons in the direct line of their Houses, carrying sword and shield and facing off against each other, is like an orgy to them. I don't exactly reason with the Furies. There is no logical way to counteract the emotions of elemental beings, but I offer up the ritualistic peace that comes with this sacred space. This is a place of justice. A place where honor is met with honor. It helps quiet them a bit.

Except for the fact that I can *feel* a dishonorable intent in one of the combatants on the sands, and so can the Furies.

Corvus. That bastard. He knows better than to try to cheat. If he wrongs this space, the protection it affords us by helping us silence the Furies so we can fight honorably will be gone, and there will be no stopping...

Want to kill... want to cut... want to burn...

Somewhere through the screams in my head I can hear the clang of metal on metal. I open my eyes and see the flurry of blows. Daedalus wields the gladiolus and a small round shield. Corvus has two blades of his own design, about the length of seaxes, with long, sharp hilts that can wound if jabbed at the opponent during close fighting. Daedalus is fast for such a big guy, a truly gifted swordsman. Balance, grace, and speed he has—so much so he rarely has to use his strength. His muscles flow into familiar shapes. There is no anger, no hatred in him. Just the easy, joyful appreciation of someone doing something they've practiced to perfection. He manages to keep Corvus back with little effort, even as Corvus pushes to get in close.

I can feel Corvus's impatience. His focus on the hilt of his blade. I can feel him pushing and wishing and wanting for the hilt to just *scratch*. I can't read minds, but sometimes desires can be so honed that they betray the thought that must have spawned them. And that's how I know that the sharp tips on the hilts of Corvus' blades must be poisoned. I reach out to Daphne and take her hand.

"You have to stop the fight," I say. Or, I try to say. Not much more than a growl can come out from between my clenched teeth. I've never had to work so hard to keep the Furies back.

Daphne has no idea what I'm trying to say, but I can feel anxiety flashing in her like a siren. "Something's wrong, Adonis," she says.

I wish I were capable of speech right now so I could agree with her. And get her to stop this travesty. If Corvus succeeds and there's a fresh kill, there will be nothing I can do to stop the Furies. This arena will turn into a slaughterhouse.

"Stop. The. Fight," I whisper, forcing each word out with guttural huffs of breath. This time Daphne hears me and somehow understands what's going on.

She jumps to her feet, but just as she does, I can feel Corvus' triumph. There is a moment of confusion. All hearts press toward the sands, in between feelings.

Waiting. Hoping. Expectant.

"No!" I hear Daphne shout.

I open my eyes and see Daedalus staggering around. It's like his legs aren't working. He's fending off Corvus as best he can, but Corvus is following him around the ring like a jackal, nipping at him with the tips of his blades. Blood is flowing freely from several small stabs all over Daedalus' body.

Betrayal, murder, injustice!

The Furies scream so loud I almost pass out. Then I see Daphne at the edge of the fight sands. She's yelling something into the ring. Can't hear her over the crowd. Can't even hear much of the crowd over the Furies who are a blazing cacophony of hatred in my head.

Castor comes running into the ring, unarmed. He tackles Corvus, blindsiding him and knocking him down. Castor swiftly disarms Corvus, taking away his blades and inspecting them. Daphne has jumped into the ring, too. She goes to Daedalus. She starts calling for help.

And now my sister is up and dragging me along behind her. She's yelling for everyone to get out of her way as she pulls me with her into the ring. But my head is killing me and if I don't sit down soon, I'm going to pass out or drop dead, and I definitely can't do that because I'm the only thing holding the Furies at bay.

The Furies. They've become visible to me. Three young girls, tangled black hair unbound, shivering in their torn clothes, weeping gore. Ashes in their hair. Ashes everywhere.

I can't pass out. I can't pass out. I can't pass out.

Rage, horror, desperation.

I can't die. I can't die. I can't die. If I die, they all will. Leda. Daphne...

14

DAPHNE

I don't think Daedalus is going to make it.

He's bleeding from, like, *everywhere,* and the blood that's flowing from his many wounds isn't slowing as it usually would for a Scion. Maybe he's a hemophiliac or something? But that's impossible. Scions who don't heal fast die fast, and Daedalus is in his mid-twenties or so. He's practically old for our kind.

I press down on the wounds nearest his heart, but I only have two hands and no one from his House is helping me. His frigging dad is standing two feet away from us like this is somebody else's problem. Like if he gets too close, he'll get failure on his shoes. What a dick.

"What's wrong with him?" Bellerophon asks.

Uh, multiple stab wounds? I hold my tongue. A human girl my age probably wouldn't talk back to someone like Bellerophon. Not unless she was very, very dumb.

"This is not normal," Castor says. He turns to Corvus,

holding up one of his small swords with the wicked looking hilts. "What did you put on this?"

Corvus looks truly shocked. "What are you suggesting?"

A small scuffle nearly breaks out as several people from Athens and Rome step forward and start hurling accusations at each other. Leda pulls her brother behind her as she strides onto the sand and Adonis, gray-faced and shaking, falls to a knee.

"Stop," he whispers. "I can't—"

"We need a doctor, or he's going to die!" I shout. I purposely don't use the word Healer—a mortal girl wouldn't know what that was—but my distraction works. The arguing stops and Adonis looks somewhat relieved. For now.

If Daedalus dies, it will be a fresh kill, and there is nothing anyone would be able to do to stop the Furies from overtaking us all.

"Carry Daedalus to the *Valetudinaria*," Leda says vaguely, like she's still a bit dazed from using her powers. Dark shadows have bloomed under her glassy eyes.

"He needs a Healer," Castor says, holding his hand out to her. She gives him her cellphone, identical to the one I saw Adonis use, and Castor runs for the exit to get aboveground and make his call.

"Lift him up," Leda says, directing two dark-haired Athenians to stoop down and collect Daedalus.

"Stop," Bellerophon orders, and the Athenians freeze. "You think we're just going to let you take him so you can finish the job?"

"Finish the job?" she repeats, like he's an idiot. "If your son dies, our Houses will fall on each other in a frenzy and fight until there's only one of us left. Do you think I'm stupid enough to believe that last person will be me? It is in my best interest to keep Daedalus alive."

Bellerophon leans back on his heels and nods once. The Athenians continue lifting their prince. As they carry him out, Leda's eyes flick over to Corvus. He's doing a marvelous job of looking baffled, but the way Adonis is staring at him tells me Corvus did it.

And if *I* know it, Castor and Bellerophon will know it soon, too. Unless we cover it up somehow. I go to Adonis and throw his arm over my shoulder.

"We've got to keep this quiet," I whisper to him as I support him out of the colosseum.

He nods, his lips pressed together tightly. He's paper white and sweating. A blood vessel has burst in one of his eyes, painting it red. "I can't handle the Furies much longer," he whispers back. "Athens has to leave."

"Okay," I say, glancing around for some other Roman to take over for him. "I'll handle it."

I hurry Adonis through the double doors labeled *Valetudinaria*, deposit him on one of the two rows of hospital beds I find inside, and then catch a glimpse of the red-headed sentinel. As I chase after her, I pass Leda, Castor, and Bellerophon who are questioning Corvus.

"Take my blades! Test them! Test Daedalus! You will find no poison!" Corvus proclaims in a loud, almost showy way.

They will *find* no poison. Not that there isn't any. Smart to word it like that. Especially in front of Castor, when it's widely known that there's a Falsefinder among the Delos brothers, but few know which of them it is. Corvus is dangerous, but of course I can't speak up. I'm supposed to be a clueless mortal, and anyway, it would just be a reason to start a war.

I touch Leda's arm as I go past. "Adonis is in bad shape. He said that those guys in blue need to go," I tell her. "He says he can't hold on any longer. Whatever that means."

I try to look as innocent as possible while Leda eyes me for a moment, then she cranes her neck and finds her brother, slumped on a hospital bed and I'm forgotten. Her eyes widen and she looks at Castor, who shares a blank look of fear with her. I leave them to it and chase down the redhead.

"You've got to come back," I tell her. "Bring anyone else who can control the Furies."

"But, even fully rested I couldn't possibly—" she begins.

I cut her off. "If you don't get in there and do something, Adonis is going to black out, or maybe even die, and everyone in that room is going to start tearing each other apart."

Well. The cat's out of the bag now. There are other mortals who know about Scions, but they are usually married in and have kids involved, so their silence is assured. Hopefully this situation is chaotic enough that my understanding of the Furies will be over-looked, but I can't help but feel like the mousetrap is whirling and clicking away around me again.

The redhead dashes away, calling out the names of other Romans with a slightly hysterical pitch to her voice. At least she understands the severity of the situation. I make my way back to Adonis, who is sitting on the bed where I left him, quietly collapsing in on himself. He's soaked with sweat and trembling, like he's been crawling through his own private hell over here.

"Is there anything I can get for you?" I ask.

He shakes his head but holds out his hand to me. I take it in mine and sit next to him, uttering meaningless but hopefully comforting things like, "It'll be okay," while he tries to say something to me.

"Check. Daedalus," he finally manages to grind out. He points across the room. "Phaon."

I see a human doctor in a white coat darting around Daedalus with urgency. There's still a bit of a crowd around him and the doctor is telling everyone to back off so he can work. At the top far corner of the bed, ever so slightly in the shadows, is Phaon. He's standing there unobtrusively, his hands hidden at an odd angle behind his body and he's drawing nearer to Daedalus a millimeter at a time.

In the back of my mind a distant lesson from my uncle Deuce surfaces. *The Medicis poisoned half of Florence and no one knows how they did it. It's said all they had to do was brush up against you and you were dead.*

The Medici were House of Rome. Instinct tells me not to let Phaon touch Daedalus.

"Don't die," I tell Adonis.

"Hurry! I can't—" He doubles over on himself, and I really am afraid that the Furies are going to tear him apart from the inside out.

I don't have a lot of choices in this situation. Phaon is too close to Daedalus. I must remove him immediately without calling attention to either of us. Whatever I do I have to do it fast or I'm afraid both Daedalus and Adonis are going to die. I come up behind Phaon while he is completely focused on Daedalus and electrocute him.

It's tricky because I never really know how much juice a person can handle, and I can't kill this guy even if he deserves it.

Luckily, I use the right amount of lightning. Phaon stiffens and then lists into my arms, immediately unconscious but not dead. I hold him upright, taking his weight, as I glide him into a back room of the hospital. I'm careful not to let his hands touch me in case there is some poisoned barb on them that I can't see. At that moment a sudden influx of Romans run into the room, led by the redhead, to manage the Furies for Adonis. This causes enough of a commotion that no one notices Phaon's head lolling on my shoulder.

The back room turns out to be a surgical theater. I lay Phaon out on the operating table and get the hell out of there before someone sees me. The Athenians have left. I start back toward Adonis, but slow when I see Castor and Leda standing around him as he sits on his hospital bed, drinking from a jar of honey. He still looks terrible, but it doesn't seem like he's trying to hold back a tidal wave anymore. Adonis sees me wavering, and he gestures for me to come to him. Castor looks me over closely as I sit on the bed next to Adonis.

"She's good," Adonis tells Castor as he takes my hand possessively. He's soaked with sweat and the hand he puts in mine is weak and cold. I put my arm around him.

It's an act, of course. Easier for Castor to think I'm Adonis' mortal girlfriend than get into some elaborate lie that would explain my being here, but it still feels strange to play another guy's girlfriend in front of my real boyfriend's brother. I was okay when it for Leda, but this is odd. Why do I feel guilty?

"I didn't mean to stare," Castor says to me politely. "I thought I knew you for a second." He shakes it off and addresses Leda, getting back to what they were talking about. "Thebes has labs for our antiquity preservation projects and Scion scientists that can test for poisons without having to bring the police into it. The question is, will Bellerophon believe us if our tests come up negative? Corvus gave over those blades of his a little too quickly for me to think there's anything there."

"I don't trust Bellerophon to test the blades. He'll make *sure* he finds something," Leda replies.

"I had to give him one," Castor says, shrugging like his hands are tied. "And he's going to test it."

"Thebes needs to test the other, then," Leda insists. "If you find nothing, you have to vouch for us." He goes to turn away and she stops him. "Castor. Who's to say Daedalus wasn't faking it?"

Castor's eyes dart away as he considers it. He suddenly shakes his head, making up his mind. "I don't believe that. And you don't either."

Leda puts up her hands in a surrendering gesture. "I'm willing to swear in front of your Falsefinder that I had nothing to do with it."

A tall man with dark blond hair and the look of the House of Thebes about him enters the *Valetudinaria* flanked by three Romans.

Castor lifts a hand in greeting towards the man. "I believe *you*, Leda. But you aren't Corvus," he says quietly, and then goes to join his kinsman.

Leda curses under her breath after Castor is out of earshot. She looks at her brother. "I'm going to kill Corvus for this."

"That'd be awkward. For the Head of the House to be an Outcast?" Adonis shakes his head. "Better pay someone else to do it."

Leda walks away to join Castor at Daedalus' bedside, and it's only then I realize they're kidding. At least, I hope they're kidding.

"I can't stay upright anymore." Adonis lies back, pulling me down with him. "You might as well get some sleep," he tells me around a very large sigh.

"I'll take the bed next to you," I say, trying to peel myself away from him.

"Can't," he mumbles. "You've got to stay close to me while I sleep, or my sister will feel the Furies." He forces his eyes open and looks at me. "The Furies are gone between you and Athens, though. You saved Daedalus' life, you know."

"I did?" I look over my shoulder to the door that leads to the operating room. "Phaon was *actually* going to murder him?" Adonis doesn't reply and when I look back at him, he's fallen asleep.

I lie down next to him, still thinking about Phaon, his flat eyes and unsettling comments. Scions are all killers. I've killed someone. Even Ajax, who hates violence, killed my uncleDeuce because he had to. The Fates have always put us in situations where it's kill or be killed, but there's something different about what Phaon was about to do to Daedalus. There's something wrong with him. Something that makes me very happy that I'm not lying here alone.

My gaze is drawn across the aisle to Ceyx, working on Daedalus. His hands glow blue in the low light. Everyone has left, except for Leda, Castor, Ceyx, and the mortal doctor. I try to sleep but the most I can manage is to fade in and out of moments. Voices and footsteps draw close, and I open my eyes to slits.

Catching the edge of their argument, it seems that Ceyx is chastising Castor and neither of them is comfortable with that. This isn't their usual power dynamic, I gather. They both tilt away from each other as they reassess their tones.

"I'm sorry I dragged you into this," Castor says. "But if Daedalus had died, that would have been it. Are you really ready for the war to start tonight?"

Ceyx throws one of his long, thin hands through the air in a dismissive gesture. "It's *going to happen*, and if Athens and Rome destroy each other first, it means less Thebans I have to save. From *them*. Shit, Caz," he says, staring at Castor like he doesn't recognize him.

Castor drops his head, and Ceyx softens. "We're going to have to do something about your overdeveloped sense of justice," he says jokingly before growing serious again. "I can't keep this between us, you know."

"I'll tell my father," Castor says, nodding. "This won't fall back on you. I promise."

Ceyx watches Castor for a moment. "They aren't your friends."

Castor snorts. "Friends? I don't even like Daedalus."

"I meant Leda and Adonis. Be careful, Caz." Ceyx leaves Castor staring after him.

In his sleep, Adonis throws an arm over me and snuggles his face into my neck. Castor notices the movement and narrows his eyes at me through the low light like he's still trying to figure out how he knows me. I close my eyes and pretend to sleep until I do.

15

DAEDALUS

I didn't feel any pain. Not even when I saw Corvus' blade going into my skin. Shock. Had to be.

The world telescoped away after that first cut. I'd swing my sword arm, or bring my shield up to block, and it was like I was watching a mortal do it. Every move was so slow. It was kinda funny, even when I saw that blood was pouring out of me like I was a plastic bag full of the stuff and Corvus was poking holes in it. Red, watery ketchup fountaining out of me like I was a damn cartoon. Somebody stick a finger in me, I thought.

I was distantly aware of the fact that I was blundering around the arena like a wounded animal until Castor jumped in the ring and called it off. Castor Delos. That prick. He can't even let me die without trying to steal the spotlight. He's gotta swan in and be all noble and shit, tackling Corvus like some prep school quarterback. Cue the cheerleaders with the pom-poms.

Then some strange girl was pressing down on my injuries, trying to save me. Not that I could feel her doing it. I just saw her above me, like I was watching it on a screen. And... Leda. So lovely. She looked worried, but not about me. About me dying. That would send the whole lot of us to hell. I'm talking monkey shit fight at the zoo if I died. Strange. I worried about her making it out alive even though I'm the one who was dying.

Just behind her was my dad, jettisoning me as easily as ballast. I'm a loser. He has no need of me anymore. At that point I was happy to black out or die or whatever it is I did.

Because now everything is blue. Grecian blue, but not like water. Like sky. It *is* sky. Nope, it's light. I open my eyes and see some Theban-looking dude standing over me with his face screwed up in concentration, and his hands glowing blue. I guess I'm not dead, but that makes sense. I've never been given the easy way out. And *now* it hurts. Not a lot, more like an itchy, throbbing, achy hurt. Healing hurt, I guess is what it is, and I'm also guessing the Theban is one of their legendary Healers. Wish we had one of those. But Athenians don't heal their wounded. We disown them. No one from my own House is even here to watch over me. I could be a drunk, a murderer, a thief. I could beat my wife and kids if I had them, and no one would even blink at that in my House. But lose a fight? I'm a pariah now.

"I've found no poison in him," the Healer is saying to Leda and Castor. "But that doesn't mean it isn't there."

Wait. Poison? They're turned slightly away from me and haven't noticed I'm awake yet.

"How can that be?" Leda asks. Interrogates is more like it. She's so charming when she crosses her arms and glares at people. Well, charming to me. Maybe not to them.

The Healer shakes his dark blond head. "He has a highly unusual enzyme imbalance that caused his blood to stop clotting, but I can't tell you why or how that came to be."

"Enzyme imbalance. But no poison," Leda presses.

"Nothing I would classify as poison, but..." he trails off and shrugs. "You have to understand, anything can become lethal if administered improperly. Even vitamins."

"She's asking if you found anything like arsenic," Castor clarifies, though he needn't. The Healer knows what she's asking. Gods, that guy can be such a know-it-all. Spelling out biology shit to a Healer like he knows better.

"An enzyme imbalance of this magnitude doesn't usually happen without some kind of catalyst. But no, I didn't find anything obvious like arsenic."

"Because he wasn't poisoned!" Leda insists. "Is his blood clotting normally now?"

The Healer glares at her for moment before walking away saying, "He'll live. I guess that means Rome will too," in an aggravated tone. Castor follows him.

"You're awake," Leda says. I realize she's looking at me now. She's pale, and for the first time I can remember her hair looks messy. The skin around her eyes is drawn with fatigue, but she smiles at me anyway.

I try to answer her, but my tongue feels like it's twice its usual size and covered in glue. She sees me swallowing and gets me some water. The bottle she hands me is opened already. I give it a long, hard look.

"Oh for god's sake," she snaps.

I chuckle. I know it's not poisoned, and she takes my teasing like a pro, but laughing makes me cough and *damn* my lungs hurt. I think one of them was punctured or something. She swoops in and puts an arm behind me to lift me and lean me forward so I can drink. I feel like such a baby. I have no strength. I can't even hold myself upright without her help and it bugs me that she's seeing me like this.

"You can go," I say. Judging by the injured look on her face, I sounded harsher than I meant to.

"I can't," she replies. "Someone has to control the Furies."

Castor comes and stands next to her. And I know I should probably say something nice to him about how he stuck his neck out for me. He called a *Healer* from his own *House* for me. Never heard of Thebes doing that before.

Meanwhile, no one from my House is even here to see if I'm dead. My father is probably hoping I am, so he can skip to the part where he gets to pillage. About every twenty years or so the Houses come to the brink of war. There are skirmishes. Rich Scions, usually not in the direct line of descent, of course, get slaughtered and their treasures taken. Athens has always made out well during these dustups. We're about due for another, and my father's been looking for a way to instigate one without starting an all-out war. It's tricky, though. My death would give him an excuse to attack Romans and carry off some loot, although it would be overkill (haha). For an Heir to die would be more than a dustup. It would be all out war.

Either my father is too dense to understand that, or that's what he wants. An all-out war with the other Houses. I don't see how he thinks we could win that, but my father is all brawn, no brain. Maybe he doesn't care.

"I know it wasn't you two, neither of you benefit from a war. But someone else could." I look at Leda. "If you and Adonis got killed tonight, that would leave Corvus the Head of the House of Rome, wouldn't it?" I ask. She nods in response.

"Back up," Castor says, shaking his head. "If Corvus meant to kill whatever Athenian he faced tonight with poison, he would know that the Furies would take us all. It would have been a bloodbath. How would he escape with his life?"

"Trapdoor," Leda whispers. "Under the sands in the ring. There are several of them. He would have gotten away just fine."

I stare at Leda. She's working through all the scenarios in her mind, and none of them are pretty.

"You tell me," I say to her. "Would Corvus pull something like this on his own? Attacking an Heir is a big risk, and doing it tonight with so many people's lives on the line if the Furies broke out?" I stop and think about this for a second. It's huge. And it would definitely start a war. "Would he do that?"

Leda's eyes are distant with thought. She looks afraid. "Maybe. I don't know how deep it goes yet."

"Whoever was involved didn't care if you lived or died in the fallout tonight. That's practically a coup," Castor says to Leda. "If Corvus has allies, and he was trying to get you killed, you aren't safe in your own House."

Leda snorts delicately. "I never have been," she mumbles.

She must be tired to be so honest. Castor is shaken by her revelation. Of course he is. His brothers and cousins would die for him and he for them, but Leda and I weren't raised in Houses where everyone was cherished and told they were precious little miracles.

"You need protection," Castor says, looking like he's offering.

"What are you going to do about it, Thebes? Tuck her in at night?" I scoff. While he tries to backpedal, I talk over him. "We'll figure it out together, okay? I'm going to find the bastards who set this up. It's my right."

No arguing with that. If poison was involved, and I think Leda, Castor, and I are past the point of pretending with each other that it wasn't, I was dishonored. I can't let that go, and they know it.

"But we keep it quiet," I continue. "No talk of poison, or my father will go to war."

"So will mine," Castor agrees. "He's looking for anything. Rome trying to kill the Heir to Athens would be enough for him to justify taking Rome out," he says to Leda. "And the Hundred Cousins will agree. I won't be able to talk them out of it this time."

"*This* time?" Leda replies, rolling her eyes. "How many times have you had to walk your family back from killing off mine, by the way?"

Castor gives her a wry smile that's just a little too dashing for my liking. "You'll get your revenge," he tells me. "Leda will get her House cleaned. And I'll tell my family that I'm still searching for Atreus with the two of you. Deal?"

"Deal," Leda and I say together, though I have no idea how Castor became the tacit leader in this. It was my frigging idea.

"Now get the hell out of here and let me get some rest," I say.

Castor shakes his head at me. "You're welcome," he replies, and leaves.

Leda goes to the bed next to mine and starts pushing it toward me. "Why does he get under your skin so much? He's a good guy. He demanded a rematch between you and Corvus."

"I'm sure he made a big show about it so he could wiggle out of facing Corvus himself," I comment unfairly. Leda is pushing a bed over toward mine and she looks up at me, about to argue. "What are you doing?" I ask before she can tell me how amazing Castor is yet again.

"I need to sleep," she explains. "The only way I can protect you from the Furies while I sleep is if I'm right up against you."

She climbs on top of the bed and rolls onto her side, facing me. She puts her palms together and slides the hand-sandwich between the pillow and her cheek, like I've seen little kids do. It's her eyes, I decide. Green is so much warmer than the icy blue ones I have. The heat in them makes you think she cares about you, but she doesn't. She could be lying here next to anyone and look at them like that.

"Castor," she says, undeterred. "Why does he irritate you so much?"

"Right now, you're the one irritating me."

She actually laughs. She didn't take it the wrong way or get all offended because I'm such an insufferable grouch. Maybe she even thinks I'm funny, which would be a first.

"He *wants* you to like him, you know," she says.

"Only because he's not used to being disliked, and it makes him uncomfortable," I rebut, and I see surprise and possibly even a bit of respect in her expression, like she's thinking maybe I'm not just some mindless ox.

"You want to like him, too," she says. "But you won't let yourself."

"Do you and Adonis have the same mother?"

"Yes," she answers, her brows drawn together in confusion at what seems to be a shift in the conversation.

"Do all of your siblings have the same mother?"

She shakes her head vaguely, her eyes searching mine. "It's just me and Adonis. Our mom died when he was three."

"Do you remember her?"

"Yeah. Adonis doesn't, though."

"All I have are half-brothers. My father separated us from our mortal mothers after each of us were born." I don't go into detail about the different methods that my father used to get rid of our mothers, because it really depended on how attached each of them were to us. Essentially, how hard or easy it was to convince them to disappear from our lives. But I think Leda understands what I mean.

"Your half-brothers. Nilus and Lelix," she says, naming the brothers of mine she knows about and inviting me to continue.

"They're close to each other, but I'm nothing like them," I say. "Truth is, I can't stand them."

She stares at me for a while, trying to figure me out. "And *this* is why Castor annoys you? Because you don't like your half-brothers?" she asks, her lips tilted in a wry smile.

I guess it makes me feel better to know that she may be able to read and even control hearts, but she doesn't always understand them. At least, she doesn't understand mine. Yet, anyway.

"Maybe," I reply, rolling over and ending the pillow talk before I do something ridiculous. Like try to kiss her.

🐝 16 🐝

DAPHNE

I wake up pasty-mouthed, and I smell the mushroomy, metallic dankness of dried blood. Daedalus' blood. I didn't scrub with soap and water, just sort of wiped it off before I fell asleep, and I'm regretting that now. Not that I slept deeply.

Adonis complains when I poke him. I know he's still spent from last night, but I don't care. The sun is coming up, I feel disgusting, Ajax will be getting worried about me soon, and I have this urgent need to get the hell out of here. I keep glancing at the door to the surgical theater, expecting to see Phaon come out of there any second. I know he didn't see me electrocute him. I was careful to come up behind him, but I was the only strange face in his inner circle last night, so he's bound to suspect me anyway. I'll just never use this face again and he'll never... why am I freaking out about Phaon?

"Get up *now*," I tell Adonis. "I've got to go."

He moans about it, but he does get up. Before leaving he

checks on his sister, who looks quite comfortable spooning Daedalus. He raises an eyebrow.

"What?" I ask, catching his looks. "Doesn't she have to be close to him to protect him from the Furies?"

"Yeah, but she doesn't have to like it so much." He studies them for a moment.

"He is quite attractive." I notice.

"Sure. When he can't glower at you."

I glance at the back doors. "Come on. Let's go."

Adonis glances down at my chest, reading my heart. He gestures to the surgery doors. "What's back there?"

There's no point in trying to hide it from him. I know Adonis well enough now to know he'll keep pestering me until I tell him. It's weird how quickly I've figured him out. "That's where I left Phaon after I electrocuted him."

Adonis walks over and pushes the doors open despite my shushed protest. "He's not there," he tells me when he comes back, which doesn't make me feel better. Adonis does another one of those heart-checks on me, and I try to cover my chest with my hand.

"That's really obnoxious," I say, but he ignores me.

"You're scared of him." He looks surprised.

"Move it." I start to push him out of the *Valetudinaria*.

"It's Corvus you should be afraid of," he tells me, allowing himself to be rushed. "He's the one who holds Phaon's leash."

The thing that bothers me the most about that analogy is how easily I can picture it. Phaon is like an attack dog with his flat eyes and unpredictable viciousness. Also, the image of Phaon on a leash in a leather-fetish dungeon flashes through my head and now I want to wash my brain as much as my body.

"Where's your place?" I ask.

Adonis takes me up to one of the penthouse apartments in the same building. There's a great view of the park, which he ignores on his way to the bedrooms. "There are towels in the bathroom, clothes in the closets. Shoes. Help yourself," he says and then leaves me.

He's got a varied selection of single-serving sized toiletries. All high quality, matching sets of unopened little bottles. I feel like I'm at a hotel, which is less comforting in some way. Like it's not people who use this room but clients. I shower, dry my hair, find a new toothbrush in the cabinet, and brush my teeth before going to the closet. There's a little bit of everything in here, from sweats to ballgowns. Any possible occasion is covered. Lots of different sizes, too, and it's not just kitted out for women. Adonis has quite a few things in there for men as well. I'm getting the feeling Adonis entertains a lot.

When I'm jeaned, sweatered, and booted, I go out to the kitchen to see if he's got anything to eat. I'm surprised to find him in there cooking.

"Coffee's ready," he says, nodding at a French press that's steeping for me while he drinks from a mug of his own.

"I thought you'd go back to bed," I say, sitting at the counter across from him.

"When I'm up, I'm up." He flips the omelet with a flick of his wrist.

"I'm the same way. Ajax can fall asleep anywhere, anytime. Drives me nuts," I say while I slowly push down the plunger on my French press.

"So rude of him," Adonis agrees, smiling softly as he butters some toast.

I sip my mug of coffee and watch Adonis plate our breakfasts with practiced ease. I can tell by the way he has everything timed perfectly that he cooks often and that he enjoys doing it. This is nice. Homey. *They aren't your friends* floats thought my head. Ceyx was warning Castor, but it applies to me as well.

We eat in near silence. There's no way for me to hide what I'm feeling from him, but judging from the plethora of single-use items in his guest bathroom, he's probably used to getting through awkward mornings with people who are realizing that, sadly, he will not be a part of their lives from here on out. My reasons may be different from those of his usual guests, but the result will be the same. He gives me space to eat and drink my coffee, and in the meantime I steel myself against wanting him for a friend.

"I like that you're trusting me with your real face," he says, looking at his plate.

I hadn't noticed I was wearing my real face. "I'm more comfortable with you than I should be," I admit.

"I think I can see through the disguise now anyway. I've always almost been able to." He's pushing his eggs around, not eating them. "I'm not doing it to you, you know," he says. He sounds defensive, so I look over at him. "I'm not influencing you in any way."

"I didn't think you were."

"I don't go around screwing with people's hearts just because I can," he continues. "Especially not people I... like."

He lets it drop, but I can tell it's still bothering him. He wants proof I believe him.

Everyone seems to think he's this blithe party boy because of the way he looks. I know how that feels. I've spent most of my life being judged like that. I know this is a risk, but I've already decided I'm going to trust Adonis. I pull out the Cestus of Aphrodite that I wear in the guise of a heart necklace and explain it to him. How Helen got it from her sister Aphrodite before the fall of Troy. How it's been passed down from mother to daughter since. That it makes the bearer impervious to weapons and allows her to change her appearance at will so she can become any woman in the world. Finally, I tell him how it can influence emotions.

"I can't do what you do, or anything even close," I say. "But I know you're not manipulating me because I know that doesn't last, and that there's usually blowback."

I tried to use it on my dad to get him to be normal toward me, and it only made his obsession with me worse. As a rule, I try not to think of my dad. Even when I want to remember something good about him, the memory always gets ruined by the ending.

"Where'd you go?" Adonis asks. He touches the heart-shaped charm with the tip of a finger.

I shake my head. "Just remembering some blowback." I tuck the Cestus under my shirt. I may trust Adonis with secrets that could mean my life, but I don't talk about my dad with anyone but Ajax.

It's still early morning when we leave Adonis' apartment and walk to the subway heading downtown. I'm anxious to get back to Ajax, and Adonis is just anxious for some reason I haven't figured out yet.

A train pulls into the station. We go through the subway doors, and he starts herding me all the way to the end of the car. He corners me against the last pair of doors and lifts his arm, ostensibly to reach the overhead bar, but I think it's to shield me. I touch my face unnecessarily. I know I'm not wearing my real one.

"What's the matter with you?" I ask after catching him glancing over his shoulder for the third time.

He grips the bar overhead and wrings it in his hand. "Furies," he whispers, looking around. "I keep feeling them, don't you?"

"No." I try to look around Adonis but he's being too overprotective for me to really see anything. It's both sweet and annoying. "You sure you're not feeling the Furies from me? You are *right* on top of me."

He shakes his head. "This is from Athens. And I don't feel the Furies from you anymore." I stare at him for a moment, and he nods, a muscle in his jaw flexing. "I think you saved my life when you intervened in the coliseum and stopped the fighting."

I shake my head, not understanding.

"I almost died trying to control the Furies. You saved me."

I don't feel the Furies right now and he does, so that has to mean that I really did clear my blood debt with Athens, like Adonis said last night, and apparently Rome too. I guess he passed out before he could tell me that. This is almost too good to be believed. I don't have to worry about *any* House feeling my presence when I'm disguised. It's such a stroke of good fortune I can't help but question it. I'm a Scion. We don't have good fortune, only bad. Makes me wonder what the Fates are up to. But at least now I can stay with Ajax at Ladon's cove, where I will be shielded from them.

"Well... good," I say, pleased. It really would hurt me now if Adonis died. He's wormed his way into my affections, the jerk. Didn't see that coming.

His head snaps around quickly, like he's hearing something I can't, and he grips the overhead bar a little tighter.

"Can you feel your way toward their location?" I ask.

"Over there," he says, tipping his head toward a cluster of people behind and to his right. Then he shakes his head, his eyes looking uncertain. "It's moved."

"But they haven't," I say, my eyes on the group. They're all just standing or sitting there.

Adonis makes a frustrated growling noise. "It doesn't make any sense."

I start marking everyone on the train car, memorizing their faces. No one stands out. Certainly no one who looks like an Athenian, and they are usually of a type that can't be missed. Black hair, blue eyes, tall and pale-skinned, Athenians stand out.

"Have you seen someone following us?" I ask.

"No. And that worries me." His expression gets uncharacteristically dark, and his stance lowers, ready for a fight.

"Let's go aboveground at the next stop. Draw them out," I suggest.

Adonis agrees, and we exit at Union Square and wait to see who follows us. "Recognize anyone from on the train?" I ask him after a solid ten minutes of watching.

He shakes his head, still looking harried. "I can feel them, though. Only faintly, but..." he trails off and lets out a long breath. "It's like he's hunting us. It's fun for him."

"You're sure it's a him?" I ask, craning my head around, studying every guy I see.

"I don't know!" he nearly shouts at me. I haven't seen him lose his cool like this. He fights to calm down. "We're in Thebes's territory now. We should go."

We head below ground again, insert our tokens and go through the turnstiles, and then Adonis grabs me by the jacket.

"We gotta move!" he growls in my ear and drags me to the end of the platform.

"What is it?" I say, looking around.

He's shaking his head, and his eyes are darting around trying to be everywhere at once. "Whoever it is means to kill you," he says in my ear, pulling me against his side in a panic. "And I can't *find* him!"

A train enters the station, and Adonis barely waits for there to be enough room before he's hauling me down onto the tracks behind it.

He reaches behind his back and under his clothes, pulling out a pair of long daggers. "Run!" he shouts, pushing me in front of him.

My eyes haven't fully adjusted to the sudden darkness, and I stumble. I glance back and see a figure coming up behind Adonis. Something huge and misshapen. Whatever it is isn't human.

I summon a lightning bolt. "Get down!"

Adonis drops down to the ground and I let my bolt fly, but the creature is gone. My bolt flares out, finding metal and wires to fry. When the flash of white light ends, I'm left blinded again and blinking.

I think there's a flying shape that's bobbing about like a drunk bird. It expands. Legs sprout and come to standing beneath the small body of a bat. The body, too, expands and then changes. Arms grow and simultaneously reach down to grab me and pull me toward a blobby, not-quite-formed face. The beady eyes inside the doughy ball are filled with surprise and avarice.

"Atreidae," the slug-like tongue says around newly emerging teeth.

The entire transformation occurs in less than a second, and now a hunchbacked man with twisted limbs and uneven features is before me, confining me in a tight grip. I try to break free, but he is unbelievably strong. Stronger than me. I'm summoning another bolt, stripping what little water I have left in my dehydrated body to generate the necessary charge, when the hunchback suddenly jerks and releases me. He turns around, screaming.

He reaches around for Adonis to grab him, and I see one of Adonis' blades sticking out of the creature's thigh. Adonis jumps up, abandoning his blade. He pauses long enough to reach down and haul me along with him. We sprint to the service door and throw ourselves through it. I twist my head around to look. In the darkness, I can barely make out the seething shape of the creature as it changes from a man into something else. Something much bigger than a man.

Adonis yanks on my arm, and we hurl ourselves headlong down the metal steps. We don't bother to stop and barricade the door behind us. I know how strong that creature is; he would be able to break it down.

"This way!" Adonis gasps. The cuff on his wrist glows. I can hear the creature thundering down the steps behind us, keening like a banshee.

We've come to a stone wall that's covered in ice. I round on Adonis, about to scream at him for bringing us to a dead end, when he pushes me right through the wall.

17

DAEDALUS

I wake up and everything hurts. But at least I'm not leaking blood anymore. I peel back a few bandages and examine the deeper wounds from last night. They've all closed so I'm good to go.

Leda sucks in a fast breath and wakes herself with a violent shake. Her eyes land on me, but she doesn't see me yet.

"Nightmares?" I ask.

Her eyes find focus, but they're still wild, and her body's stiff and motionless with fear. She glances around and lets her muscles loosen.

"I should be so lucky," she replies.

"Why's that?"

"Because nightmares aren't real." She yawns and stretches, looking around, but we're the only ones here. She turns her hands up in frustration. "Where the hell's the doctor?"

"Sleeping, probably." I roll myself over gingerly, easing myself out of bed. Corvus must have stabbed me over a dozen times. Most of them are small punctures, but damn.

"What are you doing?"

"Going home." Or I would if I was wearing shoes. Or pants.

"Are you an...?" she searches for a proper insult, but nothing scathing enough comes to her. It *is* early. "You can't just go. You need to be seen by the doctor first."

"I'm okay," I say, looking around for something to wear. "I came here fully dressed. Where's my shit?"

"On fire, hopefully."

She's funny. She swings her legs beneath her and stands. She looks almost as drained as I feel.

"I'm not going to get you to stay here for the day, am I?" she asks. I give her a look and she nods. "I gotta take you to get clean clothes in case..."

"There's a Roman who can't control the Furies around. I know the drill." I wrap the hospital sheet around my waist and stand. Well, mostly stand. I'm sort of bent over a little.

We shuffle down the hall like a couple of little old ladies.

"What the matter with *you*?" I ask her.

She gives me the side-eye. "Do you know how much strength and energy it takes to control the Furies? You don't. So shut the hell up."

"Jeez, you are *grouchy* in the morning," I say like I'm shocked, but really, I'm smiling. Why is it funny to me?

She walks right into the men's section of the spa that's adjacent to the arena and the *ludus*. Handy positioning. It's so the gladiators can be all oiled, massaged, and perfumed before they go out and hack away at each other with swords. We have fight cages in the House of Athens, and we dedicate a lot of time to training, but we don't do massages and aromatherapy or whatever all this shit is. The Romans have always been decadent and perverse. True to form, there are a couple of naked dudes sitting, standing, and otherwise hanging out in the fragrant steam of the spa, but Leda doesn't seem at all phased, and neither do they. One or two of them tuck up a bit, but to be honest, I think it's more because of me than her.

She goes straight to a locker, opens it, and starts pulling out expensive-looking track gear. When she's satisfied with the cut or color or gods know what, she hands it to me.

I wait for her to leave, remember that she can't, and say, "Turn around."

She rolls her eyes, but does as I ask anyway. The naked Romans stare at me, inspecting every inch. And I do mean *every inch*, though they mostly focus on the cuts left by their kinsman. Some of them look like they feel bad about it, or bad for me, I guess. I still look like I fell into a blender, and it'll be another day or two before all the angry red marks fade to nothing. I ignore the naked brigade and try to dress as fast as I can, but I'm so unsteady I have to concentrate on not falling over. I get the pants on, but I feel like I'm going to barf.

"Here," Leda says, reaching out for me.

She makes me sit down on one of the benches, and I realize I'm shaking all over. She puts a shirt over my head, guiding my arms through the holes for me, then kneels in front of me and starts putting socks and shoes on my feet. I'm so stunned I let her do it. I don't remember anyone ever dressing me before. Not even when I was a kid, but I can tell by the way she doesn't even have to think about it that she's dressed someone else plenty of times.

I recall that their mother died when Adonis was three. She must have taken care of him when they were little. Anyway, that's just the impression I get. She's dressing me like I'm her kid.

Leda finishes tying my shoelaces and stands. She holds out a hand to me. "Come on. I'll take you home."

I take her hand and let her lead me out of the *ludus*. She stops at the front part of the spa area, goes behind a counter, and comes back with honey. Then she takes my hand again and leads me out of the building, and onto the street. I don't know why she's still holding my hand, but I don't mind it. It feels right. She hails a cab and gets in with me. I should say no, but I don't. I just give the cab driver my address, then I open the jar of honey and gulp it down in several swallows without tasting it.

"Are you controlling my emotions?" I ask when we get to about 23rd St.

She gives me a baffled smile. "Of course not. Why would you even think that?"

I shrug, then look out the window for the rest of the ride downtown. As soon as we pull up, I see my mom pacing in front of the door of my building. She's strung out.

"You should go," I say, getting out of the taxi, but Leda can sense the sudden flood of adrenaline in me. And she can see how I keep glancing nervously at the junkie who's muttering to herself and itching her forearms compulsively.

Leda scoots across the seat of the cab and puts her feet out on the curb before I can close the door on her.

"Dae?" my mom calls out.

Great. Just frigging kill me now.

"Is that...?" Leda asks.

"My mother," I mumble, turning away. Leda follows me over to my mom, who goes to hug me, stops herself and then glances at Leda.

"It's okay, Mom. Let's go inside."

My mom holds onto my wrist, shaking her head. "He's back. He's in my apartment. I can't go home."

I let out a huge sigh. Regroup. Try again. "Mom —"

"You have to come to Brooklyn and get him out!" she says, her voice inching its way towards hysterical. Leda's eyes are wide with sympathy, and she's trying not to stare or look away. Most people try not to see my mom. They try to pretend she's not there so they don't have to see her ravaged face, her too-skinny limbs sticking out like a doll's from her bloated midsection. Leda does the opposite. She tries to see her, to notice her, without turning her into a freak show. But it's hard.

"Okay," I say, soothingly. "I'll come and get him out." Even though I know this is just another one of her hallucinations.

"Wait, what the hell?" Leda says, her hand shooting out to stop me. "You're not going anywhere. You need to lie down right now."

I pull Leda aside. "She won't stop until I go with her. She's not... in her right mind, as you can see."

Leda stares at me disbelievingly. "You're about to keel over, and she's in no shape to take care of you. If you die, Rome is screwed."

Oh. That's all she cares about. Right. "I'm not going to die," I reply, turning away.

She stops me. "Okay. You're not on death's doorstep, but what if someone *is* in her apartment? What if you have to fight?"

"There's no one there, trust me," I say, about to lose my temper. I run a hand through my hair. "She does this. She sees things, always has."

Leda crosses her arms stubbornly. "I'm going with you."

I can't let her come. I just *can't*. I turn away from Leda and take my mom by the elbow, guiding her down the street. I hear Leda following us. I stop and face her.

"Go home, Leda," I warn.

She doesn't reply. Just stares at me. I start walking away again and she follows. And now I've had it. I spin around and grab her by the shoulders, pushing her back. "You can't come, okay!? Go home!"

She tips her chin up at me. "Make me," she says, calling my bluff like we're nine or something. She's not even a little bit scared of me. That's a first.

I'm just too damn tired, and I've started trembling again. I sigh and let go of her. "Fine," I say. "But don't say I didn't warn you."

We hail a cab, and I give the driver directions to Bay Ridge. He's not happy about having to go to Brooklyn, but he hits the meter and goes anyway. My mom starts in on her crazy babble about the cat that can turn into a person. I let my head fall back onto the top of the seat and close my eyes.

"But how does he get into your apartment if you always keep the window closed?" Leda asks. She's trying to reason with my mother, which she'll soon learn is pointless.

"I saw him turn into a spider once and crawl in through a crack. He can be anything," my mother whispers back, excited. She's got a rapt audience for her insanity and she's not going to pass it up. "He's always watching me."

I open my eyes and find Leda looking at me, worried. It's only going to get worse, though.

We get to my mom's place after forty-five minutes and a massive cab fare, and I can't tell if the elevator takes forever because I can't wait for this to be over with, or if it really has gotten slower since the last time I was here.

We go inside my mom's apartment, and it's about what I'd expected. Overflowing ashtrays. Empty bottles and takeout containers on every surface. Vodka, gin, Jack Daniels, 40's, two-liter bottles of Coca-Cola. One spilled, and now the brown liquid has dried into a sticky amoeba shape on the floor. Sink full of dirty dishes that have been there so long they've gotten dusty. And of course, my mom's gear still laid out on the table. Hypos and blackened spoons, a length of rubber tubing and a lighter. The windows are shut and taped up and it smells like sickness in here. Like someone rotting from the inside out.

Leda is stiff with shock for a moment, just staring at the filth, and I think *this is when she runs away screaming*. But she doesn't. She crosses to the windows and starts pulling off the tape. My mom yells at her to stop, but Leda has a plan.

"Oh, I'm *looking* for him. I'm going to squash him," she tells my mom.

After a beat, Mom nods nervously. "Okay," she agrees. "But what if he bites you?"

"I'm not afraid of spiders," Leda replies, getting back to opening the windows. "Dae, go check your mom's bedroom."

Dae. I watch her for a second, throwing herself into looking for that frigging spider, and I want to kiss her. Really kiss her, long and slow, right here in the middle of this shit hole.

I check my mom's bedroom for spiders. While I'm in there I change the sheets and toss my mom's dirty laundry together in a pile in the hall. I tell my mom to lie down on the fresh sheets and she curls up almost instantly and passes out, like she's been waiting days for me to get here just so she could sleep.

When I come out of the bedroom, Leda is wearing a pair of rubber gloves and throwing the empty bottles and moldy take-out containers into a big black garbage bag.

"You can go now," I tell her, standing there with my arms full of dirty clothes. "You shouldn't have to do this."

"I'm coming with you to the laundry room," she insists, taking off the gloves. "*You* shouldn't be alone right now."

I can't tell if she means mentally or physically. Little bit of both, maybe. She tries to get me to sit down, to rest, to order some food, but I can't sit here and let her clean this place by herself. And honestly? Even though I've just started a heal and I should be ravenous enough to eat a small car, the condition of this place makes the thought of food nauseating.

When she finally accepts that there's no way to stop me, we put the laundry to run in the basement machine and do the bathroom next. Leda puts the gloves back on and scrapes mildew scabs off my mom's shower walls while I scrub the toilet. It takes us three hours to get this disgusting place back into livable shape. Leda doesn't try to pretend this is normal or okay, she just gets it done. It doesn't feel like pity to me. I don't know what it is, actually, or why she's doing it. I can't figure it out.

"Thank you." I manage to say as we're tying up the trash bags and getting ready to leave.

Leda nods and doesn't make a big thing about it, but I know it is. She's Head of her House, runs a dozen restaurants and night clubs, and even dabbles in human politics. The society pages always have her in them, at some fundraiser or something. She's got plenty of places to be that are incalculably nicer than here.

"Will she be okay alone?" she asks.

"Not really, but there's nothing I can do about it." I look around at the apartment. "She grew up in this neighborhood, so no one will hurt her if they find her on the street. I make sure the rent and utilities are paid, and there's always money in her bank account. Never too much at once, for obvious reasons, just a little every week. I keep hiring people to come in and clean for her, but my mom scares them all away. It's like I can't keep up. The last person must have left weeks ago, and she didn't tell me."

I don't talk about my mom. Ever. Except with Ladon, and

even then, it's not like he's ever been inside her place and seen how she actually lives. He's never seen her in the middle of a freakout, either. Don't know why I'm telling Leda all this stuff. It just came out. Maybe I'm trying to explain it so she doesn't think I let my mom live like this because I'm a bad son. But there's really no way to explain my mother so I shut up.

Leda frowns and shifts on her feet, trying to figure out how to word her next question. "Does she hallucinate because of the drugs, or does she take drugs because she hallucinates?"

That's probably the most insightful thing anyone's ever asked me about her. "I've always wondered that. She's schizophrenic. In and out of hospitals her whole life, but she's also done drugs her whole life, too. I don't know which came first. But it's why my dad let her live after she had me. Nobody believed her when she said I could move the sofa when I was an infant."

"What's her name?"

"Gina. Gina DeAngelo."

"Italian?" she asks. I nod, and Leda nods with me. "This whole neighborhood used to be Italian. And Greek," she adds, lifting a wry eyebrow.

I laugh at that under my breath even though it's not ha-ha funny. Just something Leda and I get that maybe other people wouldn't. A long silence stretches out between us. I heft my garbage bag and reach for hers, but she won't let me take it.

I realize how close I'm standing to her. I can feel the warmth of her skin and see that one of her hairs is stuck to her lower lip. I want to reach out and free it, then touch her cheek, and then I want to do all kinds of things to her. With garbage in between us. In my junkie mother's living room. How romantic of me. I turn and leave, and she's forced to follow me out.

We bring the trash to the dumpster, and I expect Leda to go, but she doesn't.

We take a cab back to my apartment, and I expect her to stay in the cab and take it the rest of the way uptown, but she doesn't.

She gets out with me and leads me into a deli downstairs from my apartment where she orders about ten sandwiches, slices of cake, buckets of coleslaw, and potato salad, and bags of chips. She practically cleans the place out and has everyone who works there jumping to get what she wants. Two of the guys even help carry the stuff up to my place. She pays and tips everyone like she's a millionaire, which maybe she is, and then starts unpacking the food while I just stand there like a dummy.

"Do you want to start with the pastrami?" she asks, pulling out the wax paper-wrapped sandwich. "It's still warm."

She realizes I'm staring at her, and she stops moving.

"What are you doing here?" I ask.

She doesn't answer me right away. She just keeps pulling food out of the paper bags and laying it on the table I've got in the area next to my kitchen. I wouldn't call it a dining room. That would make it seem fancy, which it isn't, just a decent table with four matching chairs, even though I've only ever used one of them because I've never had people over for dinner. I don't have a lot of furniture. Or stuff in general, except for books. My father didn't let me go to college, but I read a lot.

My apartment is a new re-mod. Converted warehouse space. Good view, large and open with interesting, reclaimed floorboards and dimmable track lighting. I wanted it to look like an arty space in Soho, so I took over one of my family's run-down waterfront properties, picked an architect, and did it. I had no idea how to decorate it, though. No idea what kind of stuff people have to have in order to turn raw spaces into homes. Pillows and coffee tables? Rugs and paintings? I can't tell. So apart from my bookshelf, which covers an entire wall, my place is so empty it echoes, and the crinkling of the wax paper in Leda's hand is unnaturally loud.

"I'm hungry," she answers me at last, quietly. "And you still look terrible. You should have eaten hours ago."

I take a step toward her. "But what are you *doing* here?"

She looks up at me, shaking her head. "I don't know."

Now I'm scared. Whatever is going on here, she knows it's not what *should* be going on here, and so do I. But I'm not going to stop it.

Then, she sits down and opens the pastrami. "If you don't eat this, I will," she warns.

I take it from her, and now I'm laughing a little, though again, it's not like what she said was ha-ha funny, and I start eating. I don't stop until all the food is gone and I'm falling asleep at the table.

And then she puts me to bed and leaves.

18

DAPHNE

I pitch forward, trying to stop myself from hitting a wall that isn't there, and skid across the dry, parched ground on the heels of my hands.

Unable to halt his momentum, Adonis trips over my back, tumbles, and then sprawls out beside me. My muscles still throbbing with adrenaline, I twist over, kicking away from... nothing. Nothing is behind us, no monster. Just a stone wall.

We are on the shore of a huge body of water. I would call it an ocean, but there are no waves. Can a whole ocean be becalmed? A thin light surrounds us. It's not nighttime. I can see well enough, but it's as if there is no sun, just the bare minimum of gray, filtered light by which to see.

"I've never been here," I whisper.

Adonis pushes himself up on his forearms. "Cimmeria. Not quite Hades, but close," he says.

"The Cimmerians. They're in the *Odyssey*." My voice is raspy. After making a bolt of lightning, my body is always drained of fluids. I look at the ocean, which I know now is the great Oceanus, but I wouldn't drink from it even if it weren't salty. That water isn't really water. It's the body of one of the beings before the Titans. It's one of the original Elementals, like Gaia the earth, or Uranus the sky.

"Never met one. It's not a very cheerful place. I imagine they don't go out of their way to welcome visitors." He rallies his strength and stands.

"What was that thing that attacked us?" I ask as he helps me up, though he's in worse shape than I am. The last twelve hours have not been kind to him.

"I've never seen anything like it," he replies tiredly. "Come on. We can't go back through this portal."

As we start walking, Adonis explains to me that in some parts of the Underworld time stands still. We could wait for days, go back through, and no time would have passed in our world, which means the shapeshifter would still be right about to grab us.

"I don't know if time is frozen in Cimmeria like it is in Hades, but I don't think we should risk it."

"Where's the next portal?" I ask.

"The nearest one I know about is in the Land of Dreams. It might be far. But Morpheus is cool."

"Wouldn't want to hang out with a god who *wasn't*," I comment, razzing him a little. Adonis nudges me with his elbow, taking the joke. "How far is it?"

"Oh, gods, it depends," he replies, groaning. "The Underworld is elastic. Convince yourself it's just a few minutes away and we'll get there soon. Get depressed about it and it'll take forever."

I don't really understand what he means, but I go with it. I begin imagining that any second now we'll enter the Land of Dreams. The landscape works against positive thought, though. It feels so desolate here. And not desolate and beautiful like an Ansel Adams photo of the California desert, but desolate and oppressive, like a photo of the Nevada desert after the atomic bomb tests. Adonis is struggling, and I try to perk up for both of us, but I'm so thirsty from generating lightning that it's hard to stay optimistic.

With Adonis thinking *never* and me thinking *right now*, the Underworld seems to split the difference between us. It takes a few hours of walking before I see glowing globes, like soap bubbles with candle flames inside them, floating in the distance. My heart lifts. Stars shine and twinkle in the indigo sky and a breeze ruffles my hair. I feel a weight lift from both of our shoulders.

"Finally," Adonis says, picking up his pace.

We pass elfin people dancing in the dark among vaguely glowing mushrooms, and poppies that are dewed with little points of sparkling nectar. On the constant gentle breeze, I hear sighs and whispers, fragments of thoughts set adrift in the starry night. I feel at peace.

No one needs to guide Adonis and me to the marble columns atop the hill. We just know that's where to go, and we climb the gentle slope to the open-air temple. Gauzy curtains waft and occasionally snap near the burning braziers, but there is no fear of fire here. Incense hints the air with resinous scents that empty and calm the mind, and in the middle of the Doric columns, under the open night sky, is a bed.

A god with moon white skin and long, black hair that lies like a sheet of poured black glass among the silks of his bed rolls over and stretches his slender limbs overhead. His almond shaped eyes crinkle at the corner as he smiles at us like we are dear friends.

"Two of my favorite faces," he purrs, luxuriating in his giant bed.

He peels back the corner of the top sheet and Adonis slides in next to him, pulling me along with him. Somehow I don't feel strange about getting into bed with two men who aren't Ajax. Everything is okay here. It's just a dream. Morpheus shifts me over his body to the other side of him, and I lie my cheek on his bare chest with Adonis across from me.

"I'm exhausted," Adonis says on a sigh.

"I know, love," Morpheus replies, dipping his mouth down to kiss Adonis.

I feel like I've been here before, done this before. Adonis falls asleep and I suppose I do, too. Or maybe we don't sleep at all, but we both feel completely rested after lying in the god's arms for however long we do. When I "wake up," I'm not thirsty anymore. My feet are no longer sore. Everything is perfect. It doesn't seem to last long, though. A blink, a breath, and too soon it seems to me, Morpheus is sitting up.

"I'm sorry, pets, but we must go now," Morpheus says, taking our hands as he slides out of bed. "You've been here longer than is wise."

It felt like five minutes to me, but it's easier to follow than to ask a bunch of questions. I drift alongside Morpheus, lulled by his gentle presence. The poppies nod their heads as we pass, and the glowing globes bob like bumble bees in the soft breeze. But a few more steps and the warm, soft air turns cold and dry, and the carpet of dewy grass turns to packed clay.

Up ahead is a bare tree with claw-like branches that cast reaching shadows, and under the tree is the figure of a tall man, bare to the waist, with a Corinthian helmet on his head. My feet slow and I glance behind Morpheus to see that Adonis has fallen back in trepidation.

The Land of Dreams is twilight dark, and pleasantly so. It is the deep, not-quite-black-blue of summer evenings. But the darkness that crouches under the tree and that crawls around the helmeted god is the dark void of fear.

"Come." Morpheus beckons. "Hades wishes to help you."

Adonis and I share a nervous look but continue walking until we are standing under the tree opposite the god of the dead. I hear chittering things scraping across the branches above. Shapes dart too quickly to be seen, making the brittle wood creak. Shivers run down the back of my exposed neck and it's all I can do to keep my quickening legs from running away.

Hades does not remove his helmet. He wears a black chiton tied about his waist, and like a paragon of classical beauty, his bare torso is smooth and muscled, though obscured by the ever-present shadows that seem to pour out of him.

"You have already been here too long," Hades says.

Adonis and I look at each other.

"We didn't know we were on a schedule," he replies, touching the cuff on his wrist possessively, as if frightened Hades might take it away from him.

Even with the helmet and the shadows obscuring him, the similarities between Hades and Adonis are obvious. They could be twins, and I'm not the only one who can see that. Adonis keeps trying to peer inside the eye slits of Hades' helmet, though he knows what he's looking at. Himself.

Hades continues. "I mean no reproach, but time has been passing swiftly outside Morpheus' land. You have cast your lot with Nemesis, and against her sisters, the Moirai, and even now the Fates seek to crush you. You must go." He lifts a hand to banish us, and I step forward.

"Wait," I say. "What do the Fates want? How do we stop them?"

Hades pauses to consider. "Only Nemesis knows how to stop her sisters. Stay close to her heir, Ladon. As to what they want, it is as it has always been since Zeus defeated his father Cronus, who defeated his father, Uranus, before him." His eyes are unreadable inside the eye slits, but his body angles toward Adonis, his spitting image. "They want the children to replace their parents. That is the cycle of the cosmos."

I have more questions, especially about the thing that chased Adonis and me down here, but Hades doesn't give me the chance to ask. With a wave of his hand, we are sent from the Underworld.

19

TANTALUS

I hear tapping at my window and reach for the dagger I keep under my pillow.

Slipping out of bed, I pad to the window, ease apart two slats of the blinds to peer outside and find Ajax floating in midair. I get the window open and yank his weightless body inside.

"Are you crazy!" I whisper-scold as I pull him into a tight hug. I can smell her on his skin, like he's saturated with her. I have to throw the image of her face out of my mind. Ajax. He's the one who matters to me.

He moves away, glances over my shoulder at the bed, then back at me. "I can't find Daphne."

There's no reproach in his voice. No suspicion. I shouldn't be insulted by his perfect faith that nothing would have occurred between Daphne and me, even if she were in my bed. But I am. I latch on to the more urgent problem here.

"How long since you last saw her?" I ask.

"Last night at ten. She was going uptown to stay at Harlow's for the night."

I keep close tabs on Harlow, though I've never told that to Ajax and Daphne. Harlow is a mortal, and she knows about our family. So far, she hasn't said a word, but I'm watching.

"Was Harlow expecting her?" I ask.

"No. But she's not there."

It's past one a.m. now. That means Daphne's been missing for over twenty-four hours. "Dammit, Jax, what took you so long to come to me?"

"I couldn't risk being seen—" he whisper-yells back.

"All right." I cut him off and take a moment to let both of us calm down. "Tell me everything."

"All I know is that she left with Adonis Tiber."

It takes me a moment to wrap my head around that. "Willingly?" I ask.

"It's okay," he assures me.

I put the pieces together in my head. "I think I know where she was last night," I say.

I get Ajax up to speed on what happened in Roman territory, and how Castor saw Adonis at the fight with a girl. Castor said she was a mortal, but that she seemed familiar to him somehow. The girl stuck in his head. It had to be Daphne.

"Does Adonis know who she really is?" I ask, though I know he'd have to. Adonis would feel the Furies around her, and I know that some Romans can tell the Houses apart this way. Adonis is rumored to be one of the strongest Romans ever. There's no way he wouldn't be able to identify Daphne as an Atreidae, but still shield her from other Scions, so they would have no idea she was anything other than mortal. I've experienced first-hand in inter-House meetings how he can completely silence the Furies. I know

Adonis is remarkable, and that there is no way Daphne could hide her true identity from him. I only asked this to give Ajax a chance to explain how the hell it is that Daphne and Adonis are going off together at ten o'clock at night.

"He knows," Ajax replies, but he doesn't say more as I'd intended.

"Where are you staying? Maybe she couldn't get back to you for some geographical reason?" I try. He shakes his head, unwilling to answer even that question.

I let an uncomfortable pause build. Silence breaks most people. They'll do anything to fill it. Not Ajax, though. "How can I help you find Daphne if you won't give me anything to go on?" I ask, trying the *help me help you* interrogation style.

"There are going to be lots of things I can't tell you about our lives," he says. "You know why."

Again, there's no blame in his voice, and that's worse. Like what I feel for her is no threat to him. For the first time I feel anger toward Ajax. It's like a bright flash in me, feral and consuming. It makes my breath catch. It's gone as fast as it came, but it was there, and Ajax sensed it.

"Maybe she's still with Adonis," I say, turning away from him. I'm going to dial the phone, yeah, but I also can't look at him right now.

There's a second party service we use when we want to contact someone from another House. I pick up the phone by my bed to dial that number.

Ajax is shaking his head like something doesn't make sense to him. "If they were still together, she would have gotten word to me. Unless something happened to her."

"*He* could have happened to her." I narrow my eyes at him. "You're acting like you trust him with her. He's our enemy, Jax."

He tips his head to the side, considering. "I trust him to do everything he can to keep the peace between the Houses. That's what he wants. He won't hurt her."

"How do you know what he wants? Are you friends with Rome now?" I ask, dialing the service. He doesn't reply to this, either. But he should have said no.

I leave a cryptic message for Adonis, and we wait in silence for the service to call us back with his reply, but we don't have to wait long. It's Leda. She's called our house line directly, skipping over the service. She doesn't know where her brother is. She's worried, and I hear no lie in her. She wants to meet in Central Park. Usual place.

"I'm coming," Ajax says. Before I can fight him on it, he adds, "I'll stay back."

It's such a bad idea. A thousand things could go wrong. "I can't go alone. I'll have to take Castor. If he spots you—"

"I'm not asking," he says.

That's when it hits me. Ajax has changed. He's grown up, but unlike Castor and Pallas, he isn't mine to command. He's outside the House of Thebes now. Not an Outcast, certainly, but something I can't figure out yet. He doesn't have to take orders from me and he knows it, too. That bothers me.

"Castor and I will be there in ten," I tell Leda and hang up.

Ajax acknowledges the time and jumps out the window. What I wouldn't give to be able to fly like that. He always was the most gifted one—given a little bit more than the rest of us. More strength, more talent, more common sense. Daphne. She was given to him by fate, but what if she'd met me first? Would she have loved me, or is Jax just so much better than me that she would always choose him?

I pull on some dark jeans and a black pullover and wake

Castor. Groggy but compliant, he dresses and follows me. He's in a world of shit for the stunt he pulled calling Ceyx to heal Daedalus. The smartest and strongest of that whole backward clan of troglodytes, the main reason Athens is a threat to Thebes, and Castor couldn't just let him die. He'll do anything I ask right now without questioning it.

Leda is there when we arrive, pacing and chewing on a thumbnail. She's brought no second, no one to watch her back, yet instead of being terrified of us like she should be, she looks relieved when she sees Castor. I watch him greet her with an ease they shouldn't have, and I wonder, not for the first time tonight, what the hell is going on in my House.

After she acknowledges me, I step back so I can watch them interact. They launch into a relaxed back and forth, neither of them guarding their answers or searching for the most misleading ways to ask their questions. They are honest and upfront with each other in a natural way.

"The last I saw of Adonis he was unconscious in the hospital bed with that mortal girl," Castor says. "Who was she?"

"No idea. Didn't even get a name," Leda says, shaking her head. "Last night was the first time I met her, but she seemed strangely okay with everything that happened."

"And not squeamish about blood," Castor agrees.

Leda continues seamlessly, offering up information without being asked. "The security cameras in the *Valetudinaria* show Adonis going upstairs to his apartment with her around five a.m., then it shows them leaving the building together at six. Not a peep from my brother since."

Castor bites his lower lip, thinking. "It's a new relationship. Could they have taken off to be alone?"

Leda's already shaking her head. "My brother was *wrecked* last night. Controlling the Furies in that situation was enough to kill a dozen other Romans with that ability, and he knows what kind of shit we're in because an Heir nearly died in our territory. He wouldn't have just run off with some girl."

"I've heard stories."

"He's not like that," she insists.

"Okay, okay," Castor allows. "The question is, who *was* she?" he says, not asking, just venting because he can't figure it out. Watching them, I can't help but wonder if Castor and Leda have slept together. I've heard Romans who can control the Furies can and have had affairs with members of the other Houses. Would Castor be that stupid?

There's a lull in their conversation. They look to me and realize that I'm more interested in them than in the mystery girl. Castor sees my disapproval and remembers himself.

"We should split up and look for them." he offers, subtly altering his posture so it's not completely open to her.

"Look where?" she says, discarding the suggestion. "I was hoping Thebes had some more information about that girl. That's why I asked you here."

It's good that she's dealing with Castor. Leda can't hear a lie like I can, but I suspect that she can sense when someone is being dishonest, or when they're hiding something if she's looking at them.

It dawns on me that she asked us here in person for that reason. She needs to see us to read our hearts accurately, but Castor hasn't realized that yet. He's just exchanging information with her like things are equal between them when they are far from it. She's getting much more out of him than either of us know.

"Have you spoken to Daedalus?" Castor asks, still disconcertingly frank with her even though he has reeled it in a bit. Maybe it's just the way he is, but I can't help wondering what our House would do if I were to die. Our House would fall to him. Castor has all the qualities of a leader except for subterfuge. He's not devious enough to lead.

"Last time I saw Daedalus he was about to face-plant into his potato salad," Leda replies. "I doubt he's done with his heal yet."

"That girl, she was trying to call off the fight before I jumped into the arena." Castor seems to recall.

Leda raises an eyebrow. "Conveniently saving Daedalus' life."

"Do you think she works for Athens?"

She frowns. "My brother's better at reading hearts than anyone. He'd know it if she were a spy."

Castor chuffs. "Your brother? The one who's missing, last seen with said strange girl?"

"Point taken," Leda admits, looking worried now.

They defer to me. "Seems Daedalus has some explaining to do. Why *would* this girl save his life?"

"I'll go see him," Leda offers.

"I'll come with you," Castor says.

"If you're not back by sunrise I'll hold Rome responsible." I tell him.

Leda smiles tightly at me. "Always a pleasure, Tantalus."

They leave and I wait for Ajax to come out of hiding, which he does sooner than he should. "Why didn't you go with them?" he demands, keeping his voice low.

"I'm Heir to our House. I can't help Leda find her brother. But Castor can, and you can follow them. But stay out of sight," I add needlessly.

Ajax jumps into the air and is gone.

Maybe Daphne will come to me. She usually does when she's

in trouble. I hurry not to the home I share with Mildred, but to Washington Square, where she knows to come, imagining that by some miracle she's sleeping peacefully in my bed when I get there. Like Ajax had thought.

She isn't. But I'll keep waiting for her. I will always wait for her.

🜍 20 🜍

DAEDALUS

It's such a treat to wake up to the sound of someone pounding on my front door. Especially when I'm still healing. I try to ignore it until I hear Doris' voice on the other side. I haul myself out of bed, nauseous with hunger and weak in the knees.

I open the door just a crack. "What?" I growl through it.

"Good. You aren't dead," Doris teases, giving me a half-smile. She's alone, which is strange. Athenians usually travel in packs, like dogs. Or dolphins, which are way more bloodthirsty. "Are you going to let me in?"

I swing the door open. She's brought some food for my heal, which for our family is downright touching. She must have been really worried about me. It was supposed to be her fighting Corvus instead of me, so I guess maybe she feels grateful. Or guilty.

"What time is it?" I ask as she brings the large brown bag filled with Chinese take-out to the table.

"After midnight," she tells me, unpacking the food.

Doris is barely older than I am, but technically I think she's my second or third aunt. One of my father's uncles is her dad or something. Doesn't matter. Her last name is Attica, like mine, and she's the only other person I can think of in the family who's fit to lead. She's not in line to inherit the title, unless all my brothers, my kid sister, and I die, but she's my choice for a second. My dad's, too. If he doesn't delegate a task to me, it's given to Doris because unlike Nilus and Lelix she gets shit done, and she's smart enough to figure out what to do on the ground if a situation goes sideways. My dad usually gives her the shadier tasks because he knows I'll ask a bunch of questions he doesn't want to have to answer, but not Doris. My dad says "march" and she puts her boots on.

"You're mostly healed," Doris notices while I dig into one of the white fold-up containers with a pair of chopsticks.

I nod and swallow. "Leda brought me home. Fed me. Made sure I didn't pass out on the floor."

Doris' thick arms are folded across her chest. She's built like Pallas Athena. In fact, she's the spitting image of the monumental sculpture made to the goddess that was once enshrined at the Acropolis. Today, skinny women with no hips or ass are considered the ideal, but a few thousand years ago men put altars in front of women like Doris and piled gold on top of them. She's intimidating, even to me.

In recounting the previous night to Doris, I've left out the detour Leda and I took to my mother's. From the way Doris is staring at me, waiting for me to continue, I can tell that she knows, though I can't figure out how. There must have been someone following Leda and me from my apartment. I like Doris, or at least I respect her, but I know she doesn't work for me. She works for my dad, and he doesn't want me to have anything to do with my mother. I poke at my food with the chopsticks and give Doris the same expectant look she's giving me. I'm not talking about my mother with her.

She chuckles and puts up her hands. "Okay. That's your story," she says, accepting it.

I dig back into my food. She lets me eat for a while in silence.

"Atreus isn't extinct," she says.

The food in my mouth turns into a tasteless lump while Doris tells me that someone from the House of Athens saw Adonis Tiber in the subway tunnels with a girl who shot lightning out of her hands.

A bolt-thrower. No one's seen a bolt-thrower in decades, that I know of at any rate.

"We're pretty sure it was the same girl who rushed into the ring and tried to stop the fight. Probably at the request of Adonis. We believe she's his girlfriend."

I lean back in my chair, staring at Doris. "Who saw them in the subway tunnel?"

"One of the Hidden Ones." She uses the old name for the spawn of Gaia that have mingled with our bloodline. It's more respectful than calling them monsters, I suppose.

"Who?" I press, scared it's Ladon. There isn't much in this world that can kill him, but lightning could. Zeus' lighting defeated Typhon, the greatest dragon ever. "Who saw them, Doris?" I demand when she doesn't answer.

"No one you know," she assures me. "It wasn't much of a fight. Adonis left a knife in our soldier's leg, and he and the bolt-thrower got away." She produces a stiletto from one of the many folds of her black cloak-like coat and tosses it on the table. SPQR is engraved on the hilt.

She waits while it all sinks in for me. How big of a chump I am. Letting her dress me while her brother is hiding an Atreidae. I'm such a joke.

"Do you have plans to see Leda soon?" she asks.

"I'll take care of it," I reply.

She nods and stands, only pausing for a second to put a hand momentarily on my shoulder before she leaves. Can't decide if she was attempting to be sympathetic, or if she was telling me to suck it up, or what.

I sit there for a long time. Getting it all straight in my head. It's hard to shift your perspective of another person until you see them again. Like they're stuck halfway in between the person you thought they were and the person you've just learned they really are underneath. You need to see them again so you can affix a new face on them. The face of a liar.

Something tells me Leda will be back soon. Tonight. She needs to physically be with me to manipulate me. I'm still trying to work out what her endgame is when there's a knock on my door.

That *was* fast. I leave the stiletto on the table in plain sight and go get the door.

She's out there with Castor. Is he a dupe, too, or is he in on it? Thebes and Rome working together to bring down Athens? I can't quite see what their play would be with Atreus, then. I let them in. Leda immediately launches into a sob story about how her brother is missing.

"Well, he was healthy enough about an hour ago to stab someone from my House in the leg with that," I say, pointing at the table. Leda's jaw drops. She recognizes the blade and knows it belongs to Adonis.

"Where is he? Is he injured? What happened!"

I chuckle. "Boy, you're good," I tell her. I gesture to Castor.

"Does he know that your brother's girlfriend is a bolt-thrower, or are you playing him, too?"

I study them carefully, and I swear they look genuinely shocked. Castor's not faking it. Leda? Who knows.

"Have you lost your mind?" she asks me. "That girl, who suspiciously saved *your* life?"

I scoff at that, shaking my head at her. "Your brother and that girl got into a fight with someone from my House in the subway tunnels. She threw a bolt. You're telling me that your brother didn't know she was House of Atreus? While he was suppressing the Furies the way you are now?"

Leda's eyes swim. She sits down suddenly at my table. I see her jaw working as she clenches her teeth. Grinder. That's a tic of hers. Something she does without thinking about it. Shit, maybe she *is* telling the truth.

Castor pulls me aside. Tells me about how Leda asked for help finding Adonis. "My brother Tantalus is a Falsefinder. He would have heard it if she'd lied to him. She has no idea where her brother is. She's telling the truth about that at least," he says.

So, it's *Tantalus* who's the Falsefinder. I knew there had to be one in their House, and it's a shame it's him, but it makes sense. I pull out one of the other chairs at my table and plop down into it because I'm tired and shaking again. I've never sat here before, and it feels weird, but Leda's in my chair.

"Okay, let's assume Adonis doesn't know she's an Atreidae." I offer, even though it makes me the biggest fool in the world. The trouble is, I want to be able to believe her. Too much.

"No," Leda says immediately. "He would know she's from House of Atreus from the names the Furies would whisper to him. Furies he can block from me so that I never hear them." She makes a little noise of frustration, her hands in claws next to her face like she wants to tear her hair out.

It's the information that makes me think she might be telling the truth, more than her behavior. Why admit her brother would know if she didn't have to? Unless she is that many steps ahead of me, in which case, I've lost already. Castor sits down opposite me. He's buying her story. Maybe because his brother already vetted her. Or maybe it's because he's working with her.

"Okay, so we've established that Adonis knew." Castor says, taking charge again, like he's the one who's calling the shots. Pompous ass. "He knew she was an Atreidae, and he hid it from you. We need to know, why?" He looks at me. "What subway stop were they at when they fought your kinsman? We need to find them."

The thought occurs to me that this is officially the most people I've ever had at my dining table. Which is disturbing, considering the company.

"I don't know," I reply, too tired to figure out everyone's motives anymore. I can't even figure out my own. "There is someone who might know where they are, but I have to go see him alone."

"Why?" Leda asks.

"He doesn't come aboveground, and you can't swim there," I reply.

They try to fight me on it, but there's no way I'm telling either of them about my brother. Finally, they accept that I'm not going to budge on this and go.

I leave my apartment, walk across the street, and jump into the Hudson River before I can think too hard about what a sucker I am.

All because she pretended to look for a spider.

21

DAPHNE

Hades sends Adonis and I directly to Ladon's cove. Ajax isn't here.

Ladon tells us that we've been gone for a full day and half the night while we were trudging through the Underworld. It's nearly dawn now. Ajax went to Tantalus for help hours ago and he's not back yet. Daedalus was just here asking Ladon about the creature Adonis stabbed in the leg. So Athens knows there's a bolt-thrower running around because we left that shapeshifter alive, and Thebes does too because Daedalus told Castor. Fantastic. Ajax and I are inches away from being found out. We can't have any more slip-ups.

"Can you describe what you saw?" Ladon asks, intrigued. Adonis launches into a quick explanation, but Ladon is stumped. "He changed into other creatures?" he repeats, then shakes his head. "I know all the Hidden Ones down here, and none have this shape-shifting power. There are some Athenians who can take the form of a horse—the avatar of Poseidon. But a bat?" Ladon shakes his head. "Not even the children of Apollo can do that, and a few of them have several avatars they can adopt."

"I heard the Furies for the House of Athens. He wasn't Theban. He changed into a couple of things while I was looking at him," Adonis insists.

"Then he has been well hidden."

"Or maybe not," I say, looking between the two friends. "If he can change his shape he could have been around your whole life, and you never would have known it."

"I would have scented him," Ladon says, shaking his head. Then his expression changes. "But I'm sure my father would have anticipated that and he would have taken precautions if his intention was to keep this Hidden One's abilities a secret from me and Daedalus." Ladon smiles weakly. "My brother thinks our father is not a smart man, but he is quite clever in his own way. He has kept many secrets from us in the past."

"Ain't family grand?" Adonis drawls. "Well, I should go check in with my sister before she starts a war with Athens," he adds.

"If Ajax returns while I'm gone, tell him to stay here until I get back, okay? I'm going to see if he's still with Tantalus," I tell Ladon as I make for the exit with Adonis. Ladon throws up his hands, like that wouldn't be the choice he would make. "I can't just wait around," I call when I see his disapproving look, and it's true. I'm worried and angry. Ajax never should have left Ladon, no matter how long I was gone.

Adonis and I part ways when we get aboveground. "I'll come back to Ladon's later," he promises, giving me a quick hug.

I tell him that Ajax and I will be there. "I'll try to get Antigone to come, too. Maybe she can help us figure out what the hell is going on."

He takes off, running uptown through the nearly empty

streets of pre-dawn Manhattan. This may be the city that never sleeps, but at this hour it's like it's on pause, if not in slumber. Standing across the street from the Delos' front door I'm forced to hesitate. It's too early to ring the doorbell.

I see a dark shape that I think is a bird at first. It stoops so steeply I think it must be a falcon, but as the shape grows closer it proves to be too big to be a bird. It's Ajax, moving fast so no one has the chance to see him in the dim light. He hovers in front of his brother's window and reaches to open it. I see Tantalus on the other side, waiting for his brother. I step into the street and risk calling out rather than wait until Ajax comes back out to intercept him.

And then it starts to happen again. The mousetrap. One thing leads to another in a series of perfectly logical, yet unbelievably improbable events occurring in a row. It's like watching falling dominoes.

I don't say his name. I'm not stupid. I step forward and raise a hand, trying to get his attention.

And a face appears in one of the other windows. A girl's face. It's Pandora. She's like, *eight,* and there is absolutely no reason for her to be awake at the crack of dawn. Ajax is hovering outside, just a few feet away from her at another set of windows. Tantalus' bedroom windows, I suppose, from their position all the way at the end.

I can't allow Pandora to see Ajax. She worshipped him, and it would destroy her if she ever found out we had deceived them all. I do the only thing I can think to do. I summon a blinding pitchfork of lightning. I mean for it to fall between them and break her line of sight long enough so Ajax can fly away, and it works. Pandora shields her eyes and turns away. But the bolt also hits Ajax.

Not entirely. Not enough to kill him. Just one errant fork of lighting manages to break free in its search for the ground. It's enough to blow him back and knock him out of the sky as he loses consciousness.

He falls into the road at the exact moment a garbage truck is passing. A car wouldn't be enough to kill him, but a big truck would. I'm aware that I'm moving forward, trying to swim through the air with arms and legs, like I'm hoping to claw out the scene unfolding in front of me. The driver was blinded by the lightning, too. I can see he still has an arm thrown over his eyes as the truck continues to move forward. He runs right over Ajax.

The truck jolts and bounces. Knowing he hit something or someone, the driver stomps on the breaks at the worst possible moment. Ajax is still underneath the truck. By this point I'm there, reaching for Ajax underneath the truck before the back wheels can skid across him as they skip sideways on their way to the curb. I clasp Ajax's body to me and heave. I get him out from under the axel just in time for the wheels to hit the curb and for the back of the truck to start to twist and tumble.

It's going to fall on us. Holding him on top of me as I scramble back, kicking furiously with my heels, I barely clear his legs in time. The truck falls on its side, and Ajax and I are trapped by the top of the truck in front of us and the metal fence that stands between the brownstone and the sidewalk behind us.

I hear the driver shouting. He's jumping out of the truck, calling for help. Ajax is still unconscious, thank gods, because I can't even think about how injured he is right now. I pull him closer to me and push against the truck with my legs. The truck doesn't budge, but the fence bends enough that I'm able to stand and sling Ajax over my shoulder.

"Wait! I'll get an ambulance!" the driver shouts. But I run away as fast as I can while carrying Ajax.

I have to get him away from here. Away from his family's eyes, and more importantly away from the mousetrap. There's only one place to hide Ajax from that. I run through the park to the subway station. It's early—barely dawn—and the commute hasn't started yet, but there are always people around in New York and I can't move fast enough carrying Ajax so that the mortals can't clearly see what's happening. Ajax is a mess. A lot of people who are up at this hour are, but this much blood is unusual even for this city. I don't care if I make a scene. I jump the turnstile first, and then the tracks.

I hear people shouting and calling out to me, but now that the numbness of shock is passing, fear has me by the throat and I'm scrambling in the dark. I'm tripping and falling down onto my knees and getting back up, and all the while I can hear my breath harsh in my ears. I finally find the service door. I start running down the metal staircase and I'm already making a deal with Hades in my head, measuring all that I have and all that I am and ready to trade every bit of it for Ajax.

22

DAEDALUS

It's dawn and I really should be in bed, recovering. But instead, I'm at my father's door, telling my dumbass brother to wake him up.

"You know he hates being woken up," Lelix says, yawning.

I push past him and into the room. It's a converted warehouse by the water, of course, but my father has put even less thought into the design and decoration of his space than I have of mine, and so it's just one step nicer than a storage unit. Second and third cousins hang around. Some of them are asleep on the mismatched furniture and some are smoking and drinking, playing cards at fold-out tables. It's like a scene from one of those old mob movies where the boss is holed up and all his goons hang out, guarding him, but instead of zoot suits and fedoras, Athenians lean toward denim and leather.

"Where's Doris?" I ask the room full of goons.

A pair of shoulders detaches itself from the wall of shiny black hair and shiny black leather dusters and tips toward me. Behind

Doris is Ion. I think that's his name. He's a fourth or fifth cousin of mine, I think. I actually have no idea who his parents are. He's hardly ever around, but it's not like we're missing much. He's strong, but he's not a very good swordsman, as I recall, which is probably why he's favoring a leg like he's nursing a recent injury. Looks like the injury is in the thigh. Huh. I bet he was the one who encountered Adonis and the bolt-thrower. That's interesting. I don't get a chance to ask about Ion, though.

"You should be in bed healing," Doris says, but what she really means is *you shouldn't have come.*

"I have to talk to my father," I reply, suddenly unsure about that, so I double down and say it firmly. Like a bonehead who can't take a damn hint.

She shakes her head and gestures for me to follow her because she can't deny me in front of the goon show, or she'll make me look weak, which Doris wouldn't do to the Heir. All of this tells me I'm not going to like what happens next. Doris takes me to a door at the back of the open warehouse space and knocks on it.

My dad is getting out of bed when I enter the smaller room. It's dark in here, but Athenians see best in low light. We're built for dim, underwater worlds and have to remember to turn lights on when we're around mortals so we don't come off as strange. Well...strang*er.*

Bellerophon, Head of the House of Athens, Son of Poseidon, and my father, swings his legs out of bed and puts his back to me. He clears his throat and makes a bunch of chewy noises in his mouth around the gobs of oyster-like phlegm. He's doing it to express his disdain for me, I guess. Classy.

"I see you're already better," he says in a dismissive way. He stands up and reaches for his robe.

"I'm fine," I reply.

He twists his head around to look at me through the stygian gloom. His eyes glint, flat like pewter. "You're fine, huh?" he repeats. He faces me, tying his robe, his nose in the air and a look of distaste on his face. "So you were faking it then."

I stand there for too long, wondering how anyone could fake bleeding to death, while my father walks past me out into the main room. He's careful not to touch me as he passes.

"We didn't find any poison on Corvus' blade, so we're gonna have to say we did," he informs me when I finally follow along behind him. "Seeing as how you lost. To a Roman."

He says it like he can't grasp the concept of a Roman defeating an Athenian. Making a show of it. I glance at Doris, whose face is stony, but she doesn't look back at me. My ears are ringing, and the back of my neck is hot. I have to take it. Swallow this humiliation or Athens will destroy Rome.

"It wasn't poisoned," I lie, the sound of my voice foreign to me. I have to do it, though, or my dad will start a war. And the first head he'll hunt will be Leda's.

"Coffee," my dad says to my aunt Calais and she scurries to the kitchen area. She's younger than my dad. Has a couple of kids who aren't fully grown yet. One of them is close in age to my little sister, Cassiopeia. Can't remember the kid's name, though. My dad sits down and spreads out. The room is quiet. We can all feel his displeasure.

"Not poisoned," he says to me, sucking his teeth as if he's mulling it over. "And you want people to know that? Because I sure don't want any of the other Houses to know my Heir is a loser."

The ringing in my ears gets louder and my face gets hotter. I could say that Corvus got a lucky shot in; try to weasel my way out of this without admitting there was poison, but it would only make me look weaker. Instead, I stick to the facts. Calm down, stay logical, and don't let emotions get in the way.

"Castor Delos has the other blade. His family will test it and they won't find poison. Castor's honor will compel him to make you swear before his Falsefinder brother, Tantalus, who will hear your lie. Athens will be shamed even more. *You* will be shamed, personally, for lying," I say.

My father picks up his head. "Tantalus is the Falsefinder?" I nod in response and though this is valuable information it only makes him angrier. "How is it Paris Delos was given so many useful sons, and mine can't even die right?"

Lelix guffaws, and I look over at him, confused. He's enjoying my humiliation, but he's such an idiot he didn't catch that it includes him, too. Now he gets it. His face falls. My father continues as if he didn't even notice Lelix's hurt. Which he doesn't, probably.

"Paris has an Oracle, and all I have are losers," he laments to Calais as she delivers my father's coffee.

"An Oracle would sure come in handy," Calais says, steering him away from all the loser talk. I wouldn't say she's been nice to me over the years, but she hasn't been openly cruel, and this is the best she can do. Deflecting my father's hair-trigger temper is the best any of us can do.

"An Oracle would win us the war." He sips his coffee, staring at me over the rim. "How are you going to make this right for Athens?" he asks me.

"There will be a rematch. And I'll defeat Corvus," I say, trying not to sigh. If there was real honor at stake in this, it wouldn't be so ridiculous to me. But all this stupid saber rattling to save face we don't have is tiring.

"Really?" he asks.

Now he's just pissing me off. "Really," I reply. He knows he's gotten a rise out of me, and he likes it.

"Because I want you to kill him."

No one is supposed to kill anyone in these contests for territory, and he's conveniently forgotten that. It would disqualify our House if I were to kill Corvus, not to mention drive everyone present at the match into a Fury-driven free for all, but my father won't be satisfied unless I get him his pound of flesh.

This is why my House has never been able to rise from last place. I could win the most valuable plot of land in all of Manhattan for us, a territory that would mean we'd have Thebes surrounded, but he'd have me throw that away to kill one man. I force my stiff neck to bend in a close approximation of a nod. I'll walk him back from this terrible decision later, make him see that winning the territory is far more important than Corvus' life, but I know he won't hear sense right now.

"And after you kill Corvus, I want you to kill Castor."

Doris takes an involuntary step forward as if even her body knows she should object to this, but I gesture low with my hand at my side, indicating she should step back. I don't want any of this spilling over onto her. Because if I die in this useless pissing contest, she's the only one with enough sense to lead.

"To even get a chance to kill Castor in the ring, I'd have to spare Corvus," I say. My voice is steady. I'm not afraid of my father or of killing, but killing Castor would be wrong, and I won't agree to it. "If I kill Corvus, the contest for the territory will be over because we will be disqualified," I say loud enough for everyone to hear. The Furies would have all driven us mad and we'd have ripped each other to shreds anyway. But my father is too much of a moron to remember that.

He stands, his chest puffed up. "Did I give you an order?"

"You gave me two. And one of those orders makes the other impossible," I reply. "You have to choose. Corvus or Castor."

He rushes me like a bull. I half expected it. Whenever I say too many words at him, my father has always resorted to violence, especially when my words prove what a fool he is.

He never let me go to college, not because it wasn't good for our House, or because with a decent education I would have been able to grow our business and our wealth, but because he was always afraid that I'd turn out smarter than him. Better than him. For all his talk about how useless his sons are, he can't stand the thought of one of them surpassing him in any way. I take the blow and let myself fall back, no resistance. I can taste blood in my mouth.

"You will kill who I tell you to kill," he growls, pointing down at me.

I spit to the side and stand. "When you choose which of them you wish for me to kill, I'll do it."

His face twitches with rage. "You're trying to stop this war from happening, aren't you?" he accuses.

"I'm trying to win us the best position on the field before the war begins," I reply. "Lincoln Center. The heart of Manhattan. That could be ours, but only if we're smart about it."

His top lip lifts in a sneer. "What're you implying?" he asks, ready to strike me again.

"Let me fight Corvus the right way. Then Castor. I can beat them both honorably, and then Athens won't have to battle uphill as we always have in the past. You're still going to get your war," I promise. "But with Lincoln Center, you might actually win it this time."

My father shifts on his feet. Then he nods once. The bare minimum for agreement. "Go on, get out of here," he orders.

I wipe the blood off my lip and go. This is the only way for him to reverse his orders to kill Corvus and Castor and still save face. I'll do it the right way and he can either claim that it was his idea later if it works, or disown me if it doesn't. Regardless, I'm on my own as usual.

Maybe it isn't hot-headedness or stupidity that has kept Athens in last place for all these millennia. Maybe this is the real reason. Castor has family that would stand with him to the death, and all my family seems to want me to do is go away and die alone.

23

ION

Guessing correctly that his Heir would make an appearance today, my father had me take the human form he prefers and stay close to Doris. To watch, he said.

My real human body is misshapen, but Father does not allow me to wear my real body when I'm human. It's no matter. One body or another, I can look like anything. Though, I don't like being human. Clothes are uncomfortable, but they aren't as annoying as other people are.

Humans never leave each other alone. They are always prodding, always looking for something from each other. Status, recognition, entertainment, sex. They are always tugging on each other when they are in a group. Needing. Bumping up against each other's edges to test them, making "jokes" or talking about stuff they have no control over like politics, the weather, the lives of celebrities, what's going to happen tomorrow. It's very irritating.

When I take the shape of an animal, I still have my human mind, but other creatures ask little to nothing from me—unless they ask for my life. When I am a rat, a dog will chase me for my blood because that is what a dog is for. I quickly disabuse it of that possibility, and it leaves me alone again. Simple. There is no hidden meaning in anything a dog does.

But humans never go away, even when you bite and scratch. If you are near them, they always want something from you, and it's rarely a simple thing. They want something complicated, and usually it's something that they don't even know they want. All that humans feel is a restless lack of something they can't name, but that they hope you will give to them. Or that they can take from you. I've never seen a human get this elusive, unnamed thing they want, and yet never once do they consider that what they want might not be found in others at all. Or worse, that maybe it doesn't exist. It's because they don't know what they are for.

Doris bothers me the least of all the people I'm forced to be around. She knows how to be quiet and keep her thoughts to herself even when she is in company. She seems to need less from others, but when she does need something, she is direct about it. She will tell me to follow someone as a bird. Watch someone else as a cat. Be a fly on the wall. A spider in a web. Usually, she has me follow mortals that orbit our family. Nilus' or Lelix's lovers. Daedalus' mother. Report back, she'll say.

I told Doris about Leda helping Daedalus clean his mother's apartment. They never found me because I changed into an ant, and they were looking for a spider. She was not happy to have that information, and Doris told me that I wasn't to tell my father about it. She protects my father from information that will make him upset, and I think this is wise. She's a very wise person. From Doris there are no teasing jibes that are angry underneath, like there are from so many of my other kin. There is no jostling for dominance. She is the boss of everyone save a select few, and she need not prove her dominance every time she speaks. She knows what she is for.

Apart from my father she's the only one who knows that I have the same ability as our ancestor Proteus. She's also the only one who knows that I am a prince of the House Athens. I am Disowned, of course, because I am one of the Hidden Ones, but being Disowned means little to me. I don't care about status. I do what my father tells me to do because I imprinted on him.

And I think he must be imprinted on me in a way, too. Humans do not imprint, I know this, but he did not turn me out as a baby as he did my eldest brother, Ladon. My father used to keep me as a pet—a snake, a ferret, a parrot, and many other kinds of animals. Whatever struck his fancy. He did this because he wanted my company. He did not want Ladon with him, but he wanted me. That is why I think my father imprinted.

When I got older, he insisted I be a man more often because animals are not allowed in most places in the city, and I cannot change from an animal into a man unless there are clothes nearby for me to put on. But sometimes I still play his pet for fun.

I hold a special place in his heart. I know this because he holds a special place in mine. Let Daedalus, the handsome, clever one, take the throne of our House. I will go to the grave with our father and have him with me forever because I am special to him. This is what I am for.

Right now, our father is very angry with Daedalus. He hits him. They disagree often because Daedalus does not know what he is for. His purpose is to follow our father, not try to cut in front of him and lead before his time. He will make a good leader someday, I think, and I am sorry that he does not know how to wait. Why he will not kill both of the other enemy Scions like my father is asking is beyond me. I will kill them if father wants me to, but no. Father wants them killed in the light of day, not in the dark where I do my killing.

I almost killed an Atreidae in the dark last night. I was a disguised as a fly, following her and the Roman, and when they jumped down onto the tracks, I saw the most amazing thing. Her face went from one to another.

She is like me. She can change. I can still see her real face, framed in lightning. It was like no face I've seen before, and it has stayed in my mind's eye as if burnt there by one of her lightning bolts.

I must see her face again. Even though she was Atreidae I did not feel the Furies when I looked at her. This must mean she was meant to be mine. I do not know if she can become anything in the world like I can, but still, we are alike. I never thought I'd find someone like me. The Fates have given her to me, and I will take her into the water with me, and keep her there in one of the deepest caves, so I may look on her face whenever I like. That is what she is for.

But later. I will do it later because right now my father needs my help to start a war.

As Daedalus leaves, our father sits and gestures me and Doris forward. We both walk to stand before him, waiting for him to speak.

"This Corvus," he says, not looking at Doris, but tipping his head in her direction while he scans the room, making sure everyone else keeps their distance so our conversation is not overheard. "He seems to want this war to get going, doesn't he?"

"I would guess so," Doris replies. "If Daedalus had died in the ring by his hand, it certainly would have started the war. And I know everyone is saying poison wasn't found, but that don't mean it wasn't there." My father narrows his eyes at her and she shrugs. "I've sparred with Daedalus, and he's no bleeder. Corvus did something to him. That wasn't a fair fight."

My father goes back to brooding for a bit but does not dismiss us. "Can Corvus control the Furies?" he finally asks.

Doris gestures to me, engaging my participation. "We can find out."

"Do it. And if he can control the Furies, bring him to me."

Doris seems uncomfortable with this. "He might put up a fight," she reminds him.

"If he does, kill him. It is our right to after what he did."

Doris frowns because even I know what my father is saying would break the rules between the Houses, but she doesn't speak against my father's decision because she knows what she is for. Her purpose is to follow my father's orders.

"I'm sick of waiting for this war to start," my father says. "But this time, we're not going to be left scrounging for the scraps. This time I'm going to know how it ends before it begins."

Doris straightens, liking this less and less. "What do you have in mind?" she asks.

"The only thing better in a battle than having good field position, is knowing what's going to happen before it does."

Doris looks frightened now. "But ... there's no way to get to the Oracle. Thebes would die to the last soldier for her. She's sacred—"

My father holds up a hand. I think he means to soothe her, and she certainly does seem to need it. I don't know if I've ever seen her so agitated outside a fight.

"Just get me a Roman who can silence the Furies. Let me worry about the Oracle."

We're dismissed with a wave of my father's hand.

❦ 24 ❦

DAPHNE

The creatures hiding underground can sense when something's injured.

As I carry Ajax down through the levels, I see them creeping out of hidey-holes, or snaking their heads out of burrows. There are too many eyes and claws and hisses from the dark. Since I'm carrying Ajax, I can't summon a bolt and hold it, glowing, in my hand to frighten them away. I settle for kicking at them and yelling, "Get back!" when they skitter too close.

It reminds me of the first time we came down here. The Hecatoncheires, and how they frightened me. They're not here now, but some hysterical nostalgia for anything even remotely familiar makes me almost miss them. By the time I get to Ladon's cove I'm stony with shock.

"What happened?" Ladon calls out as soon as I'm close enough for him to smell the blood. He races to me and takes Ajax from my shoulders. I resist. I don't know why, but I don't want to give him over to anyone. "It's okay. I have supplies to heal him," Ladon coaxes, his voice low and calm.

I let Ladon have him and mechanically repeat what happened. The domino-fall of events. Ladon carries Ajax to a smaller cave off the main cove. It has a bed and a matching chest of drawers. The bedspread is white and girly. I strip it off before he lays Ajax down.

"I'll be right back," he promises, and then is quick to return with a leather apothecary bag. He opens it, revealing an inside full of tinctures and bandages. Both the bag and its contents seem part old-timey doctor, part witch.

I try to remove Ajax's clothes. I'm shaking so badly that Ladon puts a hand over mine and tells me to go sit down. He can do this faster than I can. I nod and back away as he lifts and turns Ajax's inert body easily with his strong arms.

"Get some water," he says.

Yes. A task. I take the pitcher from the matching washbasin on the dresser and stumble out of the room, following his instructions to a rivulet that runs down the far wall of the cove. It's fresh and clean, still chilly from the Catskills melt. I fill the pitcher and bring it back to the small room to find Ladon already working on Ajax.

Ladon says. "I'll have to re-break his leg."

"Do it now while he's out," I say.

Ladon is mercifully quick and his hands are sure, but still my back teeth squeak together at the sound of Ajax's snapping bone. Ajax screams, and then passes out again. A cold sweat breaks out on my upper lip and on my back between my shoulder blades.

"The water was for you, so you don't faint." Ladon says as he takes a glass off the nightstand by the bed and hands it to me.

I'd be insulted he assumed I'm a fainter if the edges of my vision weren't turning black. I pour myself a glass of water and gulp it. Ladon splints the leg efficiently and then moves on to the red Lichtenburg mark from my lightning strike on Ajax's chest. The mark begins on his left pectoral muscle, right over his heart, and then branches out, looking like a red feather lying under the top layer of his skin as it travels down to just above his belly button.

"It's actually quite lovely," Ladon says. He taps gently at the seared flesh with a cotton ball soaked with a blue solution from one of his crystal-stoppered vials.

"I've scarred him for life," I reply. Usually Scions heal completely and without scars. But I don't think this will ever go away.

Ladon turns the human top part of his body over the serpentine lower half to look at me. "I dug this room out of the granite, learned how to tend even the most serious of wounds, and acquired all of these medicines—some of which are magical—for Antigone," he says. "In case I injure her. Again."

His razor-sharp scales are iridescent and beautiful and just as deadly as my lightning, I realize. I stay back in the chair by the arched entry, careful to keep out of Ladon's way. The Cestus protects me from weapons, but it doesn't stop me from accidentally cutting myself on sharp objects, like Ladon's tail, and he needs a lot of space to move around. It's not until after he has Ajax bandaged and covered with a less ornate blanket than the frilly white one that we hear Adonis calling out for us by the exit tunnel.

I'm too shaken to talk. When Adonis joins us, Ladon recounts what happened, and Adonis stands there stunned for a moment.

"Well, that's it then. Ajax can't leave this cave until we have a solution for the mousetrap," he says at last.

I will the words *what if there is no solution* away, but I can't help but think it. The Fates are trying to kill Ajax. How does anyone run away from that?

"I can't do this anymore. I'm just waiting for the ax to fall. I need the Oracle to tell us what's going to happen," I say. "Even if she sees Ajax's death, at least we'll know when and where it's supposed to happen. At least I won't be—"

Adonis steps forward and takes my shoulders in his hands, flooding my body with warm feelings. "We're going to figure this out." He pulls an incredulous face. "Even *Hades* is helping us. I don't think he'd do that for people he knows are going to die soon."

I finally feel the knot in my chest loosen. "Thank you," I say.

"Anytime," he replies, and I feel another push of warmth from him.

"Really, I'm okay," I say.

Adonis releases me abruptly, like he's just realizing that he's still holding me. He steps back, turning quickly to look at Ajax. "Do we want to wait for him to wake up before we get Antigone?" he asks, shoving his hands into the back pockets of his jeans.

"I'll get her," Ladon offers.

"You have to stay here with Ajax," I insist. Then a thought occurs to me. Not a lot of dragons running around New York. At least, not aboveground. "How *do you* get her, by the way?"

"I don't reveal myself," he assures us hastily. "There's a manhole cover near her front door. I turn it one way when I'm waiting beneath, and the other way when I'm not there."

"And you just wait there for her?" Adonis asks, looking charmed.

"She taps on it five times, and then we meet up in the subway tunnels."

That's what Antigone was doing out in the middle of the street, I think. "But it's nighttime. Wouldn't she be asleep already?"

"Night is when we usually meet. She'll be looking out her window for my signal soon," Ladon replies.

Adonis sighs. "Where is this manhole cover—and don't tell me I have to schlep through a sewer to get to it."

While Ladon takes Adonis into the main area of his cave and gives him instructions on how to get to there, I crawl into bed next to Ajax. I think I'm just going to shut my eyes for a moment, but I'm so drained. I fall asleep. When I wake, the cave is quiet and Ajax is on his side, facing me.

I can smell honey on his breath and the sting of antiseptic on his bandages. A lump starts to form in my throat.

"I'm okay," he says, but I'm going to cry anyway.

"Why did you leave the cave?" I ask. Tears blur my vision and then spill sideways onto the pillow.

He watches me cry with a pained expression on his face. "Because it hurts more to worry about you than it does to get struck by lightning."

I sniff back tears and reach out to touch his face, tracing the edge of his lip, and the tiny golden hairs that gild his cheekbone. "We can't keep this up."

"No," he agrees. He frowns in thought, his eyes unfocused. "I couldn't stand it anymore and I just... walked out of the cave to find you. I wasn't thinking. I just did it."

I nod, knowing I would have done the same thing. There's no

point in scolding him for looking for me, or apologizing for not meeting him here at the cave when I said I would. Ajax and I are past blaming each other for any of the bad things that happen to us. It might not have been the Fates controlling him, because he was with Ladon and shielded from them, but we know the mouse-trap is going to put down cheese we can't resist reaching for. Instead, I tell him everything that happened while we were apart. The shapeshifter, the walk through the Underworld, Morpheus taking Adonis and me to meet Hades. Everything Hades said to us.

"Nemesis," he whispers when I'm done, mulling over how she fits into our current situation. I wonder why his mind latched on to that one tid-bit out of all the things I told him. "She's on our side?"

"I guess. I think it's more like we're on *her* side. I didn't know she worked against the Fates, but it makes sense," I mumble, too tired to say anything intelligent about the fact that, to the Greeks, nemesis didn't mean "enemy" like it does today. Nemesis, the sister to the Moirai, was the embodiment of Righteous Anger. She exists to balance power because nothing, not even Fate, should be all-powerful. But my brain is mush at this point, so even though I'm thinking about all of this erudite stuff, none of it comes out of my mouth.

Ajax smiles. "They *are* siblings, and siblings are usually either alike, or exact opposites." His face falls at the thought of his own siblings. "I followed Caz for a while last night, while I was out looking for you."

I weave my fingers into his, knowing how much he misses his family. Which reminds me. "Tantalus. He saw you get hit."

"He knows you'll take care of me." Ajax closes his eyes and controls his breathing. He's in terrible pain, I realize.

"I'll get you some food," I say, sitting up. He holds onto my hand.

"Just lie down with me," he says, turning his face into the pillow.

I relax back onto the bed and hold him as well as I can around his bandages and splinted leg while my mind turns over all the bits of information I've been given. I find no pattern to it, and no solution to our problem before I fall asleep again.

I dream of a woman with a veil covering her face. She's trying to talk to me. I think she says, *I'll be there at the end,* and I try to tell her that the end is too late, but no matter how hard I scream, no one can hear me.

25

ADONIS

What the hell am I doing in a sewer?

I should be kissing my sister's ass right now, trying to make up for the fact that I lied to her about who Daphne really was, and that I'm still lying to her about what I'm up to, rather than escorting our enemy, the Oracle of Delphi, to the underground lair of another enemy to help two more enemies. It's like an enemy sandwich down there. And I'm the meat.

Leda is furious with me, and she has every right to be. I brought the Heir to the House of Atreus into our territory, and I didn't tell her. Well, she knows now. Leda does not know about Ajax, though. Or Ladon and Antigone. There's a lot of secrets still, but I feel like if I tell her about all those other pieces on the chess board there's no way we'll beat the Fates. And the Fates will most certainly use Leda against me if I involve her. We've all tacitly agreed that it's better to keep this whole crazy scheme—the details of which are still hazy to me—between as few people as possible for as long as possible. Daphne didn't tell Tantalus, Ladon hasn't told Daedalus, and I can't tell Leda. I've got to find a way to keep her out of this.

And, yeah, I feel bad about that. My sister pulled the whole *we promised each other we'd stick together* line and she's right. It's been Leda and me against the world since our mom died, and I feel like a piece of garbage for lying to her. She was hurt way more than she was angry, which means I'm the lowest kind of garbage. Especially since I went right back to lying to her not two seconds after I apologized. *Gods*, I suck.

But what can I do? The bigger I make the web, the more likely we'll all get caught in it. Hades—the frigging *god of the underworld*—warned me that I was in a fight against the Fates, and I don't want that level of shit anywhere near my sister. Even if it means she never really trusts me again. Wow, it hurts to even just say that in my head.

"Are you okay?" Antigone asks me.

"Peachy," I reply. "I love traipsing through a sewer."

"No, I mean, you seemed really sad for a moment."

She's a tiny thing with a girlish body, but she's not as young as she looks. In fact, right now she seems older than I am and I'm like, a *thousand* on the inside. Feeling everything that everyone around you does ages you quick. It occurs to me that the only thing that could age me faster would be knowing the future.

"I am sad, kid," I say.

"I'm not a kid."

"I know." I nudge her. "I also I knew it would annoy you enough that you would change the subject."

She eyes me. "I'll remember that."

"It's a good trick."

We walk for a while down the freshly cleaned tunnels, courtesy of Ladon I'm sure, before she blurts out, "I'm seventeen. Old enough to be in a relationship."

She's killing me with that aching heart of hers. So much longing. "I know it, kid," I say.

She tries not to laugh, because it genuinely bothers her, but she can't help it. "You're such a jerk," she says, chuckling.

"Yup," I reply. "Easier that way."

"Maybe for you," she grouses. She's funny. Most of those Apollo brats take themselves too seriously, all honor and beauty and truth, but this girl is cool.

"I get why he loves you," I say, though I probably shouldn't have. Confirmation of her fondest wish makes her heart glow with a hazy, golden light. It's stunning. But all that beauty will probably turn to bitterness because of three old hags with some string and a pair of scissors. I really hate the Fates, and not just because of what they've done to me.

Well, okay. Sure. Mostly because of what they've done to me.

Why Daphne? *Because it's ironic* is the correct answer, but that's more like a punchline than a reason. Adonis, the most powerful Scion of the Goddess of Love, and he's in love with someone who will never love him back. I'm like Narcissus, without all the narcissism. I guess I'm destined to pine away until I die. Awesome.

We get back to Ladon's cove and everyone's fallen asleep because it's the middle of the night and most people sleep in the middle of the night, except for me now. Frigging Daphne. If she's not ruining my sleep getting me chased by shapeshifting monsters, she's ruining my sleep because I can't stop thinking about her. It's a good thing owning so many nightclubs has given me plenty of practice staying up all night. Though it also makes me need to sleep all day, which I haven't had a chance to do since *she* came into my life. And completely wrecked it.

Ladon wakes before we enter and forces himself not to run to Antigone. Even though his body stays where it is, his heart flies to her, like it's jumped out of his chest. I can see it arrowing toward her. I just love that guy.

I peek into the back room because I can't help it. She's there with Ajax. They're on their sides facing each other, their hands entwined between their bodies. The glow of love around them is pierced by needles of worry. I feel my heart fly to her and think how stupid I am because, clearly, she is madly in love with Ajax. They couldn't be more joined if they were actually making love right now. Speaking of, in my pocket I have the potion that will make him sterile. It's a tasteless white powder, easily dissolved in liquid. I eye the water on his bedside table. I could slip into the room, and...

Daphne wakes and lifts her head, first scanning him to make sure he's okay, and then turning her head to the door where I stand. There goes my chance. For now, anyway.

"Is Antigone here?" Daphne whispers to me.

I nod and she disentangles herself from Ajax, completely unaware of how I feel for her. Which I'm grateful for. If she knew how I felt she'd shut me out entirely, and I wouldn't get any part of her. At least this way I get something. Maybe even a little of her trust. It isn't enough, but better than nothing.

If she knew I loved her she'd think what I feel is obsession. Her curse enacted. Another casualty to the Face that Launched a Thousand Ships, but that's not it. I know what obsession looks like and I can see my own damn heart, and it looks like a heart in deep, pure, once-in-a-lifetime love. Which usually never happens when it's one-sided like this. Usually, love is like a circuit. It takes two or it stops flowing, but apparently, I'm an exception to this rule. I know with shocking certainty that I will love Daphne as long as I live, even though I know with equal certainty that she will never return it. At least my love is a rare one. That's all it's got going for it, though.

It crept up on me, which is just another layer of ridiculousness to this whole debacle. I know emotions. I understand them. I get how they grow and change, and why and how, and when they do both. But she ambushed me, and I didn't know that I was in love with her, never even considered it, until I woke up with her poking me on the forehead in the *Valetudinaria*. The Furies were gone, I could see through the fake face she was wearing over her real one, and I wanted to both kill her for waking me up and kiss her just for being her. I mean, seriously. Who pokes someone on the forehead to wake them up? And I knew I was in love. Like the massive tool I am.

We join Antigone and Ladon. Daphne intercepts Antigone, who tries to go straight to the back to check on Ajax.

"He's okay," Daphne says. "Let him rest."

Antigone relents, and then mercifully gets down to the reason I sat under a manhole cover for half an hour to bring her here. "I've seen some strange things over the past few days," she says.

"Prophecies?" I ask.

Antigone shakes her head. "Visions."

"That's the one that's like watching a movie with the sound turned off?" I ask, just to be clear.

As far as I can discern, both visions and prophecies are going to happen no matter what, but prophecy is a bunch of words coming directly from the Fates, and the Oracle can't remember them. They need to be heard by others to be recorded. A vision is something the Oracle sees or dreams in her mind's eye, but without context. Both prophecies and visions are completely literal, but they are rarely understood in full until after they happen. Which makes me think maybe they're both more trouble than they're worth.

"It's like seeing a few seconds of a movie I've never seen before with the sound fading in and out at random moments," Antigone clarifies.

I sit down, rolling my eyes. "And the Fates couldn't possibly twist that to their own use."

"What did you see?" Daphne asks, ignoring my sarcasm and sitting next to me on Ladon's couch.

"Two things." Antigone takes a breath, checks herself, and then tries again. "First. I think I saw you two."

"Us?" I ask, gesturing between Daphne and me.

"But it wasn't you," she adds.

"It's so refreshing when you're specific like that," I say, and Daphne smacks my arm with the back of her hand without even looking at me. Shit, I love her.

"I think it had to be Helen—who we believe is Daphne's future daughter," Antigone continues. "She was with someone who looks so much like you, Adonis, it was freaky, but she called him Orion."

"Brother and sister?" I ask hopefully.

Antigone shakes her head. "They were a couple."

"How do you know that?" Ladon asks.

"Another vision a while back. They were kissing," Antigone answers, not able to look at him when she says it.

"Are you sure he didn't look like Daedalus' kid?" Daphne presses.

Ladon nods. "Lucas," he says. "I met him, too."

"Helen and Lucas were in love," I add. "Really, deeply, completely in love. Trust me, I know these things."

"Orion looked like Adonis, and he and Helen were in bed together, and they were all over each other. I did not see that incorrectly," Antigone insists. "He was also wearing your cuff," she adds, pointing to my wrist.

"He'd have to be a direct descendent of Aeneas to wear it." I let that sink in for a bit. "Orion is my son?" I ask. I mean, I knew Daphne and I would never be together, but if my son and her daughter are dating it means we have kids with other people. Which means I really don't get Daphne in the end.

Antigone shrugs. "I don't know."

I can't get too upset about it because I know I'll never see this vision come to pass. If Orion has my cuff, that means I'm dead anyway. What does that give me? Twenty, thirty years tops, depending on when we have these hypothetical children.

"What?" Daphne asks me, knowing something's up.

"I'll tell you later," I say, shaking it off. "Okay, so our kids get together in the future. Why is that important to us?"

"Because they were using the fact that I'm an Oracle to contact us now in the past."

"So you could watch them screw around and tell us about it?" I ask, confused.

"No! That was a different vision! Okay," Antigone breaks off, frustrated. "Let me start over. Helen and Orion were sitting on a couch like they were facing me. Helen clearly said, *This message is for Daphne.*" Antigone rubs her palms on the tops of her thighs.

"I can't tell you how strange it is to have someone speak to you across time."

"Actually, that's what you do to us in a way," I say.

Antigone tips her head to the side, considering, before she moves on. "Anyway. Helen kept talking like she knew I could hear her. Which in and of itself is strange because the soundtrack in visions isn't usually so complete. I normally only get a word or two."

"What else did they say?" I ask.

"That when Helen turns seventeen Daphne had to do everything in her power to get her away from Lucas before she falls in love with him. Helen said that the future depended on it, and if you failed at first, that you were to do everything you possibly could after that to keep them apart." Antigone looks troubled. "She hates him. Helen hates Lucas. The way she said his name it was like he was the enemy."

Definitely not what I expected.

"I'm supposed to stop her from falling in love with Lucas?" Daphne says, just to be sure.

Antigone nods emphatically.

"Why?"

"It must be to keep the Houses separate," Ladon says. "Lucas looks just like Daedalus so he must be Athenian, and she's Atreidae."

"But if Orion is wearing this cuff," I lift my wrist, "then he's Roman. How is Helen and Orion being together any better than her and Lucas?"

Daphne just sits there, shaking her head vaguely. "How do you keep two people from falling in love?" she asks, like that's the more pressing problem.

"The only thing that works is to not let them meet," I answer.

"Or if Helen meets Orion first, she'll probably fall for him instead. Especially if he looks like me."

Daphne hits me again without even glancing at me (*gods* she's perfect) and skips to another problem. "Wait, I thought you couldn't change anything in the past. Doesn't it create a paradox?" she asks.

"This isn't the past. It's our present," Ladon replies. "All Helen's Oracle is instructing you to do is act in your future, which is exactly what Oracles always do when they make a prophecy, when you think about it."

I look for something to throw at Ladon because that's just bullshit. "They're asking us to change something. Helen was in love with Lucas. She wants Daphne to change that. That's changing the past for Helen."

"They're asking Daphne to behave a certain way in her future. The only difference is perspective, and isn't our perspective just as valid as Helen's?" Ladon asks, refuting my point. "Helen telling Antigone what the future holds to elicit specific behavior is no different from the Fates telling Antigone what the future holds to elicit specific behavior. Antigone is delivering a message about the future, as she always does. It's just from a different source. A source I'm more inclined to trust, by the way. Helen and Orion are Scions. They're more likely to be on our side than the Fates are."

I can feel my brain liquefying and sloshing around in my head. "I need you to shut up for a second," I tell Ladon, standing. "I need a drink."

They continue to debate the notion of prophecy as a time-traveling, paradox-creating message from the future that changes the past, and therefore shouldn't exist in the first place, and I honestly don't have the strength to listen to this nonsense sober.

It's all semantics. A thing is a thing is a thing, even if you call it a doohickey. Helen is telling Daphne to do something so she can change something. Or is she? Maybe Helen is just telling Daphne to do something she already *did*. Now I'm doing it. I have to stop hanging out with Ladon. He's too philosophical for my own good.

I scrounge though his carefully arranged shelves at the back of the cove until I find some whiskey in a crystal decanter, and help myself. Ladon doesn't drink. The only reason it's here is because, magpie that he is, he probably wanted it for the sparkly prisms it makes. But the whiskey is excellent.

When they've talked themselves out, Antigone pulls Daphne aside before leaving. Whatever Antigone says creates a flare of panic in Daphne's chest that is so bright I can see it through her back. Ladon goes to check on Ajax after Antigone leaves, and I motion for Daphne to come to me where I'm still sprawled out on the couch.

"What'd she say to you?" I ask. I keep my arm cocked behind my head like a pillow so I don't reach out for her. I want to soothe her, but that's probably just an excuse I'm making for myself so I can touch her.

Daphne sits on the edge of the couch next to me. "She told me that Lucas is going to kill everyone in the world."

"O-kay. So, definitely keep him away from your daughter," I joke, but only because it strikes me as ludicrous. "He seemed like such a nice guy. Didn't have a *murderer of billions* vibe to him at all."

"Yeah," she replied, distracted.

"What else did she say?" I ask.

"She told me what I wanted to know. Now... I wish I could un-know it," Daphne replies evasively.

I watch as her mind ticks through dozens of different scenarios. Damn that face of hers. I've decided why I think it's divine. Not because it's sublimely symmetrical or flawlessly sculpted, although it is both of those things. It's because her face is the perfect conduit for her thoughts. I'm used to emotions moving all the time and being able to watch that inside other people, but I can see Daphne's *thoughts* at work through her face. I don't know exactly what she's thinking, like I know what people are feeling, but I can tell she's probably two or three steps ahead of anyone else. It's mesmerizing.

"You said you wanted to know Ajax's death," I prompt. She's surprised I remembered. "I pay attention. Sometimes." She'd laugh at that if she wasn't so sad. I tap her with my knee. "Tell me."

"Antigone said that in her vision Ajax and I are separated by something I can't cross. She couldn't tell me what it was because the thing separating us is in shadows; she just said that I'm stuck in one place, and he's in another. I can see him, but I can't get to him in time. I have to watch as..."

Her tone is even, but her heart is swimming in fear. I can't help it. I reach out and rest my fingertips on her wrist, siphoning off some of the fear inside her. Daphne has an uncommonly deep well of darkness in her, but I think it only makes her shine brighter because she's managed to rise above it.

"When does it happen?"

"She said we don't look any older in her vision than we do now."

"Who kills him?" I ask when she doesn't continue.

Guilt piles on top of Daphne's fear. Guilt and shame and self-hatred, dragging her down in a spiral toward that well of darkness. I can't stand it, so I sit up and tug on her wrist until she faces me completely. I give her arm a little shake, bringing her back to the here and now.

"Daphne. Tell me."

"Tantalus," she whispers. "Tantalus kills Ajax. Because of me."

26

TANTALUS

"Ceyx hasn't been called upon to heal anyone," I tell my father.

And he should have been. I know Ajax was terribly injured. I saw the flash of lightning. Pandora screamed because she was startled, but she didn't see anything. Just lightning, blinding her.

There was blood on the sidewalk. The driver told me about the young man and the girl—Daphne, no doubt—and how she carried him away like he weighed nothing. Adrenaline, he kept saying. He'd heard a story about how a woman lifted a car off her kid, and he was sure this was the same thing. It's amazing how mortals will swallow any story to keep the world as it is.

I hope Daphne knows what she's doing. She'd never endanger Ajax, but I still don't know why she hasn't contacted me. She shouldn't be trying to heal him alone. She needs my help, but maybe she can't get to me.

Castor and Pallas had a few questions about the lightning, and Castor knows that a bolt-thrower from the House of Atreus has been seen. I was considering sending them back to Athenian territory to find out more about the bolt-thrower because I had no other choice. It would have been suspicious if I hadn't. But Thebes got summoned to an inter-House meeting in Central Park, and I gladly sent them to that instead. I still don't know why Daphne has been firing bolts off at everyone. She's getting desperate and erratic. She needs my help. She could be trying to come to me right now.

"And you're certain that none of the Hundred Cousins were outside tonight?" my father asks me.

"Must have been a mortal," I reply.

The description of the injured kid fits with the House of Thebes type, but a young blond man is a pretty common sight here near the NYU campus. All the family knows is that there was a bolt of lightning that blinded a truck driver who hit a young man and wrecked his truck right outside our house. The injured young man was carried away by a young woman. Luckily, no one in my family had even come close to putting any of these descriptions together with Ajax and Daphne, but my dad hasn't let the situation go yet.

"Getting hit by a garbage truck would have torn a mortal apart. They'd still be out there mopping him up," my father counters.

"I'll check the Cousins again," I say because I know he won't stop until I've counted every single head. Why won't he dismiss me? I need to get away from my family so Daphne can contact me.

He starts pacing again. "It was Elara. I know it. Last I saw her it was like she hadn't aged a day, and in the dark, she could still look like a teenaged girl. Did Castor say it was a teenaged girl with Adonis? Or older?"

"I don't know."

"I didn't feel the Furies tonight. Did you?"

"No."

"And you didn't see anything out the window?"

"I already told you. I didn't."

He's obsessing now. Prowling like an old lion, his feet padding across the Persian rug in the center of his office silently. He's always worshiped beauty and surrounded himself with it, like a true son of Apollo.

"She's the bolt-thrower from the subway. It's Elara."

He says the name carefully, holding every letter in his mouth. Am I that bad? Do I make up excuses to say Daphne's name? It's not that he didn't love our mother. They were close, closer than I'll ever be to Mildred, but my father hasn't remarried. Not because he still loves my mother, but because of Elara. He's waiting for her like I'm waiting for Daphne.

But I can't be waiting for her. The only way she could be mine is if Ajax were dead, and that's unthinkable.

I stand up. "I'll find out," I promise. He gives me a nod, dismissing me. I'm nearly at the reinforced door when he stops me.

"Son? Don't kill her."

"I won't," I say, and it's not a lie because she's already dead.

Pandora is waiting in the hallway outside our father's office. Her nightgown is getting too short. I can see her skinny ankles peeking out at the bottom, and I make a mental note to stop by Macy's for some new clothes for her. Yet, even though she's growing, she's still so tiny. I don't think any of us boys were ever that small. I think Ajax was born bigger than Pandora.

"What are you doing up?" I scold.

"Was the bolt-thrower trying to kill me?" she asks.

I sigh and pick her up. "It was just lightning. There was no bolt-thrower," I lie, carrying her upstairs. "You never have to worry about anything like that, okay?"

"Does it hurt? Getting struck by lightning?"

"I don't know. Lightning happens so fast maybe you don't even feel it."

She nods, like this is a very sensible answer. I put her back in her bed and pull up the covers. I make sure her windows are locked, and that the curtains are shut tight more for her peace of mind than for mine.

"You won't let her kill me like she killed Ajax, will you?"

My throat closes off for a second. She thinks I failed him. That I'm going to fail her. "I got Ajax's killer, remember?" I lie.

"Oh yeah," she says, screwing up her little face.

"I'll never let anyone hurt you, Pandora."

She smiles and snuggles down, closing her eyes. I make sure she's on her way to sleep before I leave, shutting her door behind me.

I need to find Daphne. I'm worried that she got injured in the wreck, too. I can't think of any other reason she hasn't come to me. She always comes to me. I'm nearly out the front door to look for her when I see Castor and Pallas making their way to me, just getting back from their meeting in Central Park with Daedalus and Leda. They're picking through the vestiges of the wreck. Shattered glass. Ajax's blood. That's too much blood for him to heal without help. He should be with Ceyx.

"Inside," Castor says, his jaw tight.

"Something happened," I say. It's not a question, but an opening for them to fill me in.

Castor and Pallas don't reply, they just keep walking past me. They aren't twins, but they may as well be. The two of them were born eleven months apart and though physically they are different, with Castor being thicker and taller and Pallas as pretty as a girl, they walk the same, hold themselves the same. They even communicate without talking most of the time. Just glances and gestures. Their non-verbal communication is convenient for when they take their animal forms, though I've always been left out of that. I don't have the talent to take on any of Apollo's avatars. When they both stonewall me like this, I have to wait for them to silently work out whatever it is they're working out because neither of them will speak first unless I make them.

We go back inside, through the kitchen and down to our father's secure level. Pallas is staring at Castor. He's angry with him, and behind the anger is worry. I want to ask questions, but I don't. Patience is power.

Our father is in his bedroom. We take our usual places behind the chairs in the sitting area of his bedroom, but none of us take seats. This is not a chat between father and sons. This is a discussion between a general and his soldiers.

"Did you find her?" our father asks too eagerly.

Castor and Pallas do that thing where they glare at each other, daring the other to go first until Castor finally speaks.

"The House of Athens has issued a challenge," Castor announces. "Daedalus wants a rematch for the Lincoln Center territory. Rome is to host it at their coliseum."

Our father straightens with anticipation. Not the news he was hoping for, but good news all the same. Expanding our territory to Lincoln Center would give us the high ground. "And you accepted, of course."

"Castor can't beat Daedalus," Pallas says, stepping forward.

"He's not frigging Achilles reborn," Castor growls at his near twin.

"You said he was faster than you!" Pallas shouts.

"I can still best him!" Castor shouts back.

They nearly come to blows and I step between them.

"Castor will fight," our father decides.

"Father, listen to me," Pallas pleads. "It's not about winning or losing. The Athenians are using this as an excuse to kill Caz!"

"Daedalus doesn't want to kill me," Castor argues. "He may be a dick, but he knows that doing so will start the war."

Smart. Pallas is onto something with this even if he's too angry to articulate it right now. I do it for him.

"Bellerophon *wants* the war to start, and he can order his son to do it," I say, addressing Castor. "Killing you would be a sure way to start it. And if the Athenians have all four of us penned in at the coliseum, they could very well take us, and the Hundred Cousins would go to war without a leader, which would be disastrous for our House."

Castor turns his glare on me now. "You're assuming I won't *win*."

"If Daedalus is fighting to kill, you'd have to kill him to win. With a fresh kill, the Furies would overtake us all. Same result," I reply.

"Then don't come," Castor says. His pride is hurt, and rightfully so.

I don't know for certain who would win between the two of them, but we've all heard stories about Daedalus Attica, about his strength and speed. There were a few Outcasts from the House of Athens—*true* Outcasts, and not just disowned, who had killed kinsman and needed to be brought to justice—and Daedalus did it. He captured, subdued, but didn't kill the Outcasts, which showed remarkable strength and self-governance.

How he managed to ignore the Furies so he didn't kill them and become an Outcast himself is a feat most Scions wouldn't be capable of. And he was only sixteen when he did it. Castor is strong, and he's had less opportunity to prove how good a fighter he is, but our kind don't create legends unless it's earned. Daedalus seems to have earned his, and he's Castor's age.

Which is why Castor wants to fight him so much. His whole life he's been compared to this guy without any opportunity to prove how he measures up.

We wait for our father to decide. Pallas still thinks he's going to stop this, but I know better. Our father loves us, but he loves his House more.

"When?" he asks.

"In three days," Castor replies.

"Then in three days you fight," our father says. Pallas opens his mouth to argue, and Father lifts his hand for silence. "Pallas, you will help your brother prepare. It's on you to make sure he's ready."

Pallas turns on his heel and storms out instead. Dismissed, I grab Castor by the shoulder and pull him to the door with me.

"Go after him and don't let him do anything stupid," I say quietly as we leave. Castor and I both know that Pallas will probably go looking for a woman to distract himself, and our family doesn't need that kind of complication right now. "This isn't about how good a fighter you are. He's scared he'll lose you too."

Castor's face falls, remembering Ajax, and he goes after Pallas. If I dole it out a little at a time and use it subtly, the specter of Ajax's death could keep the two of them under my control indefinitely.

It's way too late for me to go out and search for Daphne now. I'll have to wait for morning, though I know I won't sleep. Not until I know she's safe.

✣ 27 ✣

DAPHNE

Come mid-morning, Ajax is well enough to sit up and eat, and then I'm kept too busy getting food for his heal to think about Antigone's vision.

I debate not telling him, but in the end, I know I have to. He and I are in this together, and if I start hiding things from him, I'm lost. I decide to tell him after my second trip to the surface.

"If this isn't enough food for you, I'm going to let Ladon harpoon you a whale like he offered," I tell Ajax as I set down the overstuffed bags and take off my jacket.

Ladon lifts his head, hopefully. "She's joking," Ajax insists hastily.

I start sorting through the takeout containers. I'm stalling. Ajax watches me, his chewing slowing down and his brow furrowing.

"What is it?" Ajax asks.

I look at him too brightly, and smooth my hands over the hip pockets of my jeans anxiously. "What do you mean?"

He gives me a look, pokes his fork into his linguini, and puts it aside. "Ladon, can you give us a moment?" Ladon leaves, and Ajax motions for me to join him on the bed, scooting to the side with some effort. His leg is still splinted. "What is it?" he asks, putting his arm around me when I sit next to him.

So, I tell him. I withhold nothing about Antigone's description of his death. Ajax listens, his expression going from concerned to blank as I talk. When I'm done, he shakes his head vaguely.

"It's gotta be a mistake," he says, shrugging like the matter is settled. "There's no way my brother would ever do that to me. I mean, *why?*"

Does he honestly not know? I shut my mouth and turn away from him. "I think we should leave Manhattan. Get back on the *Argo* and go."

"What about the mousetrap?"

"I think the mousetrap was the Fates maneuvering us back here. Where Tantalus is."

"He's not going to kill me, Daphne."

I go to get off the bed and he takes my hand, not letting me stand up. I look back at him over my shoulder, not saying anything because what I need to say to him is just too hurtful. He thinks his brother is set in stone, unchanging, and he doesn't see that Tantalus is different. I've made him different. But I can't say any of that to Ajax.

"Please," I ask.

"Okay," he replies, no more fighting. Because he and I are in this together. And no one else, not even his brother, matters more to him. "We'll go."

"Thank you."

I relax and let Ajax pull me into bed next to him. I should

stop him for his own sake, but I want the comfort of his body. I need to feel that he's whole. I slip my hands under his shirt and push it off over his head. The red Lichtenburg marks are already fading, despite my fear that I'd scarred him for life. He kisses me and tries to shift me under him, but his splint stops him from getting any further with me.

"I've never taken this long to heal," he says, kicking at the blankets tangled on his leg in frustration.

"You got struck by lightning, and run over by a dump truck," I say, and get out of bed.

"Where are you going?" he complains, pouting and trying to pull me back in with him. "Come on, nurse. I need a sponge bath."

I almost giggle my way back into bed with him, but I manage to pull myself together. "I have to sort out your food situation with Ladon, and get the *Argo* ready," I reply when I finally wrestle free of him. It's amazing how many hands he seems to have when he's in the mood. "We shouldn't have left it for as long as we have."

"I'd help you get it ready, but..." He gestures pathetically to his injuries.

I throw a pillow at his head and leave him laughing, yelling after me.

I take care of the *Argo* first. I'm not afraid as I go uptown on the subway. I've cleared my debt with all the other Houses and the Furies are gone for me. I can go wherever I want. I can change my face and walk anywhere in the world without fear of being spotted or discovered, without even worrying that I will be possessed by rage. And though I am afraid for Ajax, and I know that the clock is ticking, I'm enjoying this. Because I'm free of the Furies for the first time in my life. Maybe the first time in any Scion's life.

There has to be something special about this, some way I can use this rare ability to help other Scions who are trapped by the Furies. I don't know what to do with it yet, but for the first time I feel like I've found a higher purpose for myself, something outside of the basic survival mode I've been imprisoned in my whole life. Something outside of Ajax and his art—noble as supporting him is—this is mine. I think this ability to be with any Scion from any House might be my life's calling. If I can figure it out how to use it to benefit others.

Outfitting the *Argo* takes me the whole day, but there are two more places I have to go to before I turn in for the night with Ajax. I take a downtown train to Greenwich Village and wait outside the Lycian brownstone, staring up at Antigone's window. I know I won't have to wait long. Soon, she's going to look out that window to check the manhole cover that serves as a signal between her and Ladon.

When she does, I step out of the shadows and raise an arm. She sees me. She glances over her shoulder, then holds up a finger as if to say *wait*. Another fifteen minutes go by and she opens her window. I climb up the side of her brownstone and pull myself inside her bedroom.

"What are you doing here?" She mouths the words more than says them, staying as quiet as she can. "If you get caught in here—"

"I need to know if you've seen anything else. Ajax and I are leaving... and we're not coming back."

She casts around, not sure how to answer me. "Bits and pieces."

"About Helen?" I specify and she clams up pretty fast. "Antigone? What aren't you telling me?"

"She's not Ajax's daughter," she blurts out, almost like she wants to get it over with. "Sorry. I told him we shouldn't tell you, and here I am telling you."

"He knows?"

She nods. "I have no idea when you have Helen, though. It's not like there's a time stamp on any of my visions. You could be with Ajax for years."

The only way I'd ever be with another man, is if Ajax is dead, and even then, I still can't imagine it.

She looks sorry for me, but not very. "At least you get to have the one you love, even if it's just for a short while. That's more than some of us will ever have."

I do feel bad for her, but that doesn't mean I'm content with the idea that one day Ajax is going to be taken away from me.

"I wish I could go with you," she says. "Away from this prison."

I reach out and touch her arm briefly. "Are you sure it's such a good idea to sneak out to see him? You're going to get caught one of these days, you know that."

"He's my best friend," she says simply.

How could I ask her to give that up? It would be hypocritical of me, even though we both know that if she gets caught, so will Ladon. And what's going to happen to him?

"Are you going to him tonight?" I ask.

"If he wants me to."

"Be careful," I say, giving her a hug goodbye.

My last stop is Washington Square. I don't need to pick a shadow to hide in this time. I need to be seen. I wait for him under the Arch. Even though I'm not wearing my real face, he'll know it's me and come out eventually.

I don't have to wait long. After about twenty minutes I see the front door to the Delos' brownstone open. Tantalus comes out with no jacket on, though it's getting chilly as night falls. I can tell by his measured steps that he's forcing himself not to run.

"Were you hurt?" he asks.

I shake my head.

"Is Ajax okay?"

"He's recovering."

He visibly relaxes. "Come, walk with me."

I take a step back. "I came to tell you we're leaving," I say.

He looks like I slapped him. "Come inside. We'll talk." I shake my head and take another step back, and he takes a step toward me, reaching out.

"Don't," I say, making sure there are still people around. He won't make a scene in public. He has more self-control than that. "We have to go. Ajax is in danger here."

"From what? And who?" he asks, looking more and more desperate. "Tell me. Let's go up the street, to a café. We'll sit down and talk it through. Whatever it is, I'll help you, you know I will."

I chuff with frustration. I can't tell him that *he's* the danger because I can't tell him what Antigone saw without telling him how I'm in contact with her and therefore give away Ladon and Adonis. I'm painted into a corner. It's the mousetrap again, I realize that, but I'm not quick enough to see if the net is descending right now or not. I have to get out of here.

"I just came to say goodbye."

I turn to go. "Don't walk away from me," he warns. His chin tilts down and his hands clench into fists.

"Seriously?" I ask, equal parts shocked and hurt.

"Shit. I'm sorry," he says. He moves closer to me, like he wants to put his arms around me, but he stops himself.

Everything I do hurts him. Staying, going. It doesn't matter what I do, I'll always hurt him.

"I'm angry, but not at you," he explains. "I just... I get the feeling that if you leave right now, you'll never come back, and it bothers me, that I can't handle that."

I'm such an idiot. Why did I come here? Did I think saying goodbye would make it easier for him? It probably would have been better for him if he thought Ajax and I had died.

"I shouldn't have dragged you into this."

"It's not your fault," he says, trying to comfort me. Absolve me. "None of this is your fault. Please, let me help you."

I run for it before I make it any worse. The only way out of this is if he never sees me or Ajax again. And the sooner never begins, the better for all of us.

28
ION

It was a stroke of luck, really, that the Oracle slipped out her front door intent on doing something and didn't see me. She went right out into the street all by herself and tapped on a manhole cover. She didn't even glance over her shoulder. It was as if she was begging to be taken.

We were only there to mark the Lycians' patterns and observe who from the Hundred Cousins is stationed downstairs to guard the Oracle. We thought it would be days before we would be ready to move on her. The original plan was to be ready when the fight between the Houses over the disputed territory was scheduled to take place; that way Thebes would be distracted, but this opportunity was too good to pass up. My father always says that when something like this happens, it's fated to be.

With Phaon from the House of Rome in the parked car controlling the Furies, no one in the Lycian brownstone was aware that enemy Scions were near. I was standing outside on the street, watching. As soon as I saw the girl emerging from the front door alone in the dead of night, I simply walked up to her and took her.

How easy it is to steal a little girl. Even though my leg is still bothering me because my Roman adversary twisted the blade when he stuck me in the thigh, the girl was no trouble to lift. I put my arm around her and covered her mouth with my hand. Then I picked her up in my arms and got into the back of the car that Doris was clever enough to drive up right beside us. It didn't take more than five seconds altogether. The girl had so conveniently positioned herself right there in the middle of the street, with not one guard from her House even watching her from the front door!

Why has Rome never done this before, I wonder? Some of them, like this Phaon character, can control the Furies for brief periods of time. It seems to me they could have done this themselves.

"Come on, let's go!" Phaon says, hitting his hand on the dashboard, though Doris is doing a fine job of driving away at a fast but still inconspicuous speed. He spins around in his seat to yell at me. "We were only supposed to watch!"

Phaon is afraid. *That* is why Rome has never attempted this before. They knew that Thebes would've declared war over the Oracle, and they did not want that. But that was before. War is what we all seem to want now. Or at least, some of us do. Thebes will suspect Rome because the Furies were not felt when she was taken. That's why Phaon is afraid. Thebes' retribution will be swift and permanent. For taking the Oracle, Thebes could wipe the House of Rome from history. But with Athens here to take the blame, Rome can say we made them do it, and Thebes' anger would be directed at us. It's all very confusing, but I know what I am for. My purpose is to follow my father's orders, and he wants the Oracle taken. In a way, Rome would be right in blaming us. Rome would never have attempted this without Athens to hide behind.

"I was told to take the girl," I reply.

I wish my father would order me to find the Atreidae girl as well. She would not be so easy to take, but perhaps one of my forms would be able to endure her lightning. Yet, if my father were to order me to take her, I do not think he would let me keep her. He would have some purpose for her in mind, and I do not want to give her to my father. I want to keep the Atreidae for myself.

"Doesn't look like we're being followed," Doris says, I think to calm Phaon down. It works. His shoulders drop and his face is less twisted with fear and anger after she says it. Doris looks at me through the rear-view mirror. "You're holding her too tightly," she says. "The girl can't breathe."

Doris is right. I let the girl go. When she recovers her breath, she screams. I put my hand back over her mouth because I do not like the sound, but I am careful not to cover her nose this time.

"I thought you said they guarded her," I say to Doris.

"They can't guard her from herself," Phaon answers for her, twisting around again from the passenger seat to stare at the girl. "What were you doing sneaking out at night, tapping on that manhole cover?" he asks her in a sly way, like he's in on her mischief.

I let go of her mouth, but she doesn't answer Phaon. She sniffles and starts to cry.

I see Doris' eyes flick up to the rearview mirror a few times, her attention divided between the crying girl and the road.

"So much fondness in you as you tapped on that manhole

cover. Do you have a pet alligator in the sewer?" Phaon teases. The girl cries harder, her head bent with weeping.

"Leave her alone," Doris says. The way she says it is enough to make Phaon stop. Doris is very good with people.

Phaon knows what he is for. He is for following orders like I am. Corvus was very eager to team up with us. We went to him as my father ordered, but we did not have to kill him or even threaten him, though I notice Corvus did not risk coming himself. Phaon is better at controlling the Furies, he said. I think it is that Phaon is better at following orders.

We take the Oracle to my father. He is surprised to see us so soon. He did not think we would be returning with his prize, but he is happy to welcome the girl.

"You won't have me for long," the Oracle says. She looks at me and her eyes narrow like she sees something I cannot. Whatever it is she sees, she likes it.

"Is that a prophecy?" Phaon asks, eager to play with her. "I wonder if you're any good as an Oracle. After all, you didn't see us coming."

The girl shrinks, ashamed. "I was distracted," she says. "But I'm not anymore."

My father looks troubled. "You may see the future, Antigone, but yours won't come until I'm through with you," he says. Phaon likes that.

"Until we are both through with her," Phaon adds. He stares at the girl's pale limbs as if deciding which he should like to eat first.

"It's already been decided between Corvus and me," my father says, sensing a challenge. He faces Phaon and throws his chest out. "What you get from this deal is the territory. Lincoln Center. Athens gets the Oracle."

Phaon broods over this. He wants the Oracle for himself, like I want the Atreidae. He wants to keep her. He likes to play with little things like her, though I do not think she would like it very much. He looks to me like a fed cat with a mouse. He would bat at her for as long as she could stand it, and then she would die. This would be wasteful, and I do not like waste. For a cat, playing with things until they fall apart is what they are for, but it is not what humans are for. I decide I do not like Phaon. He is not natural.

"You'll still need me here to control the Furies for you," Phaon says. My father hadn't considered that. There are often things that take him by surprise when he is negotiating, but Doris usually has something to say that fixes the problem.

"And Ion and I will be right there with you," Doris promises in a cheerful way, as if we're all going to have a nice time. My father likes this, while Phaon does not. He knows Doris will not let him play with the girl.

"Now all we have to do is hide her until she tells me how this war is going to go. And after the territory dispute is settled in Rome's favor, of course," my father says, changing the subject. Phaon is not appeased, but he is thinking of how he might still get what he wants.

"We should get her out of the city," Doris suggests.

My father shakes his head. "I want her close by in case we have to act on anything she might say."

"If she's here someone from the House of Rome will be able to find her," Phaon objects. "Adonis and Leda know the names the Furies whisper even better than I do. They will be able to identify the Furies of Thebes in the territory of Athens if they are near enough to her."

My father had never heard of this before. It makes him angry that Rome can do this. Doris thinks deeply on this problem because she knows what she is for. She is for fixing my father's oversights so that he may have everything he wants.

"How far away from them, physically, does she have to be so they can't hear her Furies?" Doris asks Phaon.

He considers. "Adonis is strong," he says, though he does not like to admit it. "I would guess that he'd be able to feel her if he was within a thousand feet?"

"Most city blocks are less than three hundred feet. That would leave nowhere to hide her from him if he were to walk through in quadrants," my father says. He starts pacing impatiently.

Doris picks her head up. "*Walk* through. On the *ground*," she says, smiling.

And I know she's figured it out, which makes me glad because the sooner we can settle this, the sooner I can go looking for the Atreidae.

❧ 29 ❧

DAEDALUS

There's a knock on my door, and the first thing I think is *Leda,* because I am an idiot. There's no way she's on the other side of the door. This fantasy I have of her coming to me, professing her feelings, and then falling into bed with me is not only ridiculous, but dangerous. It's also the only thing I think about anymore.

I start unwinding the tape from my hands, blinking the odd drop of sweat out of my eyes on my way to the door. I've turned my living room into a fight cage to practice. Hard to practice alone. Doris is on some secret mission for my father, so she couldn't train with me tonight, and I don't intend to lose the fight for Lincoln Center.

It really is just like my father to deprive me of my training partner right when I need her the most. There's no sense in half the stuff he does. As I'm opening the front door it occurs to me, too late, that there's no sense in what *I'm* doing, just letting in whoever is on the other side, because although I don't feel the Furies, and I know no enemies could be out there, it might be difficult to explain why my apartment looks like a kinky sex dungeon.

I open the door to find a gorgeous blonde girl on my doorstep. And when I say gorgeous, I mean *shit*. Her face is haunting.

"I'm Daphne Atreus. And I come in peace."

My perception of the world shifts. "Daphne, daughter of Elara?

"I don't have time to explain, but your brother Ladon really needs to talk to you right now. It's an emergency."

There are so many things wrong with what she just told me. "But... if you're an Atreidae, where are the Furies? And how do you know about my brother Ladon?"

She shakes her head as I barrage her with questions and holds up a hand that's sheathed in blue sparks, proving her House of origin.

"You have to come with me, now," she says, somehow managing to look like she's asking rather than threatening even though she's waving a mini thunderbolt in my face. A bolt-thrower. Wow.

"How do I know you're not luring me out to ambush me?" I ask.

"Why lure you out? I could kill you right here." She's looking at me strangely, like maybe I'm an idiot. And maybe I am because I feel like I can trust her. She's not here to kill me. She extinguishes the bolt and puts her hands in her pockets. "Quickly," she urges.

I must still be in shock because I start following her like a sleepwalker.

"Shoes. Shirt," she reminds me, and from the belabored way

she says it I get the feeling this isn't the first time she's had to remind a guy to put some clothes on after sparring.

Makes sense, considering who she is. She looks so delicate, but I bet she's a beast in the ring. I can tell by the way she stands that she's trained in combat. She holds herself like a panther. She's also mouthing the words to the song that I'm blasting, and it's not some happy pop jingle.

Head like a hole. Black as your soul. I'd rather die. Then give you control.

"You like *Nine Inch Nails*?" I ask as I tie my shoelaces.

She nods. "I've got rage."

That makes me nod with her in understanding—what Scion doesn't have rage—but it also makes me worry about Ladon again. Lightning is the only thing I know of that can kill a dragon, and she's got it. I turn off my CD player.

"Is my brother okay?" I ask as I pull on a shirt and slide my arms into a jacket.

"Physically, he's fine, but emotionally he's freaking out. So am I, actually," she says, turning and jogging down the steps. "I'll let him explain, though."

We run across the street to the water, too fast for mortals to see us, and jump over the metal guard rail. Crab walking down the steep slant of rocks to the water's edge, I see my brother's head bobbing on the tide. I float out to him.

"What happened?" I ask, treading water next to him. He's never done anything like this before.

He launches into a whole thing about how he was waiting under a manhole cover, and how she tapped back, and then he heard her gasp followed by the sound of heavier footsteps.

"The footsteps were uneven, like he had a limp. When I lifted the manhole cover, I saw a car driving away with a large man hunched over in the backseat of it. It was Ion. I smelled Ion," he says, trying to speak clearly as the words come tripping out of him.

"Ion?" I ask. "Walking with a limp?"

"I smelled his blood. He's been injured recently in the leg."

I'm pretty sure that Ion is the shapeshifter from the subway tunnel. But that can't be because the descendants of Proteus are only in my father's direct line, which would mean... Wait. Who are Ion's parents? I can't recall ever being told that.

"The House of Athens has taken her! He must have had someone from the House of Rome with him in the car because he didn't seem possessed by the Furies, and none of the Thebans inside the house came out! They must not have felt him!"

"Back up," I say. "Who did Ion take?"

He says her name like it's the most important word in the world to him. "Antigone!"

I don't have to ask, but I do anyway. "Antigone Lycian, the Oracle of Delphi, is the girl you're in love with?

"Please. You must get her back from Father."

What has our father done? We're all going to die. "Doris and Ion went on a mission tonight, with this Roman, Phaon—"

"What!?" we hear Daphne say from the rocks. She comes down to the edge of the water but is careful to not so much as put a toe in it. "Phaon's involved?" she asks, clearly enunciating his name in case she heard me wrong.

"I don't know. But they were together."

"You have to get Antigone away from him."

Ladon grabs my arm. "Help me get her back," he pleads.

My mind turns through all the ramifications. If I interfere, my father will definitely disown me. But I can't let him do this to Ladon. Or let him plunge the Scions into war.

"I have no idea where they've taken her, but I know Doris. She won't let Phaon do anything to Antigone," I tell Ladon.

"We have to get her back before anyone from Thebes notices," Daphne says. "If we return her before anyone gets killed, we might be able to convince them it was a misunderstanding."

"And if we can't?" I ask. This could all be too little too late. Thebes could be attacking my family right now for all I know, and once the bloodshed starts, the Furies will make sure it doesn't stop.

"I'll speak with Tantalus, but only if she's back unharmed," Daphne promises.

"Wait, didn't he kill you?"

She rolls her eyes and sighs, backed into a corner. "He helped us fake our deaths, so Ajax and I could run away together." she says.

"You're just full of surprises, aren't you?" I ask her, but my sarcasm is a knee-jerk reaction at this point because I'm reeling.

Putting aside the problem of the Furies, which a ton of Scions obviously *have* somehow, if Daphne and Ajax are in love, they join Atreus and Thebes. If my brother could ever consummate his love for Antigone that would join Athens to Thebes. And if Leda and I ever... What am I saying. She'll never love me. If anything, I should be more worried about her and Castor. That would join Rome to Thebes, and all four Houses would be united under the umbrella of Thebes. The gods would be released from Olympus, and the final war—not one of the usual battles that we Scions have with each other about every twenty years or so, but the big one between the Scions and the Olympians—would be upon us. But one catastrophe at a time. I focus on my brother.

"We need a Roman to help us." I say. "They can track Scions using the Furies."

"Adonis," Ladon says. "He's coming to my cove tonight."

"What the...?" I start, but my brother waves me off.

"I'll explain on the way." He disappears beneath the water, leaving me with Daphne.

"The fastest way to my brother's place is underwater," I tell her holding out my hand. "I can swim you there."

"Hells no. I don't even put my head underwater in the bathtub. I'll meet you there." And she takes off.

Does everyone know where my brother lives? "Shit," I say to myself, and then I join my brother beneath the surface.

30

ADONIS

Ajax and I stare at each other in Ladon's cave. He's brought me up to speed, and all he and I can do is sit back while Daphne and Ladon try to convince Daedalus to help us. Assuming he's not in on it. Athens took the Oracle. With Rome's help.

"Well, that's it," I say, throwing myself down on the couch. "The war is officially starting."

I turn my cuff around my wrist. If Thebes starts hunting down the other Houses, I have the ultimate panic room ready to go. I'll take Leda, of course. We'll hide like we used to when we were kids when one of our cousins was going to try to hurt us. We'll keep Rome alive, outlasting Bellerophon and Paris. I don't want to spend my entire life stumbling around the Underworld, but better that than dying and releasing the gods from Olympus. We can hang out with Morpheus if we get bored. It'll be great.

"Maybe not," Ajax says, floating himself over to the couch perpendicular to mine.

His leg is still healing and he can't put any weight on it, but he doesn't need to because he's a flyer. How frigging jealous am I? Having a helicopter doesn't even come close.

"If we can somehow get Antigone back tonight before my aunt goes to wake her up in the morning, and notices she's gone, it'll be like it never happened," he says.

"I can find her if I'm given access to Athenian territory," I offer. "Leda will help."

"We should do this in groups," Ajax says. "I don't think whoever's got my cousin is going to just hand her over, and don't take this the wrong way, but you and Leda shouldn't be —"

"Romans are lovers not fighters, is that what you're saying?" I finish for him.

"You should each have someone with you who can handle themselves, in case there's a fight. Not even Daphne should go alone," he says judiciously. "And she's the best fighter I've ever seen."

"I haven't had the pleasure of seeing that side of her. Although, that incident in the subway —"

"The shapeshifter?"

"She told you?"

"About Hades, too."

I hate how open they are with each other. I've never been able to tell someone *everything*. Not even my sister. Ajax watches me struggling.

"What?" I ask, posturing.

"Look, I know how you feel."

"How *do* I feel?"

"She has that effect on everyone."

I stand up, acting offended, but I have no idea where the hell I think I'm going. Just somewhere away from him.

"Listen, don't worry about it," he says. He should be jealous, but he's not. Wait. Is he...?

"Are you feeling *sorry* for me?" I ask, disgusted.

"Kinda," he admits.

"Thanks. Prick." Childish, I know, but I'm not used to being the one who's emotionally unbalanced. I'm used to doing that to other people.

And I should be the one with the upper hand here. This guy has all his cards on the table. He's facing me, showing me his heart. I can read everything that's going on inside him, and I still don't understand him. I've never met anyone like him, and that just winds me up even more, because I think I could have fallen in love with him as easily as I fell in love with Daphne if I'd met him first. No wonder his brothers lost it when they thought he died. He has the most beautiful, complicated heart I've ever seen.

"Do you have any idea what it's like for me?" he asks— and he's really asking. This isn't rhetorical bullshit. He's wondering if I, as a Roman who can read emotions, understand how he feels. I don't, so I take a closer look.

His heart is so full of love I want to punch him. But on the edge of that love is fear. Like, top of the roller-coaster fear. The kind you know you asked for because you willingly got on for the ride, but that you're not sure you can physically handle. Just looking at it makes me feel dizzy and I have to sit down.

"Well, she loves you and no one else," I say. I don't mean to sound as bitter as I do, but I wish it was me.

"I know," he replies. There's no ego there, just responsibility. "But we didn't fake our deaths because we thought it would be romantic. We did it because other people would kill me to get to her. And one of these days someone is going to succeed. But I'm not scared for me."

I'm confused for a second. "You're not scared for yourself that you're going to die? Walk me through this."

"You've looked into Daphne's heart," he says. "Now, imagine her after I've been killed."

He's right. Daphne is capable of things other people aren't. Her strength is hypnotic, and potentially horrifying if it were ever corrupted by desperation or grief.

"After she lost her uncle Deuce, who was the only other person besides me she really loved, she..." He finds it hard to continue.

"Grief can be the garden of compassion, or an anchor that weighs you down."

Every Scion knows that Ajax Delos killed Polydeuces Atreus, bearer of the Aegis of Zeus, but only I can see what a mess it's made of Ajax.

"You have to promise me something," he continues.

"What?"

"If I don't make it, I need you to promise me that you'll help her get over me. That you'll use your talent to make her love you, if that's what it takes. Just make her move on, or I'm afraid she's going to do something terrible, either to herself or to a lot of other people."

I know without a doubt that he's right. Daphne stood before Hades, fearless. I was terrified. Not only because I look exactly like him, and I have no idea what that could possibly mean, though I'm pretty sure it can't be good; but because Hades *feels* like death. Daphne was fine with that. She doesn't seem to have any problem with looking death in the eye. Backed into a corner, with nothing to lose, she may very well become a weapon. A bitter, vengeful weapon bent on destroying whatever it was that took him from her.

But I could fix that.

It's not impossible, not in this case. The reason no one can change true love is because when you really love someone, you fall in love with them a little bit every time you interact with them. Seeing them, talking on the phone, even just getting a letter from them is enough to make you fall in love even after a long separation. But if Ajax were dead, Daphne would never be able to interact with him again. I couldn't ever make her feel true love for me, but I could make her feel something close, and maybe the rest I could earn.

"It's wrong to do that to someone, you know," I say, far more tempted to agree to his request than I should be.

"I know," he replies, looking pained. "And the fact that you don't want to do it makes me feel better about asking you to. I'm not asking because it gives me some weird possessive thrill to dictate who she's with after me. I ask because I think she'll kill people if you don't."

"*Neither* of us should be with Daphne," I say. "Keeping the gods on Olympus where they can't send humanity back to the Bronze Age should be our priority."

"I know," he says, looking just as guilty as I feel. "But the Houses can only be united by blood."

The rules I learned as a kid left a lot of gray area. This is how it was explained to me: The Trojan war was instigated by the gods on purpose, either with Helen's kidnapping or with that whole business with the golden apple, so that the gods could get the Scions to kill each other off. The gods were making a lot of babies, and that was problematic for them because every generation we Scions got stronger and more plentiful. The gods were getting anxious that we'd overthrow them, and so they designed a huge war where all the Scions were set against each other to cull us. But then they got so involved in the Trojan war that Olympus was nearly torn apart by infighting. At the end of the war, the Scions insisted the gods imprison themselves on Olympus and stay out of the mortal world, and the gods insisted the Scions would never unite and become so powerful that they could threaten the gods again, or they would come back and kill us all and subjugate the earth. That sort of thing.

The actual deal the Scions made said that the gods would be released from Olympus when there was only *one Scion House left*, but either by union or war was unspecified. I always got the feeling that it was left unclear like that because it favored the gods who don't want to spend too long on boring Olympus. They knew we would be haunted by the Furies for our sin of kin-killing at Troy and they bet we'd eradicate each other in a few generations. Which we almost did. But no one really knows why the vow on the River Styx was made the way it was; just that it left us in this war of attrition for over three thousand years.

"Antigone made a prophecy that only Daphne heard. She said that *blood* is the only way to unite the Houses," he continues. "Although she didn't say whether blood means bloodshed, or bloodline. Falling in love and getting married isn't enough to break the Truce."

He looks down, but I can still see his heart. It's bruised as hell. "Antigone also said that Helen will be Daphne's daughter, but I'm not the father," he says. "Some mortal named Jerry Hamilton will be."

Now this is upsetting because who the hell is this Jerry character? But it's also a relief because now I don't have to worry about the Houses uniting through Thebes and Atreus. Or about carrying the guilt of making Ajax sterile. Before I can ask any more questions about Helen's eventual father, like, does Daphne care about him, is he a good dad, and what's his stance on three-ways,

Ladon surfaces in the cove, followed by his brother. I silence the Furies that arise between Daedalus and Ajax.

"Promise me you'll do it," he says.

I want it too much and he's handed me too good of a reason to resist.

"If I have to, I will," I reply. But as the two brothers join us, I feel like I've made the wrong kind of vow.

"What the hell?" Daedalus is saying to Ladon. "Were you ever going to tell me about this?" He waves a disdainful hand at Ajax and me.

Ladon looks tortured. Daedalus should know better than to pick on Ladon. He can't handle this kind of pressure.

"Back off, would you? Ladon and I met by chance in the tunnels, and I kept showing up here until he either had to kill me or make friends with me," I say in Ladon's defense. "And he hid it from you because I guilted him into it. Anyway, we never discuss House politics, if you're worried that he's betrayed Athens."

Daedalus looks shocked. "That's not what I meant."

Clearly, it's never crossed his mind that Ladon would betray him. He's hurt, plain and simple, because Ladon didn't tell him about me. Okay, I can see why Leda thinks he's hot. When Daedalus' tender underbelly is showing, like it does around his brother, it's obvious he has a big heart and that he's been starved for love his whole life.

"We've all kept secrets," Ajax says. The way he says it, with humility and regret, embodies the apology we all owe someone we love while gently reminding Daedalus that he can't be blameless. He's a Scion. He's bound to have lied to loads of people.

"Alright, alright," Daedalus says, letting it go as he shakes off the water. "Let's figure out how we're going to save Antigone so we can all go back to hating each other like we're supposed to."

🜲 31 🜲

DAEDALUS

It's decided that we need to split into groups and start searching immediately. Adonis brings me uptown to get Leda.

After a quick explanation that leaves her staggered, he tells Leda that she's got to stick close to me because we're going to be searching for the Oracle in Athenian territory tonight.

"Call me if you find her," Adonis says, patting the cellphone in his pocket. He turns to me, looking uncharacteristically severe. "Don't let any of your backward, banjo-plucking relatives hurt my sister."

I'm angry, but not about the *Deliverance* reference, which I think is dead on and kind of hilarious. But because it's too easy for me to imagine one of said backward, banjo-plucking relatives hurting Leda.

He glances down at my chest. "Oh, boy. That's bound to be problematic," he says, frowning. I hate it when he does that, like he knows more about me than I do. Then he punks out and goes back downtown to meet up with Daphne and Ajax.

Leda stands there in the middle of her lavish apartment, bare-foot, hair all over the place, wearing monogrammed silk pajamas and an eye mask that's pushed up on her forehead.

"I'm gonna kill him," she mumbles to herself.

"It's not his fault."

"Not him. Corvus." She rips the eye mask off her forehead and starts pacing. "He's going to destroy our House—*my* House!" she yells. "He's been trying to undermine me for years, and this time, he's not getting off with a reprimand."

I feel a flash of the Furies. Whispering. Irrational anger. Her neck is so slender. I bet I could snap it with one hand.

"Sorry," she says, taking a step back. She must have lost control over the Furies for a second there.

That was frightening. I could almost feel the column of her throat under the pads of my thumbs. I turn away from her in case she can see what's in my heart. I don't want to scare her.

"Yeah well, you can kill Corvus later. Better yet, I'll do it for you," I say. "Just go get dressed. We need to hurry."

She glances down at her pajamas like she's realizing she's still in them. They're cute. Tailored like boy pajamas, but colored lavender and pearl gray. I squint to read the monogram; it says SPQR, and of course she's not wearing a bra. I look away quickly before I see too much through the pale silk.

I'm shaking all over. It was that brush with the Furies. Her body. I'm too amped up and it's all one big blaze in my head. What the hell is wrong with me? It's not like I've never seen a nipple before.

She jackrabbits out of the room, and I hear drawers sliding and some thumping around. I take some deep breaths to calm myself. That slip-up with the Furies reminded me that we're on thin ice. I shouldn't get too comfortable around her, or I could hurt her.

Her place is clean, but still homey. Decorated, but lived in. Little photos in matching frames and everything smells nice, like her perfume, or maybe it's all the fresh-cut flowers in crystal vases. The furniture is obviously expensive, but it's clear that someone, probably lots of people, have sat on it. Now I'm thinking about all the guys she's probably had over. Sitting on her furniture. Smelling her flowers.

She didn't shut the door all the way, but I'm not peeping or anything. My attention is naturally drawn to the motion as she starts throwing her clothes around the room like a magician pulling handkerchiefs out of a hat. Some of the clothes must land on her body and stick amidst the whirlwind she creates because a moment later she comes out dressed in jeans, boots, a black t-shirt, and a dark, stylish trench coat like I've seen that supermodel Christy Turlington wear on the cover of fashion magazines. Behind her, the devastation is shocking. I point into the room.

"You're just going to leave it like that?"

"I got the feeling you were a neat freak," she accuses, turning me around by the shoulders and pushing me out in front of her.

"What?" I ask.

"Your apartment. It was sanitized within an inch of its life," she says, grabbing her keys, wallet, and phone and shoving them into various coat pockets.

"So? What's wrong with that?"

"Come on," she says, stressed out about everything like I would be if I wasn't so distracted by her. "Let's find the Oracle before the House of Thebes comes marching up Madison Avenue to kill me."

We run for it because running at Scion speed is faster than any other transportation in the city. We're crossing through Theban territory when she puts out an arm and stops me.

"Should we get Castor?" she asks.

"Why?" I ask, baffled. "We're trying to get the girl back *before* Thebes find out she's gone."

She's nodding like she understands all that. "Hear me out. We're probably not going to find her in," she looks at her watch, "four hours when the sun is up. If we can get through to Castor before time runs out, he might be persuaded to talk to Tantalus on our behalf. He'll know you and I didn't do it, and that we're all working towards the same goal. Maybe Tantalus will be satisfied if we hand over Corvus."

"What about my dad? Are we going to hand him over too?" I ask, squashing her hopes.

"I didn't think about that," she admits, frowning.

"Right. You forgot. Or maybe you just wanted to see Castor so you could *persuade* him?"

"What?" she asks, confused. Then she recoils from me, disgusted, when she gets my meaning. "Let's just go."

"I'm—" I try to apologize but she starts running again, and I've got to move to keep up with her.

I wouldn't blame her if she didn't want to speak to me again after tonight, but even still, she can't go into Athenian territory alone. She might be able to control the Furies, but everyone in my House knows what she looks like and if she's spotted, she'll be in real danger. Every time I get near her, she speeds up. I don't care if she hates me, she's in too much danger. I catch up and grab her arm.

"Would you stop!? I'm sorry!" I shout at her as I spin her around to face me. She's fuming.

"What is *wrong* with you!? And here I thought that there was an actual person in there!" she yells, hitting my chest as hard she can.

"There is," I say quietly. "Just not a very smart one."

"Why are you so insecure?"

"I don't know. But it's worse when I'm around you. So, it's kinda your fault."

Then she does something that absolutely blows me away. She laughs, and then kisses me.

She fits against me perfectly. So soft she could spill right through my fingers. I'm careful with her, breathing her in like she's smoke or magic, and then I'm lifting her up, looking for a wall, anything solid to brace her against or I'll just keep falling into her.

It's New York. A wall is never too far away, and when I have her against it the rough contact snaps her back to herself and she says, "Wait, wait, wait," a bunch of times, and she's pushing against my chest. She unwraps her legs from around my waist and I set her down. I back off, but I still feel like I'm falling toward her and I wonder if that feeling's ever going to stop. Damn, that happened fast.

She has her hands over her mouth and her eyes are wide. "Shit," she says, confused, nodding a lot and pacing around. "We can't do this."

"I know."

"W-we should keep moving," she stammers.

"Yeah," I say, but I'm looking at her and all I want to do is pick her up and put her against that wall again. She can see what I want without trying.

"Stop it!" she scolds, smacking my arm playfully, and I'm so relieved she's not angry with me. Then a wave of guilt hits me and I want to apologize again for what I said earlier. But she can see right through me, and she won't let me waste time by getting into it.

"Later. Come on," she says before I can speak, and she breaks into a run, grabbing my arm and pulling me along with her.

Adonis had divided downtown into two sections, saying he would take the east side from Mott Street in Little Italy over, and she should take the west. That way he ends up taking the lion's share, which I don't mind. We work top down, starting on the edge of Theban territory in Soho at Canal Street. The plan is to move south in a grid until we hit the Battery. Going block by block, we can't so much as jog or Leda might miss something. At this pace, we're not even going to make it south of Chinatown before the sun comes up, and we both know it. Are the street lamps always this bright? Her face glows every time we pass under one. Her beautiful, unmistakable face surrounded by all that shiny, bouncy hair.

"Why didn't you bring a hat? You're like a beacon out here." I say, sounding just as grouchy as I feel. She doesn't get defensive because of my rotten temper, though.

"Yeah, it's not suspicious at all when someone wears a hat at night," she replies sarcastically. "Should I have worn sunglasses also? Maybe a ski mask?"

I chuckle at that. "Maybe," I reply. "Stay on the inside." I move her to the inside of the sidewalk in case Athenians drive by.

"I'll feel them before they spot me, you know," she says, though she lets me do it.

I realize a moment later I still have my arm around her back, and I pull it away. Usually, I don't like it when someone stands too close to me. It makes me feel smothered, even more so if it's a girl. I like my space. But it feels natural to have her right up against me. In fact, I'm the one who's practically walking on top of her. I want her under my jacket. In my pockets. I want to cover her with my thick skin so no one can hurt her. We proceed like this, with me hovering around her anxiously for about another hour, clearing the grid at a glacial pace. I'm getting more and more tense every second, and we've barely gotten into Tribeca.

"No, not down there," I say when Leda nearly turns down Jay Street. "My brother Nilus lives on that block."

"All the more reason we should check it," she says.

We pass his building and are continuing our sweep to the water when two guys round the corner from Greenwich. They're just shadows at the end of the block, but I still know even before Leda stops dead next to me that they're Athenian.

I take her hand, acting like a normal person out on a date, but it's too late. They saw her hesitate. I don't know who from my House is coming toward us, but now they're coming fast.

"They're not where I thought they'd be," she says apologetically, and somehow, I get what she means. She sensed that Athenians were near, but she thought they were inside the building, not rounding the corner outside of it.

"It's okay. Go back," I say, trying to move her in the other direction but when I turn, I see that there are two more Athenians coming up behind us.

"Daedalus?" Boreas, one of Nilus' goons, speaks for the group. They're all teenagers. One of them is little, too. Younger than fifteen, I'd say, and a bit of a runt on top of it.

"Shit," I whisper under my breath. They're all armed, but I'm not worried about that. I just don't want to hurt a bunch of kids. "What are you all still doing up?" I ask, trying to keep it light. "Don't you have school tomorrow?"

"Nah. Tonight's a big night," he says, and the group at large guffaws. It's obvious they've been drinking, killing brain cells they don't have. "You out celebrating?" he asks, gesturing to Leda, his eyes oozing all over her like pollution. He hasn't recognized her yet.

"You heard?" I ask, trying to drag attention away from her. Seems like even these little ones know about the Oracle's kidnapping. Wonder why they know and no one from our House thought to tell me.

"You pissed you're not going to get to fight tomorrow?" Boreas asks.

"Why wouldn't I have to fight?" I ask.

Boreas shrugs at his cronies. "Because we got *her*. *You* know. All bets are off now 'cuz we've basically won." He's nervous talking about this in front of Leda. He thinks she's a mortal. What a dumbass.

I nod. "Yeah, well, I'm still fighting, so don't make any plans for tomorrow night," I say, taking Leda's hand and making my move out of here.

Of course, it's the runt, the one who's probably thirteen, who narrows his eyes at Leda and points. "Hey, aren't you—"

He squawks when I grab him and put him in a headlock. Knives come out. The guy with Boreas isn't even holding his correctly. Who trained these boys? I kick him in the wrist and his blade goes flying.

I see a flash behind Leda. One of the punks that came up behind us, I think his name is Ocean, goes to take her. I let go of the runt, and capture Ocean's forearm, pinning it to the wall beside us before he reaches her. His blade is in his hand. He was going to stab her in the back, I realize.

I look at him, surprised at first, and then I'm so angry I have to work really hard not to break his arm when I hit it against the bricks to make him drop the blade. Then I twist his arm around him and, grabbing the back of his head by the hair with my other hand, I bend him in half, twisting his hair in way that makes it clear to everyone that I could snap his neck in a heartbeat. Whoops. I do break his arm. I accomplish all of this before Boreas can do more than take a step toward Leda. Bunch of kids. Never been in a real fight before.

"Back up," I say quietly to Boreas.

"Where are you going to go?" Boreas asks me, shocked. "We're your *family*."

He's got a point there. I have no place else to go. "Leda Tiber is in Athenian territory under my protection," I say, invoking my right as the Heir. "Now back up."

None of them would dare disobey me, but they're not happy about it. I let Ocean go and move Leda away from them.

My dad is sure to hear about this. There goes any chance I had of returning Antigone safely to Thebes and claiming I had nothing to do with it.

"I'm sorry," Leda says when we're a few blocks away and I still haven't said anything. She is silent for a while, just feeling bad for me, I guess. She knows I'm in trouble.

This is the strangest thing about her; no matter how testy or off-putting my behavior, she either ignores it or thinks it's funny. She never takes the bait and gets defensive, or scared. That's what it is. She isn't scared of me, and nearly everyone else is. If they aren't scared of me physically, they're scared of my taciturn nature. Leda doesn't buy into any of my crap, and I don't know what to say to her, unless I'm willing to be my real myself around her. That's the only version of me she hears. The real me. And who wants that?

"How bad will it be for you?" she asks, not letting up.

I don't have an answer for her, but by my silence she can

assume the worst. I certainly am. I don't think my father will have me killed or anything like that, but disowned is bad enough. I'll be sent to live among the mortals, alone for the rest of my life. Easy for the other Houses to pick off.

"I've been alone my whole life anyway," I say. I don't mean to say it out loud, but hearing it does give me an odd sort of comfort. "Shit, I barely even recognize half the people in my own House. My dad made sure of that by keeping me separate. Probably so I couldn't gain support, then rise up and depose him."

"I know what that's like. Not being able to trust your family. Corvus has been trying to have me killed since my dad died and I inherited the title." She threads her arm through mine. "But if you're disowned, you won't be alone."

She can't mean her. That would be ridiculous. But she's looking up at me with those green eyes of hers and I stop and face her. I want to kiss her.

No, I want *her* to kiss *me*. I want her to hold me. Wrap herself around me and keep me safe. It feels nice to think about it for a moment before I consider that's probably all it takes to unite the Houses.

What is a union, anyway? Marriage? A child? Amazing sex? Or is it that even just a mutually beneficial business arrangement would be enough to unite the Houses and free the gods from Olympus? It's unclear, and it always has been. All those prophecies and rules that we have to follow have been handed down after they've been translated, mashed-up, and purposely misunderstood to fit into some ancestor's personal objective over the course of more than three thousand years. To be safe, it's drilled into every Scion's head from an early age to avoid anything that even remotely feels like a union with someone from an enemy House.

What about this? Because even looking at Leda makes me feels like I'm joined to her. Everything about this is so wrong. Knowing that does nothing to make me want it, or her, less.

I let myself touch her face. I run my thumb over her lower lip, remembering the hair that got stuck there when we were cleaning my mom's apartment. But this can't happen, so I let her go.

We walk a few more blocks with our hands shoved in our jacket pockets and our strides matched to the inaudible rhythm of New York, the one you feel thrumming up from the pavement that makes everyone in this city walk a little faster to meet it.

"The Furies are gone between us," she says.

"What?"

"You saved my life back there. Your blood debt with the House of Rome is cleared."

I'm so surprised I don't know what to say. "Is that what it takes? You have to save an enemy's life?" I ask.

She nods. "But I don't think that's going to matter very much in the next twenty-four hours."

She's right. Because the sun is coming up and soon a mother is going to walk into her daughter's room, find an empty bed, and a war will be declared.

32

DAPHNE

The sun is coming up.

"Anything?" I ask Adonis for the thousandth time. He glares at me in answer. "All right. Sorry," I say, acknowledging that I'm being annoying. I'm so tired.

"This was a long shot anyway," Ajax says. "I'll go see Tantalus. See if I can talk him out of retaliating."

"Talk about long shots," Adonis comments, looking as tired as I feel.

Ajax just needs to do something, anything, so he doesn't go mad with worry for Antigone. He's been threatening to go to his brother for half an hour now, and so far I've been able to keep him here with me. He doesn't believe in Antigone's vision, but I do. We should be on the *Argo*, sailing away from Tantalus. Yet, here we are. Somehow the mousetrap has kept us in New York. I haven't forgotten that, even if Ajax has. It's like none of this is really sinking in for him. I couldn't even get him to stay with Ladon tonight no matter how much I argued. He said he couldn't sit around and wait, and I buckled and let him come. I'm surprised he hasn't been hit by another dump truck yet. He disengages gravity, but I grab his arm before he can fly away.

"Wait," I say, my mind spinning with half-formed excuses. "Walking around hoping we'd get lucky *was* a long shot, but someone knows where Antigone is." I turn to Adonis. "Where's Corvus?"

He raises his brow. "Can't say for certain, but I know where he usually is."

Ajax nods decisively. "Okay. You two go to Roman territory and look for Corvus. I'm going to go to Tantalus and try to buy some time."

"You can't," I say, pulling him back down to earth.

"Daphne," he says, alighting and taking my face in his hands. "He won't hurt me." I make a disbelieving sound and Ajax continues. "Antigone's vision was of you witnessing him killing me, right?" I nod in response. "Then we know it's not going to happen now," he continues, "because you won't be there to see it."

He kisses me briefly in goodbye, but I hold onto him. "What you should do is go back to Ladon's cove," I say, trying to come up with anything to keep him away from his brother for as long as I can.

"I will. Right after I speak to Tantalus," he promises and then he gently disentangles himself. "If I don't at least try to stop him from starting the war, I'll never forgive myself." He flies away.

I stare after him until I feel Adonis touch my arm. "Let's go."

He calls Leda and updates her, and then he and I go uptown to the same building on 92nd Street that houses both the colosseum and Adonis' apartment. He reminds me to change my face when we're still a few blocks away so that I don't show up as myself on any of the security cameras the Romans have in the vicinity of their hub.

"Do you all live in the same building?" I ask.

"We all have apartments here and elsewhere," Adonis replies.

"Should we be warning your House to run?" I ask, and Adonis considers this with a grim expression.

"It would leave my sister and me unprotected," he decides. "Look, it sucks, because Corvus and Phaon betrayed all of us by doing this, but my sister and I can't run, and we can't face the Hundred Cousins alone."

In the end, Adonis chooses to tell everyone. We wake up a lot of Romans. No one seems to know where Corvus is, though everyone seems to have just seen him in the building recently. No one has seen Antigone or Phaon, either. We put everyone in his House on alert about what Corvus did and how Thebes is likely to retaliate. It takes us hours to question and notify everyone. I can't help but admire Adonis for doing this. He tries to act like he doesn't care about anything, but I'm starting to think he cares about *everything*. Every person he walks by on the street, and every window in every building soaring above our heads in Manhattan that are so easy for the rest of us to ignore, he feels a whole person there, someone with feelings and needs. It must be overwhelming.

"Are they going to leave town?" I ask after we've covered the building.

"Most will because it's the smart move. But you might be surprised. When my House isn't stabbing each other in the back, they can be weirdly loyal and idiotically brave."

I hope so, for his sake.

We move on to some of Corvus' favorite haunts, asking if anyone has seen him or someone who fits Antigone's description, grabbing breakfast and coffee as we go. It's past lunch by the time we give up, and at this point we're starting to look over our shoulders, expecting a Theban to attack at any moment.

Adonis yawns. "Let's go back to 92nd Street and check the spa," he says when we've run out of ideas.

After yet another fruitless search of the spa, the fight cages, and other various and somewhat shocking training and pampering areas that the Romans endure or enjoy depending on your perspective, Adonis and I sink down next to each other on a very comfy sofa in the reception area.

"I'm exhausted," Adonis says through another huge yawn. "Why is it I've gotten less sleep in the week since you arrived than I usually do in a day?"

"You could jump into one of those ice baths," I say, gesturing to the locker room we just left. "That'll wake you up quick."

"My life was perfect before you showed up, you know."

"It's not like this is my fault," I argue, insulted by his insinuation.

"It's *all* your fault," he complains dramatically. "Everything is your fault." He lets his head tip to the side and rest on my shoulder. "Why do you think I look like Hades?" he asks, out of the blue.

"I don't know," I reply. I think about it for a few moments. "He said the Fates want the Scions to replace the Olympians."

"And you think I'm supposed to replace Hades because I look like him?" he asks, hoping I'll gainsay this.

I run a finger over the golden cuff that encircles his wrist like a shackle, and I can't help but think that it's as if he's been unwittingly training to replace Hades his whole life. He knows the Underworld and how it works better than anyone alive. I can't imagine how horrible it would be to know you were fated to become the caretaker of that place, though.

"Thanks," he says bitterly, reading my heart and seeing the pity there.

"None of this is fair. We're just actors in some pointless cosmic cycle that's been on repeat since the beginning of time," I say, turning sideways on the couch to face him. "Look at my face. It's supposed to start a war. Why? Because it happened before. What kind of a reason is that? None of this makes any sense, but we don't have to go along with it. I've never done what I'm supposed to do, and I'll bet you haven't either."

He smiles at me, heartened. "Yeah, but I'll bet that's just what Oedipus's father thought," he adds quietly. "The Fates wait until you think you're in the clear, and *then* their prophecies bite you in the ass. What if they win, and get the Greek tragedy they've been trying to make out of our lives for thousands of years?"

I face front and settle down into the cushions next to him, our shoulders touching. "We're all going to end up in the Underworld someday, but at least you won't have to die first. You get to retire there, the head honcho, with a fabulous palace and lots of servants." I think about that for a second. "They'll probably be zombies," I add, "but we'll give them names like Ted and Burt and Earl."

He laughs and allows himself to relax. Both of us know the Underworld isn't like this at all. But joking about it helps.

"You know what would be cool about it, though?" he asks. I shake my head. "I'll be able to give people back to each other. You had an uncle who died, right?"

"Yeah," I reply, my voice catching a little. "My uncle Deuce."

"I could bring him back to life for you." His words hang

there, too stunning for me to reply. Then, he chuckles. "I wouldn't even make you sing to me first."

I chuckle with him because I know he's referring to Orpheus, but really, I'm trying not to cry. "Wise choice. I couldn't carry a tune in a bucket," I quip, but only to hide how overwhelmed I am.

"And if this war happens, and you ever need a place to hide, I've got a good one." His voice shakes a little. He holds up his cuff, reminding me of that cavern of his behind the submarine door. I wonder what's behind that door for everyone who doesn't have a key to the Underworld. I run a finger over the leaf design again. It really is beautiful. And so is the offer.

"Thanks," I say quietly.

We fall asleep and I dream of Morpheus, but it's only my spirit that's in his land, not my body. I can't hear him or feel him as I drift. All I can see is a dim eidolon of his face, shouting something I can't understand.

🜲 33 🜲
TANTALUS

Ajax wakes me at dawn.

He tells me that Antigone has been taken, but he won't tell me how one of the other Houses managed that, or even how he knows. His main objective in informing me seems to be asserting the innocence of Daedalus and Leda. Our enemies.

This is partially my fault. Letting him be with Daphne and allowing him to believe that there was some other way forward besides war was wrong of me. I've always known there was only one path that we could take. And now that our Oracle has been kidnapped, today is the day we start down that path.

I get out of bed. I pull on some clothes. I pick up the phone. Ajax keeps saying the word innocent over and over. He's got ahold of my wrist. He's trying to stop me from calling our father downstairs in his bunker and waking him. He knows that once I do, we go to war.

"They were betrayed by one of their own!" he pleads. "It was

Corvus, and some Athenian named Ion. Daedalus and Leda had no part in it. They've been out all night looking for Antigone."

He explains to me how Leda and Adonis have been using their ability to distinguish between the Furies to feel out where Antigone might be. I stare at him, trying to reconcile the man in front of me with the boy I knew—the boy I raised, practically. I was more of a father to him than ours ever was. Father never understood him the way I do, and now I'm starting to wonder if I ever did. Ajax has always argued for peace, but I thought he grasped what this was all about. I thought he knew the survival of our House had to come first, whether specific members of the other Houses were "innocent" of any aggression towards us or not.

"No one is innocent, Jax," I say when he's done. "That's what the Furies have been trying to tell you your whole life. We're all guilty, and every single one of us deserves to die."

He recoils from me. "Including Daphne?" he asks.

He watches me carefully, reading my expression. My heart is painted on my sleeve. *No*, my expression says, *not Daphne*.

I feel that I'm losing him and if I lose Ajax, I'll lose Daphne. I can't allow that to happen.

"War is fated. You know this, Jax. What you're forgetting is that it's just the first step." I grab him by the back of the neck and bring his eyes closer to mine. "We will replace the gods, and we will be *better* at it than they were. This is the Fates' plan. Uranus was replaced by Cronus, who was replaced by Zeus, who will be replaced by us. Every cycle the ultimate beings have come closer to earth and have had more compassion for the human condition. We Scions are the final cycle. We are the mortals who will become gods."

He moves away from me. "I don't want to be a god."

"Why not? You'd make a better Apollo than he did. The so-called god of truth and beauty raped half of Greece." He's still not getting it. "This is our real fate. Not war. Our fate is to become the kind of gods that humans need. Not vengeful punishers who use mortals for amusement, but gods who help them. Gods who actually *answer* their prayers. Our fate is to make the world the paradise it could be."

I nearly have him. He wants to believe in me, but more importantly he wants to believe in this future that I'm offering, because he's a good person and he wants to help other people.

"Only if we destroy most of it first," he replies bitterly.

I shake my head, disappointed he still won't let himself believe. "It won't be like that."

He takes a step closer toward the window. "You don't know what it will be like."

"I will," I say. "As soon as I get the Oracle back."

"The Oracle? She used to be Antigone to you." He keeps moving away from me. "You're going to get our whole family killed," he says, and then he flies out the window.

He might be right about that, but I can't let it stop me. I can't, in fact, stop it even if I tried. It's all in the hands of the Moirai now. I go downstairs and give my father the news. He is properly pious about it, assuming the mantle of the Hand of Fate as is right for the House of the Oracle, but behind that I can feel his impatience. His battle lust rising. This is what he's been waiting for his whole life. There's only one thing that spoils the moment for him.

"We need to secure the Oracle," he says. "She must be with us before we attack."

"Yes," I agree. "As long as Bellerophon has her, he has the upper hand. We can't risk an all-out assault until she's home."

"I should call your aunt," he says as an afterthought, though he obviously doesn't relish the thought of telling his sister that her daughter is missing.

I leave him to it, then I go and wake Castor and Pallas. They don't even consider that the war is starting. The only thing that concerns them is getting Antigone back.

"Can you reach out to Leda?" I ask Castor.

He throws himself out of bed and starts pulling on clothes to go meet her without giving it another thought. "She'll help us. I know she will," Castor replies, as he tucks a sheathed Bowie knife into the back of his jeans.

"I'm coming with you," Pallas says, already standing.

"No. I need you to help me gather the Hundred," I tell him. They both pause to stare at me. I rarely ever split them up like this because they are much faster as a team, but in this case, speed is not my main objective. I need Castor to set a trap for Rome. Though he won't know it.

"Castor can't go alone," Pallas argues.

"He'll be fine," I say. "Leda won't let anything happen to him. She has feelings for him." Castor stops and turns to gauge my expression. He looks guilty. I think he *did* sleep with her, but I'm not going to push the point right now. "You're with me today, Pallas. Most of the family is out of town, and we're calling in everyone."

They both accept their orders without further question, though it is dangerous for Castor despite what I said. But if I don't separate them, they might find a way to return Antigone peacefully and with no bloodshed. Alone it will take Castor longer, giving me more time to get the Hundred Cousins into position. He will be on alert, too, less confident without Pallas watching his back. Easy prey for his hair-trigger reflexes to take over when I maneuver it so that someone from the House of Thebes kills someone from the House of Rome. Then, the Furies will take care of the rest. With a fresh kill reigniting the vendetta between Thebes and Rome, Castor will kill Leda where she stands whether he wants to or not. And she won't see it coming, because he won't.

She's not a Falsefinder like I am, but I know how she works. How she relies on her ability to sense honesty, and I know how to manipulate that strength to turn it into a weakness. The only way to entrap someone who can feel lies, is to tell the truth.

34

ADONIS

I'm having a lovely dream until Morpheus chucks a neon walrus into it. *No way to sleep through that* I think as the giant, impossibly colored mammal goes soaring through my brain.

I wonder why Morpheus would be trying to wake me up. Usually, he enjoys my company, and we have a lovely time painting pictures with my mind. He must be really anxious about something to make me dream of a neon walrus.

That's a *bad* thing, I decide, and I shake myself awake.

Daphne is lying on top of my chest, wrapped around me in an exceptionally comfortable way, and I'm tempted, just for a millisecond, to let her keep sleeping and pretend she's mine. But I don't because that would be creepy.

"Hey," I say, shaking her lightly.

She's momentarily startled, but she orients herself quickly and with only a modicum of embarrassment for having mistaken me for Ajax. Apparently, I smell like him and I know why. One of the gifts of Aphrodite is that her offspring's scent alters with each person, so that they smell like the thing that turns their partner on the most. Which for her is Ajax. Which for me is heartbreaking. But I've got bigger problems than my disappointed body and soul right now. I can hear a familiar voice coming down the hall. It's Corvus. I yank Daphne up and shoo her behind the bar.

"I'm about to lose you, I'm going into the spa," Corvus shouts down his cellphone. He's stopped on the other side of the spa entrance so he can finish his conversation.

"It's Corvus," I whisper.

"Why are we hiding?" she whispers back. She wants to jump out and fight him and blow this chance to possibly overhear where they're keeping Antigone.

Well, I can't blame her for not being as good at spying as I am, but even if she didn't grow up in a House full of backstabbing sneaks, doesn't she know that when you're given the opportunity to overhear any conversation your family doesn't know you're privy to, you should find something to hide behind and listen? I don't have time to explain any of that, so I just clamp a hand over her mouth and wrestle her down next to me.

"Of course I'm training. I'll be ready for the fight," Corvus continues, stopped halfway through the door, "and if Thebes and Athens don't show, then they forfeit, and Lincoln Center is ours. Why do you think I had you kidnap the girl in the first place?"

"Phaon," I whisper, to let her know who Corvus is speaking to if she's not following the context clues. She rolls her eyes at me, so I guess she is.

Corvus ends his conversation and pushes the rest of the way through the doors. I keep Daphne down, even though yet again she tries to spring up and rip Corvus' face off. There's a better way to do this.

"What the hell?" she demands when I finally let go of her

mouth.

"He just spoke to Phaon, which means he knows where they're keeping Antigone. We need to get that information out of him."

"Oh, I'll get it out of him," she says. I reach out and grab her by the back of the shirt before she goes barreling after him and reel her back to me.

"He's going to go into the bath. Disarm. Disrobe. Don't you think that's the best time to interrogate him?" I pause dramatically, letting a few moments pass while she tries not to scream at me. "Aaaaand now we should follow him," I say, drawing out the words.

She shakes her head at me as she turns to go like she's annoyed, but I know she's enjoying my little show. At least I amuse her.

When we enter the baths Corvus has undressed, as intended, but is not intimidated by me and my companion. Though, to be fair, he doesn't know who she is. She's wearing the face of the mortal girl who I suppose everyone assumes is my girlfriend. Would that she was that and more. I want to be with her every day and every night. I want children with her. A pack of lightning-throwing, heart-manipulating wiseasses that we call our own, though that would certainly unite our Houses, violate the truce with the gods, and bring everyone one step closer to the shitting in a bucket scenario I can't allow.

And it just occurred to me that I don't know what I want anymore. I'm not used to that because usually my problem is that I can have anything and anyone I want, which makes me not want it or them anymore.

Now I know exactly who and what I want, and I shouldn't want either. It's official. Daphne has ruined my life.

"Cousin!" Corvus shouts happily from the Jacuzzi. "I hear you've been looking for me."

"You and Antigone," I reply, strolling up to the side of Corvus' bath. I dip a finger into the Jacuzzi and suck in a quick breath, like I burned myself. "Seems like you've gotten yourself into some hot water."

Corvus looks at Daphne. "He's cute, right?" he asks her, trying to use his influence to sway her heart in his direction.

I block him, and I'm not nice about it. He glares at me, feeling the fear and discomfort of knowing I hold his emotions in my proverbial hand. I smile back.

"It almost makes up for his stupid jokes," he finishes.

"Where's the Oracle?" Daphne asks oh so quietly. She walks to his clothes and starts rifling through them. She takes out his cellphone and presses some buttons.

"You can dig through that all you want, you'll just see numbers with no names." He taps his temple. "I keep it all up here."

Daphne looks up at him. Her eyes crackle with lightning. "Good. I'm much better at digging through skulls."

Corvus freezes, and well he should.

"If you kill him the Furies will set us against each other," I warn, because right now I don't trust that she wouldn't kill him without a verbal reminder.

She nods once but doesn't look at me. "I don't have to kill him," she says, every feature on her face immobile. I don't even know how she's accomplishing speech to be honest. She's gone as still as a tiger in the brush.

I believe Daphne is a good person. The truth is most people are good because they aren't capable of doing anything all that bad. I believe Daphne is a good person because she *is* capable of doing absolutely terrible things, and so far, has chosen not to. But that doesn't mean she always will. Ajax's warning about what might become of Daphne if he were to die comes back to me.

"Who are you?" Corvus asks her.

"I'm the girl you're going to tell everything she wants to know," Daphne replies, taking silent steps toward him. It's very clear to both Corvus and myself that she is the one in charge here.

He waves an arm magnanimously, feigning nonchalance, though I can see his insides shaking like Jell-O. "Ask away."

"Where's Antigone?"

"No idea."

Daphne holds up a glowing hand. "Ever touch your tongue to a battery?" she asks. "Because this is going to hurt much worse."

Corvus is out of the water in a moment, but he doesn't get far. Daphne is fast. She has him on his knees in front of her, her hands wrapped around his throat. She's choking him, thank gods, and not electrocuting him because I don't think I could handle the blood-curdling screams of agony.

"Dearest?" I say, tapping her on the shoulder. "He can't answer you when you have your thumbs stuck in his windpipe like that. If you could just... there you go," I say as she loosens her grip a bit. "Sorry, Corvus, but this isn't going to pan out the way you want it to. Look into her heart. What do you see?"

He looks and nods. He sees murder, just like I do.

"She'll kill you if you don't tell her. It's that simple."

"Antigone is on a rooftop," he gasps. He lets go of her wrists long enough to hold up his hands in a surrendering gesture. "I don't know which one. All I know is that it's on a very high rooftop somewhere in Athenian territory. So high up that if even *you* were walking right below..."

"...even I would still be too far away to feel the Furies," I finish for him through a sigh. "All that walking around last night and all I had to do was look up. Very clever."

"It was Bellerophon's idea," Corvus says, and he's not lying.

"Surprising," I reply. "You can let him go," I say to Daphne, who gives me a disbelieving look. "He's not hiding anything," I tell her. "He's told us all he knows."

Daphne releases him and then wipes her hands on her jeans as if they've been soiled by touching him. Corvus stands clumsily and gets a towel to wrap around himself, and then he takes a seat on one of the teak benches to catch his breath.

"What does it matter, anyway?" he asks. "You're too late. The war has started."

"The difference is that we're going to get Antigone away from that twisted little psychopath, Phaon," Daphne replies.

Corvus laughs. "He's had her for almost a full day. So, yeah. You're too late."

It's as if Daphne's arm shoots out of its own accord. She punches down on him so hard she pile-drives him into the teak bench beneath him and it *breaks*.

Corvus lays in the splintered planks and doesn't move. No, no, no. I look up at her. Please, no.

She's staring at Corvus, a hand to her mouth. Then she looks back at me, pleading.

"I didn't mean to... is he dead?" she asks, her fake face dissolving into her real one and her voice high and young with regret.

I love her so much. I couldn't bear to hate her. I can control the Furies, but only up to a point. If there's a fresh kill, I will attack her. She'd destroy me, I have no doubt about it, but that's okay. I'd rather die than hurt her.

I wait, but nothing. No Furies. I look at Corvus' chest and see movement. "His heart's still beating," I say, clasping mine. "Don't ever scare me like that again."

She breathes a relieved laugh, coming towards me with a smile. Then she throws her arms around me in a fierce hug. I'm shocked momentarily; then I allow myself to really hold her. But only for a second.

The hug didn't mean to her what it meant to me. She goes and stands over Corvus' awkwardly sprawled body, tilting her head. "What are we going to do with him?"

"Nothing. He'll be fine," I reply. "We need to get downtown pronto."

"Where, exactly? I'm not sure if you've noticed, but there are a lot of tall buildings downtown. How are we going to check on top of all of them?"

"Easy. We just need to fly by her location close enough and I'll feel her."

"Well, Ajax isn't here, and I can't fly. Can you?" Daphne asks.

I take her shoulders and spin her around, then gently push her into a walk ahead of me.

"They're called helicopters, darling, and I happen to own one." I say it close to her ear, knowing it will send a pleasant shiver down her spine.

"We'll aren't you Mr. Bigshot," she says in a way that makes my heart skip around like a schoolgirl, even though she's not flirting with me. She's just joking around. The difference is intent, and I can clearly see that her playfulness is not romantically moti-vated. She's simply enjoying our camaraderie. It occurs to me that I've become special to her because she doesn't have any other friends.

And how could she? Everyone wants something from her. Including me. I'm just better at hiding it.

35

ION

I've been in this form for too long. I don't like being human, and when I am, I especially don't like being in this pretty package my father insists on. This skin sits so tightly on the body and the clothes are stiff and confining. I'd much rather be in fur. I keep sliding my edges along rough surfaces, like a snake trying to shed its skin.

Human forms are made to do many things. They can run, crouch, jump, climb, swim, even burrow if they have to. There are not many animal forms that can do all the things that a human body does, but being generalists means that humans do nothing very well in specific. A horse is made for running, but it cannot climb a tree. A shark is made for swimming, but it cannot scratch its own tail. Yet even though they are limited, those forms know what they are for. The human body is not meant for *one* thing, and because of that it does not know what it is for. Maybe that is why when I am human, I find it harder to remember what I am for. And I do not like this feeling.

My father orders us to watch the Oracle until she makes a prophecy about who will win the war. Antigone tried to tell him that she cannot control when the Fates will speak through her, and my father replied, *then what good are you?* He does not know what she is for, and he doesn't like that. My father is like me in this. Everything should know what it is for.

He ordered me, Doris, and Phaon to stay with her before storming away. The fact that he can't immediately have the prophecy he was expecting has left my father quite distracted, and I'm wondering if he's forgotten about us up here. There is a lot on his mind at the moment. Those trapped in human form often have to think about things like the future, which is why they value Oracles and prophecies so much in first place.

I do not wonder about the future. Someday we will all die. That is what we are for.

I cannot disobey my father, but I will not be able to endure this much longer. Three times I've gone to take my pants off, and Doris has shaken her head at me in warning. My father does not wish for Phaon to know of my abilities, so I must not change my form, but it's been nearly a whole *day*. How do regular humans stand it?

"Can you make him sit?" Phaon snaps at Doris.

"Can I make you shut up?" she replies. It silences him, but only for a moment.

"Is someone bringing us dinner soon?" Phaon whines.

"Any minute now," Doris mumbles, gazing off into the distance.

She's watching the sun lower. When it's down I wish I could turn into a bat or an owl and fly out into the darkness. Doris looks like she wishes the same.

We have been hiding on a rooftop in our territory for hours. I suppose a human would consider this patio garden quite nice and hospitable. It is well furnished with padded outdoor chairs that are striped blue and white like the colors of Greece. Large, canvas umbrellas are deployed to shield us from the sun. Though it is not summer, they do keep some of the breeze off. I am not cold, but I believe that Antigone has been quite uncomfortable. Doris gave her a jacket to wear, but the girl wears only a nightgown underneath that. We did steal her in the middle of the night, after all.

Unable to keep his mouth closed for more than three minutes at a time, Phaon gets up and crosses over to Antigone where she is sitting on the floor in front of her chair. She is rocking back and forth, holding herself.

"I told you not to bother her," Doris shouts to him.

Several times now Doris has had to intervene. Phaon seems to be doing something to Antigone, either with the quiet words he has been whispering to her or by using his Roman talent to influence hearts, or possibly both. Doris has told him repeatedly to stop, and once she came close to striking him. I think, when we are done with this business, that she will kill him.

I think Antigone would like that.

Whenever she looks at him, her face twists as if she were looking at something vile. He enjoys her discomfort, too. I've seen him smile while watching her crying softly to herself.

The door to our rooftop garden opens and we all turn to see who comes. It is a girl named Cassiopeia who I am told is my half-sister. I do not know her except to recognize her. She looks a bit younger than Antigone. Or maybe she looks the same age? I'm not certain because sometimes it is hard to tell with humans. She must be about thirteen or fourteen years old based on when I was informed of her birth, and she is carrying two large brown paper bags that smell strongly of food.

"Who is *this*?" Phaon asks. His eyes spark with interest and Cassiopeia blushes.

Doris groans and gets to her feet. "Why would they send *you*?" she asks Cassiopeia.

She stammers and tucks her long, black hair behind an ear. "My father tried to send Ocean out to get the food, but Ocean said his arm still hurt from when Daedalus broke it against the wall."

That's another thing distracting my father. It appears Daedalus was seen in Athenian territory last night with Leda, the Head of the House of Rome. He attacked some young members of our House and gave Leda his protection. My father was not happy about that at all. Phaon believes that Daedalus and Leda were working together to try to find us, and bring the Oracle back to Thebes before she was discovered to be missing. But if they were trying to do that against my father's wishes, they did not succeed. Thebes has no doubt declared war already.

Doris curses. "I'll make Ocean's arm hurt. Go on, get out of here," she tells Cassiopeia.

"Let her stay," Phaon says, sliding closer to her.

"Is she okay?" Cassiopeia says, looking across the rooftop at Antigone.

"She's been kidnapped. Of course she's not okay," Doris replies with her usual plainspokenness.

"Maybe I can make her feel better, if I stay and talk to her?" Cassiopeia asks.

She looks genuinely worried about Antigone, which is something I've noticed in several warm-blooded species. They tend to empathize most with those in their immediate age groups, although I don't understand why. Empathy belongs between a parent and a child who imprinted on each other. Peers will not ensure the survival of your line.

"Aren't you a sweet young thing?" Phaon says. I think he's giving Cassiopeia a compliment, but Doris still doesn't like it. Also, he called her "young", but I don't think Phaon is that much older than she is. He can't be older than Daedalus, although that is a full ten years older than Cassiopeia, at least. Among teenaged humans that is too many years to be mates, I suppose.

Doris seems to weigh several options in her mind, and finally says, "All right. Try to get her to talk to you. If we get even one little glimpse into the future out of this, it might make it all worth it."

I don't know what she means by that. This must be worth it already because it is what my father wants.

Cassiopeia brings food over to Antigone. She sits down next to her even after Antigone shakes her head in refusal. She has taken no food since we stole her, and she will weaken if she continues on like this.

Cassiopeia does not sit too close. She gives Antigone space, and mirrors the other girl's posture, with her knees pulled up to her chest and her arms wrapped around them. Humans do this a lot. They copy one another's bodies and faces when they are trying to understand them. They don't even notice they are doing it most of the time.

I know why they do it. The forms we take make us feel what it is to be that thing. To understand a leopard, become a leopard. To understand Antigone, Cassiopeia is trying to become her. But she can't. This is why humans will never really understand each other. It occurs to me that maybe this is another reason humans poke and prod at each other so much. Why they always want what the other has. They cannot become the other, so they jostle and shake each other, trying to understand what it is that makes the other what they are, like they would with an unknown object in a black box they will never be able to open.

Antigone refuses to speak to Cassiopeia at first. She just sits there, limp, as Cassiopeia tries to talk her into eating something.

"You know, you could have told my dad anything and he'd have believed you. It's not like he knows what he's talking about."

"That would have been lying," Antigone says.

Cassiopeia looks at her incredulously. "And you never lie?"

"Even if I lied your father would have believed it to be the truth, and sometimes people make things true when they believe in them hard enough."

Cassiopeia is silent for a while. "Gods, I hope you're right," she says fervently. "Maybe I'll grow some boobs."

Antigone finds humor in that, before falling silent again. When suddenly, a convulsive shiver racks her body. *"You won't have the chance,"* she says, but her voice is strange.

Cassiopeia jumps back from her, crab walking on her hands and heels to move away.

"You will die before the war is over. And so will she," Antigone continues, pointing at Doris, *"and so will he,"* she finishes, pointing at me.

Doris is rushing to Cassiopeia now, and I suppose I am too. Doris gets to her first and so I stand over the Oracle, amazed by what I see. At first, I think that she can shape-shift like I can, but then I see that her body is not changing, but that there are shapes that are pushing against her skin from the inside. I look closer and realize that they are hands and faces. It's as if the girl were nothing but a thin membrane between this world and another, and three old women were trying to break *through* the fragile skin of Antigone to get here. It looks very painful.

Cassiopeia is screaming. Antigone is screaming. Phaon is shouting, too, but he looks happy.

"Everyone here from House of Athens will die during the war, but I will *live*! That means House of Rome wins!" he's saying triumphantly, taunting Doris.

I don't like all the noise. I cover my ears.

❧ 36 ❧

TANTALUS

It's late in the day by the time all of the Hundred Cousins are assembled. It's better this way. Staging an assault during the day makes us vulnerable to human detection. Most Scion battles take place at night for this reason.

My father is leading the lion's share of our warriors downtown to Athenian territory, and I am bringing the rest uptown to Roman territory in a dual-pronged attack.

My father has always had a special hatred for Bellerophon. Maybe because they're the same age, or maybe because they are both responsible for killing the other's father during the last House war twenty years ago. Or maybe they just don't like each other. Whatever it is, their dislike is both virulent and mutual, and I have no problem with letting him take the harder fight. He is Head of our House, and the honor should be his anyway, but I doubt he will be successful tonight. I don't think my father is in danger, I just don't believe he will completely defeat the House of Athens in this first salvo.

I will succeed, though. Castor's description of the building on 92nd Street with its hospital, coliseum, and spa, leads me to believe that it's their forum. Romans just can't resist building town centers for themselves and taking residences around it. If I can capture the building, by dawn I will be able to claim their territory as ours. They shouldn't put up too big of a fight, either. Romans prefer to negotiate, and if that means giving ground first and then bargaining later, so be it. Most of them have probably run away by now, anyway, though I hope not all. I still need one.

Pallas stands next to me as we wait for our car to come to the front door. He doesn't fidget or glance at me. He's been in enough fights now to know how to handle his nerves.

"We're not going up there to take prisoners," I say as the car pulls around.

"I know," he replies and follows me outside. I'm happy to hear that his voice is even and without resentment.

We get into the second car of three that stop in front of our brownstone. Our motorcade makes its slow way through rush hour traffic. We could get there a thousand times faster on foot, but the cars are necessary in case there are injured. We have Artemis, one of our few precious Healers, coming uptown with us. My father took Ceyx because he is the strongest Healer. If Bellerophon fights back instead of retreating into the water, as I suspect he will, there will be more casualties on that front than this one. Still, we need the cars so our Healers can work on any potentially injured members in privacy. We can't expose ourselves on the streets, but cars are a hassle and we'd be faster on foot. Pallas' leg starts bouncing before we're past 10th Street. He's anxious without Castor.

"Did Caz call you before we left?" he asks, as if my thinking of Castor has brought him to Pallas' mind.

I've always wondered about that. There is no god with the gift of telepathy, except maybe Morpheus who can both see and shape our dreams. Regardless, no Scion has ever had the ability to hear another's thoughts. Even what I do as a Falsefinder does not entail reading someone's mind. I hear a jarring, off-key sound in someone's voice when they lie, but I don't hear their thoughts. Yet, how is it my brothers and I often think the same things at the same time?

"He did. No luck," I reply.

This war was always going to happen, but I don't say that because then why would I have sent Castor to recover Antigone? It won't be beneficial for either of them to ever know that I've set Castor up as an unwitting mole. Especially if I need to set him up like this again.

The only problem with my plan could be Daedalus. Castor told me that he was with him and Leda, searching, though I have no idea why. I don't think he'll get in the way though. It benefits Athens to get rid of Leda.

"Did you call off the search?" Pallas asks.

"Of course not," I reply. "Even if it's too late to stop this, we can't just leave Antigone with her kidnappers."

"We're going to get her back." He looks out the window at the buildings as they crawl by, determination on his face at last.

His thoughts have returned to why we are fighting, which is what I intended. I want him focused on Antigone not as the Oracle, but as our little cousin. He and Castor will need emotional justifications for what's to come. I don't want to break them completely. I love that my brothers are so honorable, and I want to keep them the heroes they should be all the way through to the end of this war, but it does require extra effort on my part.

We arrive at the building on 92nd Street and the foot soldiers exit the cars simultaneously, leaving the three drivers to circle the block with the Healer, playing a shell game that keeps her protected and at the ready. I look up at the building. Night has fallen, yet all the lights are off. The windows are completely dark.

In truth, there could be dozens of Romans in there and we wouldn't know it until they'd hit us. We Scions have grown so accustomed to finding each other by using the Furies that Rome has been able to exploit their shielding abilities to our detriment. A Roman is the only Scion who can sneak up on another and stab him in the back. Luckily not all of them have the ability, but it's a safe bet that anyone left in this building tonight will be able to.

I nod at one of the Hundred Cousins and he kicks in the front door. My team sweeps into the building with our swords drawn. "Watch your corners," I remind them.

The downstairs is configured as Castor described, and I send four Cousins into the *Valetudinaria* and keep the rest with me to check the spa. We don't go far before we find two Romans in the bath. One is unconscious and lying nearly naked among the planks of a broken bench and the other, fully-clothed younger one is trying to revive him. One of them must be able to control the Furies because while I feel them, I'm not overwhelmed.

"It's Corvus," Pallas says, indicating the injured Roman, and I remember that he's had dealings with Corvus in the past. I myself don't recognize him. "Castor said he believed Leda when she told him that it was Corvus who arranged the kidnapping."

"Get Artemis," I order. I turn to the younger Roman. "And who are you?"

"Pyramus," he says, his voice cracking. He's just a kid.

A small group of us waits for Artemis to revive Corvus while I send the rest of the soldiers out to scour the building. When

Corvus is awake the Furies flash in all of us as he momentarily panics and his power falters.

"Please, wait," he says, warding me off as if we are about to kill him where he sits. The Furies lessen to an unintelligible whisper as he gets control. "I know where your Oracle is. I can take you to her."

I nod, though my teeth are on edge from the sound of his lie. "Corvus. You were the Roman who was supposed to fight for Lincoln Center?"

"I am," he admits.

I look him over. "Is he recovered?" I ask my Healer.

"He is," Artemis replies.

"Good. Arm yourself, Corvus." I stand.

Pallas puts a hand on my shoulder. "Ask him about Antigone," he says.

I shake my head. "He lied. He doesn't know where she is."

We both look down at Corvus, who is pulling the towel tighter around himself as if it could offer him some protection. He shrinks, falling into a hole of fear that's opening up inside him.

"You're the Falsefinder," he says, realizing his error.

"And this is my brother Pallas. You will face him in your coliseum and fight for Lincoln Center. And the rest of the territory belonging to Atreus and Rome. Or you can die now." I lift my sword, pointing the tip at his bare neck.

He raises his hands. "Even if I fight him, you won't get the rest of my House to agree to that. I don't have the authority to hand over Roman territory to you if I lose."

I look around pointedly. "I don't see anyone here to refute it. Now get up."

"You've chosen a champion. I have every right to choose one for myself."

He does. It's something I can't dispute. To do so would lessen me in the eyes of my soldiers. "There is no one here but you," I say.

Corvus grins. "Pyramus will fight in my stead."

A blank, frightened look freezes the boy's features.

"How old are you, boy?" I ask him.

"Fourteen," he squeaks.

"He's too young," Pallas says, shaking his head.

"He is whole and I am injured. Far fairer that he fights," Corvus says as he takes up some clothes. I can feel his cowardice like it's my own. It really is remarkable how the Romans can do that. How they can seed their feelings inside of you and make them bloom.

I do feel pity for him though as I watch him dress, and I wonder if I'm being unfair. I'm forcing this terrible situation on him after finding him unarmed. Helpless. It's not like he meant me any harm. I should reconsider—

I walk over to him and hit him in the face. My pity evaporates instantly, replaced by disgust for what he just did to me. "Do that again and I'll kill you," I tell him as he reels, clutching his mouth.

"You broke my jaw!" he shouts with garbled speech.

Now I understand why Romans usually stick to merely influencing others, rather than trying to twist them completely like Corvus just tried to do with me. If they fail, the result is the opposite of what they intended and they only make things worse for themselves. Now I want him dead, and I don't care how it happens. It's become personal, whereas before his death was just an unfortunate necessity.

The look Corvus gives me is strangely detached. Like he got

caught doing something regrettable, but no more than that. If he feels pain, he knows how to live with it. If he feels fear, he knows how to shut it off. All the emotions I read in him up to this point were a show.

I raise my fist to hit him again but then I hear a strange, digital song. Corvus perks up. "Wait! That's Phaon." The digital song sings again from a pile of clothes on another bench. "He's with Antigone."

"Find out where she is," Pallas says. He holds out his hand for the nearest soldier to throw him the ringing cellphone and catches it as it sails through the air. By the third ring he's handing it to Corvus.

"Yes," he says into the black, glowing instrument. "Okay. That's great. I'll come to you. Where are you? I know you're on a rooftop. Where? What building?" He listens and then says, "I'll tell you later." He lowers the phone and presses a button under the small green window.

"Where is she?" Pallas asks.

"It's so hard to talk with this jaw," he says.

I grab his wrist and twist his hand backwards. I don't break it, but it does hurt so much that Corvus' torso curves around to alleviate the strain on his tendons. He shouts out the address. It's a building downtown in Athenian territory. Almost at the very tip of Manhattan. He isn't lying.

"Good," I say, letting go of his wrist. "Let's go." I wave a hand toward the coliseum.

Corvus frowns. "I gave you want you wanted," he says.

I look at him, pretending to be puzzled. "The fight is for your territory, not the location of my cousin, although I'm glad you did the right thing and told us." I lean close to him. "You're still going to fight, Corvus."

"I have chosen my champion."

"I can't beat him." Pyramus says, touching Corvus' arm, but Corvus shrugs him off.

I push them both in front of me toward the coliseum, barely restraining myself from beating him further. Pallas falls in beside me silently. I can tell he feels this is wrong, but he says nothing.

The boy takes up a gladiolus and goes out onto the sand. He looks like he's sleepwalking.

I pull Pallas aside before he enters the ring. "Remember what I said earlier?" Pallas is momentarily confused, then his eyes widen with surprise when he understands my meaning. He almost argues with me. "We're not here to take prisoners," I repeat.

He stares at me. He doesn't like my decision, but he won't disobey me. I clap him on the shoulder and leave him. I jump over the railing that separates the arena from the stands and take a place next to Corvus.

Pallas presents himself to Pyramus and both of them turn to the audience, raising their swords. They don't say, "We who are about to die salute you," as the ancient Romans insisted their gladiators did, but they do pause for a moment. To this day it's part of every fighter's ritual to salute the crowd before a fight. Even modern-day boxers do it, though they don't know why.

"Begin," I say.

They square off and start to circle, taking each other's measure. Pallas steps in and initiates the first exchange. He's faster, stronger, better trained. The boy can barely keep up.

Pallas looks at me as he circles back around. I shake my head at him and he stays fixed on his objective. He goes back in for another exchange and this time he draws blood.

Pallas looks at me again after having drawn first blood, and I gesture with my head to continue. Pallas' mouth tightens in displeasure, but he goes on the attack and injures Pyramus again. In the leg this time. He can't make himself kill him, but injuring the kid is only going to prolong the torture.

"Don't take too long," I call out to Pallas.

"Blood has been drawn," Corvus says, like that's the end of it. When I don't reply Corvus begins to understand.

"If you kill him, the Furies will overtake us. I won't be able to stop them," Corvus says, frightened now.

"Finish him," I order Pallas.

"I surrender!" Pyramus shouts.

Pallas replies by going in for the death blow, like he's had enough of this. Pyramus parries just in time, and I see shock on his face.

"You can't kill him! He surrendered!" Corvus shouts at me. Like rules still apply.

"Your House started this war. You *should* die first," Pallas says, breaking his silence. He glances at me, and I nod. He steps forward and puts his sword through Pyramus' chest.

Pallas is no coward. He does not turn away from the sight of death. He watches grimly as the boy falls to his knees in front of him and collapses into the sand.

"You think you know what the Furies feel like? Wait 'till you feel a fresh kill. Rome will tear Thebes apart for this!" Corvus cries.

I see Pallas' face contort with remorse as he stumbles back away from the pair, stricken. I am paralyzed with pity. We all are.

And then Corvus disappears.

We stand stock still, unable to process what we have seen. Pallas takes a few stumbling steps forward. He turns in a circle. "Where is he?" he says, as if awaking.

I feel life come back into my grief-numbed legs and jump over the railing to join him. I go to the spot next to Pyramus' body where Corvus was last seen and begin kicking at the sand. He's got to be here somewhere. No one can just disappear.

"Trap door!" Pallas shouts, spotting something. There is a faint seam in the shape of square beneath his feet.

"Find a way to open it!" I call out to my soldiers.

They hurry in several directions at once, but I know it's too late. If this coliseum is anything like the real one in Rome, Corvus has already made his escape through one of the many passageways that honeycomb the area beneath the sands. I don't feel the Furies, which means Corvus is far away from here. I wonder how long we stood frozen, trapped in the emotions he forced on us while he ran for it.

Pallas is staring at Pyramus. He looks up at me from the boy's body, his mind putting together pieces that the hectic pace of today had kept him from seeing altogether. Until now.

"Castor," he says, looking right at me. Remembering that Castor is with Leda right now and that the Furies will overtake them.

And I can't tell if he knows I did it on purpose or not.

37

DAEDALUS

By nightfall, I've hit my limit on the amount of time I can spend with Castor Delos.

I mean, sure, I feel bad for him. He's obviously beside himself with worry for his cousin and it doesn't help that Leda freaked out about the fact that Phaon is the one who took Antigone. Leda tried to be calm about it, but in the end, she felt she had to be honest with Castor and let him know that she suspects Phaon is a child molester. I really wish she hadn't. It's not like knowing that was going to help us find her any quicker.

I get that he's worried, I would be too, but I told Castor ten times already that Doris would never hurt a little girl, and she sure as shit wouldn't leave one alone with a pedophile. He doesn't seem to believe me. It's insulting, actually. Not every Athenian is a bottom-feeder. And it's not like Thebes has the corner on honor and justice. We've circled back up to Tribeca at this point. I'm so tired and hungry I want to hurt someone.

"We should keep going west," I say, turning my body in that

direction. "We were distracted the last time we swept this area. We might have missed something." I think of our run-in with Ocean and Boreas.

Nobody argues with me, surprisingly. We set out in that direction, avoiding Jay Street this time, and taking Duane Street instead. We're nearly at the water, and I'm between the two of them when it happens. It's dumb luck, really, because it's like a bomb going off inside of both of them. One second, we're walking down the street and the next second Leda is trying to claw her way through me to get to Castor.

"What the—" I push her off of me while she screams unintelligibly.

And Castor comes barreling into me, trying to get to Leda. I shove her as far away as I can, sending her sailing, and Castor hits me, knocking me into the street.

Bright lights stun my eyes. I hear car horns honking and brakes screeching and then Castor is on me. Punches and kicks and we're going at it right there in the middle of West Street. I'm still trying to figure out what's going on, but I can tell it's not really me he's after. He's not in his right mind right now, and all he knows is that I'm between him and Leda.

Leda comes running back to us, insane with rage, and I finally get it. Someone in Thebes must have killed someone in the House of Rome, or vice-versa. They're both like animals right now and I'm the only thing stopping them.

"Leda! You have to run!" I howl at her, but it's no use. She can't hear anything but the Furies. Neither can Castor.

Leda's going to die if I don't get them apart. Scion strength or no, she's not a match for Castor.

I rush Castor, taking him to the ground, and Leda jumps on top of us. She's snapping with her teeth like a rabid dog and tearing at us both with her nails. I don't have a choice. I hit her. Hard. It knocks her out. Then I just have Castor to deal with, and he's enough.

He pulls a Bowie knife out of a calf sheath, and *damn* he's good with it. Lucky for me he's going for her. I stop his forearms with my own repeatedly. I'm a little faster, at least, and I manage to block, but there's no way I'm getting that knife away from him. He's too skilled, too quick with his exchanges from hand to hand. I get my leather jacket off in time to use it to wrap up the blade just long enough so I can get behind him. Then I slip an arm around his windpipe and try to choke him out.

Castor throws a devastating elbow into my solar plexus, and I know I'm not going to be able to take another one of those. The only thing I can do is get him in the water. That's the only way I can save Leda.

I strong-arm him off the ground and run for the Hudson. If it weren't just one block away, I'd never make it, but I manage to get there before he shakes loose. I chuck us both off the pier and into the water.

I'm in my element now. I can overpower him and drag him down with me. I hook an arm across his chest, and I swim with him underwater as fast I can uptown. I feel him stop fighting me and I know that there's enough distance between he and Leda that he's not under the Furies' control anymore. But now we're far enough away from Leda that the Furies rise between Castor and me.

I swim us both to the surface and he lunges for me, reaching like he wants to strangle me, and it takes everything I've got to swim away from him. I dive down beneath the surface, and he follows.

He's a really good swimmer, gods-gifted even, and I'm

wondering *how*, but even still he's no match for me down here. I cavitate the water so not only am I pushed back in Leda's direction, but Castor is pushed away from me. I feel the Furies between us dissipate somewhat, and I know that I either stunned him or put enough distance between us so he could come to his senses and swim away from me.

I feel the effect of the Furies lessen even more. I concentrate and feel through the water, sort of asking it where Castor is going. I get the sense that he's moving uptown, toward his territory, and he's moving fast. He's probably worried about who in his family was in a fight to the death and whether or not they survived, and he's rushing home to find out.

My thoughts turn back to Leda. I left her unconscious by the side of the road.

I pull myself up onto the pier and banish the water from my clothes and skin to instantly dry myself. I run to where we fought. She's not here, but she can't be far. The headlights of passing cars keep messing with my night vision as I search up and down the West Side Highway. I don't see her.

I start to jog, looking down the other side streets. Finally, I see a tall, slender shape moving east. She's hunched over, head down, her steps uneven.

"Leda!" I call out, running to her. She staggers to a stop.

I spin her around and she nearly collapses against me. Gods, she's a mess. The whole left side of her face is swollen and bruised. Her mouth is bleeding, too. I think I knocked out a few teeth.

"I'm sorry, I'm so sorry," I say stupidly, putting a supporting arm around her. I look around for a place she can sit, but I can't find anything. "Come on," I decide aloud. "I'm taking you to my place."

"Castor?" she asks, her voice thin and ragged.

"He's fine," I say, trying not to snap at her. I know she's concussed but why is her first thought about him? It's not like he asked about her. He doesn't care about anyone outside of his family. I carry her back to Greenwich and hail a cab. "Keep your head down," I tell her and hope the cab driver thinks she's just drunk.

I get her into the backseat and hold her across my lap, her head tucked into the curve of my neck as we ride the few blocks to my apartment. Hating myself, I brush her hair across her face with my hand so the driver can't see what I did to her in the rearview mirror. Why did I hit her so hard? I keep whispering *I'm sorry*. Don't know why. It's not like saying sorry is going to make her better. I just can't seem to stop. I wait until I've got her through the front door to pick her up and carry her to my apartment so the driver doesn't call the cops on me for assault and probable kidnapping. I bring her to my bed and lay her on it.

"I'll be right back," I say, smoothing her hair away from her face. I can't believe I did that to her. She looks deformed.

I run to the kitchen to get some ice. My hands are shaking as I empty an ice tray into a kitchen towel, and I see that the back of my fist is bloody and swollen. I think I broke my hand on Leda's face. I grab a jar of honey and curse myself the whole way back to her. I see that she's trying to sit up when I get to the bedroom.

"Hey. Lie down," I say, sitting on the edge of the bed next to her. I try to put the ice on her cheek, but she pushes against me.

"My brother," she says. "I have to know if it's him."

"Okay. Give me your phone. I'll call him."

"I already tried that," she says, slurring her words. "He didn't answer. The death was Roman. I know that. I can't hear the name yet, but I felt the Furies so violently. I *know* whoever died was a Roman who was close to me."

"Here, have this" I say, handing her the honey. I stand up. I have no idea what to do. I start pacing because I think better when I'm moving. "Where does your brother live?"

Leda pauses, swallowing some honey before speaking. "Thebes has probably invaded Roman territory. You can't go there if Thebes is there."

She's right. The Furies will overtake me.

"Adonis was with Daphne." I'm reaching here, looking for any logical reason that the death that occurred between Rome and Thebes couldn't have been Adonis. "She'd have his back, right? I don't think Daphne would let anything happen to Adonis," I say, "And with her lightning it would take a lot to bring her down."

There's an uncomfortable moment between us. I think this is what sinning feels like to a Catholic because I want to climb into bed with Leda and hold her.

"What happened with Castor?"

"I let him go," I say.

"How did you resist the Furies?" she asks.

"I had to get back to you."

She looks like she feels sorry for me. She now knows for a fact that I love her. There's no way I can hide it. I'm facing her, wide open, and I don't even care if she pities me because she can't love me back. It is what it is and I'm done hiding what I feel.

"This isn't right," she whispers.

"I know." I stand up, but she grabs my hand before I can leave the room, the same hand I broke on her face. She kisses it, then draws me back down next to her and holds my hand to her chest, and I sit there, trying to figure out what the hell is going on.

She's crying now and I don't know what to do, so I give her a hug. "It's okay. I know you don't feel the same."

"Why are you so thick?"

I know I'm thick, that's a foregone conclusion; but I'm still confused because she's pressing herself against me like she wants me.

She looks into my eyes. "Of course I feel the same way."

"Don't play with me, Leda." I blurt out. And then she kisses me.

"You have to take me to my territory. I need to find Adonis."

"Okay," I agree. I can't say no to anything she wants right now. "But the streets aren't safe. Would you trust me to take you underwater?"

"Of course," she says.

I take the ice pack out of her hands and feel her chilled fingers in mine. She looks like she wants to say something, but she stops herself because what the hell can either of us say to fix this? I bend down and scoop her up.

I carry her down the stairs of my apartment building and across the street to the Hudson. I swing my legs over the railing and start side-stepping carefully down to the water's edge.

"Daedalus!" calls a familiar voice.

I look out into the gloom and find Ladon's head bobbing between the swells, where he's probably been waiting for hours. His expression is tortured. He's got to be going out of his mind with worry for Antigone.

"I'm coming," I call back to him.

"Who's that?" Leda asks.

"My brother, Ladon," I tell her.

"Ladon? Like the dragon?"

"Yeah," I reply, wincing. She's still too far from him to see the rest of his body beneath the dark water. "About that. Athens is a little different from the other Houses."

Talking about the Houses makes me remember. Antigone is

House of Thebes. Phaon is House of Rome. I think Leda must be reading more than my heart because I hear her gasp.

"Oh no. Antigone's with Phaon," she says, remembering that the bomb of violence that went off between she and Castor must have gone off between Antigone and Phaon as well. If Doris wasn't able to keep them apart, one of them is surely dead.

My brother sees my expression. He knows something terrible has happened and I explain to him about the fresh kill and how no one from Thebes and Rome can be near each other now. I look between him and Leda, torn. I don't know who to help. Or if I even can help either of them.

Leda's jacket pocket starts playing a bubbly little tune that makes her sound like an ice cream truck.

"Adonis!" she says, scrambling to answer her phone.

She tries to berate him for not picking up earlier. I can hear him shouting over her and what sounds like a storm blowing in the background. She holds the cellphone away from her ear. He's yelling that he's taking their helicopter and then he clearly recites the address of a building that overlooks Battery Park.

"Antigone is on the *roof*!" Adonis hollers. Then the connection ends.

I see my brother move to dive beneath the waves. "You can't go, Ladon!" I shout before he gets away from me. "She's on a rooftop. You won't even be able to get up there."

I put Leda down and turn to her. "You're still injured," I begin.

"Don't even *try* that on me. I'm going!"

"Antigone is House of Thebes," I remind her, and she deflates. "You can't be around her. And without a Roman, neither can I."

"I can," Ladon says. "I cleared my blood debt with Thebes by saving Antigone's life once. Her cousin Ajax is in my cave. I'll go now and tell him where she is. He'll rescue her."

I nod. "I'll go to the area. I won't go in the building, but I'll try to make sure the rest of the House of Athens stays away from it. Give Ajax a chance to get Antigone back without any more bloodshed."

"Be careful. Don't get too close," Ladon warns, then dives below the surface to swim away. His dragon tail flukes up in the water after him. Leda sees it and jumps back, making a little yelp that's adorable to me.

"Full of surprises, your family," she says.

"Yeah," I reply, but I'm not ashamed or worried she'll think less of my brother because he isn't wholly human. She met my mom. If that didn't scare her away, I don't think anything is going to.

Now that Leda knows her brother is alive, she can rest. I carry her back up to my apartment, set her up with more honey and some ice water, and leave my spare keys with her so she can come and go as she pleases. I take my sword out from underneath the bed. She watches me do it and I know she's wondering if I'm going to end up using it on anyone from her House. I'm wondering the same thing.

"I love you," she says to me.

"I love you too." I tell her, which catches me by surprise. I've never said that out loud to anyone before. Not even my brother.

I kiss her before I go even though I shouldn't. Then I run across the street to the water and dive in.

38

ION

My hands are covering my ears, but I can still hear the screaming and the chaos created by the Oracle's prophecy. Then the screaming changes suddenly, and I know something is wrong.

Everything is a bit wrong already, but it gets much worse when Phaon's pretty face twists grotesquely and he attacks Antigone like a lion attacking a cheetah cub. I have not seen such genuine behavior from Phaon before. He is pure action now, completely removed from thought, and it is exhilarating to see him so free. Still, I cannot let him hurt my father's prize, and so I have him by the back of the neck and I'm carrying him away from her by the scruff as if he were a kitten.

He squeals at the pain of it because he is not, in fact, feline. And then, shockingly, the Oracle snarls and jumps up to attack *him*.

"The Furies have them!" Doris shouts. "There must have been a fresh kill between their Houses. Keep them apart!"

And, yes, I am trying to do as she says, but I also notice that now that Phaon is past sense, he is not using his power to shield me from the Furies I feel towards him. I wrap my hands around his neck and squeeze.

I can't help it. I want to pop his head off like a daisy. Everything will be better when he is dead.

His eyes widen as his lungs are deprived of air. Now he sees his death clearly enough that his bloodlust is diminished, and the grip the Furies have over him is lessened. In an act of desperation, he manages to calm the Furies in me somewhat.

"Get me out of here!" he gasps, and I see the sense in his request.

But also, I do not. If he is gone, Doris, Cassiopeia, and I will kill the Oracle and my father would not like that.

It is a conundrum. While I am considering it and becoming more convinced there is no way for this to end without me killing everyone present who is not Athenian, I hear the sound of a helicopter approaching. Normally I would ignore this sound, but it is getting too close to our rooftop to be a coincidence. I look up and see in the insectoid bubble of the cabin the stunned face of the Atreidae.

She is mine and I will have her.

I let go of Phaon and I am running toward her, but the helicopter is being flown by someone else. Someone in crisis, by the looks of his face. The one who stabbed me. Ah—I understand. He is Roman. He wants to kill the Theban Oracle as much as Phaon, but the distance between them has preserved enough of his senses that he is able to make the helicopter veer off suddenly to be set down on the next rooftop.

The Atreidae is so close. I want to go to her. Then I remember that I must first deal with the Oracle. My father will be very upset if she dies. I need to secure her safety, and the only way to do that is to remove her from the presence of both Athens and Rome.

The Oracle is struggling with Doris, who is struggling with herself not to kill the girl. I grab the girl away from Doris and leap with her over the side of the building.

She screams as we go over the edge, but there is no need for her to fear falling. I change from man to giant ape along the way.

I am not disobeying my father by changing form. He specifically said he did not want Phaon to see me change, and Phaon did not. In this form I can both carry the Oracle and climb down the side of the building. I keep her over my shoulder as I grip tightly to the masonry, climbing around to another side before I descend. If anyone on the roof looks over the edge we jumped from, they will not see us. They will think we disappeared. I still feel the Furies in me, and their screams to kill the Oracle grow louder every second. I must not stay in her presence long or I will kill her, but I will find someplace safe to put her before I go to the Atreidae.

Beneath the roof there are a few levels of arched windows, abutted by Doric columns. At the base of each column there is a slight ledge. I leave the Oracle on this ledge, with her arms wrapped securely around a column. The ledge is deep enough that she will not fall if she does not move, but also high up enough that she will not be able to get down and run away. The windows pose a slight risk of escape, but they appear to be the kind that are not meant to be opened and this girl is too weak to break them. She is both hidden and trapped until I return to get her, which I will do after I claim my Atreidae.

There are more Scions arriving at the base of the building. Their black cars pull up, and fast-moving teams pour out of them in unison. They are many stories below, yet I know they are not

Athenian. From their numbers, and the brazen way they fan out as if claiming ownership on territory simply because they have set foot upon it, they can only be the Hundred Cousins of Thebes.

I hear the Oracle screaming down to them, and if they manage to hear her over the city sounds below, they will come to rescue her and I will not be able to reclaim her for my father later. Yet, I cannot stay here with her and guard her. I want to silence her, but this urge must not win. I must not kill her.

"Be silent!" I roar at her. This form is not designed for speech. The girl's screams drop down to a whimper. She is very frightened of me.

"Let me go!" she demands. Though she is afraid, she is no coward.

The Furies wail at me and gnash their teeth, but I must not kill her. I tear myself away from her with the thought of the Atreidae. I will go to her, and by leaving, I will spare the Oracle's life. As I start to climb down, I hear the Oracle calling out above me.

"Ajax!" she cries.

I look up and see another Theban alighting next to Antigone. He's a flyer. I didn't think any of those existed anymore, but there he is, soaring through the air with impossible grace. Only animals should fly. The human form is not meant for it.

I cannot tell if it is the Furies that are enraging me anymore, or if it is because this Ajax intends to take the Oracle away from my father, but I am climbing back up the side of the building to kill him. I nearly have him when I hear a voice shriek from the rooftop on the building across from us.

"Look out!" screams the Atreidae.

She warns him. She is not Theban, yet she warns him. I see her face though she is far away, lit at an angle by the floodlight from the helicopter, and even though she struggles with an opponent of her own, she cares more for Ajax's safety than the fight she is in with the Roman who stabbed me.

She does not know what she is for. She thinks she is for Ajax, but she isn't. She is for me.

Ajax, my rival, is much stronger than his little cousin and he breaks the glass of the window with a fist he's wrapped in his shirt. The shards shower down on me and I must cover my eyes. I decide that this form is wrong because if my rival can fly, I must be able to fly as well. While I am in the middle of my change, Ajax helps the Oracle into the building through the broken window. I become an enormous falcon and first fly up, gaining altitude and speed, and then I stoop with my talons extended. But he eludes me.

My strike misses because he has flown back away from me. I tumble in the air and right myself, but the opportunity has passed. The Oracle is inside the building now, already running through a door, and Ajax is outside it, flying off. I have lost the Oracle, but not him. I decide to chase him. He is very fast. I don't know if I can catch him.

I will chase my rival away and when he is gone, I will return for the Atreidae.

39

DAPHNE

It's all I can do to keep Adonis from running down the stairwell and across the street to fight every Theban amassing in the building across from us.

It must have happened while we were getting the helicopter. A fresh kill between Thebes and Rome. As soon as Adonis got close to Antigone on the rooftop, he was able to hear Pyramus' name in the screams of the Furies and he managed to tell me what happened. He almost crashed us, and as soon as we got out of the helicopter, I put him in a headlock because he begged me to. He can't control himself without my help, and that means that I can't help anyone else.

I see the shapeshifter from the subway. Ion, Ladon had called him. He takes Antigone away from a big, black-haired woman who is choking her. I know that woman. I fought her and Daedalus' brothers months ago.

And then Ion jumps over the side of the building.

It's so shocking I can't look away. I nearly strangle Adonis as I drag him with me to the edge of the roof to peer over. I see a huge gorilla-like creature clinging to the outside of the building with Antigone, who's screaming, slung over one of his massive shoulders like a dish rag. Adonis wriggles free and I have to jump on top of him. When I can look across the street again, I see Ion has found a nook next to a huge window that looks far too precarious to be safe and he's *left* Antigone there. He's starting to climb down the side of the building. Where the hell is he going?

"I have to get her," I'm saying, and then I see Ajax flying to Antigone.

I have no idea how he knew to come here. Adonis called Leda right before we got in the helicopter and Ajax had been in Ladon's cave for hours by then. None of this adds up. I can't see the individual steps and how they lead from one to another, and I'm afraid. I'm afraid the mousetrap has grown so large it's become too big for me to see. I'm scrambling now to figure out how to get Ajax out of it and back to Ladon's cave.

Ion starts to climb back up toward Ajax and Antigone. I remember how strong Ion was. He'll kill Ajax. I lean over the side of the building to shout a warning.

Ajax hears me, but so does Ion. The shapeshifter looks right at me and give me such an odd look. He's just staring at me. Ajax uses the time to his advantage. He takes off his shirt, wraps his hand with it and breaks the window. I see Ajax help Antigone inside the building and to safety.

Adonis chooses this moment to wrest himself free again, and now it's a race. I chase him to the door to the stairwell and tackle him from behind.

"Don't let me go!" he pleads through clenched teeth. He's fighting with everything he's got against the Furies and it's still not enough.

"I won't!" Dammit. I'm going to have to hit him. I really don't want to do this. I give him a little jab, just to test out his skill level, and he blocks. Okay. He's been in a fight before. Now I go in with a slightly quicker combo, but he does a good job of dealing with it.

"Yeah, fight me," Adonis says eagerly, like fighting could help him.

He sweeps my leg and tumbles me under him. I pull guard, and then it's a wrestling match. Maybe if he works out some of his aggression on me, he'll be able to fly the helicopter out of here and away from anyone in the House of Thebes and the Furies and I won't have to really hurt him.

Last resort is my lightning. Or knocking him out. If I even *can* knock him out. He's a good fighter, and I have to concentrate to keep him on the roof. One moment he's fully focused on fighting me, and the next it's like the Furies wheedle into his brain and he suddenly loses focus and tries to get away from me. I manage to turn him around so he's not facing the door to the stairwell, and I get a chance to briefly see what's happening on the other rooftop.

Tantalus has arrived. He's up there with one other Theban soldier. I don't recognize him. But an Athenian is there to meet both of them. She's the big woman with black hair. She takes out the Theban soldier with impressive ease, and she and Tantalus run at each other; swords drawn.

"Wait!" I shout at Adonis, but he's already tackling me and taking me down. I can't see what's happening. The fight with Adonis is becoming desperate.

He's whispering things, and his expression is going from violence to apology to self-loathing back to violence and more than once I worry that I won't win this without killing him. I've hit him half a dozen times but he won't go down, and I don't want to hit him hard anymore because I'm afraid I'm going to really hurt him. At one point we both hear a falcon screeching overhead as if it is going to land on top of us, but it veers off suddenly and goes to the other building. I need to know what's going on over there. I have to end this fight with Adonis.

If I use my lightning I might kill him, but I'm running out of options. It's hard to control a bolt when you're flooded with adrenaline and trying to stay alive, but I concentrate, take a breath in between the barrage of kicks and punches and I grab hold of his forearm and let the current flow.

He spasms grotesquely, his body convulsing, and I pull my hand away from his seared skin as he falls down, his arms and legs stiff while he flops around like a fish in the bottom of a boat. Branching out right over his golden cuff are the red lines of a Lichtenberg figure that go up his arm.

"I'm sorry, I'm sorry," I keep repeating, reaching out to touch him, and then pulling my hands back, fearful they'll hurt him more.

Finally, he stops shuddering. I touch the pulse point on his neck and feel a faint, irregular thudding. He's alive, at least. The sound of ringing swords makes me look away from Adonis and across to the other rooftop.

I can't believe what I'm seeing.

Ajax and Tantalus are fighting.

I run to the edge of the building, but it's too far for me to jump. I could try to hit Tantalus with another bolt, but I don't know if I could control it. I might hit Ajax.

From this angle, I can only see Ajax and Tantalus from the waist up. Ajax still has no shirt on and there's blood covering Tantalus' sword all the way up to the hilt. I don't see blood on

Ajax's bare skin. Tantalus must have killed someone else already. The woman with the black hair.

I don't understand why they're fighting, though. Ajax is behaving as if he's possessed. Did he attack Tantalus?

I look across the expanse of darkness separating me from Ajax, and I know it's happening just like Antigone said it would. There is a dark space between us that keeps me from getting to him exactly as she described. I don't dare take the time to run down the stairs of this building, cross the street, and run up to the other rooftop. I can't help Ajax or do anything to stop it. All I can do is watch. I scream and scream. I don't know what, but I'm screaming something.

And then it's over.

With one elegant arc of his blade, Tantalus cuts off Ajax's head.

40

DAEDALUS

I rise up out of the water and stay low until I'm into the sparse cover offered by Battery Park. Before I'm even all the way through the park and to the street, I feel a faint whisper from the Furies and know that the Thebans have spread out around the base of the building.

This is only going to draw more Athenians to them, and if they were hoping to snatch the Oracle and get out of here, they're going about it the wrong way. I'm guessing the Oracle isn't the only thing they want anymore, though. I think they are ready to fight an all-out war right here, right now.

I wonder briefly where my father is, but I didn't listen to my answering machine for a reason, even though I had over a dozen messages waiting on it. I'm on my own with this. I haven't changed sides, that's impossible, but I'm no longer working under the assumption that I'm fighting for the House of Athens anymore.

My father wants this war. I'm still trying to stop it from

starting.

It might already be too late, but I have to try. I can never have Leda, I know that, but I'd kill my whole family before I'd let them hurt her. Everyone except Ladon.

And that's where fate has me by the balls. The Furies could make any one of us kill any one of them, even if it was the last thing we wanted to do; and if I were to start killing Athenians to protect her, I would become an Outcast. The Furies would set me against my own brother. Kin-killing is the ultimate sin, and the Furies would hound us. He could probably resist. I know I couldn't.

That's what happened to the House of Atreus. That's why they're nearly extinct.

But what do I care anymore if Athens goes under? I've fought my whole life to keep it afloat, and for what? Right now, I'm just trying to keep me, Leda, Ladon, and my mom, alive. I'm going to find a way to do that. Somehow.

I keep my distance, skirting the edge of the park for a little bit of cover until I can pinpoint where all the Thebans are and what their rotations are like. I've got to hand it to them, they run a tight ship. Working the docks for my dad in some of his not entirely legal enterprises has taught me a thing or two about how to secure a building and how to space out muscle, but this is like a military outfit. They even have the military gear. The all-black outfits and the walkie-talkies. Must be nice.

I'm just here to make sure that they get the Oracle back, and that's it. It's not right that my family took a teenaged girl like that. I'm also here for Ladon, because he loves her. Maybe his love for Antigone is not the same as my love for Leda, but it's just as valid. So, yeah, I'm betraying my House, but I'm still doing it for the right reasons.

I see a swarm of Thebans exit the building. Among them is one of the Delos brothers. I'm pretty sure it's Pallas. He's hustling out of the front door with his body hunched protectively over a small figure who is wrapped up in a big coat. They got her. I peer closer. She's walking on her own. I don't think she's injured, just shook up. Two of the three big black cars I've clocked as theirs come around the block at a fast clip and both screech to a quick halt right in front of Pallas and Antigone.

While this small group of Thebans are making their exit, I see another Scion shape come running from up the block. He or she is moving fast. I tense, worried the new Scion is Athenian, but when the figure stops, I see his face over the hood of the car. It's Castor. He looks relieved, and I'm happy for him when he hugs his cousin.

There's a moment between Pallas and Castor. Pallas' head is bent and he looks devastated. I watch closely. Something happened to him and he tells his brother about it. Castor is stunned, maybe even a little repulsed, but he hugs Pallas, comforting him, before he makes his little brother get in the back of the car with Antigone. Castor closes the door and the black cars speed off leaving only one circling for the remaining Thebans, which can't be more than two or three of them, Castor included.

So it's done. I can go back to Ladon and tell him that his totally platonic sweetheart is safe. I don't know how it is that my family hasn't gotten wind of this, but they haven't showed up. Doesn't matter. The rest of the Thebans should be leaving soon, and I'm not going to look a gift horse in the mouth.

Castor is going inside the building, and I'm turning away when I feel it.

It doesn't cross my mind that it's dishonorable to come running out of the dark and cut down an unarmed man. I'm not considering or thinking anything. I am nothing but motion. There's been a fresh kill between our Houses.

Castor felt it too. The Furies make him turn and meet me. We collide in the middle of the street, and I was wrong about him being unarmed. He was carrying a gladiolus that I couldn't see because the car was blocking most of his body, but I'm glad he has it. This way the fight will last longer. I want it to last. I want him to be tired and nearly bled out when I finally run him through.

This has been coming for a long time. We're the same age, so he and I have both been training since we were kids for the day when we would eventually fight. I would go rounds with Doris, or my dad, or one of my old uncles who used to train the younger generation, in preparation for the day when I would meet Castor Delos. And he's good. Technically, he might be a better fighter than me. He was worth all that hard work for all those years I trained to be right here in this fight. This feels amazing, and I know he'd agree. But he also feels that I'm stronger and faster, and we both know he is going to tire before I do.

The first exchanges are so fast I don't use my eyes; I just know where his edge is going to land and I know when he's going to shift his weight. I feel when he's going to slice and when he's going to thrust. I don't have to think about it. I'm past thinking right now. Saying I'm angry, or even enraged, doesn't cover it. This is what I was made for. I am an instrument of blind fury.

Castor is slowing down, while I'm just hitting my stride. Now will come the tricks. The things he learned to make up for the fact that I was always stronger, always faster, and always waiting in the wings. But I can handle whatever bait and switch he's got in his toolbox. I'm focused on him completely, so much so that even though I hear a woman screaming, it's not in my universe.

Then I see Daphne hurtling into Castor. She blindsides him,

knocking him to the ground from behind so he never sees her, and she hits the back of his head with her elbow so hard he's out like she hit a switch. Just like that. I look at her, too stunned to understand exactly what she's doing.

Because he's mine. Castor is *my* kill. I raise my sword to finish it but she jumps up and catches my wrists in her hands. She's so strong I can't bring down my arms even one inch. Then I feel a shock running through my body and everything goes white.

She's screaming something at me, and I have no idea what she's saying. I can't understand anything. She hits me. Knocks me nearly into next week. She pulls my gladiolus out of my hands, grabs me by the back of my head, gripping my hair, and pulls me behind her. I stumble, barely able to keep my feet under me, she's moving so fast.

Once we're inside the building, the wailing of the Furies, which I guess has been blocking out the sound of everything else up to now, abates enough so that I can understand what she's saying.

"I can't leave you there unconscious. There are still Thebans driving around, and I have to get up to the roof, okay?" she's shouting back at me.

She lets go of my hair, but twists one of my arms behind my back and holds my own sword to my throat. I have the strange feeling she's doing it for my own good, but it's still painful.

"What the hell!" I scream over my shoulder at her. I can barely speak. She hit me so damn hard my tongue went numb.

"No time," she utters, and now we're running up the stairs. Or she's running and carrying me is more like it.

I still feel the Furies pushing me, and it hurts. It hurts and I want to find the nearest Theban and kill him. I have to kill at least one of them. Have to.

But we get to the roof and she lets go of me. I realize I can't stand on my own and I drop to my knees. That shock she gave me. She must have electrocuted me. I'm still shaking from it and seeing spots. When the blue and white blobs finally clear from my vision I can see that there's a dead Theban up here, lying on his side.

And Doris. She's here too. She's dead, lying in a seeping halo of her own blood. She deserved better.

Near Doris, there's another shape. It's a man's naked body without a head. The body is lumpy and twisted in a strange way. It takes me a moment to follow the spine and realize that he's a hunchback. A few feet away is the severed head. The face is away from me and all I see is black hair. Like mine. He's Athenian. Ion was with Doris. They pulled this job together. Ion the shapeshifter. Who was his father, I wonder? And then I just know. My father was always complaining about his bad luck when it came to sons.

Everything is blurry. I hear something and brace myself on my arms, forcing my eyes to focus. Someone is charging me, and I hear the wailing of the Furies but I can barely stay conscious right now. Tantalus. It's Tantalus Delos who is charging me with his sword raised. I think I'm going to die right here next to Doris. Wouldn't be too bad, actually. A warrior's death, next to one of the few relatives I actually liked.

Daphne steps in front of me and uses my sword to block him.

The exchange she has with Tantalus is fast and vicious. I can't see half the moves she makes, but she beats him back and then she winds up and kicks him in the chest so hard he goes flying ten feet through the air, landing in a heap on the other side of the roof.

"Where is he!?" she screams at Tantalus. She stalks forward, lightning crackling around her in icy-blue webs and lifting her hair up from her scalp. "Where's Ajax's body?" she demands. Sobs shake her so fiercely I can see her back heaving and her legs shaking.

Tantalus is rolling around on the ground in agony, clutching his chest. She's just as big a beast as I thought she'd be. Unstoppable. How could anyone fight that? She probably broke his sternum and several ribs with that kick, and she's still moving toward him like she's going to finish the job. And she would, too. She'd kill him.

"He... wasn't... Ajax!" Tantalus manages to point to the beheaded hunchback. "It changed... while fighting!"

It crosses my mind that I never told Leda that I found my mother's spider. I wonder if I'll survive this and see her again.

Blood comes pouring out from between Tantalus' lips. Daphne looks around, baffled. Her lightning changes into sparks and they spill from her fingertips and from her eyes like diamonds. The sparks dance across the rooftop, bouncing around like pieces of magic.

Tantalus looks up at her sparkling face, enraptured, and then I understand everything. He loves her. His little brother's woman, and he wishes she was his. That's why she thought Tantalus killed Ajax. Because she knows he would.

"It... was a —" Tantalus is trying to speak, but he can't.

"Shapeshifter," Daphne finishes for him. Then she runs forward and gets down on her knees in front of him. "I'm sorry," she's whispering. "I thought—"

"I know," Tantalus says as Daphne tries to tend to him. "I would never... hurt my brother."

But he's lying. He *would* kill his own brother for Daphne. That's the last thing I'm sure of, and then everything goes dark.

❧ 41 ❧

TANTALUS

This is bloodlust, and I understand now why my father was so eager for this war to begin. He wanted to get back to this feeling.

There's something pure about it. Clean. It is one emotion, sustained, and when does that ever happen? Every other emotion I've ever had was either so fleeting it left me as soon as I turned my inward gaze on it, or it was not one emotion, but several occurring all at once. This is fury and only fury, untainted. Hot and bright and singular, like an opera singer's high note that she extends past the boundaries of normal human capacity until the soul is transported by the sound of it.

I've never been in a trance, though as I fight this big, black-haired Athenian, I imagine this is what one must be like. She is a remarkable opponent, a specimen of a woman, and I love her as much as I hate her. She and I are locked together. United. The Furies have us and we are neither responsible for our actions, nor do we blame the other for what we feel. It's natural, what we are doing.

I have never been as honest with anyone as I am with her when I put my sword through her heart. She is just as honest with me when her eyes meet mine. She dies for me and no one else. It's beautiful, this gift she gives me. The one and only life she'll ever have.

Then I see her at my feet, and my love for her has not gone away. But now I also feel the loss of her, and it hurts. How can that be? Is this the real curse of the Furies—to feel such kinship with the one you have killed? I don't even know her name.

I hear the unmistakable shriek of a bird of prey. I feel a fresh surge of fury and lift my sword to it, soaking it in. Another opponent, but this one is a falcon. It's larger than any bird I've ever seen. It's impossible.

The bird is changing. I'm still trying to make sense of what I see when it becomes a man. He's naked and his body is misshapen, but his hair is Athenian black and his eyes are the bright blue of the ocean. He is overwhelmed by the Furies. He comes staggering toward me, incoherent with wrath.

"You killed Doris!" he says, and I am grateful to have her name.

"Pick up her sword!" I yell at him, flushed with this indescribable feeling.

He takes her sword and rushes me, swinging wildly. He is not the warrior Doris was, and it saddens me to know that I may never have such a perfect kill again. He knows he is not a good fighter, but he has other abilities. He starts to change again. He turns into Doris.

By taking her form he has taken on some of her grace, but none of her skill. After a few exchanges he abandons her body, and he becomes me. But I'm not afraid of myself.

He then runs through several different bodies. Bellerophon, Daedalus, some random woman I've never seen.

Then he becomes Ajax.

I reel away from him.

I can't kill Ajax, though I have dreamed of it. My guilt makes me falter. My shame and my fear for what I might do paralyzes me. I would never hurt Ajax.

But this is not Ajax. This creature is strong, but he's nowhere near as good a fighter. Somehow that snaps me out of it. He may look like Ajax, but he's nothing like him. He presses forward, sensing the advantage this body gives him over me. It doesn't take me long to find my opening now. I see it, and cut off his head.

From far away, I hear someone screaming.

The creature changes back as he hits the ground, dead. I stand over him, panting, staring, making sure he doesn't change back into Ajax again.

I'm tired. My body feels both empty and heavy. I can't seem to lift my arms, and it's funny to me that emptiness can weigh so much. This urge to laugh is hysteria setting in.

This is the madness that comes after the bloodlust. The ancients warn of it. Hercules went mad, so did Odysseus. Scions are prey to it, and I used to fear that Ajax would succumb to it one day, consumed by the fire of his genius. I can't allow madness to be my downfall. Not now when so many people count on me.

I feel the Furies rising again. I realize that Daphne is here, but she isn't the source of this ecstatic rage. She's looking at the corpses on the rooftop, searching, but all I see is the Athenian she brought with her. He's injured and he can't even stand to fight; still, the Furies thrill through me, filling up my empty limbs, and I'm running at him with my sword raised.

And then I'm fighting Daphne. It's not the Furies between us, it's just her desperation, and I'm screaming *no* on the inside, but nothing comes out of me but more blows and more parries and I can't stop fighting her, or I'll be killed. She's magnificent. The best fighter I've ever seen. Our exchange doesn't last long. I'm exhausted, but even fully rested I would be no match for her. She kicks me.

I feel my chest cave in, and I see the ground rushing up to meet me. The pain is like a wall. I can't see over it or around it or through it.

She strides toward me, turned into an angel of death. She's covered in light and crying stars. I worship her, but she wants Ajax. She thinks I killed Ajax, and she will kill me if I don't speak. I manage to blurt out some words that get across what really happened.

Then she's next to me, touching my face, and running her fingertips over my chest to see how badly she hurt me. She's crying, saying she's sorry. But I would suffer this pain a thousand times to see her look at me with so much loving care again.

"This is going to hurt, but I have to move you," she tells me. "We're still in Athenian territory, and with a fresh kill they'll feel you here. They'll be coming for you soon."

I shake my head, but that's no better than talking. "My father. He's got Bellerophon... pinned down."

"You can't fight even one," she tells me and her meaning is clear. She'd kill for Ajax, but not for me, and not for territory. I'm going to have to retreat.

She lifts me up and carries me downstairs, disguising her face on the way. The last of our black cars pulls up. I ordered the other cars to leave with Antigone and stayed with only one Cousin to take care of the last Athenian on the roof myself. Doris, my sweetest kill, killed him in three moves. We'll have to negotiate for his body later.

Castor is in the car with only the driver. When did he get here? He isn't moving and I struggle to reach out to him.

"He's alive, but you both need healing," Daphne says, easing me in next to him.

I nod, knowing this must be the end of the fight. For now. Daphne closes the door and disappears.

42

DAPHNE

I'm shaking with adrenaline and relief and guilt. All I've done tonight, it seems, is hurt people I care about.

I put Tantalus in the car and make sure the Thebans are gone before I go back for Adonis. Daedalus should make it. I left him on a roof surrounded by dead bodies, but at least he's in his own territory. Adonis isn't. And pretty soon he's going to be surrounded by angry Athenians who are going to blame Rome for tonight's debacle.

But Ajax is alive.

I get back up to the roof to find Adonis still unconscious. I have no idea how to fly a helicopter. I'll have to leave it. I pick up Adonis and with the last of my strength I run him uptown to 92nd Street. Plenty of mortals see us. There's nothing I can do about that now. There's no way I can run fast enough to escape detection, not carrying Adonis and not in the shape I'm in.

I get to Adonis' building and find the front door kicked in, and blood on the floors. I hesitate, wondering if this is a safe place to bring Adonis or if it's been captured by Thebes, but then I see a Roman opening the doors to the *Valetudinaria*. It's that red-headed girl who can control the Furies. She must have seen us coming in on one of the surveillance cameras and she rushes out to meet me.

"Oh my gods, is he..."

"He's alive," I finish for her as I hand him off.

I can barely walk behind them into the *Valetudinaria*. Nearly every bed is filled, and not only with the injured. There are some dead bodies in here. Their faces are covered by sheets. Why do we do that? Why do we cover people's faces when they're dead? Dehumanizing them. Making them anonymous. I notice blond hair peeking out from under some of them. Those are Thebans. I look under the sheets to make sure I don't know any of them. Thankfully I don't.

Adonis was right. A surprising number of Romans stayed and fought, and after Tantalus left to get Antigone, the Romans were able to take their forum back. Maybe this show of force will make Tantalus back off. As soon as I think it, I know how ridiculous that is. Tantalus will never back off now.

"Do you need something?" the redhead asks me. She's brought Adonis to the mortal doctor and now she's back to check on me. That's nice of her.

"Water," I reply, and she gets me both water and honey and disappears to help someone else. I'm anxious to get back to Ajax. I drink quickly and then I leave the *Valetudinaria*, but someone else stops me before I get out the front door of the building.

"Wait," Leda calls from the stairwell. I stop and turn around, allowing her to see my real face. "It's you, isn't it? You're Daphne?"

"I am," I reply, watching her study The Face. She nods to

herself, as if understanding something she hadn't before. *Her* face is badly bruised and her lower lip is split, but she doesn't seem harmed otherwise.

"Did you see Daedalus?" she asks, her voice shaky with worry.

I give her all the important details. Leda visibly deflates with relief when I tell her that he was safe enough when I left him on the roof. She loves Daedalus, that's obvious, though I don't know how long that's been going on. I'm not surprised. They are yet another attempt by the Fates to mess with our lives, bring the Houses together, and start the war with the gods so we Scions can replace them. Well, the Fates failed this time around with me. I know that if Tantalus had killed Ajax, I would have killed him, and then probably all of Thebes once the Furies had me. Who knows when I'd stop?

"I'll get him," she says.

"You can do that?" I ask. I try to remember if anyone from Rome killed anyone from Athens, or vice versa.

"Our Houses don't have a fresh kill between them. Yet," she replies.

"Is it going to be Athens and Rome uniting against Thebes?" I ask.

Leda shrugs. "I think before it's done it's going to be every House for themselves," she replies. "What is Atreus going to do?"

"Nothing. Ajax and I are leaving and we're not coming back."

"My brother will be sorry to hear that."

I guess what she must mean by that, but she's got it all wrong. I shake my head. "Adonis and I are friends."

We both let it pass, although it does stick with me. "If you ever need us, we owe you one," she adds.

"Good luck," I say. She wishes me the same, and I go.

I take the subway downtown because I don't think I can walk

that far. The honey and water revived me somewhat, but I'm dead on my feet and the only way I know how to get into Ladon's cave is by going through the subway station by Washington Square. As long as Ladon didn't kill any Thebans, his blood debt is still cleared and he won't feel the Furies towards anyone in the House of Thebes, nor they towards him. I'm pretty sure Ajax must have flown directly to Ladon's where the Fates can't see him, or how else could he have escaped the mousetrap like he did? Because it was closing. It almost had him. But not quite.

Then it hits me. Antigone's prophecy happened. It came to pass, but not in the way we thought.

It's over. We're free.

I sit there on the downtown 6 train, smiling to myself like I just got a joke someone told me weeks ago.

I make it to Ladon's cave and pretty much fall into Ajax's arms. The only thing I want to do is curl up on his chest and sleep for about a thousand years, but first I tell them the events of the night. I describe what I saw between Ion and Tantalus.

"The last thing I saw was Ion chasing me. I circled wide before coming back here," Ajax says. "I knew Antigone was safe, but I felt the Furies everywhere and I knew if I went back, I would end up killing someone."

"I saw you go, but I was struggling to keep Adonis from attacking anyone in the House of Thebes. Then I saw *you* fighting Tantalus. At least I thought it was you. And then it happened, just like Antigone described it to me."

"Only it was Ion. The shapeshifter," Ladon says, mulling it over. "That's usually the way prophecies go, though, isn't it? Correct, down to the letter. And not at all what you thought they would be."

The three of us look at each other, scared to say it out loud. Finally, Ajax does.

"Did we beat fate?" he asks.

"I think so." We're giddy with happiness, but only for a moment. I have to tell Ladon what happened to Doris, and how I intervened in the fight between his brother and Castor. "Daedalus was in bad shape when I left him on the roof, but Leda said she would go get him. I know she'll take care of him," I finish, still feeling guilty.

"You did what you had to do," Ladon says, letting me off the hook. "My brother is a survivor. I'm more worried about Adonis."

"Me too," I admit.

Ladon congratulates us and then he slips beneath the water, probably to wait underneath the manhole cover for Antigone, though I think it will be a long time before anyone in her family lets her out of their sight again.

Ajax and I fall asleep in Ladon's spare bed, finally together and whole again after a hellish week, and for the first time in months I don't feel like I'm sleeping under a sword.

When we wake there's a moment where we both forget to be happy. A million worries rush in, and then we remember again.

"We're free," Ajax says, staring up at the rocky ceiling. He looks over at me. "Can we even say that?"

"I think so." I look over at him, our heads on the same pillow. "Let's get out of New York."

"Today," he agrees.

"We can go anywhere," I say, getting excited.

"Where?"

"Somewhere sunny. With gorgeous beaches. I want to collect seashells."

"The Bahamas," he says, his smile warming with his thoughts. "I'll make you a necklace from the pink shells."

We watch each other's faces, slowly letting ourselves believe we can have this. He rolls on top of me, fitting me under him. He doesn't kiss me right away. He takes a moment to look at me, his eyes tracking over every angle. He always sees more of me than other people do, both inside and out.

"I love you," he says.

It's such a simple thing to say to describe something so complicated, but that's why it works. Nothing else in our lives is clear, but that is.

"Always," I reply.

43

DAEDALUS

I've never been an optimist, but I'm trying.

It's been three months since the war started with Pyramus' death at Pallas' hand in the colosseum, and since then my brother has barely gotten to see Antigone. She's been a prisoner of her own family, and they have used her ability to prophecy to whittle away at the other House's numbers, picking us off one by one. It's been torture for her, wracked by the Fates nearly every day now that she's separated from Ladon. I saw her a week ago when we finalized this crazy plan, and she looked half dead already. Selling her death by suicide wasn't the hard part, as nearly everyone in the House of Thebes suspected she would do it eventually. The hard part will be her surviving it.

Ladon spent months perfecting a potion that would convince even Ceyx, the top Healer in the House of Thebes, that she was dead. It was a tall order, but Adonis had just the thing. His House is known for their poisons and love potions and with a little digging into some old family recipes he came up with one that really kills you but then revives you three days later. Or so he says.

"You know, if she doesn't make it, Rome is better off," I remind my brother. "Without the Oracle, Thebes can't ambush Rome the way they have been." *Or us* I add silently.

Romans can feel that members of the other Houses are present before we can feel them, and that's always given them the edge on getting away during these inter-House wars. Like Corvus got away. And Phaon. No one has seen or heard from those two since the start of the war, but Leda is sure they're alive and that they're going to pop up eventually. Corvus won't stop until he is Head of the House of Rome, even if he's the last member of his House standing, and Phaon is just an animal who's enjoying all of this carnage.

Somehow the two who deserve to die the most have managed to escape detection from the Oracle, even though Thebes has counteracted Rome's ability to feel the other Houses coming for them and get away by using Antigone's foresight a dozen times now. She's been able to tip Thebes off as to where key members in the House of Rome were going to be before they did, laying an ambush, and killing them. Adonis has every reason in the world to need Antigone dead or at least separated from her family, even if he genuinely likes her. I know my brother trusts Adonis, but I know Adonis will do what he has to in order to defend himself, his sister, and his House. That guy may act like a punk who doesn't take anything seriously, but I get the feeling that's because he takes everything a little too seriously. Especially things like preserving the Truce.

"Just keep digging," Ladon replies. Then, after a few more minutes he adds, "And if she doesn't make it, it will be because I brewed the potion incorrectly, not because Adonis intended to really kill her."

Even though we're underwater and it changes our pitch a bit to speak down here, I can still hear a wobble in his voice. I drop the subject and keep digging because I hate seeing him like this. He's half out of his mind with worry.

I shouldn't even be here. If Leda is wrong and the Furies aren't appeased when I revive Antigone, I might attack her. As far as we know, no Scion has ever tried to engineer a life-saving situation to intentionally rid themselves of the Furies, and what if it doesn't work? I know Ladon is strong enough to stop me even if I am overcome with bloodlust because he's done it before. But I'm not sixteen anymore, and what if he has to kill me to stop me? He'd never forgive himself, and *that* sounds to me like something the Fates would do just to make our lives even more miserable.

I think this whole plan is a disaster waiting to happen, but like I said, I'm trying to be optimistic for Ladon's sake, and maybe for my own. It hasn't escaped my attention that if this contrived life-saving works and appeases the Furies, Leda and I could use it to rid ourselves of the Furies we feel towards Thebes. We could run away, knowing that the Furies wouldn't lead Thebes right to us, which they always do if they haven't been appeased.

I'm just spit-balling here. We won't run away, of course. Neither of us could live with ourselves if we abandoned our Houses. I haven't even touched Leda since she came to get me on that damn roof, though it's just about killed me not to.

"You're thinking about Leda," my brother says. I don't know how he always knows, he just does. I don't say anything because there's nothing to say.

"You could—" he begins.

"Have a platonic relationship with her?" I counter, cutting

him off. My tone makes it clear how ridiculous that is to me. Maybe Ladon can handle that with Antigone, but I know I can't.

"You don't have to have a child with her," he finishes calmly and I realize how harsh my tone is.

"It doesn't matter what we do to avoid it. The Fates will make it happen."

Ladon nods because he knows it's true. What I feel for Leda isn't an accident. It's fated. We were meant to bring Athens and Rome together, and if I give in to what I feel for her, one thing will lead to another, and then we *will* have a child. If we use the pill, condoms, both, everything all at once it won't matter. We won't be able to avoid fate. Then Adonis will be bound by an oath every Roman takes to hunt down that child and kill it. While I was recovering from Daphne's bolt, Leda told me all about it. Rome has laws concerning the children of two Houses, who they call Rogues, just like Athenians have laws about Earthshakers and the Hidden Ones. I guess Rome has dealt with enough Rogues to have protocol for them, which makes sense considering Romans are the only Scions who can be in a relationship with someone from another House. Their laws demand that Rogues born within the House of Rome are to be hunted down and killed, usually by the next of kin.

I could never put Leda through choosing between killing her brother or letting him kill her child, so I stay away from her as best as I can. When I do see her, which happens pretty much every few days because the Fates love to screw with me, I'm cruel to her. I'm just doing it to push her away. She'll forget about me soon and find some adoring mortal who treats her like a goddess. I hope anyway. I want her to be happy. I just don't want to have to see it.

Ladon and I finally dig through the floor of the Delos family crypt, deep beneath their residence on Washington Square Park. I hold the water that wants to gush up into this room in stasis and we pull ourselves up into the crypt. Antigone told Ladon about this burial chamber, describing every aspect, even where her body would be placed. Ladon cracks a fresh glow stick, looks around, and rushes to the central pillar in the middle of the room, where all the Oracles are entombed one on top of the other as if in multi-layered bunk beds. He starts to scrabble at the stone that bears the name *Antigone* written in Greek.

"Don't damage it!" I hiss through a whisper, though I don't know why I'm keeping my voice low. It's not like anyone can hear us down here. "We have to put it back the way we found it."

He forces himself to slow down and remove the gigantic stone carefully, placing it on the ground without so much as a scuff. He doesn't even break a sweat, either. I wonder for the thousandth time how strong my brother is. I'm one of the strongest Scions, and not even I could handle a six-foot-long three-foot-deep slab of marble as if it were made of Styrofoam.

Inside the niche Antigone lies completely still, covered by a thin drapery of linen. It does not move around her nose and mouth at all. Ladon pulls it back and I feel his heart fall. She looks really dead, not play dead. Dead dead.

"You do it," Ladon whispers.

I reach in and pull Antigone out of her niche while Ladon busies himself with the body he stole from gods know where. I see a flash of straight black hair as he shifts the body from his coils and consider that he may have swum all the way to India or China to find a dead girl who would be a suitable replacement. To us, it's a sin to disturb a body once it's been interred, but you never know. What if Thebes decides to move their crypt in a few decades? We need to have bones and hair in here that could pass for Antigone's just in case.

"I'll take care of it," I tell him. "You start closing up the hole."

I don't want to undress these girls and switch their clothes. I'd rather have Ladon's job covering up the tunnel we dug, but I'm supposed to be the one saving her. Her skin feels cold and rubbery, and I can't look at either of the dead girls while I stuff them into each other's dresses as delicately and respectfully as I can. I put the strange girl into Antigone's niche and give her Antigone's obol, hoping I'm not leaving Antigone with nothing to give to Charon. Ladon seals the strange girl up, and we get the hell out of there, swimming back to Ladon's cave.

I surface behind Ladon, carrying Antigone. Leda and Adonis stand from their seats in Ladon's subterranean living room with anxious looks on their faces. It's always the same when I see her, like something's exploding in my chest, but it's worse when I'm not expecting it. Then I have to go through a list of reminders about what I'm doing and why I'm doing it just to give me enough energy to mean mug her. It's so tiring.

"What are you doing here?" I ask Leda, striding past her and toward the back room where Ladon has a bed and medical supplies ready for Antigone. "If she wakes up, you guys are going to attack her. Ladon can't protect her from all of us."

"We can control ourselves around Thebans now. The effects of the fresh kills have worn off. Mostly," Leda replies, rolling her eyes as if everything Furies-related requires a qualification now. "We're here in case *you* attack her."

I put Antigone on the bed and face Leda. "Adonis can handle that just fine on his own. You can go."

Her eyes round with hurt and another piece of me shrivels up and dies. "I was hoping to..." she trails off and tries again. "Maybe if we both save her, both of us will be free of the Furies towards Thebes."

DAEDALUS

I don't even have to fake the sneer on my face. "So you can hang out with Castor again."

Her jaw jumps as she grinds her teeth. "So I can survive this gods-damned war!" she volleys back at me.

I shake my head, looking away. I hate acting like this. "Fine. It's probably not going to work, though."

"Just a ray of sunshine, aren't you?" Adonis says from the doorway. He looks upset with me. Genuinely upset, and not like his usual sardonic self. He's worried about Leda, I realize.

I really look at her, rather than just glancingly so I can spare myself the trauma. She looks exhausted. I move closer, but stop myself before I touch her.

"What's going on?" I ask instead. I keep my voice low so I don't sound all gruff and angry like I normally do.

"Oh, I don't know," Adonis answers for her. "Maybe my sister and I have been shielding members of our House who can't block the Furies night and day so Thebes can't find them? Ever consider that?"

"Adonis," Leda chastises, frowning and shaking her head.

The truth is, Thebes *is* finding them. I know that three more Roman have been picked off. It must have been members who weren't shielded by Leda and Adonis. That must feel horrible for her, to know that not being with someone every second of the day could mean their death.

"How are you holding up?" I ask her.

Adonis makes a frustrated sound, and I glance over at him to see that he's looking at my chest. "Like we need another thing to deal with," he says, meaning the love he sees in me. "You know broken hearts are like catnip to her, right?"

"Don!" Leda snaps. He pushes off the doorframe and leaves

us. She glances at me, her arms folded. "We're both exhausted," she says by way of apology for her brother.

"I didn't know," I say. Then I roll my eyes at how much of an idiot I am. "Obviously," I add.

She cracks a brave smile. "I haven't slept in days," she admits. "The last Roman that Thebes killed was fifteen. Just a kid."

My hand cups her elbow, pulling her closer to me. I'm not even doing it, I swear. It's like parts of me are acting of their own accord now. She cants toward me slightly and that's all the invitation I need. I take her in my arms. She lets her head rest against my chest and I wrap her up, laying my cheek against her hair. She feels thinner. Hollowed out. But still perfect.

"I'm sorry to interrupt," Ladon says, bustling in with his apothecary bag.

We break apart and move to opposite sides of the bed while he fusses with Antigone. "Aren't *we* supposed to watch her?" I remind him gently.

"You may need a few things," he says, opening his bag and putting it on the cot next to Antigone's bed. We all know this is just an excuse so he can check on her. He lays out a few tinctures and oils, all of them brightly colored and housed in sparkling crystal vials, explaining what each one is for. "Rub this on her hands and feet. The heat it makes might help restart her circulation. This blue liquid is to clear her lungs, in case there's any fluid in there from her time underwater. If she wakes and coughs, give it to her."

By the time he's finished, there are half a dozen jewel-toned medicines lined up on the bedside table. Leda and I finally kick him out and close the door.

We sit opposite each other for a while, not saying any of the hundreds of things we want to say. She's so wiped out she can barely sit up in her seat. I go and get the extra pillow and blanket my brother keeps in the bottom drawer of the dresser.

"Come here," I say, spreading out the blanket on top of the spare cot.

"What are you doing?" Leda asks, coming around to me.

"Lie down," I tell her, holding up a corner of the blanket. She starts to argue, but I'm not having any of that nonsense. "Just lie down, okay? I'll wake you if it seems like she's coming around."

Practically delirious with fatigue, Leda lies down on top of the covers and I put the blanket over her. She curls up on her side with her hands sandwiched under her cheek. She falls asleep so fast it's more like she's passing out than resting. I watch her for hours. It gives me plenty of time to think, and what I think is that I'm done with this shit. Why the hell am I trying so hard to stay away from Leda when Thebes is going to kill us all off anyway? We probably won't even get a chance to make this hypothetical Rogue kid I'm so worried about. The truth is, the Hundred Cousins outnumber us, they're better organized than us, and they are hell-bent on being the last House standing. The gods are coming. It's fated. So why the hell should Leda and I suffer in the meantime?

I hear Antigone make a very disturbing clicking sound in the back of her throat, and I grasp Leda's shoulder to wake her.

"Sit her up," I say, coming around the bed to help from the other side.

We get her propped up, but she's limp and still making that clicking noise. Leda opens Antigone's mouth and sticks her fingers in there, fishing around.

"Her tongue feels swollen," Leda says, using her index finger to press down an air hole in the back of Antigone's throat.

"It means she's breathing at least. Or trying to," I say, turning to Ladon's tinctures, tying to remember what all of them do. Antispasmodic. Anti-nausea. Circulatory stimulant. Nothing here for strange noises in the back of the throat. I give up and turn back to Leda. "Her heart. Is her heart beating?" Leda looks at Antigone's chest and shakes her head. "Keep her airway open if you can," I say, tilting Antigone back onto the mattress.

I start chest compressions while Leda has her fingers stuck halfway down Antigone's throat. I have no idea if this is going to work, but I keep going anyway.

"It's beating!" Leda says.

My brother is hovering frantically in the doorway. I can hear his tail thrashing around out there, scraping against the rock. "Stay out of here!" I yell at him over my shoulder. If he comes in it'll be havoc.

It takes forever, but we keep going until Antigone is coughing and flailing, and Ladon is yelling, "Give her the expectorant!"

What the hell is an expectorant? But Leda understands and takes the blue bottle that will clear Antigone's lungs and dumps it down her throat. The coughing turns to retching. She's weak and struggling and I honestly don't think she's going to make it, but it turns out she's stronger than she looks.

After a paroxysm of coughing, Antigone settles down. Her breathing is still labored, and Leda tells me that her heartbeat is elevated, but she's alive. She struggles to open her eyes.

"Where's Ladon?" she whispers.

"I'm here!" he calls out behind me.

I look at Leda. "Do you feel the Furies?" I ask her.

Her eyes unfocus for a moment, and then she shakes her head.

"They're gone," she says quietly, like she's too hopeful to say it out loud. She looks past Ladon at Adonis. "Do you still feel them?" she asks him.

"Yes. But you two saved her and you're both free," Adonis replies, sounding content with that outcome.

Unable to contain himself any longer, Ladon comes into the room, his tail coiled tightly against his lower body, and displaces me. Leda and I leave him to watch over Antigone and join Adonis out in the main living area. Adonis takes his sister aside, saying a few things quietly to her while shooting me looks that are alternately regretful and mistrustful, and then leaves us to go back to the surface.

"I should be going too. Do you want me to swim you back up?" I offer.

She narrows her eyes. "So, you're being nice to me now?"

I manage a half-smile. "I'm sorry."

She gets it now. Her cheeks and the tip of her nose get red. I get the cheeks, but I have no idea why the tip of her nose gets red when she's angry. I frigging love it.

I catch her hands and pull her toward me. She struggles while I reel her in, but we both know who's going to win this. She gives up and kisses me and then she starts to laugh. No idea why so I stop and look at her.

"You know why that worked?" she asks. "I could see you still loved me, even when you were being the worst to me. But hatred isn't always an emotion."

I nod because I know why it worked, too. "You can love someone in your heart and decide to hate them in your head. I just can't do it anymore."

She sighs and threads her fingers through the hair at the back of my head. It feels so good. "What are we going to do?" she says, more to herself than to me.

I've already decided. Everyone else is doing it; why not us? "Fake our deaths and run away?"

"My brother would never let us—"

"Your brother doesn't have to know."

She looks almost hopeful. Her eyes get this faraway look as she runs through all the scenarios in her head until she lands on something that stops her. "I can't abandon my House. And Adonis can't protect everyone on his own."

I nod and draw her against my chest, holding her. She's not ready. "Okay," I say, adding a silent *for now* in my head because I know I'm going to bring this up again. I'm not going to wait around for Thebes, or possibly my own House, to kill her. "But Thebes won't stop until we're all dead."

She pulls back, a thought occurring to her. "Until they *think* we're all dead," she corrects.

What she's suggesting is insane. We can't fake that many deaths. "We won't be able to save everyone," I say.

"I know." And then I kiss her. I'm going to make this work, for Leda.

I've never been an optimist, but I'm trying.

44

DAPHNE

We live on a sailboat, surrounded by water.

Ajax and I got aboard the *Argo IX* and left New York. For us, the war was over, though it was just beginning for everyone else. We were given a second chance, and we weren't going to stick around and blow it. I think there are only so many times anyone can reasonably expect to beat fate.

We focus on us. Our lives. Our second chance. Ajax is a fantastic sailor. Me? Not so much. What I *am* good at is selling his art.

It's been three years since that night on the roof. We've sailed all over the world together. When we need money, or when I find that I'm tripping over too many unsold paintings, we dock and I go ashore as Mina Fury, art agent extraordinaire.

Mina has one client. He's a genius, a once-in-a-generation kind of artist. He doesn't have a name or an address, but anyone who knows art knows "Mina's Client" and they pay through the nose for his work with as much begrudging humor as they tolerate his eccentricity. There is a rumor that he is horribly disfigured. Mina divulges only the truth—her client has the most beautiful soul she's ever been fortunate enough to encounter.

Mina's Client's paintings are hanging in the Guggenheim and the Louvre. Everyone is hungry for a meeting with him, especially a family of art dealers in New York. The Delos brothers, Castor and Pallas, are desperate to buy one of his canvasses, although in the last year there's been no request. The whole Delos clan has been preoccupied with something other than art.

Mina won't sell to them, or even meet with them. If they want to see his art they have to go to a museum, she tells them. She's a harpy. She doesn't even tell her client that the Delos brothers want to meet him.

Because I know how he'll grow sullen and silent if he even hears their names.

We've been in Europe for nearly a year, and only just returned to the US. We've weighed anchor off Nantucket, not to sell any art, but for our yearly meeting with Tantalus.

We never would have made it without Tantalus, and apparently, we escaped just in time. Both of us feel partly responsible for the war that went into full swing after we left, though we knew the war was coming no matter what. It's a kind of arrogance to say we caused it, considering Tantalus and Bellerophon had been spoiling for a final fight for years.

There were many times we thought about coming back. When we heard Antigone died, we almost did.

Anyhow, it was a brutal war. Last time we had any news we learned that the other Houses were nearly extinct. Paris and Bellerophon both got the hero's death they envisioned, as did most of the Hundred Cousins and supposedly all of the House of Athens. No one's seen Adonis in over a year, but it's assumed he's dead. I know better. He had the ultimate hiding spot ready. I only hope he managed to get Leda and Daedalus in there with him, but I don't think he did. The war is supposed to be over and the House of Thebes is supposedly the only Scion House left. The gods aren't here, obviously. So I'm holding out hope that at least Adonis, Leda, and Daedalus made it out.

Because if they didn't, it would mean that I'm reason the gods aren't here.

The war has changed the Delos brothers. Tantalus most of all. The last time we saw him there was an edge to his voice I didn't like. I think this will be our last visit with him. I just don't know how to bring it up with Ajax.

When I'm done shopping for groceries on Nantucket, I take the rented motorboat out to the place we've anchored the *Argo*. We didn't rent a slip on the island and risk being seen together by some nosy neighbors looking to pop by for a sundowner. Tantalus has become something of a public figure over the past three years, dipping his toe into human politics, and Ajax looks too much like him for me to let anyone see them together.

As I pull alongside the *Argo* I see a figure on board. Ajax isn't supposed to be back for hours. I cut the engine, reach into the compartment at my right, and pull out my gladiolus.

I drift alongside the *Argo* and a blond head peeks over the side. I shade my eyes to see him, but I already know who it is by the shape of his huge shoulders.

"You beat me," I call up to Tantalus. "I was going to go back for you after I cleaned up a bit."

"I got to Nantucket way earlier than I told you I would, so I swam out," he shouts back. He's smiling down at me as I stow my sword.

"Swimming is unnatural," I say, and hear him chuckle. That

water nymph blood of theirs still creeps me out. Years of living on the water hasn't stopped me from fearing it.

I climb up the ladder and Tantalus greets me with one of his enveloping hugs. I can tell something's wrong. He's too tense and his breathing is elevated. I pull back.

"You okay?" I ask. His eyes are darting everywhere to avoid mine. He finally meets my gaze but he can't really smile.

"Where's Jax?" he asks in return.

"He flew to Maine to scout a safe spot for us to spend the summer. He won't be back for a few hours. We thought you were coming later," I reply.

"I'm sorry. I guess I was a little too eager to see you," he says, shaking his head. Tantalus smiles brightly. "Let me help you get the supplies aboard."

He always wants to help me. I stopped needing it years ago.

We get the groceries put away and open a bottle of wine, chatting the whole time. I'm suddenly very aware of Ajax's absence. I can feel Tantalus' eyes on me and the look of desperation that steals over his expression when he thinks I'm glancing away. I cut some fruit and ask a question about Mildred and their son, Creon, hoping to bring him back to himself.

"He's just like her. Greedy. Impatient," Tantalus says dismissively, staring broodingly at his wine. I don't know what to say. His ambivalence toward his own son is just... not like him. Not like the House of Thebes, really. It reminds me too much of my own mother, and I'm ashamed to realize I dislike him for it.

"Pallas and Aileen are going to have their son any day now," he says, quickly changing the subject. "They're going to name him Hector."

"She's pregnant?" I swallow my own disappointment. "That's great news," I say firmly. His face only darkens more. I lean

DAPHNE

toward him across the galley table and try to salvage this conversation. "What's really going on?" I ask seriously. He doesn't respond right away.

"They're all gone," he says quietly. "The other Houses. They're gone."

It takes me a moment to process what he's implying. If the other Houses are gone, then the gods should be released, but it's clear that the gods of Olympus are not among us. So the other Houses can't be gone. Or at least, not entirely.

Because there's still me.

Or at least that's the conclusion Tantalus has come to. I won't gainsay him, either. If Adonis is still alive, I'm not going to set the House of Thebes on his tail. But I have to give him something.

"The House of Thebes and The House of Atreus will only be united when Ajax and I have a child," I say. Tantalus' eyes narrow. "Marriage isn't enough. The blood must mix in order for the Houses to join."

"How long have you known this?" he asks after a moment.

I look away. "Since before we were married. Antigone—" I break off when I see him flinch. Her death left the House of Thebes without an Oracle, but worse than that, her death looked suspiciously like suicide. I soften my tone. "She told me."

He's too still. I don't even think he's breathing. "Does Ajax know?"

I nod my head. "We've been trying," I say. I look up at Tantalus and meet his silent accusations. "I *will* have a daughter."

He can hear it's the truth because he's a Falsefinder. "You're so sure. What aren't you telling me?" he asks.

I laugh to myself and shake my head. Where to begin? "All I'm going to say is that my daughter has been foretold."

Tantalus leans back and just looks at me. "So it's not you, it's Ajax. He can't have kids?"

I shrug, refusing to tell him what I already know. *Your union will bear no fruit*, the dryad had said all those years ago when I saved Ajax. The night he got shot by my father's goons and the Furies went away for us. I tucked that bit of information away, hoping that the dryad was wrong, but as the years passed, I've grown less sure.

"I'm not sure about anything anymore," I say aloud.

"That's not true," he says in a dreamy, detached way. "You're sure of your love for Ajax."

I drop my head and nod. "I am sure of that." When I look back up at him his face is stark with hurt.

"Why couldn't you have loved me that way, Daphne?" he whispers.

I'm remembering that night Ajax and I first said I love you. The wretched couch. Tantalus coming home. He told me to keep my name when I wore other faces because if Ajax truly loved me, someday he would call me Daphne in front of the others. Then he whispered something to himself, and right now, all these years later, I realize that he was whispering my name.

I see a thought cross his mind. He reaches for my hand. "Ajax and I are not so different."

I pull back, but the cramped space in the galley won't let me get far enough away from him, so I stand.

"Tantalus, don't," I start to say, but it's like he doesn't hear me.

"I can give you a child," he says, standing and blocking my path. "I fathered Creon. I can father your child." He's staring at my face, entranced. I don't even know this person anymore, I realize. "It's for the best. Even Ajax will understand. This way you'll still become part of our House, and I won't have to kill you."

My horror quickly turns to anger. "How can you even say that?"

He laughs, although nothing is funny, and I can see something crack in him. Or maybe the crack has been there for years, and now he's going to break.

"I think we were always meant to be together," he says. I pull my hand away from his grasp again and he gets angry, building his case. Making an argument for what he wants. "You're the Heir to your House. I'm the Heir to mine. Ajax never made any sense. You should have married me when I asked you."

I shake my head. "But I never loved you. And I never will."

He hears the truth. Telling him the truth was the worst thing I could have done. Whatever shred of self-possession that still connected him to the Tantalus I knew is forgotten.

He lunges for me. But he hasn't just forgotten himself. He's forgotten who *I* am.

I take his wrist, let a small current run through him, and he's unconscious at my feet. I regret it immediately. I regret this whole, ugly thing because it isn't his fault. The war broke him. The Face broke him. This is my fault.

"Shit," I say, running my hands through my hair and holding my head as if I'm trying to press all my thoughts back inside.

"What the hell, Daphne?"

I whirl around and see Ajax standing halfway down the stairs from above decks. Is there any way I can explain this that won't hurt him? If there is, I don't think of it in time.

"He wasn't himself," I manage.

Ajax sees the truth on my face. He comes to me and wraps his arms around me. "I'm sorry," he says. "The last time we saw him I noticed he couldn't take his eyes off you. I should have ended contact then, but I—"

"I felt it too. I should have said something," I say, feeling my guilt deepen. Seeing Tantalus even just once a year was the only thing Ajax had left of his family. The only news we got of how the Scion war was progressing. The only way we knew which of our friends had died. Now neither of us will even have that, and again, it's all my fault.

Ajax releases me and looks down at his brother. He suddenly looks away with revulsion. I can see him spinning scenarios in his head about how the confrontation must have gone between Tantalus and me.

"What do you want to do?" I ask. "Should we wake him and try to talk through this?"

Ajax thinks for a moment and then makes up his mind. "No," he says. "I'll bring him to shore, leave him there, and we'll go. Hopefully we can get far enough away before he wakes up so he can't find us."

There's a long silence.

"So that's it?" I ask.

"Yeah."

I touch his arm and make him look at me. "Are you sure?"

A pained look crosses his face. "Keeping him in our lives wasn't right," he says.

"We'll have to start over. No more Mina Fury and her Client," I remind him.

"I know."

And now I've truly taken everything from him. He picks up his brother and carries him above decks and then down the ladder to the waiting motorboat.

They don't get far before I see Tantalus jerk awake. They shout to each other over the roar of the boat.

Ajax holds out a hand to his brother as he drives. Tantalus stands up on unsteady feet. The boat suddenly spins violently, kicking up a great circular wake, and I realize that Tantalus has grabbed Ajax from behind. He has him by the throat.

Tantalus has lost his mind.

"No!" I scream, running along the deck of the *Argo*, looking for a clear shot while they struggle. Bolts turn my hands blue, but lightning is too erratic at this distance to risk a shot. I will almost certainly hit both of them from here. I'm just not sure I won't kill them both.

I look down at the water. I can't even try to swim to them. I will sink like a rock.

And here it is. The two of them fighting and the dark expanse between us that I cannot cross.

I remember Adonis saying to me once, long ago as we sat on a couch, about how fate waits for you to think you're in the clear, and then it comes for you.

Ajax wrests himself loose and tries to fly away from his brother rather than fight, but Tantalus grabs Ajax's foot and hauls him back down. He has something shiny in his hand.

My gladiolus.

I'm screaming. Just like last time, I don't know what.

My sword in Tantalus' hand arcs through the air. In the setting sun it looks like it's on fire. Blood sprays. And Ajax's head falls from his body.

The world goes white, like a flash bulb star-bursting in my eyes.

My vision slowly irises back and I see Tantalus clutching Ajax's headless body to his chest. He looks like he's wailing, but I can't hear him. I can't hear anything. A high whine, like an insect inside my ear, eclipses all other sounds.

We were wrong. We didn't beat the Fates. They waited and they won, just as Antigone described. The mousetrap won.

The sky goes black and a thunderhead spins above me, far too low to be natural. Lightning forks down around the motorboat. I've summoned a storm for the first time. I suppose I'm a Cloud Gatherer. I don't know how to control it, but I send all my hate at the little boat. A gust of wind nearly topples it.

Tantalus locks eyes with me for one brief moment of terror, and then he throws himself beneath the water where my thunderbolts can't reach him. Lightning travels across the top of seawater. It doesn't descend below it, where he's hiding. He does not resurface. But I know that doesn't mean he's dead.

Rain falls. I stare at the body in the bobbing boat.

I can't hear the sound of the yacht's engine as I position the *Argo* alongside the motorboat. I can't hear the sails as they snap, untended, in the storm I've conjured. I can't hear my feet when they skid in Ajax's blood. I can't even hear my own sobbing anymore.

I don't weigh anchor. I puncture the hull, point the *Argo* toward the open ocean, and let it drift until it sinks. In the dark, I take Ajax and the motorboat back to Nantucket.

I wash him, wrap him, place an obol under his tongue, and carry him into the interior of the island. There are moors here that are deep and wild and so flat the sky domes over you until it seems like there's more sky than earth. It's the perfect place. Even though I have to put him in the earth, the sky is where Ajax belonged.

I find a quiet spot that lies like a seam between heaven and earth and I dig deep with the sword that killed him. His body is already like clay. I bury him.

It's nearly dawn when I notice there is a woman sitting next to me. Her face is covered by a veil.

"You were supposed to be on my side," I say, not looking at her.

"For a time, your goals aligned with mine. As will your daughter's," Nemesis replies, staring at the grave.

"How are you any better than *them*?" I ask. She knows I mean the Fates.

"There is no better or worse. There is only balance, and balance has been weighted in their favor for far too long. You will restore true balance by first tipping the scales in the other direction."

Now I do look at her, but she's hard to see. Like Hades, shadows cling to her and her veil, though gauzy, only hints at features beneath without revealing them.

"What if I say no?"

She nods in thought. "That's the whole point of you. So that others might say no."

"But not me."

"No, Daphne. Not you. But maybe your daughter. If she is strong."

"If she stays away from me." I can't look at the grave anymore so I look up at the stars. "Everyone I love dies."

"There are others you love who are alive, and hidden," she tells me. "You are powerful and completely free from the Furies. It's your choice to use your gifts to help other Scions or not."

I feel a breeze stirring and I know that she's gone. Later, I feel the sun and the moon and the sun again, but it isn't thirst or hunger that drives me to get up from his graveside and find other people. It's my calling.

I will have the daughter I owe the goddess of love here, on this island, where I buried my love. I already know what to name her. Helen. I'm not sure if that was my choice, or if it was fated, but I would never name her anything else. Then I have two tasks. I will find a way to go back down to the Underworld and bargain with Hades, and I will get Ajax back.

I'm going to beat fate. Somehow. This isn't the end.

In the meantime, I will go find others like me. I will use my gift to gather all the Outcasts to me. I'll build an army of them if I have to.

I'll do whatever it takes to get to Tantalus, and I will kill him.

"Are you okay? Miss?"

I realize that I'm walking on the side of a road. It's after dark. I look into the driver's window of a Jeep and see the face of a man only a few years older than me. It's a strong face, not handsome, but his eyes are kind and his compassion for me is so genuine I decide to answer.

"No." My voice is rusty with lack of use. I don't know how long it's been since I've spoken. I don't know if the conversation I had with Nemesis was real or if it was in my head. "I'm not okay," I admit.

He unbuckles and opens his door, climbing out and coming over to me. He helps me into the Jeep. "Do you need me to take you to a hospital?" he asks.

I look down and realize I'm covered in dirt and sand and blood. "No. I'm not injured. I just need..."

He waits for me to finish, but I don't.

"I'm Jerry," he says to fill in the blank.

"I'm ... Beth," I lie, touching the heart-shaped pendant at my throat.

I meet his eyes and smile at him with all the charm the Face has to offer, but something strange happens. He clears his throat, looks at the road, and keeps his head.

That's when I know. This is a man who can resist the Face. This is a man who could raise my daughter with love.

And I always wanted my story to end with love.

ENDLESS

Please enjoy the following excerpt from ENDLESS, book
seven in the STARCROSSED saga.

Chapter One

The bass pounding out of the speakers was so loud that the
little hairs on Helen's forearms stood on end and pulsed in time.
Helen watched them, fascinated for a moment, until she shivered
suddenly from the unnerving sensation of feeling sound on her
skin.

Her mind rabbited around the fact that if she were mortal,
she'd be going deaf right now, and she reached for her drink to
derail what she knew would be a downward spiral of thoughts

that inevitably led the conclusion that if Helen were mortal her father would still be alive.

"Do. You. Want. Another." Helen yelled at Hector.

He stared at her mouth, perplexed. She raised her glass and shook the half-melted cubes around to show that they were, sadly, no longer surrounded by vodka. She watched his mouth move, apparently soundlessly, as he failed to shout down the speakers. He finally gave up on verbal communication and shook his head. Helen didn't see the cocktail server anywhere.

She stood up from their VIP both and swam upstream against the current of partygoers who were trying to navigate away from the bar with hands full of sloshing drinks and brains slippery with alcohol. Everyone in the nightclub was wasted, but that's exactly why she and Hector were there in Los Angeles on a Tuesday night at one a.m. To be just two more mammals in an undulating, anonymous herd, preferably a herd that had been so jaded by constant celebrity sightings that they looked right past any faces or bodies that were too perfect to be normal.

Helen made it to the bar by squeezing in sideways between two dude's backs and smiled hopefully at one of the all-female bartenders wearing black halter tops that said *Pour Girl* stenciled on the front. The bartenders were far from identical, but they seemed like sisters. Their body types and coloring varied. Skinny, curvy, short, tall, light, dark, whatever you were looking for there was a Pour Girl representing, but even with all these differences they had one thing in common. They were scary hot. Scary because they sort of resembled vampires with their inky eyeliner and oddly sharp teeth, and hot because they oozed sex appeal with their cynical yet flirty half-smiles, cocked hips, and scantily clad bodies. One of the bartenders narrowed her eyes and tipped her chin up at Helen in invitation, but before Helen could shout her order, a man behind the bar came up to the Pour Girl and said something in her ear. The guy looked like a young, hip Santa. He was wearing a t-shirt that said *Party God*. Helen recognized him instantly. She recognized the bartenders, too.

"Dionysus!" she shouted, pointing a finger at him. She hadn't seen him since the wedding.

The bartender-maenad gave Helen a sympathetic look. "Sorry about your father," she shouted above the din, and then gestured past Helen to engage some other customer.

Helen stared at Dionysus, not sure what she wanted to say, but certain that they should speak. She felt like he owed her something. Maybe it was an apology, though she knew that wouldn't help. Maybe it was an explanation, though she already knew his reasons for doing what he had done.

Sighing, Dionysus gestured for Helen to meet him at the end of the bar. She fought against the crowd until she got to the place where the bar swung upward on hinges. Dionysus brought her behind the bar and into the liquor storage room where barbacks were shouldering bags of ice from the walk-in cooler and changing out the lines on kegs of beers. It was quieter in there. Helen's heels sunk into the holes in the squishy, honeycomb floor mats and she nearly tipped over as she rounded on Dionysus. She'd figured out what she wanted to say.

"Where's Hera?" she demanded, throwing off his attempt to steady her.

He held up his hands, backing off. "Gone. Back on Olympus."

Helen could hear that he wasn't lying. She didn't have to look at his heart to know how much he pitied her. Even while it was happening, Helen had known that he and his maenads had wanted no part in her father's death four months ago, but the

Olympians were too powerful and Hera had forced them into doing it. Hating Hera was easy. Hating a few people had become easy for Helen. She'd never been able to stay angry at anyone before, but that had changed. The hard part was shutting it off before she did something irreversible. She balled up her hands and smothered the sparks shimmering just under her skin.

"If you see Hera, tell her I'm coming for her," she said, trying to move past him and leave.

"Does it matter?" he asked.

"Yes!" she shouted back.

"No, it doesn't. Your father's death was a parting shot from the Olympians. They're holed up on Olympus, and it doesn't look like they're coming back," he said.

"How do you know they're not coming back?"

Dionysus huffed with frustration, caught. "Because none of them are strong enough to beat you, and Olympus is a damn sight better than Tartarus." He looked at her sympathetically. "Revenge isn't you, Helen. That's how *they* did things. You're different and you know it."

It annoyed Helen to no end knowing that Hera had gotten away with it. But Dionysus was right. Hera didn't matter. Helen was using her as something to focus on, anything but what was really bothering her. She tried to push past Dionysus and leave the room.

"What are you doing, Helen?" Dionysus asked, sounding dismayed as he stepped in front of her, keeping her there.

"What do you mean?"

She knew what he meant. She just didn't want to get into it. More sparks. Her hands shook with the effort it took to hold them back. She shifted anxiously on the bad pairing of her shoes and the floor mats while Dionysus watched her struggle for control. In the low light he could see the electric glow under her skin. He knew what she could do with it, but he wasn't scared of her. Probably because he was used to being ceremoniously ripped into pieces by his maenads only to be reborn every year.

"You can't party the pain away," he said, his intimate relationship with both partying and pain apparent in his tone.

"Isn't that the whole point of you?" Helen said. "To drink and dance until you forget about your problems?"

He smiled, shaking his head, like he was so accustomed to being misunderstood he knew better than to try to explain himself. "The question you should be asking is whether or not this is the point of *you*."

Helen opened her mouth, realized she had no comeback, and stormed past Dionysus. He turned with her, making a frustrated sound.

"You're a leader, Helen," he said, raising his voice as she got farther away. "The small gods are waiting to see what you'll do. Stop wasting time the world doesn't have!"

Her throat tight and her fists clenched, Helen dove back into the sea of people on the other side of the bar. Threading through flailing arms and gyrating pelvises, she was quickly disoriented. Helen stopped in the middle of the room, trying to get her bearings, and deflated when she heard the sound of angry bellows over the deafening music. Even amidst the frantic dancing, the off-rhythm motions of a brawl were unmistakable.

"Not again," she mumbled to herself.

When she got back to the VIP booth area, she saw that Hector was letting some meathead beat on him. He just stood there for a bit, taking the abuse, before he pretty much threw the drunk idiot off of him and into someone else. This only spurred the havoc on, reeling in more drunk idiots who were spoiling for a fight.

"What did you do!?" Helen asked Hector as a new guy stepped up to him.

Hector shrugged, happier than Helen had seen him in a while, and pretended to throw a few jabs, all of which he pulled. Hector wasn't trying to hurt the guy, he just wanted to get him angrier before sending him into the general mayhem that Helen was sure he had created. Helen noticed the black-clad bouncers with earpieces and walkie-talkies making their way toward them.

"Time to go!" she said, grabbing Hector. She searched for a shadowy place to hide them while she portaled them away, but there were too many people around them. All the shadows were taken.

Cursing Hector while dodging flying fists, Helen dragged him toward the door. She had to influence a few hearts along the way to get him out of there, convincing the bouncers that they were innocent bystanders even though Hector was still pushing people into each other, trying to make more trouble.

"I can't take you anywhere anymore. You always start something," she snapped when they were out the door and half a block away.

"It's too early to go home," Hector said, still amped up and grinning. He grabbed Helen's waist and pulled her against him while they walked. "Let's go to Vegas!"

"Again?" she said, trying to push him away although he had suddenly seemed to have sprouted ten hands and all of them were trying to tickle her or lift her up or just pester her in general. There was a gust of wind that pushed her against Hector even as she tried to veer away. The Santa Ana winds were blowing, hot and dry.

"Yes, again," Hector said as he picked her up and carried her. "Come on. It'll be fun."

"For you," Helen said. "I don't get gambling."

"Vegas," he insisted, holding her tight to his chest and burying his face in her neck. He kept chanting the word until she was squirming and squealing. She finally gave in.

"Okay!" she said. She pointed to a dark doorway. "Bring me over there."

As soon as they were in shadows, Helen portaled them to Everyland first.

Hector groaned when he saw that they were in the house Helen had created for herself in her world. "Not the Vegas *here*. I always win here. There's no point."

"You have to change," Helen said, jumping out his arms. "Your shirt's ripped and that's someone else's blood," she said, pointing to a red stain on the thigh of his pants. "I could change you on the way there but..."

"Too freaky," Hector agreed, already walking away from her toward his room while he stripped off his shirt.

He hated it when Helen changed him during a portal. There was no physical bathing or handling occurring, it was just a wish-like thought that was instantly granted by Helen's ability as a Worldbuilder, but the experience was alarming. Lucas had done it to Helen once and she knew how strange it felt.

"I don't want to stay out all night," she called out, shoving the thought of Lucas back down into whatever hole in her soul it had crawled out of.

She went into her enormous closet and looked at all the clothes hung or shelved in there. She could think herself into anything—gowns, jewels, jeans, t-shirts. She could even portal herself back in a Ferrari or a yacht if she wanted, as long as she'd seen it somewhere in the real world first. Helen had a good imagination, but that didn't mean everything she imagined would work in the physics of the real world. For insistence, she could imagine a jet that looked like a teddy bear, but that didn't mean it could fly.

Technically, she didn't need a closet or garage to store anything, either, because the shift could be made in transit between Everyland and Earth, but sometimes she wanted to go through the process of selection. Deciding on clothes, makeup, cars, and shoes helped keep her from dwelling on anything emotionally damaging, which was why she had created this house and its closets to begin with. Distraction.

Her glance landed on a dress she'd seen in a magazine and had filed away in her collection a few weeks ago, but her gaze slid off the elegant garment as the exchange she'd had with Dionysus came back to her.

"You okay?" Hector asked behind her.

Helen spun around, feeling caught, like she was breaking their unspoken rule to keep it light when they went out together. She smiled at him as he approached her.

"Are you going to put that on?" she asked instead of answering, pointing at the fresh shirt he held in his hand.

He kept coming toward her, his expression neutral while he tried to read hers. "Don't," he said, taking a guess as to what she was thinking about and deciding it was Lucas.

"I won't," she replied, looking up at him.

He was practically pressing up against her and she wondered if he would kiss her this time. She wondered if she'd let him.

Over the past four months since they'd been betrayed by the people who'd claimed to love them, Helen and Hector had nearly kissed several times. They were aways touching each other, standing too close, hands straying, but nothing definitive had happened between them yet. It was as if their body language was telling everyone else that they were a couple, but when they were alone neither of them were willing to be the first one to step over that line.

"Let's go," he said, moving back to put his shirt on.

She grabbed the dress and portaled them to Vegas with plenty of cash in their pockets.

Helen knew she was technically counterfeiting, but she'd cleared her conscience of that long ago. A few thousand dollars here and there was not about to upset the world economy, and Hector needed a physical limit to his gambling. Ones and zeros in a bank account meant nothing to him, but if he had actual cash or chips that he was playing with he'd stop when he got to the end of them.

His father had already cut him off. Left to his own devices Hector would get himself into serious trouble. He was looking for it, too. Hoping to anger the kind of the people who broke kneecaps just to give himself an excuse to get into a real fight, but Helen wasn't going to let that happen. He'd never forgive himself if he went too far and killed a mortal. It was another line neither of them was willing to step over. There weren't many of those left for them.

Normally it cooled down considerably in the high desert at night, but when Helen portaled she and Hector to a quiet spot just off the strip in Las Vegas it was hot and windy. Though there was no sun in the sky the atmosphere still radiated heat like there was. In the half a block it took them to get into the casino Helen felt sweat jump to her skin, only to be sucked away by the thirsty air. It had been dry everywhere, though. It was spring, and usually it would rain nearly every day in Massachusetts, but there had been nothing.

Going into the climate-controlled lobby of the casino was no less shocking than entering another world. They immediately sought the most action, doing a lap around the casino, past flashing lights and bleeps and bloops that seemed more geared toward children who wanted to play video games than grown-ups. Helen hated Las Vegas. It was like one, big, joyless carnival where avarice and disappointment collided, and like the gaudy wall-to-wall carpeting it was only brightly colored to cover up the stains. At the moment, gaudy joylessness suited Helen's temperament just fine.

They roamed from one room to another, hardly noticing when the décor of the never-ending labyrinth changed minutely. She never knew what would catch Hector's fancy. Sometimes he played blackjack, sometimes roulette or poker. He didn't have a favorite.

They followed the sound of raucous cheering to a craps table. A group of men in tuxedos were clustered around one end of it, goading on the roller. Their energy was teetering between excitement and violence. That was the real reason Hector wanted to come here, Helen realized. He was still looking for a fight. He joined the action and placed a bet. Helen had no idea how craps even worked. She knew there were dice involved and that was about it.

A quick glance around told her that there were no women standing with this group of men, which was odd. For some reason Helen couldn't fathom, Vegas adhered to strictly misogynistic rules that were stuck in the Rat Pack era. High rollers always collected arm charms, but there wasn't a short skirt in sight at this table, apart from Helen's. Usually, Hector and Helen had to block any incoming suitors for each other and by this point Helen would be busy letting all the starry-eyed females know that

Hector already had a date. Given the circumstances, Helen decided it was okay for her to sit down.

"Not the gambling type?" asked a male voice.

Helen turned her head and found that one of the tuxedoed men was taking a seat beside her. His bow tie was undone, his hair was mussed, and he draped himself with inebriated ease over the chair and the edge of the table. Though he was loose-limbed after what appeared to be a long night, his gaze was clear and steady, like he'd drunk himself sober. In one hand he was shuffling a pair of coins, weaving them over and under each other in a smooth and constant motion. He wasn't the most handsome man Helen had ever seen, but he had nice hands.

"I've never seen the appeal," she said, answering his question.

"Then why are you here?"

She gestured toward Hector. "I'm his muscle."

Tux laughed and nodded, appreciating the banter. He took one of his coins, put the edge of it on the table and gave it a twirl, sending it spinning.

"It's all fixed, anyway," Helen continued, watching the coin blur into a sphere as it skimmed across the tabletop. "The house always wins."

"Eventually, yeah," Tux agreed. He pressed his hand flat over the coin, stopping it. "Heads or tails?" he asked.

"I told you. I don't gamble."

He kept his hand over the coin. Helen saw a preternatural gleam in his eyes. "This isn't gambling. It's chance."

"What's the difference?"

"The odds are evened. Fifty-fifty. We both risk an equal amount. There is no 'house' and no one is in control. Just—" He waved his free hand, as if to indicate something ineffable.

But Helen wanted an answer. "Fate?" she guessed.

He frowned. "The opposite, actually. Uncertainty."

A breath of a laugh escaped her. "What's your name?"

"Plutus."

"Interesting name." He was obviously Greek, but if he was one of the lesser gods, Helen had never heard of him.

"You're stalling. Take a guess," he coaxed.

"Why?"

His expression softened with a whimsical thought. "To see if you're lucky."

"Heads," she replied immediately, though not sure why.

Before Plutus could lift his hand and reveal the outcome, all hell broke loose over at the craps table. An influx of gamblers had joined Hector and the tuxedoed men, and for whatever reason the newcomers had been stupid or drunk enough to get into it with Hector. One of them was flying through the air toward Helen table. She jumped up before he landed and ran to intervene.

Starting a fight at a dark night club was one thing, but Vegas didn't mess around. Casinos were too well lit and there were cameras everywhere. There was no way for them to hide their abilities, and they couldn't just run or portal away to avoid getting arrested. Helen was not going to jail. It was a school night. She clamped onto Hector's forearm and dragged him out of the casino, her eyes seeking out cameras along the way.

"What is wrong with you!?" she growled at him. A pair of security guards stepped in front of them, motioning for them to stop. "It's okay," Helen said to them, smiling brightly until confusion clouded their faces and she could push past.

"This one was not my fault," Hector argued as Helen pulled him outside. "I was having a conversation with one of the servants of Tyche, and this jackass..."

"The *what*?" Helen marched Hector around a corner.

"Tux guys. Servants of Tyche." He pulled back on his arm, forcing Helen to spin around and come back to him.

"Who's Tyche?" Helen asked, looking up at him. He had blood on his face. Helen kind of hoped it was his.

"Lady Luck. Goddess of Chance." Hector grinned. "If *she* were on my side I'd never lose."

Helen scoffed. "The last thing you need is to go on a winning streak and draw even more attention to yourself," she said. And, deciding the night was over, she portaled them back to the Delos brownstone in New York City.

"I've seen them before," Hector said as they started climbing the stairs from the ground floor.

"Where?" Helen asked. She certainly hadn't seen a bunch of tuxedoed servants of Tyche hanging around before that night.

"Atlantic City," Hector said, his pace slowing as he reached the top of the stairs and pass the entrance to the nap room. When Helen got alongside him, she saw why. Pallas, Hector's father, was sitting on one of the comfortable couches in the nap room, waiting for them.

"Is that where you were tonight? Atlantic City?" Pallas asked.

"What are you doing here, Dad?" Hector did not choose to join his father in the nap room, so neither did Helen. They stood in the doorway, half in and half out of Pallas' ambush.

"Don't you have classes tomorrow morning?" Pallas sounded calm, but underneath he was obviously simmering.

Hector sighed. "What is this? An intervention?"

"If it were an intervention the whole family would be here. I came to talk to you."

This confrontation had been coming for a while, and Helen was actually glad it was coming from Pallas. Of all the adults in their lives, he was the least likely to make Helen feel guilty for partying too much. And if he *did* try to wag a finger, Helen wasn't about to buy it. She'd heard stories about him in his twenties—she'd even seen him back then, looking like a suave, New York party boy—and she knew he didn't have a leg to stand on.

"I know you're upset about Andy," Pallas began. Helen cringed. Leading with Andy was a terrible idea.

The details about what had happened to Andy while she'd been doing research in the Arctic had come out in bits and pieces over the past four months. Her professor on the research boat had actually been Hera, and once Andy had been separated from Hector for a few months Hera had fed the small spark of jealousy in Andy until she had allowed herself to be a vessel for one of the vengeful spirits that Hera had convinced to side with the Olympians.

When all was said and done, not only had Andy ghosted Hector, but she'd also turned against the Scions and was even willing to help Hera capture and kill Helen. Hector had felt more betrayed by this than Helen had. To Hector family was everything, and in the attempt on Helen's life Andy had attacked Ariadne. While Ariadne was still mortal, no less. Ariadne was strong enough to handle Andy a dozen times over—even before Helen had gotten Everyland back and made her immortal—but she was still Hector's little sister. Attacking his family was the worst thing anyone could do to him, regardless of what vengeful spirit was to blame.

When she's snapped out of Hera's delusions, Andy had been devastated by what she'd done. Still, she couldn't deny that she had allowed herself to become a vessel for an evil spirit. She'd tried to apologize a thousand times, but Hector wouldn't hear it. He was too hurt. She hadn't trusted him, so he no longer trusted her. He'd been betrayed, just as Helen had been betrayed by Lucas.

"Upset isn't the word, Dad," Hector said. He looked at Helen. "Can we get out of here?"

"Wait," Pallas said, grabbing Helen's arm before she could portal them away. "Kate lost him, too…"

"Oh, hell no," Helen muttered, trying to disentangle herself from his grasp. She couldn't talk about her dad.

"You think you can't screw up your life," Pallas continued, still holding her there. "That you have a solution to everything. And sure, you can party all night and make it to school the next day and phone it in, and what it's going to do to your future? Probably nothing you can't fix with a quick trip to Everyland. Look, I'm not here to lecture you about how you're messing up your future. I'm here to tell you that you're messing up *right now*. You're hurting the people who love you right now, and that's something you can't take back no matter how powerful you are." Pallas let go of Helen's arm.

Helen felt a surge of anger. She hadn't been the one to screw up her life. That had been done for her, *to* her, just hours after he'd promised to love her forever.

The words came flying out of Helen, thoughtlessly. "Have you asked Lucas to give back Aileen?"

Helen's question hit Pallas like a physical thing. He froze, staring at her, unable to answer. She felt Hector put a hand on her waist.

"Let's go," he said quietly in her ear and she portaled them to Everyland.

They stood in the middle of the living room area. White furniture and walls of glass that looked out over a sparkling cityscape surrounded them. The huge room felt dark and lonely in the night.

"I'm sorry. I shouldn't have brought up your mother," Helen said.

Hector shook his head. "It's okay. And he hasn't by the way. Asked for her back."

Helen wondered how he knew that. She supposed they all must have seen Lucas plenty of times over the past few months, though no one had spoken to her about it.

"Have you?"

"I miss her, but I don't know if it's right to bring her back." He shrugged and gestured around in a vague way. "She's been gone for twelve years. And she's in a better place."

"How do you know that?"

He looked reluctant to say it, but he finally did. "Lucas had a long talk with me, Jason, and Ari about her. He said she drank from the river of Joy. She's at peace."

Helen knew she should let this go, but she couldn't. "He talks to you?"

"He comes home every day. He has until the end of summer before he... you know."

Before he descends into Hades and never comes back, Helen finished in her mind silently. She'd never say that out loud to Hector, though. He still felt it was his fault that Lucas had traded himself for Hades in a bargain to bring Hector back from the dead. That guilt was part of the reason he was hiding here in Everyland with Helen, though she knew Lucas' vow was not Hector's fault. If anyone was to blame, outside of the Fates who had engineered the entire situation, it was Lucas. In her experience, he made a lot of choices that involved the lives and deaths of others without ever asking anyone what they wanted first.

"And you never asked to see her, or talk to her? Not even just one more time?"

"No, but not for me. For her."

She turned away from him, feeling ashamed of her own self-ishness. "I don't get that."

"I know," he said. "But you might someday."

ALSO BY JOSEPHINE ANGELINI

STARCROSSED SERIES

Starcrossed

Dreamless

Goddess

Scions

Timeless

WORLDWALKER SERIES

Trial by Fire

Firewalker

Witch's Pyre

THRILLER

What She Found in the Woods

Printed in the USA
CPSIA information can be obtained
at www.ICGtesting.com
JSHW020914140823
45669JS00001B/1

9 780999 462881